The Billionaire's
Cinderella
Seduction

The Billionaire's *Cinderella* Seduction

**MICHELLE SMART,
HEIDI RICE**
and **JULIA JAMES**

MILLS & BOON

THE BILLIONAIRE'S CINDERELLA SEDUCTION © 2021 by Harlequin Books S.A.

The publisher acknowledges the copyright holders of the individual works as follows:
THE SICILIAN'S BOUGHT CINDERELLA
© 2019 by Michelle Smart
Philippine Copyright 2019
Australian Copyright 2019
New Zealand Copyright 2019

First Published 2019
Second Australian Paperback Edition 2021
ISBN 978 1 867 23064 9

CONTRACTED AS HIS CINDERELLA BRIDE
© 2019 by Heidi Rice
Philippine Copyright 2019
Australian Copyright 2019
New Zealand Copyright 2019

First Published 2019
Second Australian Paperback Edition 2021
ISBN 978 1 867 23064 9

A CINDERELLA FOR THE GREEK
© 2016 by Julia James
Philippine Copyright 2016
Australian Copyright 2016
New Zealand Copyright 2016

First Published 2016
Fourth Australian Paperback Edition 2021
ISBN 978 1 867 23064 9

® and ™ (apart from those relating to FSC®) are trademarks of Harlequin Enterprises
(Australia) Pty Limited or its corporate affiliates. Trademarks indicated with ® are
registered in Australia, New Zealand and in other countries.
Contact admin_legal@Harlequin.ca for details.

MIX
Paper from
responsible sources
FSC® C001695
www.fsc.org

Published by
Harlequin Mills & Boon
An imprint of Harlequin Enterprises (Australia) Pty
Limited (ABN 47 001 180 918), a subsidiary of
HarperCollins Publishers Australia Pty Limited
(ABN 36 009 913 517)
Level 13, 201 Elizabeth Street
SYDNEY NSW 2000 AUSTRALIA

Printed and bound in Australia by McPherson's Printing Group

CONTENTS

The Sicilian's Bought Cinderella
Michelle Smart

Visit the Author Profile page
at millsandboon.com.au.

Michelle Smart's love affair with books started when she was a baby, when she would cuddle them in her cot. A voracious reader of all genres, she found her love of romance established when she stumbled across her first Harlequin book at the age of twelve. She's been reading—and writing—them ever since. Michelle lives in Northamptonshire, England, with her husband and two young Smarties.

DEDICATION

To all the Emmas in my life. Love you all! Xxx

CHAPTER ONE

DANTE MONCADA JUMPED into the car beside his driver, two of his men clambering in behind him. This was all he needed, someone breaking into the old cottage that had been in the Moncada family's possession for generations.

As his driver navigated Palermo's narrow streets and headed into the rolling countryside, Dante thought back to his earlier conversation with Riccardo D'Amore. The head of the D'Amore family had put the brakes on a deal Dante had been negotiating for the past six months. Riccardo ran a clean, wholesome business and was concerned Dante's reputation would tarnish it.

He muttered a curse under his breath and resisted the urge to punch the dashboard.

What reputation? So he liked the ladies. That was no crime. His business empire was built on legitimate money. He did not play the games many Sicilian men liked to play. He kept his nose clean literally and figuratively. He liked to drink and party, but so what? He didn't touch drugs, never gambled and avoided the circles where arms, drug dealing and people trafficking were considered profitable business enterprises. He worked hard. Building a multi-billion-euro technology empire from a modest million-euro inheritance, and with an accountancy trail even the most hardened auditor would fail to find fault with, took dedication. For sure, he cut the odd corner here and there, and his Sicilian heritage meant he did not suffer fools, but every cent he'd earned he'd earned legitimately.

But the legitimacy of his business was not the factor behind Riccardo's foot coming down on the deal that Dante and Alessio, Riccardo's eldest son, had spent months working on. The D'Amores had developed the next-generation safety system for smartphones that had proven itself hack-proof, out-performing all rivals. Alessio and Dante were all set to sign an exclusivity agreement for Dante to install the system in the smartphones and tablets his company was Europe's leader in. This system would give him the tools to penetrate America, the only continent Dante was still to get a decent foothold in.

Riccardo's talk about reputations boiled down to one thing. Dante's parentage. His recently deceased father, Salvatore, had been a heavy gambler and the ultimate playboy. His mother, Immacolata, was known unaffectionately as the Black Widow, a moniker Dante had always thought unfair, as she had never actually killed any of her husbands, merely leeched them for money when she divorced them. His father had been her first husband. She was currently on number five. His mother lived like a queen.

Riccardo, on the other hand, had had one wife, eleven children, thought gambling the work of the devil and sex outside the confines of marriage a sin. Riccardo was concerned Dante was the apple that hadn't fallen far from the tree. Riccardo wanted proof that Dante was not the mere sum of his parents' parts and would not bring Amore Systems and by extension Riccardo himself into disrepute. Riccardo was now in advanced talks with Dante's biggest rival about contracting the system to them instead.

Damn him. The old fool was supposed to have retired.

He had one chance to prove his respectability before the deal was lost for good, Alessio's forthcoming wedding.

Dante's angry ruminations on his business problems were put to one side when his driver pulled the car to a stop in a small opening amidst the dense woodland that ran along the driveway to the cottage. A few metres away, also cunningly hidden in the woodland, was a much smaller city car...

Dante reached into the footwell for the baseball bat he hoped he wouldn't have to use.

Flanked by his bodyguards, he neared the rundown farmer's cottage through the thick trees that hid their approach from watching eyes and rubbed his arms against the bracing chill under the cloudless night sky. The remnants of what had been an unusually cold winter still lingered in the air.

The small cottage with its peeling whitewashed exterior walls came into view. All the shutters were closed but smoke curled out of the chimney that hadn't been used in two decades, wisping upwards into the still darkness of this early spring Sicilian evening. Marcello, who managed the land, had been correct that someone was there.

Keeping to the shadows, Dante and his men approached it.

The door was locked.

Brow furrowing, he pulled his key out and unlocked it.

He winced as the sounds of the creaking hinges echoed through the walls, and stepped inside for the first time since his teenage years, when he would sneak girls there. It hadn't been his father he'd worried about catching him, it had been the girls' fathers. Sicilian men did not take kindly to their daughters having a sex life before marriage; at least, they hadn't twenty years ago.

The open-plan interior was much smaller than he remembered. The lights already on, he scanned it quickly, looking for damage. The window above the sink had been boarded in cardboard. He guessed that was where the intruder had gained entry, but there was no other visible damage, nothing to suggest his unwelcome visitor had come here intent on vandalising or robbing them. Not that there was anything to take unless the intruder had a penchant for decades-old musty furniture. An air of neglect permeated the walls, mingling with the black smoke billowing from the log fire. A pile of what looked like educational books was stacked on the small table.

He stared at those books, brow furrowed again at their incongruity.

A floorboard creaked above his head.

Adrenaline surged through him.

Keeping a tight hold on the baseball bat, Dante nodded at his men to follow and treaded slowly up the narrow staircase, cursing that each step was received with yet another creak. He could have left his men to deal with the intruder but he wanted to see the face of the man who'd had the nerve to break into his property before deciding what to do with him.

Like all men with his wealth and power, Dante had enemies. The question he asked himself was if it was one of those enemies hiding behind this door plotting against him or just a cold vagrant chancing his luck.

He nodded at his men one more time and pushed the door open.

His first thought as he entered the empty bedroom was that he was too late and the intruder had escaped. There was no second thought, for a figure suddenly burst through from the *en suite* bathroom and charged at him, screaming, with what looked like a shower-head in hand.

It took a long beat before his brain recognised the screeching figure for what it was—a woman.

Before the showerhead in her hand could connect with Dante's head, Lino, the quicker of his men, grabbed hold of the woman and engulfed her in his meaty arms.

Immediately she started kicking out, hurling a string of obscenities in what sounded like English, but with a strong accent he had trouble placing.

Dante stared with amazement at this struggling intruder dressed only in a thick maroon robe.

Her eyes fell on him. There was a wild terror in the returning stare.

'Let her go,' he ordered.

Lino removed the showerhead from her hand and released her.

As soon as she was free from his hold, she backed away from them, her eyes going from Dante, to Lino, to Vincenzo and back to Dante, the terror still there.

He quite understood her fear. Dante was tall and physically imposing. Lino and Vincenzo were mountains.

'Leave,' he barked at his men. 'Wait downstairs for me.'

Her eyes settled on him.

This woman might be an intruder, her reasons for being there to be revealed but, unless she had a gun hiding beneath that robe, which she would have already used if she'd had one, she posed no danger.

His men were too well trained to argue and left the room. Stealth no longer being needed, they thumped down the stairs like a herd of wildebeest.

Now that he was alone with her, Dante's senses became more attuned. A wonderful scent filled the room, a soft floral smell that clung around the intruder, who had backed herself into the corner of the room. The only sound to be heard was her ragged breathing.

He stepped slowly towards her.

She pressed herself more tightly into the corner of the room and hugged her arms across her seemingly ample chest, strikingly angled eyes ringing with fear at him. If she hadn't broken into his property and made herself at home, he could feel sorry for her.

He guessed her to be in her early twenties, petite yet curvy, snub nose, plump lips, freckles covering a face that was either naturally pale or white from fright. The colour of her long, wet hair was impossible to judge. Whatever the colour, nothing could detract from the fact that this was one beautiful woman.

Under any other circumstance he would be tempted to let a whistle escape his lips.

Her long, swanlike neck moved but she didn't speak. Those strange eyes did not leave his face.

He stopped a foot away from her and asked in English, 'Who are you?'

Her lips tightened and she hugged herself even harder, giving a quick shake of her head.

'Why are you here?'

But still she didn't speak. If he hadn't caught the obscenities she'd screeched when she'd exploded out of the bathroom, he could believe she was mute.

If she hadn't broken into his property, he would feel bad for her obvious fright.

'You know this is private property? *Sì?*' he tried again, speaking slowly. Dante's English was fluent but his accent thick. 'This cottage is empty but it belongs to me.'

The strange yet beautiful eyes suddenly narrowed and in that slight movement he realised fear wasn't the primary emotion being thrown at him, it was loathing.

'My backside does it belong to you.' She straightened. Her strong accent registered in his brain as Irish. 'This cottage is part of your father's estate and should be shared with your sister.'

Anger swelled in him.

So that was what this was all about? Another charlatan pretending to be Salvatore Moncada's secret love-child in the hope of grabbing a portion of Dante's inheritance. What did this make? Eight or nine fraudsters since his father's death three months ago? Or was this someone Dante's lawyer had already sent packing but thought they would chance their luck one more time and try and convince Salvatore's legitimate child herself?

As a means of getting his attention this woman had played a master stroke.

What a shame for her that it would end in her arrest and deportation.

'If I had a secret sister I'm sure I would be open to sharing a portion of my father's estate with her, but—'

'There's no *if* about it,' she interrupted. 'You *do* have a sister and I have the proof with me.'

Something in her tone cut the retort from his tongue.

Dante stared even harder at the beautiful face before him as his veins slowly turned to ice.

Did this truculently sexy woman really believe she was his…*sister*?

So *this* was Dante?

Aislin had seen many pictures of the cruel Sicilian intent on denying her sister what was morally hers but nothing could have prepared her for the sculptured reality stood before her.

In the flesh he was much taller than she'd expected, his hair thicker and darker. He had a lean, wiry muscularity she hadn't expected either. Nor had the pictures done justice to the rest of him. His thick, dark beard couldn't hide the chiselled jawline or downplay the firm, sensuous lips resting below a straight nose that could have been carved by a professional sculptor. Thick black brows rested above green eyes that could only be described as beautiful, and those eyes were staring at her with a combination of disgust and disbelief.

It hadn't escaped her attention that Dante was a good-looking man but she had not been prepared in the slightest for the raw sexiness that oozed from him.

His black shirt was unbuttoned at the neck and, while she kept her gaze fixed on his eyes, she'd glimpsed the dark hair poking through at the base of his throat.

Dante Moncada was the sexiest, most handsome man she had ever set eyes on and it thrilled with the same intensity that it repelled.

Despite the warmth she'd managed to inject into the walls from the log fire, a shiver ran up her spine, and she drew her towelling robe more tightly around her, wishing she could glue it to her body. It fell to her ankles but, with that green stare on her, she might as well have forgone it. She felt naked.

Beneath it she *was* naked.

It had been two days since she'd broken into this cottage. Two days she'd been living here, waiting for her presence to be noted and for the certain confrontation with this man to take place. But, seriously, did it have to occur the minute she stepped out of the shower?

So much for the cool, calm, no-nonsense first impression she'd hoped to make. In her head she'd created a scene where he stormed into the cottage and found her sitting serenely at the table studying, preferably wearing her reading glasses. Whenever Aislin wore those glasses, men tended to speak to her as if she had more than a single brain cell floating in her head.

Hearing the creak of the floorboards as Dante and his two goons had climbed the stairs had terrified her. She'd been instantly aware of the vulnerability of her position, thrown her still-wet body into the robe and wrenched the showerhead off as her only means of defence.

Dante must think he was dealing with a wailing banshee, an impression it was essential she correct immediately.

He took a step back, his left brow rising up and down. 'You believe you are my sister?'

She jutted her chin out to hide her discomfort at her nakedness beneath the robe. 'If you will be good enough to let me get dressed, I will explain everything. The kitchen is stocked with coffee.'

He gave a grunt of surprised laughter. 'You break into my home and want me to make you a drink?'

'I'm asking you to give me some privacy so I can make myself decent before we start arguing about the inheritance you are trying to keep for your greedy self. I'm simply pointing out that there is coffee if you wish to have one while you wait, and that I take mine with milk and one sugar.'

The green eyes flickered over her, taking in every inch of her body, before he blinked, gave the slightest of shudders and took another step back.

'I will leave you to dress,' he said curtly.

He closed the door behind him.

Aislin took a moment to force huge lungfuls of oxygen down her throat but Dante's departure seemed to have taken all the air with him. All that was left were the remnants of his cologne that even her non-perfumer self could tell with one sniff was expensive. Expensive and…sexy, just like the man it adhered to.

Knowing she needed to calm her thoughts or Dante would eat her alive, she pulled a pair of jeans, a silver jumper and underwear out of the wardrobe and hurried into the bathroom, locking the door behind her. She dressed quickly, ran her fingers through her damp hair then took one last fortifying breath before leaving the room to find Dante.

This confrontation was one she had prepared for. In theory, she had prepared for all eventualities, even if those eventualities had been cobbled together in a rush when they had learned Dante had sold the hundred acres in Florence and pocketed the proceeds into his already bulging bank account.

All she had to do was hold her nerve against this physically imposing man. His looks and scent did not count for jack. This man, a billionaire in his own right, had ridden roughshod over her sister's efforts to claim a share of their father's estate.

The stairs led into the cosy open-plan living area, where she found him sat on one of the sagging sofas, flicking through one of her university books. Two steaming mugs of coffee were laid on the table before him. His Goliath-proportioned sidekicks were nowhere to be seen.

His eyes narrowed at her approach and he waited in silence until she had sat herself in the farthest spot from him she could find.

He jabbed a finger onto the opened page of the textbook, the place where she had marked her name, as she had done since her school days. 'Tell me about yourself, Aislin O'Reilly.'

He pronounced her name 'Ass-lin', which under normal circumstances would have made her laugh.

She shook her head. For some reason her tongue struggled to work around this man.

He slammed the book on the table, making her jump. 'You claim to be my sister, so tell me about yourself. Show me your proof.'

She crossed her legs and met the intense green stare head-on. 'I'm not your sister. My sister, Orla, is your sister. I'm here as her representative.'

His brow furrowed. She could see him trying to work out what that made them in relation to each other.

'Orla and I have the same mother,' she supplied. 'You and Orla have the same father.'

Dante's lungs loosened at the confirmation that this intruder was not of his blood. The mere sway of her hips as she'd walked down the stairs had sent his senses springing to life. Dante was not particularly fussy when it came to women. He liked them in all shapes and sizes but to think he could find someone who was possibly his own sister desirable would have been enough to drive him straight to the nearest therapist.

'Where is the proof of this, Aislin?'

The lighting in the cottage against the darkly painted walls left much to be desired but now she sat close enough for him to see that the colour of the eyes ringing their loathing at him was grey. The black outer rim of the eyeballs contrasted starkly, making the grey appear translucent. Along with the angled tilt of her eyes, it gave the most extraordinary effect.

'It's Aislin,' she corrected, pronouncing it 'Ashling'.

'Ashling.' He practised it aloud. 'Aislin... An unusual name.'

The striking eyes held his without blinking. 'Not in Ireland it isn't.'

He shrugged. As unusual and interesting as her name was, there were far more important things to discuss. 'You say you have proof that... Orla? Is that her name?'

She nodded.

'That Orla is my sister. Let me see that proof.'

She got to her feet and walked to the small kitchen area, the curve of her bottom in her tight jeans a momentary distraction. From a small bag on the counter she took out an envelope and opened it on her walk back to him.

Pulling a sheet of paper out of the envelope, she handed it to him with a curt, 'Orla's birth certificate.'

Dante took the sheet from her with blood roaring in his ears. Slowly, he unfolded it.

He blinked a number of times to clear the filmy fog that had developed in his eyes.

The birth certificate was dated twenty-seven years ago. On the box labelled 'father' were the words *Salvatore Moncada*.

He rubbed his temples.

This didn't prove anything. This could be a forgery. Or, more likely, Aislin and Orla's mother—he scanned the certificate again and found Sinead O'Reilly named as the mother—had lied.

From the envelope still in her hand, Aislin plucked out a photograph and held it out to him.

He didn't want to look at it.

He *had* to look at it.

The photo was a headshot of two people, a young woman and a toddler boy.

A violent swell clenched and retracted in his stomach.

Both subjects in the photo had thick, dark-brown hair, the exact shade of Dante's.

The woman had green eyes the exact shade of Dante's.

CHAPTER TWO

AISLIN TOOK IN the ashen hue Dante's olive skin had turned and experienced a stab of sympathy to witness the penny drop in that arrogant head.

She placed the envelope on the table and grabbed the coffee he'd made for her, unable to understand why her hands shook. It felt as if her entire insides were shaking, tiny vibrations quivering through her bones and veins.

She told herself it was because of the situation, her body preparing itself for the biggest fight it had ever undertaken. It was nothing to do with Dante himself.

The value of this cottage and its land were peanuts for a man of Dante's wealth but for her sister it meant the world. It would enable her to buy a home that Finn could live in with the freedom to be as normal a child as his condition allowed. That was all Orla wanted— a decent home in which to raise her son.

Aislin loved her nephew with her whole heart. Finn *was* her heart. For months she'd sat by his side as he'd lain in that awful incubator in the neonatal intensive care nursery, willing his tiny body to grow, for his lungs to work on their own; praying that one day he would be strong enough to go home…to survive.

The little fighter had survived, but not without complications. His entire life would be a fight and Aislin was prepared to do whatever necessary to make that fight more bearable.

Dante's lawyer had blocked her sister's every attempt for recognition. Aislin had flown to Sicily determined to confront Dante in person but, again, had been blocked. The security around him was too tight for her to get a foot through it. Breaking into this cottage had been the last desperate resort.

After a length of time had passed that seemed to be stretched by elastic, Dante finally looked up from the photo.

Her heart made the strangest clenching motion when his green eyes locked onto hers. There was a hardness in his stare.

'I have never heard of this woman. My father had many lovers. Many men and women have come forward since his death claiming to be his secret love-child. You give me a photograph and claim it is my sister...'

His thick Sicilian accent soaked into her skin as if her pores were breathing it in.

'I am claiming nothing—she *is* your sister. You can see the resemblance.'

He gave a tutting sound that was pure Sicilian. 'A convenient resemblance.'

'There is nothing convenient about it!' she retorted hotly, and would have added more had he not raised a palm up.

'If she is my sister, why did she wait until after my father's death to reveal herself?'

'She didn't need to reveal herself. Your father paid maintenance for her upbringing until she was eighteen.'

He sagged slightly at this revelation but it was the briefest of movements, his composure regained in a breath. 'That is something I can discover the truth of for myself.'

'It *is* the truth and, if you hadn't stonewalled her every attempt to speak to you, you would have all the facts at your fingertips.'

'My father acknowledged one child. Me. There was no talk of a secret sister, no death-bed confession.'

'That's not Orla's fault.'

'Would she still claim to be my sister if I were to tell you there is nothing left of his estate?'

'That's because you've sold it all off!'

The look he cast her was full of fake pity. 'My father was a gambling addict. He sold everything he could to fund his debts.'

'I've seen the list of assets.' That was the only thing Orla's useless lawyer had been able to get from Dante's terrifyingly efficient one. 'He was worth millions. Orla isn't being greedy. All she wants is a small share of it. Morally, she's entitled to that, even if you and your lawyer don't agree. I'm prepared to stage a sit-in in this cottage until you either sign it over to her or pay her off.'

Before Dante could laugh at Aislin's nerve, a lock of hair fell onto his forehead and over his eyes. He brushed it back. He needed to get it cut, another thing to add to his ever-long list of things to do.

'The law is on my side. Do you really believe that moving into this cottage—illegally—will get you any-where?'

Her eyes spat fury at him. 'Possession is nine-tenths of the law.'

'Maybe in Ireland. But this is Sicily. My country. My property. My land. I can snap my fingers and have you removed from this cottage and expelled from the country.'

'Try it.' She jumped back to her feet and snatched the envelope off the table to pull yet another sheet of paper out of it. 'Try it and I will make sure every media outlet knows what you've done. This is not your land, it's part of your father's estate. All Orla wants is what she's entitled to, and this is the authority for me to handle things on her behalf.'

Dante ignored the letter, although he took note of the pretty hand holding it and the buffed, shapely nails. Then he slowly let his gaze drift upwards, over the curvy hips, the slender waist and the large breasts caressed lovingly in a soft, silver sweater. Simple clothing draped over an outstanding body. As her fragrance snaked its way back into his senses, he experienced a thickening in his loins. Disconcerted with this involuntary reaction to this woman, and at this moment in time, he reached for his coffee.

Dante freely admitted his libido was strong but the last time he'd experienced an inappropriate erection like this had been in a maths lesson almost two decades ago when his teacher had leaned over his desk to help him and her top had gaped open, exposing her cleavage.

He made a point of taking a large sip of the coffee, dragging his focus to the matter at hand. For instant coffee, it wasn't too bad, its heat a welcome respite from the cold that had settled in his spine.

The resemblance between himself and the woman in the photograph was astounding.

'Has your sister ever lived in Sicily?'

The neat, pretty eyebrows drew together. 'No.'

'Say for argument's sake that your assessment is correct and that my father really was worth millions when he died, what makes you think Orla would be entitled to anything? My father named me as his sole heir. She was not recognised as his child. You have to appreciate that my lawyer and I have been through this many times already.'

When the first fraudster had tried their hand at claiming on the estate, Dante and his lawyer had discussed all the legalities on the off-chance the fraudster was telling the truth.

'It might have been different if she had lived in my country at any point in her life. I suggest she pays a visit to a Sicilian lawyer and hears for herself that she has no rights.' He laughed, although humour was the last thing he felt right then. 'There is nothing for her to have. That list you have is old and dates from my grandfather's death. My father sold most of the assets on it. The family home never belonged to him and nor did the land in Florence—my grandparents put them in a trust for me to stop my father selling them to feed his gambling addiction.'

That hadn't stopped one of the fraudsters taking out an injunction to prevent Dante selling those assets, an injunction his lawyer had overturned in ten days. That fraudster was currently rotting in a Sicilian prison, awaiting trial for fraud.

'This cottage is all he had left and it is not for sale.' As dilapidated as the cottage was, Dante would never sell it. He wasn't a man for sentimentality but this was the one place where his childhood memories were only positive. His mother had loathed the cottage and thus it remained untainted by her long-ago desertion.

'Then pay Orla off. Even if what you say is true, and your grandparents bypassed your father, surely she's entitled to something? She knows she can't expect things to be fifty-fifty between you but morally she's entitled to something. She'll be happy to settle for the value of this cottage.'

He shook his head in a display of sympathy. Her approach was pitch-perfect, reason matched with a seeming lack of greed. The perfect cover for an outrageous act of fraud.

Dante had almost convinced himself she spoke the truth but that was impossible. His father would never have kept such a secret from him.

He was quite sure his lawyer, one of the most feared legal brains across the Mediterranean, would have been taken in too. Aislin clearly had the brains to match her beauty. She was an incredible actress.

'This cottage is worth no more than a hundred thousand euros,' he said, ensuring his voice contained just the right amount of commiseration. 'The land is worth about the same.'

'That might not be a lot of money to you but to Orla it's a fortune.'

'If it's worth so much to her then why is she not here? Why has she sent you to deal with it?'

'Because right now she doesn't want to leave Ireland. I'm portable—'

'Did she not want to face me?' The anger that had been simmering deep inside bubbled to the surface. 'Or did my *sister* think sending a beautiful woman in her place would blind me? Is that why you're here? To tempt me into giving this cottage to her?'

Her eyes widened, dark spots of angry colour forming again over the high cheekbones. 'Your mind belongs in a sewer.'

'I'm sure it does.' He rose slowly to his feet. 'You were showering when I came to the cottage. Was that deliberate? Were you keeping watch for me? Did my men being with me force you to change your plans? Did you realise then that you had taken on more than you could handle?'

He gave her no time to defend herself.

Stepping to where she had backed herself against the kitchen unit, he continued, 'Admit it, this is all a bag of lies. What do they call it in English, when a person steals another's image and passes it off as their own?'

The colour spread from her cheekbones to suffuse her entire face, the plump lips clamping tightly together as he stared down at her, daring her to tell the truth.

A sudden image came into his head of those plump lips parting for him…

Heat coiled through his loins again and he breathed deeply to drive it away, only to inhale another lungful of her beautiful scent.

Dante gritted his teeth and waved the photograph still in his hand at her. 'How long did you search for the perfect image that you could use to pretend to be my long-lost sister?'

In one sharp but graceful movement, she snatched it from his hand and stabbed a finger at the toddler's face.

'Did you not even look at the boy Orla's holding?' she snarled. 'That's your nephew.'

'Of course it is. What better than a beautiful child to pull on a man's heartstrings and charm him into giving you money? I have to say, of all the hustlers who have tried to con me, you, *dolcezza*, are by far the best.'

Her foot moved. For a moment Dante thought she was going to kick him.

Instead she spun around, grabbed her handbag and pulled her phone out.

In seconds she had it unlocked and was thrusting it in his face.

'What am I supposed to be looking at?' he asked drolly.

For someone who had to be a foot shorter than him, she raised herself magnificently. 'The photos. There must be a hundred of Finn on it and a load of Orla too.'

The coldness in his veins made a sharp return.

'Take the phone, damn you, and look!' She grabbed hold of his hand and pressed the phone into it.

A jolt ran through him at the touch of her skin on his, a charge that flowed through them both and had their eyes locking together in mutual shock.

After a pause that went on a beat too long, she moved her hand and stepped to the side, away from him.

Aislin dropped her eyes to the floor and rubbed her hands together, trying to negate the charge flowing through her veins.

Her heart beat so hard its thrum echoed in her ears.

She had not expected that. It had been like those times when she touched something and received a surprise charge of static. But those charges had always been unpleasant, something only a masochist would enjoy. The charge she had felt when touching Dante had been...

Not unpleasant at all.

'Please, look at it,' she whispered, summoning the courage to look back at him.

Aislin was not the greatest photographer in the world, and generally managed to chop the top off heads or get a partial thumb over the lens or get a blurry finish. But, however terrible the pictures were in comparison to the one she'd printed off for him, they were documentary proof that she wasn't lying; that she hadn't catfished Orla's identity; that her sister was Dante's half-sister.

Biologically, Orla was Aislin's half-sister too, but she had never thought of her as anything other than her whole sister. They'd been raised together, shared a room until Orla had left for university and been true sisters in every sense of the word. They'd protected each other, fought each other, played, loved and hated. No one could wind Aislin up better than Orla could and she knew it was the same for her sister.

Dante's Adam's apple moved a number of times before he slowly walked to the dining table and sat on the nearest chair, his focus solely on the photos of the two people she loved most in the world.

Her legs suddenly feeling weak too, she took the seat opposite him, close enough that she could hear him breathe, the deep breaths of someone whose life was in the process of being turned upside down.

Aislin knew that feeling. Orla's accident, which had resulted in Finn's premature birth, had turned their world upside down. Life as they knew it had come to a stop that day, three years ago.

She could not help but feel for Dante, trying to imagine what it would feel like to discover a family secret of this magnitude.

It must be shattering.

Her own dad had fathered two more children after his split with her mum but there had been no deception about it, just an awareness that he'd created a new family unit that Aislin was a part of, if somewhat removed from. Her mother, for all her many faults, was no liar. Sometimes Aislin had wished her mum *was* a liar. It would have saved a lot of angst and heartbreak.

'I'm not a hustler,' she said softly after a good two minutes that felt more like two hours had passed, the only sound Dante's breaths and the swipe of his thumb against the screen of her phone. 'Orla is as much your sister as she is mine and Finn is as much your nephew too. I know she'll be happy to take a DNA test if you think it necessary.'

More silence fell until he came to a photo that made him peer more closely. Then he turned the phone to her. 'Why is he in hospital? What are those things on his head?'

She looked at her darling nephew, smiling in his hospital bed. 'That was taken six months ago when he went for an EEG.'

'What's that?'

'It measures brainwaves. He was born prematurely and has cerebral palsy. One of the side effects of that, which he has since been diagnosed with, is severe epilepsy. It's the reason Orla didn't come to Sicily herself—she's terrified to leave him. Finn's condition is the reason she wants a share of the inheritance. She honestly is not being greedy. She just wants a home he can be safe in.' She was silent for a moment before adding, 'That's all I want for him too. I'm sorry for breaking into your cottage. Honestly, I'm not normally one for criminal behaviour, but we're desperate. Please, Dante, Finn is your nephew. We need your help.'

Dante expelled a long breath and put the phone on the table, then dropped his pounding head and kneaded his fingers into the back of his skull.

He felt sick.

If the evidence was to be believed—and, no matter how hard he strove to find a new angle to disprove it, the evidence appeared compelling—he had a sister and a nephew. A sick nephew.

Another wave of nausea ripped through him.

His father had lied to him.

He thought back to Orla's date of birth. He would have been seven when she'd been born. His mother had divorced his father when he was seven.

Did his mother know he had a sister? Had she conspired to keep it secret too?

So many thoughts crowded in his head but stronger than all of them was the image of the tiny boy, his nephew, lying on that hospital bed, hooked to a machine via a dozen tubes stuck to his head.

'How old is he?'

'A month shy of three.'

He didn't want to hear the sympathy now ringing from the soft Irish brogue. He could feel it too, radiating from her.

This woman felt sorry for *him*?

She didn't know him. All they shared was a sister. And a sick nephew.

He muttered a curse.

He raised his head and looked Aislin square in the eye.

Yes, there was compassion in the reflected stare, but also a healthy wariness.

He steepled his fingers across the bridge of his nose and thought hard, pushing aside the emotions crowding him, sharpening his wits and clearing his mind.

He had a business deal to salvage with the D'Amores before he could begin to think about this, never mind deal with it. The clock was ticking. Five days to salvage the biggest deal of his life. Unless he could convince Riccardo that his own playboy days were behind him and prove his parents' faults were not his, then the deal for the exclusivity agreement would be lost for good. On Monday Riccardo intended to sign it with Dante's biggest rival.

One lesson he had learned at a young age was that nothing must come before business. His father had allowed emotions and addiction to take first place and had lost everything for it.

Yet still that image of the boy, his nephew, stayed lodged in the forefront of his mind, and as he stared into the grey eyes of this woman who had just told him his entire life had been a lie, the kernel of an idea flared.

He swept his eyes again over the curvy body and imagined it dressed in expensive couture, and the hair whose colour he still couldn't determine beautifully styled.

Aislin was a stranger in his country. No one knew

her. She was clearly intelligent. And she was beautiful enough that no one would think twice to see her on his arm.

Despite her beauty, she was far removed from the women he normally dated...

'I spoke the truth. My father died penniless,' he told her slowly. 'I gave him an allowance and paid his bills but, other than this cottage, he had nothing left to his name. Under Sicilian law, your sister is not even entitled to a share of that.'

Aislin closed her eyes and slumped in her chair.

The tone of his words held the ring of truth.

Defeat loomed so large she lost the strength to correct him, to say loud and proud that Orla was his sister too.

Aislin was a penniless student. Orla was a penniless single mother still fighting the insurance company for compensation for the damage to her son. They'd pooled the spare cash they'd had between them to instruct that rubbish lawyer who hadn't even bothered to read up properly on Sicilian inheritance laws. Her open-ended return flight here and the car hire had left them skint.

If there was a loophole they could exploit to get something, they had no money left with which to do it.

'This cottage and the land it stands on have been in my family for generations and I have no wish to sell,' he continued, breaking through her defeated thoughts. 'But I am prepared to give Orla half the value. Fifty-fifty.'

She snapped her eyes back open and met his unblinking gaze. 'Really?'

He nodded. 'One hundred thousand euros. It will

be conditional on her taking a DNA test, but we can get that arranged soon. If the test comes back as positive, the money is hers.'

The relief that surged through her at that moment was enough to punch all the breath out of her.

She covered her mouth with a trembling hand. 'Thank you. You don't know what that means—'

'I also have an offer for you,' he cut in before she could get carried away with her thanks. 'An offer that is not DNA-conditional.'

'What kind of offer?'

'A mutually beneficial one.' His eyes narrowed and he rocked his head as if he were thinking. Then he gave one final nod and stilled. 'I have a wedding to attend this weekend. I want you to come with me.'

'You want me to come to a wedding with you?'

'*Sì*. And in return I will pay you one million euros.'

CHAPTER THREE

'BUT...' AISLIN COULDN'T form anything more than that one syllable. Dante's offer had thrown her completely.

His smile was rueful. 'My offer is simple, *dolcezza*. You come to the wedding with me and I give you a million euros.'

He pronounced it *'seemple'*, a quirk she would have found endearing if her brain hadn't frozen into a stunned snowball.

'You want to pay me to come to a wedding with you?'

'Sì.' He unfolded his arms and spread his hands. 'The money will be yours. You can give as much or as little of it to your sister.'

'Won't your girlfriend mind?'

As soon as the words left her mouth, Aislin wanted to kick herself.

His beautifully thick brown eyebrows rose in perfect timing with the flame of colour she could feel rising over her face. 'Did you research me?'

'I saw a picture of you together when I was thinking up ways to get your attention,' she muttered, dropping her eyes to examine her fingernails, desperately trying to affect nonchalance.

She hadn't been researching *him*, more trying to get

a handle on the man in the days before she'd set off for Sicily, trying to decide the best way to cut through the minders and hangers-on to grab his attention for long enough to have the conversation they were now having... A conversation that had taken a most bizarre turn that she was struggling to get her head around.

What she had learned was that Dante Moncada was a man any right-thinking woman would steer a million miles away from. His father had been a Lothario who had seduced Aislin's mother when she'd still been a teenager, and all the evidence pointed to Dante being of the same 'love them and leave them' mould. Dante did not need to pay someone to attend a wedding with him. She would hazard a guess that, if he asked a roomful of women if any wanted to go with him, ninety-nine per cent of them would bob their heads up to agree like over-caffeinated meerkats.

Aislin was part of the one per cent who would duck under a table rather than accept. She'd been there, done that, stupidly having fallen for the biggest playboy on campus, believing his declarations of love and respect; believing they'd had a future that involved marriage and babies, only to find him in bed with one of her housemates mere weeks after her sister's accident.

If she was ever stupid enough to get involved with a man again, her preference would be for a boring, gaming-obsessed hermit with zero libido who had an abhorrence of the outside world and would thus never be in a position or have the mind-space to cheat.

Not a man like Dante. Not this man, who was sexier and more handsome than should be legal.

She could practically smell the testosterone and

pheromones wafting from him. They soaked into her pores in the same way his amazing deep voice did, sensitising her skin and settling deep inside her in a way that was, quite frankly, terrifying.

But a million euros…?

'I ended it with Lola a month ago.' He leaned forward, a sudden, unexpected gleam appearing in his eyes.

Her heart thumped, the beat ricocheting through her like a tsunami.

It took a huge amount of effort to keep her voice steady. 'But you must have a heap of women you could take and not have to pay them for it.'

'None of them are suitable.'

'What does that mean?'

'I need to make an impression on someone and having you on my arm will assist in that.'

'A million dollars for one afternoon…?'

'I never said it would be for an afternoon. The celebrations will take place over the coming weekend.'

She tugged at her ponytail. 'Weekend?'

'Aislin, the groom is one of Sicily's richest men. It is a necessity that his wedding be the biggest and flashiest it can be.'

She almost laughed at the deadpan way he explained it.

She didn't need to ask who the richest man in Sicily was.

'If I'm going to accept your offer, what else do I need to know?'

'Nothing… Apart from that I will be introducing you as my fiancée.'

'What?' Aislin winced at the squeakiness of her tone.

'I require you to play the role of my fiancée.' His

grin was wide with just a touch of ruefulness. The deadened, shocked look that had rung from his eyes only a few minutes before had gone. Now they sparkled with life and the effect was almost hypnotising.

She blinked the effect away.

'Why do you need a fiancée?'

'Because the father of the bride thinks going into business with me will damage his reputation.'

'How?'

'I will go through the reasons once I have your agreement on the matter. I appreciate it is a lot to take in so I'm going to leave you to sleep on it. You can give me your answer in the morning. If you're in agreement then I shall take you home with me and give you more details. We will have a few days to get to know each other and work on putting on a convincing act.'

'And if I say no?'

He shrugged. 'If you say no, then no million euros.'

'What about the hundred thousand you said you would give Orla?'

'That is a separate matter and dependent on the DNA test. Your decision will not affect that.'

'Do you promise?' She knew it was a childish way of asking but she didn't care. A hundred thousand euros was too great a sum to play games with.

But a million euros… That was a figure she could scarcely comprehend. That was life-changing.

His handsome features fell into seriousness. He inclined his head before rising to his feet. 'Whatever you decide, and whatever the outcome, that money for Orla will remain separate from it. You have my word.'

She didn't have the faintest idea why but she believed him.

· *

Dante greeted the housekeeper, who made an almost convincing job of not acting surprised to see him and at such a late hour, and strolled through his old family home as he had done a thousand times before.

This was the sprawling seafront villa he'd grown up in, just as his father had. A decade ago, to prevent the villa being used as collateral against his son's gambling debts, his grandfather had signed it over to Dante.

Although the villa had been technically his for all these years, as far as he'd been concerned it had remained his father's to do with as he pleased...apart from sell it.

With his father dead, he still didn't know what to do with it. Unspoken had been his grandfather's wish that one day Dante would settle down, marry, start a family and raise them in this home.

Dante liked city life. He liked being single. What good was marriage for? All he had ever seen of it was bitterness, greed and spite. His grandparents had been married for forty-eight years until his grandmother's death. If they were a template for the longevity of marriage, they could forget it. His grandfather had spent the three years from her death until his own celebrating being rid of her. Dante had been quite sure his grandfather's shaking shoulders at her funeral had been through laughter rather than tears.

At the far end of the villa was his father's study. In the days after his death, Dante had holed himself in there, finding comfort in the room that had been quintessentially his father.

He pushed the door open and inhaled the familiar, if now fading, scent of bourbon and cigars.

This was the room Dante had sneaked into as a small boy, the desk he would hide under until his father appeared and he would jump out at him, and his father would pretend to shout in fright every single time.

He sat on the chair his father had called his own, the chair on which his father had sat Dante on his lap, held him tightly and told him his mother had left and that it would be just the two of them from now on.

This was the room his father had given Dante his first drink of bourbon in, the room in which he'd relayed the deaths of family members, the room where he'd confessed his dire financial situation and begged his only son for a loan to pay off his gambling debts. The latter had taken place so many times Dante had lost count.

A lifetime of memories, good and bad, flooded him and it took a few minutes for him to gather himself together and for the fresh wave of grief to pass.

He opened his father's laptop. When he'd opened it the first time after his father's death he'd guessed the password correctly—Dante's name and date of birth. That had been a bittersweet moment.

Keying the password in this time, all he tasted was bitterness.

Had his father really kept a sister secret from him for all these years?

Aislin claimed his father had paid maintenance for Orla. If there was evidence of it, it would be on here somewhere.

He had a sister. His gut told him that and he did not doubt the DNA test would prove a match.

But had his father known or had Sinead O'Reilly kept Orla's existence a secret from him and lied to her daughters about maintenance being paid?

Dante sent a silent prayer that Sinead was a liar and logged onto his father's saved bank statements.

Damn it, they only went back eight years.

He drummed his fingers on the desk. Where would the paper statements be from the years before that? His father had been a terrible hoarder so they would be here somewhere...

The filing cabinet, of course.

An hour later and he was sat on the carpeted floor, paperwork strewn around him. In his hand was the evidence he'd been seeking but praying he wouldn't find.

Until nine years ago, coincidentally the year Orla had turned eighteen, his father had paid the sum of two thousand euros every month to a bank account in Ireland.

Aislin hovered by the front window of the cottage, peering out intermittently while she waited for Dante.

Nerves in the form of butterflies rampaged in her belly.

Her bags were packed and waiting by the front door. She'd spent most of the night fighting the urge to flee to the airport.

A hundred thousand euros was a substantial amount of money but a million was life-changing. Orla could buy a home, modify it to cater to all Finn's needs and have change to spare at the end of it. She could take him on holiday. She could buy him a high-tech wheel-chair. She could buy a car.

So Aislin had stayed in the cold cottage, hardly sleeping, her mind whirling like a dervish, trying to understand why her instinct was to run.

A million euros to attend a wedding! All her family's problems solved in one weekend!

Restless, she paced the living area.

She'd been prepared to break into the cottage and stage a sit-in in defiance of a powerful billionaire; had been prepared to stay there for as long as it took for him to develop a conscience.

She had not expected it to develop so quickly or easily.

His agreement to give Orla half the value of the cottage and its land had proven his conscience. That he was insisting on a DNA test was not surprising and not something she could blame him for. Dante was no fool. No one who reached the heights in business he had got there by taking people at face value.

She had expected an arrogant monster and found, instead, an arrogant man who could be compelled to listen to reason.

So why was she so resistant to spending a few days with him when the reward for doing so was so great?

A loud rap on the front door made her jump and, when Dante strode through the front door, her heart jumped too, right into her throat.

She'd opened the shutters earlier and spring sunlight poured into the cottage. Dante seemed to glow with it.

Dressed in a navy shirt, snug black jeans and an obviously expensive straight leather jacket, his handsome features were more pronounced than they'd been the evening before, the texture of his dark hair thicker and smoother, the green eyes that found hers brighter.

But there was something unkempt about his appearance too. He looked like a man who had spent the night at the bottom of a bottle of rum rather than in a bed. The effect only made him sexier. A pulse set off deep inside her, warmth gathering low in the most intimate of places...

Her reason for resistance suddenly became obvious.

This wasn't mere appreciation of a handsome, sexy man. She was attracted to him.

Aislin was attracted to Dante Moncada. Properly, heart-beatingly, swoon-makingly attracted.

'You are still here,' he stated as he closed the door.

'Well spotted, Einstein.'

Okay, so she was attracted to him. That was nothing to panic about. It didn't mean her brain cells had to become goo around him. She had overcome much worse than an unwelcome attraction to a gorgeous man before. If there was one thing Aislin had it was an abundance of self-control. How else could she have sat through all those awful meetings with the patronising social workers and other officials who'd all seemed determined to deny her the right to be Finn's legal guardian, while Orla had recovered from her horrific injuries, and not have punched any of them?

The slightest spark emerged in the green of his bloodshot eyes. 'Einstein would have killed for my IQ.'

Her lips twitched to break into a smile. 'And your modesty, I'm sure.'

He grinned. 'Am I to assume you're going to accept my offer?'

'A million euros to act as your arm candy for a few days? Yep, I can do that.' She could deal with attraction. Deal with it by ignoring it and keeping her wits sharp. 'But, before I accept your deal, I should point out that no one is going to believe we're engaged. You've only just dumped your last girlfriend.'

He winked, sank onto the sofa and stretched his legs out. His legs were so long his feet slid under the coffee table. 'Anyone who knows me knows I'm a fast mover.'

'That's nothing to be proud of,' she said tartly.

'Trust me, I know when to go slow.'

Heated colour spread like wildfire over her cheeks. 'I won't accept any funny business.'

She needed to make that very clear. Just because her body reacted so strongly to him did not mean she had any intention of allowing anything to happen between them. She would not be one of those over-caffeinated bobbing meerkats.

Dante could curse himself. He hadn't meant to make innuendoes but the opportunity had presented itself in irresistible fashion. 'You are speaking of sex?'

Her face now flamed so brightly it was quite possible it could explode.

'You have nothing to fear. This arrangement is strictly business. The bride and groom both come from religious families and will put us in separate rooms for the sake of appearances.'

After a terrible night when his brain had refused to shut down, even after he'd thrown the best part of a bottle of bourbon down his neck to assist it, he'd come to the conclusion that this deal *had* to be platonic. In any other circumstance he would go all-out to seduce Aislin but seduction would add too many complications. He needed to keep his head focused on salvaging the business deal, and that was before he added the small detail of Aislin being the sister of his father's secret love-child.

If he didn't believe she was the perfect woman to make Riccardo D'Amore believe him to be a changed man he would have called the whole thing off. But she *was* perfect. Not only was she not of their world but she had a working brain in her beautiful head and a firm commitment to family Riccardo would adore.

All Dante had to do was keep his hands off her, which he had a great feeling would be easier said than done.

Promises made in the twilight hours were much harder to keep in daylight when her scent coiled around his senses. In the daylight, Aislin was more than beautiful, her beauty enhanced now her hair was dry and its vibrant colour there for him to glory in, a deep russet that reminded him of fallen autumn leaves. It made him think of a fox, which he thought an apt word to describe her. She'd stolen into his cottage like a fox. An exquisite fox.

Today she'd dressed in black leggings, an oversized khaki jumper fraying on the left sleeve and scuffed black ankle boots. These were clothes designed for comfort, obviously old and worn, yet he found them as sexy as if she were wearing a tight cocktail dress with all her currently hidden cleavage on show.

She rubbed her hands over her arms, inadvertently pushing against those same breasts he'd just been imagining. 'As long as we're clear on things being platonic then that's grand.'

'Is there anything else you want to bring up? Because we need to get going.'

Those strange eyes were back on him again, penetrating like lasers. It was the strangest of feelings; unnerving yet weirdly erotic. 'I want half the money now.'

'No.'

'I need a guarantee. A form of surety. I don't want to spend a weekend pretending to like you only to have you then refuse to hand the money over.'

'You don't like me?'

'How do I know if I like you? I don't know you, certainly not well enough to trust you.'

Her lack of sycophancy was refreshing. She was direct, her mouth as unfiltered as her inherent sexiness. 'Ten thousand.'

'That's peanuts.'

'How much money do you have in your bank account?'

'The dust of a bag of peanuts.'

He bit back a laugh at her phrasing and spread his hands in a 'there you are' gesture.

She fixed him with a stare that made him think she would make an excellent teacher. It was a look that would shut a classroom full of screaming kids up.

He shook his head and gave an exaggerated sigh. '*Va bene*. I can be reasonable. Fifty thousand up front, in cash or transferred into a bank account of your choice, the remainder on Sunday evening. Deal?'

Her exquisitely beautiful face took on the expression of someone sucking an extra-sour lemon. Then she jerked her head into a nod. 'Yes. Deal.'

He rubbed his hands together and got to his feet. '*Eccellente*. Let's get going.'

'Transfer the money and then we can go.'

'You don't want it in cash?'

'I'd prefer it transferred.'

He sighed and pulled his phone out of his jacket pocket. 'Name of the account?'

'Miss Orla O'Reilly.'

He looked up briefly with a frown. 'You don't want it in your own account?'

'The money's not for me. It's for our sister and nephew. Orla's skint and the money you're going to give her once you've had the DNA test could take weeks to come through.'

'You're not going to keep any of the million for yourself?'

'I'll get her to buy me a pizza from it.'

Was she for real? 'Are you looking for a sainthood?'

She threw her schoolteacher stare at him again.

He shrugged. If she wanted to let the entire million slip through her fingers, that was her loss. 'The account details?'

She recited them to him.

He looked up from his phone again. 'You know your sister's bank details by heart?'

'She was in a bad car accident three years ago that left her in a coma. I took care of all her finances and stuff while she was in hospital and recovering from her injuries.'

'Is that why her son was born prematurely?'

A dimness filtered over the grey eyes. She nodded.

Why this information should make his finger hover over the sum he was about to transfer, he did not know.

This time yesterday he hadn't even known of Orla's existence.

Had his father known she'd been injured?

Had his father known he had a grandchild?

A fresh barb sliced through him at the reminder of the secrets and lies his father had kept from him for twenty-seven years.

Dante stared at the beautiful redhead, knowing he had to keep his focus on the primary reason for keeping her in Sicily and paying her such a substantial amount of money. Aislin was the key to convincing Riccardo D'Amore that he was not the sum of his parents' parts. Just because they shared a sister did not mean he could allow himself to be sidetracked. Orla's accident was history...

But the after-effects lived on in her son. His nephew.

They were nothing to do with him, he told himself grimly. They were strangers to him and would remain that way. A shared bloodline did not make them family and, even if it did, Dante had had enough of family.

He'd loved his mother with all his boyish heart and she'd abandoned him. He'd been close to his grandparents but their constant sniping and bad-mouthing of each other, and their respective expectations that he would take sides, had been a drain. His extended family were just as bad. He'd adored his father. Salvatore had been a fantastic if unconventional father when Dante had been small, father and son always there for each other through all the ups and downs life had thrown at them; and now he'd learned that beneath that closeness had been the most monstrous of secrets.

His father had been a gambler and a playboy but Dante would have trusted him with his life.

Turned out his father had been the greatest liar of them all.

Why embrace a sister when every other member of his bloodline had lied, abandoned or emotionally abused him?

No more. He was better on his own.

He hit the confirmation button then went through the additional security needed to transfer such a large sum. Anti-money-laundering regulations were the bane of the honest businessman's life. 'Done.'

He held the phone for her to see. 'The money will credit your sister's account by the end of the working day.'

She peered at it with a furrowed brow. 'You transferred two hundred thousand?'

He nodded tersely. 'I've upheld my end of the deal. Now we can go.'

CHAPTER FOUR

AISLIN GAZED OUT of the car window. The drive from the cottage to Palermo had taken her from farmed fields and intense greenery to the bright lights of Sicily's capital in only twenty minutes.

Thankfully Dante had sat in the front next to his driver, enabling her to relax into the journey and not spend the trip fighting her growing awareness of him.

The gleam she'd seen in his eyes a few times had made her think he might be aware of her in the same way, but his declaration that this was purely a business agreement had put paid to that notion.

Her limited experience with men meant her instincts could not be relied on. Growing up in a small village in Kerry, there had been a shortage of boys to play with. Secondary school had not been much better on the boy front. By the time she'd started university she'd been desperate for a boyfriend but on her first day had overheard a group of boys ranking the girls on the size of their breasts, their 'spreadability' and their looks. It had been enough to make her vomit and, from that point on, she'd kept males at a distance, willing to be friends but not anything more. Some girls might have been happy to be marked out of ten on their prowess but she was not one of them.

It was in the summer term of her second year that Patrick had taken an interest her. Far from immediately trying to dive into her knickers, he'd made an effort to woo her. He'd brought her flowers. He'd asked for her help with an assignment—without a boyfriend to distract her, Aislin had soon distinguished herself as a swot—and it had filled her silly little head with pride that the most popular lad in her year was interested in *her*.

Weeks later, they'd started dating. Words of love and respect were exchanged, words she'd believed. Six months on, Orla had been driving in a heavy storm when an approaching car had lost control and smashed head-on into hers. Patrick, resenting Aislin's devotion to her comatose sister and prematurely born nephew, had wasted no time in hooking up with Aislin's housemate, a girl she had considered a good friend.

She hadn't dated anyone since. In all honesty, even if she'd wanted to, which she didn't, there hadn't been the space in her life to date.

Dante was the first man to occupy her thoughts in three years and, compared to his playboy antics, Patrick was a rank amateur.

She didn't know if it made it better or worse that Dante didn't fancy her. It shouldn't matter at all.

This deal was strictly business.

She couldn't work him out. One minute he was haggling over the upfront payment, driving down her demands, the next transferring four times the amount they had settled on.

So far, she hadn't dared tell Orla about the deal,

fearful of building her hopes up. She didn't think Dante would be able to stop the payment but he was a powerful man. Beneath the affable exterior lay a darkness. She had no idea what he was capable of.

It had been dark when she'd landed four days ago, too dark for her to appreciate Palermo's astounding beauty, especially as she'd been trying to navigate unfamiliar streets in a rental car and driving on a different side of the road than she was used to.

She'd almost forgotten about that rental car. Thankfully, Dante had given the keys to one of his goons with instructions to take it back to the airport.

Driving in daylight through Palermo was like stepping into the medieval past. Were it not for the busy narrow streets filled with people in modern dress, she could believe she'd slipped into a time vortex.

Expecting to be taken to a secluded palatial home guarded with Rottweilers and more goons of the armed variety, she was momentarily taken aback when Dante's driver pulled up in a street that was only a little wider than the luxurious vehicle they were in, stopping beside a long terrace of five-storey apartments. The street was clean and pretty, the exterior walls painted cream, iron balconies beneath all the upper windows with hanging baskets of flowers creating colour, a few scooters parked close to the walls.

Dante craned his neck to talk to her. 'We are here.'

'This is your home?'

She pressed her face against the window for a better look, certain he was having a laugh at her expense. This was an ordinary residential street. Dante was a billionaire. Shouldn't his main home—during the course of her research she'd discovered he owned a heap of opulent city apartments across Europe—be flashier?

A young, skinny lad in a leather jacket that must have cost a fraction of the price Dante had paid for his suddenly appeared from nowhere and opened Dante's door.

Dante unfolded his legs from the car, shook the boy's hand with his right hand whilst slapping his shoulder with his left and chatted animatedly with him while the driver opened Aislin's door and helped her out.

The boot of the car flipped open and the young lad broke away from the conversation to grab Aislin's suitcase and carry it to the arched door at the end of the row, a nondescript piece of wood she would have trouble distinguishing from the others.

Amusement danced in Dante's eyes as he indicated for Aislin to follow the boy inside.

She entered warily.

Was this all an elaborate hoax to punish her for breaking into his father's cottage? Was he leading her along, only pretending to believe her about Orla and Finn?

As with the exterior of the building, the interior was nothing to write home about. Plain concrete stairs led to the top floor and was mercifully free of graffiti or any pungent smells.

Instead of climbing the stairs, Dante punched the lift button. With a loud ping, the door opened.

Aislin blinked.

The lift was thickly carpeted. A whole side was a mirror without a single smear. It was the kind of elevator one would expect to see in a posh hotel.

She didn't feel any movement as they journeyed to the top floor. She followed Dante out into a small, square landing area with only one door. A grilled security partition had been drawn back from across it.

Before he could reach the door, the skinny teenager walked out of it.

Dante spoke briefly with Ciro, pressed some money in his hand then walked into the apartment as Ciro stepped into the lift.

He'd made it across the reception area before he realised Aislin had failed to follow him.

He turned to find her hovering with her back pressed to the wall beside the lift.

'Are you coming?'

'This isn't some kind of joke, is it?' she asked doubtfully.

'No joke. There is nothing to fear.'

Her grey eyes held his for an age before she blinked and made tentative steps to the threshold.

When she crossed it the whisper of a gasp flew from her mouth.

'Not what you were expecting?'

She shook her tilted head, eyes darting over the high-carved ceilings.

'Wait until you see the rest of it.' He pushed the double doors open and stepped inside.

Her gasp this time was audible.

'You like it?'

'I don't know...'

Dante always enjoyed watching people's reaction to his main home. He'd bought the first three adjacent apartments a decade ago then spent a year purchasing the other apartments until the whole street bar one

ground-floor apartment was his. He hadn't had to use
the strong-arm tactics many of his compatriots with
his wealth and power would have used to convince the
other owners to sell. Offering twice the listed value
for each apartment had produced the same results and
allowed him to sleep at night. He now employed the
elderly couple who had refused to sell to be his eyes
and ears. The remaining ground-floor apartments he
used as homes for his staff. Knowing protection was
on hand if he needed it without having his personal
space encroached also allowed him to sleep well.

All the apartments on floors one to five had been
knocked through to create a sprawling home that was
unimaginable from the outside. This was the place
Dante called home. His other apartments had been
bought for convenience and as investments.

She walked to one of the windows and peered out.
'Where's your garden?'

Of all the questions and reactions that usually followed a new visitor stepping inside, this was a first.

'I don't have one.'

The look she cast him with was more than suspi-
cious. 'No garden? Not even on your roof?'

'There's a terrace with a swimming pool on the
roof.' He'd had it enclosed to retain his privacy. If he
wanted to wander around naked on the roof, he could,
and no one on the surrounding streets would be any
the wiser.

'That's handy in the winter.'

'It's heated, but if the weather gets too bad I use
the pool on the first floor.'

'You have two swimming pools but no garden?'

'I have no need or desire for a garden.'

'What if you have children?'

'I have no wish for children.' For Dante children went hand in hand with marriage and he had no intention of ever marrying.

'Is that what we tell people?'

'What do you mean?'

'You're going to tell people we're engaged. If the guests are anything like those who attend Irish weddings, the first thing we'll be asked is when we plan to have children.'

'If asked, keep the answer vague—we want to enjoy our time together and have children in the future. Now, let me show you to your room—hopefully you will find it more to your liking than the rest of the house.'

'I never said I didn't like it,' Aislin protested, sensing his back had gone up. 'I live in a dinky house with Orla and Finn. This is a little much for me to get my head around.'

The tiny two-bed house was the same one she had grown up in. The one decent thing their mother had done for them, before she had decided to reclaim her lost youth by backpacking her way around Asia, was to transfer the tenancy of the house to Aislin and Orla. That had been five years ago. When she planned to return to Ireland was anyone's guess. Her eldest daughter's head-on car crash that had resulted in horrific injuries to Orla and the premature birth of her first grandchild had not been lure enough to bring Sinead O'Reilly back to her family.

The space in Dante's home was mind-blowing. Sunlight poured through the abundant windows and danced over the obviously expensive dark furnishings, creating light where the dark woods and dark leathers would have made it feel gloomy. She estimated her entire house could fit in the living area alone.

Seeing the richness of Dante's life with her own eyes was very different from imagining it, was so much more, in the exact same way Dante was so much more vibrant and sexier in the flesh.

'How are we going to convince anyone that I belong in your world?' she asked, suddenly anxious.

His startling green eyes held hers for a moment before his lips lifted into a grin. 'But that is the reason you are so perfect for the role of my fiancée. You're different. I am not used to people telling me my home is anything but the work of a creative genius. You are not like my usual lovers and are not from my world. Riccardo is going to love you.'

'Who's Riccardo?'

'Riccardo D'Amore is the man we need to convince.'

'But what do we need to convince him of? You still haven't properly explained why you're paying me to be your fiancée.'

They'd passed through a room dedicated to modern art, paintings adorning the walls, quirky sculptures on plinths, and now stood on a mezzanine overlooking another vast living area.

'I have been working on an important business deal with Riccardo's son, Alessio. It's an exclusive software deal that will allow me to break into the American market. My father's death attracted much publicity. All the obituaries spoke in length about his love of women and addiction to gambling. The stories sowed doubt in Riccardo's mind about my character. He believes I am too much like my father to be trusted and that doing business with me will have a detrimental effect on the D'Amore reputation. He has put a stop to the business deal.'

Dante caught the flash of outrage in her eyes. 'Can he do that?'

He nodded grimly. 'He can and he has. Alessio runs the company but Riccardo is still the majority shareholder.'

'So how will us pretending to be engaged change anything?'

'Riccardo married young, has always been faithful to his wife and had lots of babies. He believes that family is sacrosanct, that gambling is the work of the devil— I understand his point there—and that sex is for marriage. My family is famous for pursuing pleasure—in my mother's case marrying and divorcing on a whim— gambling, sex without discretion…all the things he believes are sins. He believes in family and roots. You are nothing like my usual lovers. You study, you're intelligent, you have a strong loyalty and attachment to your family.'

The textbooks on medieval Europe she had brought with her, which he had flicked through while waiting for her to dress the night before, had been well-thumbed, pages turned over at the corners, notes in a lively penmanship made in the margins. The books had been heavy in his hands, the words dense on the pages.

She stared back, drawing her plump lips in before saying, 'But how are we going to explain *us*? Sure, you say people know you as a fast mover, but this is rocket fast.'

Her lips were the perfect shade of pink, bringing to mind fresh raspberries. What would they taste like…?

The flame of desire he'd smothered since leaving the cottage earlier reignited.

Dante fought the heated tendrils snaking through his bloodstream and willed his body to remain passive.

He was not an adolescent. He was an adult male who'd had so many lovers their names and faces were indistinguishable from each other.

'We will stick to the truth as much as we can. You came to Sicily to meet me on your sister's behalf. We can pad the timing.'

'Our sister,' she corrected obstinately.

'*Our* sister,' he agreed with a sigh. He'd known Aislin for less than a day but already he was fully aware she could argue for Ireland. She had passion in her soul and was refreshingly unafraid to show it. 'We were immediately attracted to each other.' That was not a lie. Not for him. Dante could not remember ever having felt such an immediate attraction to anyone. 'In fact, we would go so far as to say it was love at first sight. You were so different to everyone I've ever known that I was helpless not to fall in love with you. In you I knew I'd found the woman I wanted to settle down with and spend the rest of my life with.'

As he finished speaking, he realised his voice had dropped to a whisper and that his body was straining towards her. There was an itch in his fingers to reach out and touch her, to brush a thumb against her cheek…

Her face tilted back as she gazed right back at him, her neck elongating with such grace his mouth prickled to graze over the delicate skin.

'Because I'm so different?' Her voice dropped to a whisper that mimicked his.

'*Sì.*' Compellingly different in all the ways that mattered. A beautiful russet fox that made his senses dance to a rhythm he'd never felt before.

He wanted to taste those lips. He wanted to touch those high cheekbones.

'And we tell the truth about Orla?'

The reminder of his father's lies and deception acted like a bucket of iced water being thrown over his head.

Breathing heavily, he stepped back, cleared his throat and said gruffly, 'Lies only unravel into a mess. Where possible, we stick to the truth. The only real deception will be in our intention to marry. Now, I have some business to wrap up before I can give you my undivided attention.

'Your room is the last on the left.' He pointed to the end of the wide corridor. 'Get settled, explore, make yourself at home and in an hour or so we can have lunch.'

An hour would be ample time to shake off the heat flowing through his veins and get his concentration back to where it should be.

He would be spending all his time with Aislin over the next five days and could not afford to let this attraction take over his rationality.

Taking Aislin as his lover would be a complication too far, even if the heavy weight in his loins begged to differ.

Dio, he'd never reacted so strongly to a woman before. This was off all the scales.

He disappeared into his office.

Stunned at his abrupt departure, Aislin stared at

the door Dante had closed sharply behind him, her heart beating so hard it felt as if it could burst through her ribs.

For a moment she'd thought he was going to kiss her.

Worse, her lips had tingled with anticipation of that kiss. More than her lips had tingled. Her entire body thrummed with an electricity that heated her core and had her fighting the urge to kick the door open.

Furious with herself, Aislin bit hard into her bottom lip.

She must stop imagining things. Just because she found him so attractive did *not* mean the feeling was mutual. And nor should she want it to be mutual.

This was Dante Moncada, Mr Love Them and Leave Them, the son of the man who had seduced her nineteen-year-old mother.

She would *not* be a bobbing meerkat for him. She would get control of this damnable attraction if it took her the entire time they were together.

CHAPTER FIVE

AISLIN'S TORTURED THOUGHTS were momentarily shoved aside when she opened the door to the room Dante had said was hers.

This was a guest room?

This must once have been an entire apartment. Inside it lay a four-poster king-sized bed, a walk-in wardrobe twice the size of her bedroom in Ireland, a huge flat-screen television and other electrical gizmos she didn't recognise. Fresh flowers had been placed on all four windowsills and the leather sofa was a caramel colour, rather than the chocolate of his living rooms, making it marginally less masculine than what she had seen of the rest of his home.

She took a look in the private bathroom and found a humongous shower *and* a roll-top bath.

Aislin stood at the huge, gold-framed mirror and stared critically at her reflection.

Fingering a lock of her hair, she grimaced at the ends badly in need of snipping. When had she last had it cut? It had to be coming up to a year. She was lucky she'd been blessed with eyebrows that didn't require upkeep otherwise she would likely resemble a werewolf.

When had she last worn make-up? Not since Orla's accident. Vanity, like everything else in her life, had been forgotten about. She'd restarted her degree last autumn but, not wanting to study away from home this time round, had opted to finish it through distance learning. This allowed her to stay with her sister and nephew and be there to help them with whatever they needed.

What she would do with that degree when she was done she no longer knew. The life plan she'd mapped out for herself all those years ago belonged to a different Aislin.

She wrinkled her nose.

Three years of neglecting her appearance showed. No wonder she did nothing for Dante.

Presumably, her lack of glamour and ordinary looks would give weight to her being *nothing like his usual lovers*, she thought moodily. It had been nothing but a roundabout way of saying that he found her plain and unsexy.

She didn't want him to find her sexy!

Dante was paying her a million euros to act as his fiancée. There was no point griping that it was being offered due to her ordinariness.

Pulling a face at her reflection, she set off to explore the rest of Dante's home.

And what a home it was.

Aislin felt like the glamorous host of some kind of 'amazing interiors' television show. But without the glamour.

She imagined herself talking to a camera and sweeping her arms majestically, pointing out that, where concrete stairs led to the top floor outside, inside the stairs were all white marble. The top three floors had been transformed into two levels with enormously high ceilings, containing a kitchen any chef would purr with delight in, two dining rooms, six bedrooms of equal proportions to her own—none of which she did more than peek into, scared in case one of them belonged to Dante—three living rooms, more dedicated art rooms and even a water feature in the centre with a river of water snaking from it. The floor below...

A swimming pool the Romans would have considered decadent, complete with a gym and spa facilities...

Her phone buzzed.

She pulled it out of her back pocket and answered her sister's call.

'Ash, I've just received an email from the bank notifying me of a credit. I've checked, two hundred thousand euros has been put in. *Two hundred thousand!* From Dante Moncada! What's going on? You said he was going to give me a hundred thousand when the DNA test's done.'

'It's actually credited?'

'Yes!' Orla burst into tears. Her sobs were so loud Aislin moved the phone from her ear until they quietened.

'Orla, breathe,' she instructed kindly.

The sobs were replaced by deep breaths. 'What's going on?'

'Well...' Aislin screwed her eyes shut as she said in a rush, 'Dante's paying me to pretend to be his fiancée for a weekend.'

'You what?' Tearful, overwhelmed Orla was suddenly replaced by bossy big sister Orla.

'It's for a business deal he's trying to salvage. He

needs to show a respectable face. Don't worry,' she hastened to add. 'There's nothing sinister or pervy about it.'

'If there's nothing pervy, why is he paying you all that money?'

'Actually…' She almost told her the grand total would be a million but stopped herself in time.

The full million was dependent on them fooling Riccardo D'Amore that they were a genuine couple. If Aislin didn't play her part well enough, she would forfeit the remainder.

'Actually what?' Orla prompted.

'Nothing. You have nothing to worry about. Dante finds me as attractive as a rhino. He needs a fake fiancée for one weekend to seal the business deal, he feels bad about your situation and wanted to do something to help.' She'd explained the night before about Salvatore dying with hardly a cent to his name and that under Sicilian law, which Aislin had checked up on herself with the help of the Internet, she would have a massive fight to get anything at all. 'By the way, you can't tell anyone.'

Her sister snorted. 'Who am I going to tell? Finn? The receptionist from the surgery?'

'Very funny. How is Finn today?'

'He's having a good day but he misses you. When will you be home?'

Aislin's heart clenched. She and Finn had a bond that was as strong as if she'd given birth to him herself. This was the first time they'd been parted since he'd been released into her care from the neonatal unit. 'All being well, early next week.'

'You will take care of yourself, won't you? Dante's reputation with women is awful.'

'I'm not his type, so stop worrying.'

'Has he said anything about wanting to meet me?'

'Not yet.' Not a single word. 'I think he wants to get this business deal done with first. It's very important to him.'

'More important than me and Finn?'

'He just needs time to process the fact he has a sister,' she reminded her gently, smothering her instinct to tell Orla it would be better if Dante remained only a name in her life. The last thing Orla needed was to pin her hopes on a relationship with a brother who didn't want to be a brother. Aislin would not see Orla hurt again. 'He didn't know you existed until a day ago. Give him time.'

When the call was done with, Aislin released an enormous breath of relief.

Whatever her doubts about Dante and his future relationship with their shared sister, the money had cleared.

That money was safe. It was Orla's.

This was no hoax or game. If they failed to convince Riccardo, that two hundred thousand would still be Orla's. When you added the DNA-dependent hundred thousand to the mix, Orla's and Finn's lives would be changed for the better, regardless of what happened at the wedding and regardless of whether Dante wanted to be a part of their lives.

Dante had done this for them.

It suddenly occurred to her that she needed to thank him.

Not giving herself time to change her mind, she

hurried off in search of the room he'd shut himself away in.

Dante was in the middle of writing an email when a knock on his office door distracted him.

His heart thumped.

It could only be Aislin.

'Come in,' he called.

She burst through the door, her beautiful face shining with a radiance the old Masters would have struggled to capture in oil.

His every sinew tightened.

Damn it, he'd finally got himself back under control, and now that control was shattered in the time it took for her to walk into his office.

He hid his discomfort. 'I'm nearly finished.'

The most captivating smile broke out on her face. 'I'm not trying to chivvy you. I just wanted to thank you.'

'For what?'

'The money has credited Orla's account. I cannot begin to tell you how happy you've made her.' She put her hands on his desk and stared at him with such force it was as if her pupils had invisible lasers pouring out of them. 'Now that I know you're a man of your word, I want you to know that I am a woman of *my* word, and that I intend to be the best fake fiancée money can buy. I will follow your lead in however you want to play things at the wedding and make darn sure that the old fool believes you and I are madly in love.'

His blood heated to imagine all the ways he could take advantage of that declaration, starting right here and now by spreading her over the table...

He pushed the heady image away with all the force he could muster and gritted his teeth. 'My only expectation is that you be you. Obviously, we will need to buy you some appropriate clothing.'

Alarm flashed in her eyes. 'What do you mean by "appropriate"?'

'Clothes appropriate for a society weekend and wedding that you feel comfortable in.'

'I don't know what would be appropriate.'

'There are stores with personal shoppers who will help and guide you. I will take you to them tomorrow.'

'Erm…' Her brow furrowed with an uncertainty he found strangely endearing. 'Are you okay to loan me the money for it? It's just that I'm skint.'

Used to women assuming he would always pick up the tab for them, it took Dante a moment to realise she was serious.

'While you are under my employ I pay for everything.' It was imperative he re-establish that this was a business arrangement and not a personal one. Imperative as a reminder to himself and the thickening in his blood and loins.

She stilled, eyes narrowing. 'So you're my boss?'

'If I'm paying you to provide a service then, yes, that makes me your boss.'

'Don't push it, Moncada.'

He narrowed his own eyes at her. 'What?'

'You're not my boss and I'm not your employee. We've come to a mutually beneficial arrangement—a quid pro quo—so please don't ruin my happy thoughts towards you.'

She had happy thoughts towards him?

That should *not* make his chest puff up.

'I did not mean it to sound so formal,' he said with a stiffness that in itself bordered on formality. 'If I have in some way insulted you then I apologise. What I meant is that you are here, in my world, at my request. My world is an expensive place to live and it is only right that I pay for the things you need that will allow you to fit into it.'

Her stillness vanished and she bestowed him with a smile of such brilliance it could have blinded him. Instead of blinding him, though, it soared through the air shimmering around her and landed in his already aching loins.

'Much better.' She beamed.

With a silent curse, he snatched his phone up and called his chef, cancelling his lunch order, then got to his feet and grabbed his jacket from the back of his chair. 'Time for lunch.'

'We're eating out?'

He gave a sharp nod. Dante could feel his control crumbling, the itch in his fingers to touch her almost unbearable.

God alone knew how he was going to survive the next five days without acting on it.

Cold showers. Lots of cold showers.

For now, he would deal with it by dining with Aislin in public.

'Do you have a favourite food?' he asked.

Her beam only widened. 'Pizza.'

When they stepped out onto Dante's street Aislin gazed up at the sun high in the cobalt sky and whipped her jumper off. She had a long black vest top underneath and the feel of the sun on her bare arms was a joy after the long winter.

As she tied her jumper around her waist, she noticed Dante looking at her as if she were a new species.

'We're not with your society friends yet,' she told him cheerfully.

'Is it not a little cold to be exposing your bare arms?'

'You must be joking. Compared to Ireland, this is basking weather. I haven't seen the sun since September.'

For all the crazy feelings surging through her, she hadn't felt this happy in years. Dante's generosity had lifted a weight from her shoulders.

The money he'd credited to Orla's account, along with the forthcoming DNA-contingent hundred thousand, would be enough to substantially better Finn's life. The extra eight hundred thousand they would receive would irrevocably change it but, for now, Aislin was thinking of more than her sister and nephew. She was thinking of Dante. She wanted to save that deal for *him*, for this man who could have thrown her out of his cottage without a cent for any of them.

They walked Palermo's cobbled streets, two of his goons three paces behind them. She inhaled all the new scents and gawped at all the new sights—the barrows of fruit and vegetables, the stalls of flowers, tables and chairs crammed on the pavements with people sat drinking coffee, many smoking, the thrum of life a beat she felt pulsating in her limbs.

'Your city is so vibrant,' she observed. 'It's like nowhere I've ever been,'

'Have you travelled much?'

'Not much outside Ireland. I've been to London a

few times and I spent a summer working in a French vineyard picking grapes but that's it. I haven't left Kerry in three years.' She grinned. 'This is very different to Kerry.'

'In what way?'

'It isn't raining for a start!' She sniggered. 'I'm doing my home an injustice. It's a beautiful part of the world and it doesn't always rain. Sometimes the sun does grace us with its presence. Our village edges a forest so you can imagine the wildlife we have on our doorstep. I remember a stag finding its way into our garden when I was about ten. Orla screamed her head off when she saw it, the wimp.'

Dante listened to Aislin's enthusiastic chatter about her home with amusement. The money crediting her sister's account had stripped the defensive, wary cloak she'd worn as swiftly as she'd stripped her jumper.

Aislin, he was learning, loved to talk.

He led her into a pizzeria, wondering how the short walk he'd instigated with the intention of exercising his desire out of him in the fresh air had backfired. Here she was, walking his streets in leggings, scuffed ankle boots, a jumper wrapped around her waist like the teenagers wore it, her hair loose and unkempt, and she was still the sexiest creature on his island. He'd had to keep his hands rammed in his jacket pocket to prevent them reaching for her.

Gio, an old friend who owned the busy pizzeria, greeted him with a warm embrace. Kissing his friend's cheeks, Dante introduced Aislin, who returned Gio's embrace and kisses as if they too were old friends, then they were led to a corner table, menus placed before them.

'Do all Sicilians snog each other?' she asked the second they were alone.

'I don't know what you mean.'

'You kissed your friend on both his cheeks. And he kissed you.'

He shrugged. 'It is the Sicilian way. We are a tactile people.'

Her eyes were wide. 'I don't know a single Irish man who wouldn't respond to a kiss by another man without a punch on the nose.'

He couldn't help himself. Dante laughed. 'You have a very unique way with words.'

'I'm Irish. It comes with the territory.' She took a large drink of the cold lager she'd surprised him by ordering.

She noticed the look he gave her. 'Don't worry, it'll be Prosecco all the way at the wedding. I won't show you up.'

'Aislin... I cannot stress this enough. I want you to be only *you* this weekend. If you want to drink Prosecco, then that's fine, but if you prefer lager then that is also fine.'

'But everyone else will be drinking Prosecco or champagne or whatever you Sicilians drink. I know you want me to be me but you're still going to have my clothing for the weekend chosen by a personal shopper—'

'A personal shopper who will *help* you, not choose for you. I want you to be able to relax this weekend and be yourself, not feel self-conscious.'

She eyeballed him for a moment then grinned and

raised her glass. 'I'm very glad to hear it. To be honest with you, grape-based drinks and I don't mix—they give me a headache.'

'Is that why you drink lager?'

'I'm a penniless student. Cheap lager is all we can afford. It's either that or cheap spirits that are as likely to contain windscreen wash in them as proper alcohol.'

Dante could not say why he found her chatter so entertaining and dragged his gaze from the wondrous lips making the chatter.

Thankfully, their pizza arrived.

Dante bit into his first slice and sighed with pleasure.

Conscious that his father's cholesterol and heart problems, which had ultimately led to his fatal heart attack, had started when he wasn't much older than Dante was now, he rarely indulged in unhealthy food, but when Aislin had ordered a spicy Sicilian-sausage pizza his mouth had watered so much he'd followed suit.

She devoured her pizza with all the enthusiasm of a starving student. But then, she *was* a student.

'I hope I'm not about to say anything insulting, but aren't you a little old to be at university?'

'Only by a bit. I had to drop out in my final year because of Orla's accident. I started my degree again in September.'

'Are you missing much by being here?'

She shook her head and took another drink. 'I'm getting the last batch of credits I need through distance learning so I can be around to help look after Finn.'

Bypassing talk about his newly discovered nephew,

he smoothly moved the conversation on. 'And you're doing something to do with history?'

'I should end up with a bachelor's degree in Medieval European history.'

'And what do you intend to do with it?'

'No idea. I wanted to be a teacher, but...' Her nose wrinkled. 'I don't think I could cope with back-chatting teenagers and all the politics. I have lost any tolerance I ever had for twaddle.'

'What was the reason for that?'

'All the rubbish I had to go through with Finn. You know he was born prematurely? Well, they had to deliver him by emergency Caesarean section. Orla was in a coma for three weeks and under sedation for around another month after that—she had massive brain trauma. She also had broken ribs, a broken arm and damage to her spinal cord, so she was stuck in hospital for half a year, then had to go to a rehabilitation place for another year on top of that. Obviously she was in no position to care for Finn, so I had to step up and be his guardian, which was not an easy thing.'

Was this where she revealed herself to be not quite as saintlike towards her family as he'd assumed? 'Because you had to give up your life?'

'No, no, because there was resistance from the authorities. I tried to get power of attorney to act for both of them but it was a nightmare. They saw this young twenty-one-year-old and thought there was no way I should be given temporary custody of a premature baby or control over my sister's finances and I had to fight them tooth and nail for it. They wanted to make Finn a ward of court.'

She waved her slice of pizza in the air as she spoke,

her indignation ripe. 'A ward of court! When I was there with him in that unit *all the time*. Three months I slept in that hospital and they wouldn't even let me name him! When Orla finally came round she was compos mentis enough to give her authority for me to be in charge of everything, but they still didn't make things easy. Honestly, the pointless bureaucracy was enough to make you weep. Whatever career I end up doing, I want it to be nothing that involves any kind of government body and nothing that involves any kind of officious stuff.'

Dante swallowed his bite of pizza down a throat that didn't want to cooperate.

He needed to learn all he could about Aislin before the wedding but this was all the stuff he didn't *want* to know and he didn't have the faintest notion why guilt weighed heavily in his chest.

When all this had been going on, he hadn't known the O'Reillys existed.

'Where was Finn's father in all this?'

'Now, there's the question.' She leaned forward as if exchanging a confidence. 'I don't know who the father is. Orla refused to say. She had some memory problems after the accident and now says she can't remember.'

He looked at her astutely. 'You don't believe her?'

'Not in the slightest. I think her memory has holes in it, but on this I'm sure she's lying, and if you ever tell her I said that I will ram a whole pizza in your mouth as punishment.'

'Are you making a threat of violence against me?' he asked, amusement bubbling so hard inside him it dampened the bile and guilt that had built up.

He wanted to ask where her mother had been during all this but held back. He didn't want to know anything about his father's old mistress and it disturbed him to think his father must have felt many of the same physical feelings towards her that Dante was feeling towards Aislin.

Dio, he couldn't rid himself of these damn feelings. Unfiltered and amusing, her voice flew down his ears and danced into his already aroused senses.

Lips twitching as she looked him right in the eye, she helped herself to another slice, lifted it to her mouth and took an enormous bite.

He suppressed a groan.

Aislin wasn't trying to be provocative, he recognised that much, but...

How was he supposed to concentrate away from images of making love to her in every way imaginable when he found her every movement erotic, and when every passing minute spent with her increased the ache in his loins and the heat in his veins?

And how was he supposed to take her back to his home and spend two nights alone with her under the same roof? He couldn't even rely on his staff to act as chaperones, banished as they all were to their own apartments on the ground floor, leaving him with his valued privacy...

But he could enforce some changes to their working conditions for the next few days and keep them visible.

His lungs expanded and his next exhale released easily.

That was the way to play things. They could continue getting to know each other well enough to fool

Riccardo D'Amore that they were a couple in love but always with the safety of people around them.

If he played things well enough, he would not have to be alone with her again until the time came for them to part ways.

CHAPTER SIX

WHEN AISLIN RETURNED with Dante to his home much later that afternoon, she was surprised to find an abundance of informally dressed staff out in force cleaning the already spotless house.

'Let us have a drink on the roof terrace while dinner is prepared for us,' he said as they strolled through one of the living rooms.

The interior of Dante's house was so incredible that she was curious to see what he'd done with the roof. 'Sure, but no more coffee.'

He grinned and showed the way to a side door that led out to an external metal staircase.

The hours they'd spent in the pizzeria had flown by. Once they'd eaten they'd stayed at their table, drunk gallons of coffee and set about getting to know each other.

Dante had told her about growing up in Palermo. He'd lived in the family home in a villa by the beach but it had been in the city itself he'd felt the most comfortable, roaming in packs with his friends, all of them trying to look cool to get the girls' attention and trying to convince bar owners they were old enough to drink. He'd then explained how he'd formed and grown his business empire and his determination to break into America.

Hearing about his jet-set life and achievements only made Aislin feel inadequate with what she had accomplished, which, when you took a hard-nosed look at it, was not much at all.

He hadn't made her feel unaccomplished, though.

She'd talked of her own childhood, her friends, her closeness to Orla, her love of musicals and soap operas, her fascination with bloodthirsty medieval Europe, learning to ride a bike with her granddad before he'd died, attending weekly mass with her grandmother—all the most fertile memories of her life. Dante had listened hard, his eyes never leaving her face. She knew it was because he *had* to remember these things and not out of genuine interest but still…

What woman's head wouldn't be turned by a gorgeous man paying such attention to her?

And then she stepped onto the roof terrace and her head was turned some more.

The late-afternoon sun warm on her bare shoulders, she gazed in amazement at the magnificent view of Palermo's colourful streets and medieval landmarks. The vista before her led all the way in the distance to the glimmering sea.

Then she turned her attention to the terrace itself. Encompassing the entire roof, it contained a huge swimming pool and adjoining hot tub, a bar that would have put an Irish pub to shame, the biggest barbecue she had ever seen, a dance area and lots of seating, ranging from sun loungers to hammocks to plump sofas scattered strategically, some in the sun, some sheltered beneath beautiful wooden gazebos. Dante might be lacking a garden but there was no lacking of greenery, the terrace given privacy by encircling hedges and trees.

She could easily imagine the decadent parties he hosted up here.

Jugs of fruit juice were brought out to them, the staff member then taking a seat behind the bar, on hand for any further refreshments they might require.

'This is like another world,' Aislin said with a sigh, then nodded at a hammock tied between two palm trees. 'Can I go in that?'

Dante spread his palms. 'You don't have to ask. Do you know how to get into it?'

'Nope.'

'I'll show you.'

The elegance of his movements as he got himself effortlessly into it made her heart do a strange clenching motion, but there was no time to worry about it, because a moment later he was back on his feet indicating for her to try.

She spread her arms out to hold the rope and placed her bottom in the centre as he'd shown. Then she swung her legs round quickly, but must have got her balance wrong, for she would have toppled out of it had Dante not leapt forward to steady her.

'It takes practice.' His warm breath danced through her hair.

Suddenly she was very much aware of the heat of his body against hers, the strong arm supporting her bottom under the hammock, the chest leaning over her to catch the other side.

Aislin's grip on the hammock tightened as his scent surrounded her and filtered through her senses.

Her heart rate accelerated, all the effects strengthening when he made some adjustments and shifted her weight as if she were as light as a newborn. The blood roaring in her ears was so loud that at first she missed his instruction to lie back.

Breathing heavily, she did as she was told and had to bite back the demand that he let her go *right now*.

But then he loosened his hold and she had to bite back a plaintive wail for him to keep hold of her.

Disorientated and confused by what was happening to her, it took a moment to realise she was lying in the hammock unsupported.

Dante turned his back on her and forced air into his constricted lungs, disturbed by the heated reactions assailing him.

He drank a glass of juice slowly, gathering himself together, willing his heartbeat to regulate itself, willing his body back under control.

These reactions were the normal responses of a healthy man around a beautiful woman. It was his misfortune that this particular beautiful woman was one he could not touch.

Dio, she smelt incredible…

Inhaling deeply, he seated himself at the round table nearest the hammock and said, 'Tell me about your university days.'

Get them back on a conversational footing. Keep a distance between them.

Look but do not touch.

Listen. Converse. Keep a distance.

This tactic had worked in the pizzeria, proving a mostly effective way of blocking out the crazy surges of lust that kept flushing through him.

He'd been surprised by how much he enjoyed her company. Aislin had such an entertaining way with words that their time in the pizzeria had flown by.

She cleared her throat. 'What do you want to know?'

'Tell me about your friends. Boyfriends...' A thought occurred to him, one he couldn't believe he hadn't thought to ask before. 'Do you *have* a boyfriend?'

'I wouldn't be here if I had one.'

The cynical part of him almost snorted his disbelief but he held it back as he remembered that Aislin was not of his world. Her world was not motivated by money.

Aislin's world was motivated by family.

His eyes drifted back to her. She looked comfortable and secure in the hammock, ankles hooked together, russet hair spilled messily all around her head.

'I've only had one boyfriend,' she confessed, her gaze fixed on the darkening sky.

He almost snorted in cynical disbelief again. 'Just the one?'

'Yes. One boyfriend. Patrick. I met him in my second year at uni.'

'Was it serious?'

'I thought so.' There was a strange mixture of anger and defeat in her tone when she said this. 'He cheated on me.'

Dante didn't know how to respond to this unexpected confidence.

But this was Aislin and, as he'd also learned in their short time together, she said what was on her mind. His question about a boyfriend had clearly taken her mind back to the man who had cheated on her.

'He promised me the world,' she said quietly. 'I

had so many doubts about him—he was a player like you—but he convinced me I was the woman he'd been waiting for and that I was special to him. We'd been together for six months when Orla had her accident. Two weeks after it happened, one of the nurses very kindly told me that I smelt and needed to go home and get a change of clothes.'

'You spent two weeks at the hospital without a change of clothes?' Amazement at her words overrode the uncomfortable stab in his guts at her blasé way of saying her cheating ex was a player like him.

'Orla was in a coma in the intensive care unit. Finn was clinging to life in the neonatal unit. I couldn't leave. It was hard enough dividing my time between the two wards. I even asked if they could be put together but it was impossible. It was an awful time. I felt like I was being split in two. I left the hospital only once in the first eight weeks and that was to pack a load of clothes for myself. I called Patrick to come and get me, but he didn't answer, so I got a taxi home. I was sharing a house with three other women. Patrick's car was parked outside. I found him in bed with Angela.'

Dante rubbed a hand over his mouth, at a complete loss at what to say.

'He knew what I was going through.' Anger rang through the rich brogue. 'He knew I needed support. He knew my mother had no intention of coming home—she's been living in Asia for five years, and when Orla had her accident she sent a few messages, but that was it from her. All I wanted was someone to hold my hand and share just a fraction of it with me. I'd begged him to come to the hospital but he made all these pathetic excuses. In the back of my mind I knew something was wrong but I didn't have the emotional capacity to deal with it.'

'What did you do?' His question came from a throat that felt strangled, his brain whirling to think how scared and alone she must have felt.

'Told them I never wanted to see either of them ever again, shoved a load of clothes into a bag and left.'

'That was it?' He'd imagined screams and smashed crockery.

Now she twisted her head to look at him. 'I was exhausted, Dante. I hadn't slept more than a few hours in two weeks and was living on my nerves. There was nothing left in me. All I wanted to do was get my stuff and get back to the hospital. It took a long time for me to even feel the betrayal of what they'd done.'

He didn't have to imagine the devastation she'd gone through; Dante was living through his own version of it. The betrayal of those you loved was the worst of all deceits.

Aislin had been betrayed by the man she'd loved and abandoned by the woman who'd given birth to her at the time she'd needed them most.

'As cruel as his behaviour was, finding them like that did you favour,' he told her, his voice colder than he would have wanted.

He could not bring himself to say anything about her excuse of a mother.

What he knew was enough for him to know down in his marrow that Aislin must take after her father.

Sinead O'Reilly was as selfish as his own mother. It was a fine line between whose behaviour was the worst.

'How do you work that out?' she demanded.

'It meant that you knew the truth. Better than being strung along on a lie.'

'I should never have been stupid enough to believe in him in the first place. Believe me, I won't be making that mistake again. The only people I trust are my family. Well, my sister and nephew.'

'Trust no one.' He'd trusted his father. Damn him.

Dante's stomach roiled with fury but this anger was not now aimed at his lying father but at the people who'd left Aislin to deal with a burden no one should have to go through alone.

It was a misplaced anger that disturbed him.

He hardly knew Aislin. He had no reason to feel such deep fury on her behalf.

'Has there been anyone serious in your life?' she asked after an outbreak of awkward silence.

'No.' He expelled the bitterness sitting in his lungs and attempted a smile. The end result was tight on his cheeks. 'Long-term relationships are not for me. I enjoy the single life too much.'

His standard answer to questions about relationships.

He saw no need to explain himself, not to Aislin or anyone.

They needed to know *facts* about each other. Nothing more.

'If I wasn't afraid of falling out of the hammock I'd raise a glass to the single life,' she said, injecting some much-needed humour into the heavy atmosphere that had developed.

By unspoken agreement they stuck to neutral subjects for the rest of the evening.

If only he could force his body to remain neutral around her too.

* * *

Aislin dipped a cautious toe into the terrace pool and found the water heated, exactly as Dante had promised. Lowering herself into it up to her shoulders, she rested her head against the rolled side and gazed up at the night sky.

The muted city noise felt distant up here, a comforting rhythm of life, completely different from the rustle of trees and the hoots and calls of wild animals she heard when the weather was kind enough to sit outside in the evenings at home.

Ciro, the young lad who'd taken her battered suitcase into Dante's house the morning before, sat at the bar playing on his phone but his was a silent presence.

She was glad of the peace. Dante had been called out on an emergency at his father's villa just as they'd finished eating dinner. Aislin had snatched the opportunity to change into the swimsuit the personal shopper had talked her into buying that day on the off-chance she would need it that weekend.

She would never have had the courage to wear it in front of Dante.

Other than the sleeping hours, this was the first time they'd been apart since he'd collected her from his father's cottage early the day before.

The two days they had spent together had been productive and she was confident they knew enough about each other that they could fool anyone into believing they were a genuine couple. Talk came so easily to them that she had to remind herself there was a purpose behind it.

Why she had brought Patrick up, she didn't quite know. The only other person she had told about finding him in bed with Angela was Orla. Aislin had to assume it was a form of self-preservation taking control, the past rising up to remind her of the dangers a man like Dante posed.

Her growing feelings for him were inexplicable. She shouldn't have any feelings for him other than gratitude at his generosity.

Patrick had hurt her badly.

Dante was cut from the same love-them-and-leave-them mould.

But there were moments when she would catch something in his eyes that made her stomach clench and a lower part of herself melt.

It had been a relief when, after breakfast that morning, Dante had taken her to Viale Strasburgo, Palermo's designer boutique Mecca, where they had been introduced to Aislin's designated personal shopper.

Dante's unobtrusive but always present staff were a calm reassurance but nothing beat having lots of other people around and something constructive to focus on to distract the mind.

Aislin had been taken into shops where the choice and richness of what she could have had almost overwhelmed her. It had been tempting to scoop everything up, but she'd stuck to the brief of buying a minimum of four casual daytime outfits, two evening dresses, one of which should be fit for a ball, an outfit for the wedding itself, shoes and accessories and a designer suitcase to put all her new purchases in.

She still didn't understand why she'd allowed the personal shopper to talk her into buying new underwear. Her own were perfectly functional and it wasn't as if anyone would see what she wore beneath the fancy clothing. But she had gone along with it, probably out of guilt for refusing the utterly gorgeous golden ballgown the shopper had insisted was perfect for her. Perfect for a catwalk model, maybe, but not for a student from Kerry.

It made her cheeks flush to imagine Dante's face when he received the bill for it all. She knew he wouldn't begrudge buying those items, but what if the bill was itemised?

Would he imagine her wearing that underwear? And why did it make a far more intimate part of herself flush to think that?

It would be easier if he'd had any input on her clothing choices but he'd been insistent that she choose for herself without any influence from him. While she'd shopped he'd kept himself busy working on his tablet, taking her out at regular intervals for coffee and more conversation.

Three more days and this would be over, and this unwelcome longing would disappear as quickly as it had come.

Nothing could come of it. Her imagination might like to see things that weren't there but, even if the look in his eyes actually meant something, meant he had an awareness for her sexually too, she would not allow anything to happen. Dante had many excellent qualities, and she trusted him to keep his word where the money was concerned, but when it came to women he was a cad. In that respect, Riccardo D'Amore was right—Dante was just like his father.

He was not above deception either. The charade he was paying her to play her part in this weekend was proof of that. It would be a foolish woman who gave her heart to Dante Moncada…

A deep male voice startled her from her thoughts.

Aislin craned her neck to see Dante talking to Ciro.

Her heart roared in her ears as he approached her, a bottle of beer in his hand.

CHAPTER SEVEN

AISLIN WAS FURIOUS with herself for lingering too long in the pool when she'd intended only a quick dip and fought to hide her embarrassment.

She hadn't felt an ounce of self-consciousness to be dressed in only a swimsuit with Ciro around but Dante... This was a man who had bedded many of the world's most beautiful women. Next to them she would look like a sack.

Her only saving grace was that the silvery evening light meant he couldn't see what lay beneath the water's surface.

'How are you enjoying the water?' he asked when he reached her. He spoke with a light tone but she sensed a tension in the tall, lean frame.

'It's lovely. Do you mind me using your pool? I'm sorry, I should have asked...'

'The pool is here to be used. You need to relax. These last few days have been a little...'

'Full on?' she supplied.

He nodded and took a swig of his beer.

'Did you get the emergency sorted?' she asked.

His lips tightened into a grim smile and he nodded again.

Aislin's heart clenched. He'd gone to fix something at his childhood home. He'd only buried his father three months ago.

'Do you find it hard going to the villa?' she asked tentatively.

Dante gazed into the grey eyes ringing at him with astute compassion and suddenly wondered why he hadn't taken the opportunity to stay away for a bit longer.

His father's old housekeeper had called about a water leak in one of the bathrooms. Usually he would send his maintenance man to deal with it. This time he'd gone with him.

He'd needed to escape.

Two full days with his Irish fox, listening to her lyrical brogue, watching her eat, drink, laugh, smile, frown, argue…catching a glimpse of the pain she carried in her…had built up in him.

As hard as he had tried to keep his thoughts platonic and his body in neutral, there seemed to be an override in his control where Aislin was concerned.

Her throat had moved as she'd drunk a glass of water during their dinner and the sudden urge to press his mouth to her neck had sent a charge rocketing through him that had sucked the air from his lungs. For a moment, all he'd been able to see was Aislin spread naked beneath him, a sensory image so strong he'd been on the verge of sending his staff back to their apartments on the ground floor. Only the ringing of his phone had stopped him.

Forget his teenage years. This was a hundred times worse.

He'd snatched the chance for escape, only to return

to find her in his pool. He was painfully aware that, submerged beneath the glimmering surface, Aislin wore a swimsuit.

He pulled one of the terrace seats over and ignored her question.

'Orla and I found it hard to go into our nan's home after she died,' she said softly into the silence, those compassionate eyes not leaving him. 'She lived next door to us and her home was our home. Going into it in the months after she'd died and seeing all her possession still there...it was hard. I kept expecting her to call out from the kitchen asking if we wanted a cup of tea and a biscuit.' Her lips tightened and she breathed out and smiled sadly. 'It took a long time before her death felt real.'

He took a long drink.

'It still doesn't feel real,' he admitted. 'I go in that house and I see him everywhere. He's there, and I want to talk to him, but he's gone.'

Talk to him and demand answers, starting with why the hell he'd kept a sister's existence from him.

The secret cut like the deepest of betrayals. It felt like losing him all over again.

He drained the bottle and signalled to Ciro for another, guilt that Ciro had had a date lined up for that evening adding to the combustible mix of anger and desire curdling in him.

Furious anger at his dead father.

Heady desire for the woman submerged semi-naked in his pool whose eyes were fixed on him, shadowed under the emerging moonlight.

'I always knew my father was a liar,' he said into the silence. 'He was an addict. Addicts lie. But he never lied to me. He could always come to me. I never judged him. I was his son. I knew his faults but that never stopped me loving him and wanting to help him. And now I find he did lie to me. He kept from me the worst secret a father could keep from a child.'

'Orla?'

'*Sì*. Orla. It makes me think, what else did he lie to me about? Who was the man I thought I knew so well?'

There was movement in the water as Aislin pushed away from where she'd been resting, swam to the edge closest to him and folded her arms on the side.

'Have you asked your mother about it?' she asked.

'No.' He took the fresh bottle from Ciro with a grim nod of thanks. 'If my mother knows about Orla, then that means she's complicit in the lie.'

He drank deeply and gazed into the distance, looking anywhere but at Aislin. It disturbed him that, even with the heavy weight of his mood and emotions, he could still feel her stare upon him, lasering through his skin, his body charged with awareness for her.

'Parents often lie to children if they think it's a subject they won't understand, or to protect them,' she said quietly. 'It doesn't mean your father lied to you about anything else.'

'It doesn't mean he didn't,' he snapped.

She rested her cheek on a slender forearm and sighed. 'When I think of Finn and all the struggles he'll have throughout his life, it makes my heart hurt so badly that if I could swap my body for his I would do it gladly. I love that boy and his mother so much, I don't think there's anything I wouldn't do to protect them.'

'Even lie?'

'There's many things I never thought I was capable of doing that I've since done,' she answered softly. 'It's only when you're in a specific situation that you can appreciate the depths you would go to or the heights you would climb for someone you love.'

He thought of her hovering by their beds in the hospital, alone without a change of clothes for two weeks. He thought of her fighting to be recognised as Finn's guardian and taking care of everything for both of them until her sister had recovered enough to do those things for herself.

Dante could not comprehend from where she had found her strength.

He tried to lighten the heaviness engulfing them. 'Like breaking into my cottage to get my attention?'

From the periphery of his vision, he caught a fleeting smile.

Aislin thought of Patrick. She'd been in desperate need of support after Orla's accident and who better to provide it than the man who'd promised eternal love? His reaction had been to sleep with her housemate instead.

Her mother hadn't reacted at all. Her daughter and grandson had both hovered between life and death and all she'd done was send a few text messages. Aislin didn't think she'd ever forgive her mother for that.

No one had been there for Aislin, not her friends or extended family beyond the obvious platitudes.

She'd carried the burden alone. It had been a hard knock to deal with. Unlike Dante and his declaration that no one could be trusted, she knew she could trust her sister with her life. But she would not trust anyone else again, not in an emotional capacity.

'Your father made mistakes, and I understand why you're so angry with him,' she said. 'It only makes it harder that he isn't here to answer your questions or defend himself but don't ever lose sight of the fact that he loved you. I would have given anything to have the closeness you two shared with one of my parents. My mum never wanted to be a mum. Orla and I were both accidents and we both knew it. She married my dad because my nan forced her to—she didn't want the shame of having two grandchildren born out of wedlock.'

'She sounds like a formidable woman.'

Aislin remembered the outwardly terrifying woman who'd had the softest heart with a smile. 'I adored her. Nan was the one who really raised us. She died six years ago and I still miss her.'

'What about your father?'

'He remarried and moved away. We get on well but it's hard to develop a bond with someone you only see for the odd weekend.'

Dante swallowed hard to loosen his constricted throat then made the mistake of looking at her.

The moon had risen high above them. Silver light poured down and cast Aislin in a glow.

Under this bewitching light it was too easy to sink into intimacy and spill his tortured thoughts out.

Seeing Aislin like this… It would be too easy to send Ciro away, strip his clothes off, join her in the pool, haul her into his arms and…

He'd revealed enough.

He got to his feet and drained the last of his beer. 'I'll see you in the morning. I'm going to bed.'

But not until he'd taken a cold shower.

How was it possible to have such awareness for someone when the demons in his head were so present and vivid?

It was the situation they were in, he told himself firmly as he strolled away. As Aislin had said, no one knew how they would react to a particular situation until they were in it. He and Aislin were in a strange place, thrown together and tasked with getting to know each other well enough to fool a wedding party that they were in love. That was bound to accelerate and heighten his attraction to her.

He'd reached the stairs when he realised he'd left his phone on his seat by the pool.

Cursing, he went back for it.

Dante stepped onto the terrace and strode past the bar at the moment Aislin climbed out of the pool.

He stopped dead in his tracks.

Dio...

A plain black modestly cut swimsuit couldn't hide a body beautiful enough to make a grown man hard on sight.

Aislin was as curvy as any man's wildest dreams.

Blood pumped furiously, pounded in him. His mouth ran dry, palms suddenly damp, perspiration breaking out all over a torso that felt as if a furnace had been ignited in it.

Oblivious to his presence, never mind the internal havoc wreaking his fully aroused body, Aislin reached down for her towel.

A groan clutched at his throat.

Only the ends of her hair were wet and she rubbed the towel gently into it then, as she spread her arms to wrap the towel around the beautiful curvy figure, she suddenly looked in his direction and froze.

Dante was too far from her to see her features clearly but even with the distance between them a charge flowed, encircling them, tightening them in its grip...

God alone knew what would have happened if Ciro hadn't appeared at that moment from behind the bar with Dante's phone.

'I was about to bring this to you,' he said, handing it to him.

Dante took it and turned on his heel.

A cold shower had never felt more necessary.

Aislin closed the zip of her new super-posh suitcase, wishing she had something to calm the butterflies playing havoc in her stomach. They weren't even butterflies, more like giant moths.

Her moonlit conversation with Dante still played in her mind but its vividness was outshone by the memory of glancing up to find he'd returned to the terrace.

The look that had been in his eyes...

The charge that had flashed through her body and raised her heartbeat... It burned her skin.

All night she'd tossed and turned, unable to settle, thoughts of Dante taking full occupancy in her mind.

The morning had brought no relief. She'd done her best over breakfast to pretend everything was fine, that she was fine, but had been helpless to stop her cheeks flushing whenever she met his gaze.

Thankfully he'd surprised her straight after by getting Ciro to take her to Palermo's most exclusive hair salon.

She hadn't seen Dante since.

She'd returned to his home and called Orla. After a long chat that had left Aislin with mixed feelings at what Orla had asked her to do, she'd donned the first of her weekend designer outfits.

When she had slid the new black lacy knickers up her thighs, she'd been helpless to stop her mind running riot, imagining Dante sliding them back off.

The days with him had found her imagination going into overdrive where he was concerned, but now she found herself helpless to stop imagining his strong body covering hers, that sensuous mouth kissing flesh that came alive with nothing more than an overactive thought.

Restless, she stood in front of the mirror again and checked her appearance for the dozenth time.

Would he think her suitably dressed for a society weekend with many of Europe's richest and most powerful people in attendance? He kept stressing how he wanted her only to be herself but she didn't want to embarrass him. She didn't want people looking at them and asking themselves what the hell he saw in her. She wanted him to be proud to have her by his side.

A loud rap on her bedroom door set her heart thumping.

Smoothing down her newly glossy hair and checking her make-up hadn't smudged—she'd used her emergency credit card to purchase a load of it after her hair had been done—she inhaled deeply and opened the door.

Dante's heart slammed into his ribs.

The slightly scruffy untamed beauty he'd last seen at breakfast had been transformed. Figure-hugging black jeans wrapped in a wide diamond-studded belt were topped with a loose striped multicoloured shirt and a smart fitted navy jacket. On her feet were un-scuffed black ankle boots with diamonds running up the heels that were a couple of inches higher than her usual boots. Her hair had been cut subtly, the style the same as before but a little neater, smoother, framing her face in a way that enhanced her high cheekbones and striking eyes.

Her raspberry-coloured lips had a sheen to them, making them appear plumper and even more kissable...

'Do I look okay?' she asked with the touch of anxiety he was coming to recognise.

Realising he'd been staring, Dante composed himself. 'You look great.'

'Are you sure? You said to dress casually for the trip over. Would a dress be better?'

'No, *dolcezza*, what you're wearing suits you. You look elegantly casual.' And ravishingly sexy, he thought with an ache that went all the way through his bones.

She blew out a breath and laughed. 'That's a relief, although *elegant* might be an adjective too far. I nearly put a dress on but I'm not ready to get my legs out yet—they haven't seen the sun in years! They're so white I'm going to have to put some self-tanning lotion on them.'

'Would you normally do that?'

'No, but I'm sure all the other women there—'

'Only do it if it's what you want, and not for them. If you want my opinion, your colouring is beautiful and does not need any enhancement. Be proud of your skin as it's part of what makes you uniquely you.'

The skin he'd complimented turned the shade of a radish and it took her a beat to say hurriedly, 'Thank you for the ego boost. Before I forget, I spoke to Orla earlier. I know you've got a lot on your mind with the wedding but I promised I'd ask—she wants to know if you'll come to Finn's birthday party. She really wants to meet you.'

Thrown by the question, disarmed by the plea resonating in the grey eyes, danger ringing like an alarm in his head, Dante chose his words with care. 'Give me the details after the wedding.'

Her relief was visible. Before she could say anything further on the matter, he said, 'Before we leave, I have something to give you.'

He kept firmly to his side of the threshold.

After a restless sleep, he'd awoken full of fresh determination to keep a distance from this woman he was so drawn to.

But that look they'd exchanged under the moonlight lingered in his bloodstream. Tight arousal had sprung back to life when she'd walked into the breakfast room, russet hair tousled, eyes still puffy from sleep.

There had been the slightest jolt in her step to see him and then her cheeks had stained with colour.

Aislin, he knew with every fibre of his being, was as attracted to him as he was to her.

If she was anyone else, anyone other than Sinead O'Reilly's daughter and Orla O'Reilly's sister, he knew damn well all their long conversations would have taken place in a bed, preferably with Aislin's legs wrapped tightly around his waist.

He could not stop himself from imagining, with increasing vividness, what it would be like to be deep inside her, the colour of the hair that nestled between her legs, the weight of her breasts in his hands, the colour of her nipples...

It was a form of mental torture that he was inflicting on himself but, as hard as he tried, was unable to stop. It took every ounce of the control he'd mastered in his thirty-four years not to pull her into his arms and plunder her mouth.

But she was resisting it too and the electricity zinging between them was charged enough for him to feel it in the roots of his hair.

Her scent filled the space around them and he had to hold himself back from filling his lungs to the brim with it.

'What did you want to give me?' She was virtually rocking on her heels, cheeks still containing the remnants of her blush, eyes for once looking anywhere but at him.

'Your engagement ring.'

Now the grey eyes snapped on him. 'An engagement ring?'

'It would be strange to introduce you as my fiancée without a ring on your finger, don't you think?'

'I suppose.'

He pulled the small box out of his trouser pocket and handed it to her. 'Hopefully you will find it fits.'

She plucked it from the palm of his hand with, he noted, fingers that contained the slightest of tremors, and pressed it open.

Dante waited, chest and throat suddenly tight, for her reaction.

He'd bought it that morning. Thinking he would buy the first decent ring he saw that would pass muster under all the eyes that would undoubtedly want to look at it, he'd strolled into the jeweller as blasé as if buying a new pair of shoes.

He had not expected to walk out twenty minutes later without buying anything.

Three jewellers later he'd finally found the perfect ring for Aislin, a large pear-cut diamond encrusted with dozens and dozens of tiny sparkling diamonds, emeralds and sapphires and centred on a band of rose gold.

It was beautiful and different, just like Aislin.

It was also the single most expensive item he'd ever bought that was not bricks and mortar.

Why he had spent such an obscene amount of money on his fake fiancée he did not know, and refused to think too deeply about. It wasn't as if he couldn't afford it.

Her throat moved before she looked up and her wide, confused eyes fell on him. 'Dante, I can't wear this.'

'Why not? Don't you like it?'

'It's the most beautiful piece of jewellery I've seen in my life. If I could have asked a jeweller to make a ring bespoke for me, then this is exactly what I would go for...'

'Then what's the problem?'

'It must cost a fortune. What if I lose or damage it? You'll never be able to take it back.'

'It's yours to keep,' he said evenly.

'I can't keep it! It's too much.'

'Aislin…' He sighed and crossed the threshold, closing the gap between them enough to take the box from her hand and pull the ring out. Not giving her mouth or his brain time to protest, he took her left hand in his and slid the ring on her wedding finger.

'Listen to me,' he said quietly, moving his gaze from the ring on her finger to stare at the ring of her eyes.

Her eyes were a thousand times more dazzling.

'This is a gift from me. I already know you well enough to know you will give every cent of the remaining money to Orla for Finn's benefit, and I admire you for that. I admire much about you, *dolcezza*, and I want you to come away from our time together with something that is yours alone. Now, I ask that you do not insult me again by refusing it.'

Only when he'd finished speaking did he notice the tingling warmth on his hand and realise he'd clasped his fingers tightly around hers, and that he'd leaned his face so close to hers he could see the individual freckles on her pretty nose.

For once, Aislin had no comeback. Her tongue had rooted itself to the roof of her mouth, the pressure of his fingers around hers setting her already ragged heart off on a rampage of heavy beats.

She could smell his skin under the cologne he wore. She could feel the warmth emanating from him. If she raised the hand not being held so tightly she would be able to press it to his chest and feel if his heart was beating as erratically as hers.

Everything inside her heated and made a weird contraction, as if her body was being reset to a brand-new mode. Suddenly she was very much aware of her sensitised skin, the tight heaviness of her breasts and the surge of damp warmth between legs that no longer felt connected to her brain. Breathing became impossible.

The eyes staring so deeply into hers darkened as they inched closer and closer...

A large, tanned hand clasped the side of her neck and she caught the flare of his nostrils before the sensuous mouth she'd tried so hard not to stare at and fantasise about caught her in a hard, unyielding kiss that sent her resistance crashing.

Awareness exploded and rippled through her.

This...

His tongue flickered into her mouth, a new dark taste filling her, and then she was moulded against the contours of his hard torso. Feelings she had never known before crashed through her in a second explosion of awareness. Deep inside, the damp warmth became a furnace of bubbling need, and she kissed him back, plundering his mouth with the same intensity with which he devoured hers, all sense abandoned as her senses took full control.

It wasn't just his torso that was hard. His arousal pressed against her belly, sending a pulse of red-hot need so deep into her that she groaned from the sensation it induced.

Every part of her body came to glorious life, all dancing with heady delight to Dante's tune...

And then the dance was over.

The kiss broke and the hard body pulled away with a suddenness that bordered on cruelty.

CHAPTER EIGHT

STUNNED, AISLIN BLINKED and tried to breathe.

Her lungs were so tight she could hardly get air into them.

For the first time she was afraid to look at him.

She was afraid of what she would see on his face.

She was more afraid of what he would see on hers.

The silence in her room was absolute.

Her legs felt so weak it took effort to make it to the nearby armchair and slump into it. She covered her mouth with her hand. Lipstick she'd applied for the first time in three years had been kissed off.

She had never been kissed like that before.

Dear God, she burned inside and out: a furnace of desire inside, intense mortification at his abrupt rejection on the outside.

Dante dragged his fingers roughly through his hair, cursing himself with all the obscenities he hadn't used since his teenage years.

What the hell was wrong with him? He'd resisted temptation many times in his adult life, mostly with wives and partners of friends who assumed his reputation meant he had no morals, and would flirt, give him the come-to-bed eyes and engineer situations at parties where they would be alone together. Beautiful, sexy women who, if they had been single, he would have taken what they were offering without hesitation. He'd resisted every one of them without hesitation.

If people were in a committed relationship then they should respect that, not go fishing for a bigger catch.

His father had had no such morals and that, until he'd discovered the existence of his secret sister, had been the only thing that had really pained Dante about him. He'd accepted his gambling addiction as an illness, but his pursuit of any female who would give him the time of day regardless of her relationship status had chipped away at Dante's respect for him.

Dante had always thought he was better than that, and yet here he was, acting on desires he'd sworn to resist. Pulling away from Aislin's arms had been one of the hardest things he'd ever done and his aching, lust-ridden body protested loudly.

When he'd gathered enough control over himself that he could at least hear himself think over the thuds of his pounding heart, he looked at Aislin, slumped in the armchair, her face in her hands.

Her back was making jerky movements.

'Are you okay?'

She slowly raised her head. 'Getting there.'

His jaw clenched. 'I didn't mean for that to happen.'

'Neither did I,' she muttered.

'I gave you my word that this deal between us would be platonic and I have broken that promise.' And that broken promise disgusted him. Damn it, he was a man of his word. 'I can only apologise.'

'Are you apologising for the kiss or for the broken promise?'

'Both.'

A flash of anger appeared in her eyes. 'I don't want it. We were both party to it and to apologise…feels demeaning.'

'I would never intentionally demean you.' He swore under his breath and sucked in a large breath of air. 'It's impossible…'

'I know. You made it clear by your actions when you pulled away that you regret kissing me; you don't need to spell it out. I might not be beautiful and sophisticated like all your girlfriends are but I'm not a complete idiot. You don't fancy me. The kiss just happened.' She jumped to her feet and put on an airy smile that was so obviously fake his heart twisted at the effort it must have taken her to make it. 'It's one of those things. Let's forget all about it.'

She went to stride past him and, without thinking, he snatched hold of her arm. 'What are you talking about?'

Her cheeks became radishes again. 'It doesn't matter. I'm being silly. I'm embarrassed, okay? You didn't mean to kiss me.'

'Aislin…' He closed his eyes and released her arm before he did something really stupid like kiss her again. He stepped out of arm's reach. 'You're right that I didn't mean to kiss you, and right that you're not sophisticated like my old girlfriends. I thank God that you're not. But you're wrong about everything else.'

There was a long period of silence then. 'What are you saying?'

'*Dio*, Aislin, have you not felt the chemistry between us?'

She stared down at the carpet. 'I thought I was imagining it.'

'Imagining it?' He could laugh at her naivety. 'Oh, *dolcezza*, no, you were not imagining it. You are possibly the most beautiful woman I have met in my life. You are loyal and funny, and sexier than any woman should be allowed to be, but I think we both know it would be foolish to allow anything to happen. Forget our family and the complications they bring, speaking only of you and me...' His mind raced ahead of him, his tongue trying to catch up on developing thoughts he realised had been there part-formed from the start. 'I'm not the heartbreaker the media portrays me as but I'm not a saint. I don't believe in love and for ever, I don't want a family and I only date women with the same mind-set. When I said you were different, I meant it. I wouldn't be good for you. You deserve better than me.'

With baited breath, he waited for her to respond.

When she finally looked back at him, there was a fire in her eyes that lasered straight through him. 'Well, I am *thrilled* you know what's best for me—it certainly saves me the bother of having to think for myself.' Then she strolled to the door, yanked it open and walked out, slamming the door behind her with a loud, 'You, Moncada, are an eejit.'

Aislin stormed all the way down the corridor to the lift and punched the button.

Heavy footsteps approached as she waited impatiently for it to reach her but she refused to acknowledge him, even when he stood beside her.

'Have you calmed down?'

'No.' She folded her arms tightly across her chest lest she punched him in the face or, worse, hooked them around his neck and kissed him.

Her awareness of Dante was so acute it muffled her indignant anger at his apology and patronising attempts to explain himself.

Had she not spent almost four days telling herself all the reasons she had to keep her desire for him locked away? she fumed.

But that had been before he'd kissed her and sent sensation flowing through her she had never imagined could exist, and before he'd said beautiful things about her she'd never been told before and then listed all the reasons why those beautiful things didn't count for jack.

That he might very well accuse her of double standards if he could read her thoughts about him these past few days only added an extra dose of frustrated turmoil to the turbulent mix eating at her.

'I've got your suitcase.'

She'd forgotten all about it.

She gave him grudging thanks.

'Am I right thinking "an eejit" is the same thing as an idiot?'

Was that amusement she detected in his voice? She refused to look at him to see.

'Yes, it is, and you, sir, are a prime example of one.'

There was a loud ping and the lift door opened.

They stepped inside and, as the door closed, she rounded on him. 'Right, Moncada, let's get a few things straight. You might be as sexy as the devil but your reputation precedes you—see? I'd already worked that out for myself because, sir, I am not an eejit.'

'What's with all the sirs?'

'They're substitutes for the names I really want to call you.' The amusement dancing in the eyes she now allowed herself to look into only made her add a few more to the choice list of them.

'Names worse than eejit?'

'Yes, sir, much worse, and I would be grateful if you would shut up so I can shout at you and get this off my chest. I resent being told what is and is not good for me. I am not a child. If I want to have an affair with you, then I jolly well will, and I would go into it with my eyes open knowing perfectly well that it would never amount to anything, and not just because you are, by your own admission, not one for anything longer term than a bluebottle's lifespan. Affairs are short-term flings, they are not a relationship. It is an insult that you think I would not know the difference.'

The lift reached the ground floor. The door opened. They both ignored it.

'I never said you didn't know the difference.'

'You implied it. All this, *"I wouldn't be good for you. I only have affairs with sophisticated women who are happy to have the end date of the relationship set before it starts"*,' she mimicked.

'I never said that either!'

'Not in so many words but that was the gist of it. Well, sir, I do know the difference between an affair and a relationship, and I also know a relationship between us is a nonstarter. My life is in Ireland with my family. Your life, when you're not travelling all over the place, is in Sicily. Never minding all the stuff with our shared sister, we are very different people culturally and morally, so why you think I would even entertain a full-blown relationship with you is, sir, an insult.'

'Have you finished?'

'No, I have not.' Frustrated beyond comprehension, and suddenly desperate to wipe the amusement from his face, she grabbed at his leather jacket to yank him to her and pressed her mouth tightly to his.

With an immediate surge of delight her body rejoiced to feel those wonderful warm, firm lips upon her again, but there was enough anger still rippling through her to ignore the delight of sensation, hold her breath and keep her mouth there for the count of three before pulling away, just as she felt his hand breezing onto her waist.

'There,' she said primly, clasping her shaking hands together and stepping out of the lift. 'Now I have finished.'

'What was that for?' The amusement had gone from his voice.

'So that I can apologise. I'm very sorry for kissing you. We made a promise to keep things platonic. I have broken it. I'm very, very sorry.'

He took the longest inhalation she'd ever heard, followed by a ragged burst of laughter.

'You still find this amusing?' she demanded.

'You would prefer me to push you back into the elevator and take you right now? Because I have to tell you, *dolcezza*, seeing as we are being honest with each other, that right now I am more turned on than I have ever been in my life.'

She squirmed as the warmth between her legs, there since before they'd shared their first kiss, heated and bubbled again, and she pressed her thighs together as tightly as she could. 'You find my insulting you a turn-on? Are you a masochist?'

Aislin thought *she* might be one. Grabbing hold of him and kissing him like that...

As her sadly deceased grandmother had been fond of saying, she didn't have the sense she was born with.

'I must be.' Dante put his hand on the exit door and blew out air. 'I keep telling myself all the reasons why I shouldn't touch you and, before you argue with me, the thing about our mutual sister is a complication that neither of us can deny.'

She made a noise that sounded like agreement.

'I need to keep a clear head to get through this weekend,' he explained heavily. 'This is the biggest deal of my life, and if we don't convince Riccardo about us then I lose it. That means I miss the profit that comes with it, miss out on breaking into America and I will lose face too, because news of the broken deal is certain to get out. I should be keeping my eye on the potential prize but all I can think about is what making love to you would be like and it is driving me crazy. Why do you think I filled my house with staff? Without people to distract us, the temptation to touch you and taste you is a battle that consumes me.'

'Is it?'

He gave an incredulous laugh. 'Five minutes alone with you without any staff in sight and I'm kissing you, so what does that tell you? That kiss blew my mind.'

She stepped to him and gazed into his eyes.

Heat pulsed through him to remember the sweet taste of her tongue in his mouth.

The succulent lips parted and her throat moved. 'It blew my mind too.'

He suppressed a groan and tightened his hold on the door handle.

'I'm sorry for overreacting,' she whispered. 'Dante, your kiss…what it did to me… I've never felt that before. It scared me—my reaction to it scared me. I forgot why I'm here and how important this weekend is to you.'

He ran a finger across a high cheekbone that flushed with colour at his touch and managed a smile he thought probably looked more like a grimace. 'Let's just get through this weekend as best as we can.'

Her shoulders rose high and she nodded.

He opened the door and they stepped into the warm spring air.

His car was parked outside waiting for them.

Aislin gaped through the car window at the sprawling concave Renaissance castle before her that made the British royal family's palaces look cheap.

Dozens of cars that even she, the least petrol-headed person around, recognised as the most expensive on the market were lined in a row to the east side of the villa, sandwiched between the beautiful cream-and-gold masonry and the towering landscaped trees.

Dante, who had surprised her by getting behind the wheel of the sleek red car that had been parked outside his home, jumped out and hurried round to open her door. He held a hand out for her.

The pear-shaped diamond ring that had so floored her with its beauty and obvious expense glittered under the high sun as she took hold of it and joined him on the gravelled grounds, so flat and even, she suspected someone must have brushed it.

She stared up at him and took a deep breath.

Green eyes bored into hers and he brought her hand to his chest. 'Are you ready for this?'

She nodded decisively and squeezed her fingers around his.

She could do this. She *would* do this.

On the drive over, he'd given her the low-down on the guests attending that he knew personally and told her in more detail what she could expect from the weekend, which basically consisted of a lavish display of wealth dressed up as a celebration. Events were kicking off with a champagne reception hosted by the father of the bride in the castle's sprawling gardens, to be immediately followed by a seven-course meal.

Neither of them had mentioned the kiss again, or where it might lead, if indeed it would lead anywhere.

It was time to get down to business and Aislin had forced her mind-set into focusing on that above all else, and it was a focus she was determined to keep.

The valet who had guided them to their parking space coughed discreetly and indicated for them to follow him inside, while another valet whisked their cases away.

As they set off, hands clasped—after all, this was show time—a two-seater sports car and a stretch limousine slowly drove past them in succession.

Inside they were led into a huge reception room where a handful of waiting staff with trays of filled champagne flutes stood discreetly, and a glamorous couple in full evening wear chatted to a small group at the far end of the room.

Aislin cringed inwardly and fought the fresh burst of panic clawing at her throat. Her casual outfit, as chic as it was, now made her feel massively under-dressed.

She was never going to fit in.

'That's the bride and groom,' Dante said into her ear as they approached them.

Shivering at the brief sensation of his breath against her skin, Aislin forced a smile to her face as the couple spotted them and broke away from the group to greet them.

Alessio and Dante gripped wrists and pulled each other in to embrace tightly and exchange kisses on the cheek, the tactile Latin nature unashamedly displayed. She noted there was a slightly greater distance between Dante and the bride, who he introduced as Cristina, and then Aislin was yanked into an embrace by Alessio and an equally effusive one from Cristina. They both grabbed her hand to examine the ring on her finger.

'You're a dark horse, Dante,' Alessio said with a laugh. 'Springing a guest on us at the last minute. When Cristina said you were bringing your fiancée, I thought she had misheard you.'

Cristina flashed the whitest teeth Aislin had ever seen at her fiancé and laughed. 'One day you will learn that I am always right.'

'Don't worry, I'm learning.'

'Good!'

That they spoke in English could only be for Aislin's benefit and she was grateful to them for it, and grateful for the warmth of their welcome. She could only hope their guests were as welcoming.

After making small talk for a few minutes, Cristina said, 'I'm sure you must be keen to get to your room, so why don't I get one of the staff to show you up so you can get freshened and changed before the reception starts?'

'That would be lovely, thank you,' Aislin replied, thinking the singular use of the word *room* was a linguistic flaw. She had a pretty summer dress to change into for the champagne reception and meal.

Cristina beckoned a uniformed member of staff over and Alessio pulled Dante to one side.

They switched to their native language but Aislin sensed by their body language that they were discussing the business deal. Alessio had the look of a man apologising.

She got the chance to ask Dante a few minutes later when they followed the member of staff up the first flight of cantilevered stairs and through the warren of corridors to their rooms. Their hands were clasped again, the show of affection they needed to perform being one that didn't allow them to drop their guards for a moment.

'Yes, he apologised,' Dante confirmed. 'Alessio is ashamed of his father's behaviour.'

'I assume he's tried to change his mind?'

'He has but with all the wedding preparations Alessio hasn't been able to sit down with him and discuss it in the detail it needs. Riccardo knows that going with my competitor will give them less profit. My terms were more generous but he is proving very stubborn on the matter.'

Dante welcomed the discussion of business, a distraction from the feel of Aislin's much smaller hand in his.

He'd had to concentrate hard on Alessio's latest apology and not think about Aislin for the whole two minutes Alessio had taken him from her.

It disturbed him how much he'd resented having to let go of her hand.

This was an act they were performing. They were passing themselves off as a couple so madly in love they were going to marry. Holding hands in these circumstances was a must, but he could not understand why it felt so damn *good*.

The staff member behind whom they walked came to a stop and checked the clipboard in her arms. 'This is your room.'

'Mine or Aislin's?' he asked.

She looked again. 'Mr Dante Moncada and Miss Aislin O'Reilly,' she read, then put her hand in her pocket and removed a large set of keys, from which she carefully selected one, unlocked the door and walked in. 'Do you require a maid to unpack for you?' She indicated their suitcases set side by side by the four-poster bed.

Dante caught Aislin's furrowed, silently alarmed gaze.

'No, thank you. We will manage.'

'Where's my room?' Aislin asked the moment the woman shut the door behind her.

He closed his eyes and swallowed back the thuds of his rampaging heart. 'This is it. We've been put together.'

CHAPTER NINE

'WHAT?' AISLIN'S SHOCKED voice echoed in his thumping head. 'We have to share? But you said...'

'That we would be given separate rooms?' He laughed morosely. 'I thought we would be.'

He heard her take a long inhalation. 'Maybe all the other guest rooms were taken, seeing it was such short notice.'

'I'm sorry.'

'Don't be.' Her own laugh was equally morose. 'Cristina probably thinks she's doing us a favour. I'll sleep on the *chaise longue*.'

'No.'

'Well you can't sleep on it—you'll never fit with those long legs.'

'I'll take the floor.'

'And get a bad back?' She opened the oak wardrobe then began opening all the drawers of the dresser.

'What are you doing?'

'Looking for spare bedding.' She muttered something that sounded like a curse then rose to her full height and raised her shoulders before facing him. 'There isn't any. We can't ask the staff for some in case it gets out and the other guests start gossiping that we don't sleep together, which will defeat every purpose of me being here. We'll just have to share the bed.'

She said it in a blasé fashion but her movements had become stiff, her gait awkward. She lifted her suitcase and put it on the bed. 'Did you want to use the bathroom before I get changed?'

Immediately his mind careered to imagining her tugging those jeans down her thighs and stepping out of them...

He replied through teeth he'd clamped together. 'No, go ahead. We've time for you to have a shower or a bath if you want.'

She shook her head violently. 'The steam will frizz my hair up and I haven't time to de-frizz it. The stylist gave me a load of stuff to put into it but I'm sure it'll take me ages to do.' She pulled out a deep red dress with pretty navy flowers patterned over it and gave it a shake, then unfolded three further outfits still encased in their protective wrapping. 'Hopefully these won't be too creased, but if they are I'm sure housekeeping will have an iron I can use.'

He had never heard her talk so quickly or avoid his gaze so much.

Aislin, he realised, was more rattled than he was about the sleeping arrangements.

Her skittishness had the effect of calming his own heightened emotions.

'If your clothes need pressing then housekeeping will do that for you.' He took the outfits from her. While he hung them in the wardrobe, she scooped a handful of lacy underwear and shoved them in a drawer, then scurried into their private bathroom with her selected dress and a large bag.

He heard the door lock and muttered a curse that he suspected was much stronger than the one she had used.

How the hell was he going to get through this?

It would be bad enough finding themselves having to share a bed even if they hadn't shared their earlier kiss but they *had* shared it and that made it all worse. Hunger was never sated by a morsel. He'd had a brief taste of Aislin and all it had done was whet his appetite.

The drive from Palermo had been torturous but they had both made a conscious effort to keep talking: about the expected guests; about the events that made up the weekend, of which the wedding itself was only a small part; about the correct etiquette, which he didn't care for, but about which Aislin had wanted to know all the details; talking, talking, talking, not another mention of that damned kiss and what it had unleashed between them.

Dio, he could explode from the heat coursing through him. He didn't know what to do with himself. All he wanted was to batter that bathroom door down and drag her to the bed.

Aislin slipped the dress over her head and, instead of checking her appearance, stared at the discarded clothes she'd thrown in a puddle on the bathroom floor.

How could she cope sharing such an enclosed space with Dante? Their appointed room was beautiful in both decoration and proportions but they might as well have been given an old-fashioned telephone box for all the difference it made. As soon as that door had closed them in alone, her body had come roaring back to life.

She could cope with her wild feelings for him when they were surrounded by people but when they were alone…?

She pulled hard at her hair and welcomed the fleeting pain. But it was nowhere near distracting enough to override the hot, sticky feelings rampaging through her.

She felt desperate enough to jump under the shower and set it to cold. Or call housekeeping and beg them to fill the bath with ice into which she could submerge herself.

And then what would happen? A cold shower or an ice bath wouldn't be enough. Soon their effects would wear off and she'd be back to where she was: having to share a suite with the man she desired so badly it was like a sickness had infected her.

Clenching her hand into a fist, she put it to her mouth and bit her knuckles, stifling a scream of frustration.

Desire was not supposed to *hurt*.

A knock on the door made her jump.

'Aislin? Are you okay?'

She pulled it open and found Dante standing there, a crease in his brow, the rest of his features taut.

Their eyes locked together.

Her heart thumped so hard a ripple spread through her body and lifted the hairs from her arms.

Time came to a stop. The room shrank.

Her feet rooted to the floor, her vocal cords frozen.

The green eyes she found so mesmerising pulsed. His chest rose high and then loosened jaggedly.

This sickness wasn't hers alone, she realised dimly, and as that thought whispered into her consciousness her feet bounded to Dante at the same moment he sprang to life and seized her.

One moment she was gazing at him, the next she was in his arms, like two puppets whose strings were controlled by a deity, being pulled together. Their mouths fused tightly and his tongue swept into her mouth, entwining with hers, his hot, dark taste sending sensation crashing through her.

Aislin threw her arms around his neck and held him as tightly as she'd ever held anything. His hands swept up her back, one reaching up to burrow into her hair, winding a thick lock of it in his fingers, the other roaming everywhere, while her fingers grazed through the soft texture of his thick hair and her nails dug into his scalp.

His taste, his scent, the bristles of his beard biting into her cheek, a pleasure mingled with pain in its own right...

They kissed like starving waifs given one last meal, a wet, feverish unstoppable force, and she revelled in the relief of it and moaned at the pleasure they were unleashing.

Her taut breasts crushed against his hard chest and she pressed every part of herself tighter against him. Her body was aflame with need, desperate for relief from this painful longing that had become such a part of her.

And he held her just as tightly. The strength and depth of his kisses, the hunger in them, the urgent possessive exploration of her body proved he had lost his head to the moment as much as she had.

Had *she* been possessed? Was that what this long-ing for him was, not a sickness but a possession?

Sickness could be cured, she thought dimly. And possession could be cured too. Sometimes the only way to cure was to purge.

Purge or not, she didn't care. What had erupted between them was a force of nature she had no inten-tion of fighting.

They'd fought it for too long, for days that with this acute yearning growing stronger inside her had felt like for ever.

Pulling his mouth from hers, Dante burrowed his face into her neck. His beard rubbed against the sen-sitive flesh and he lifted her into the air to carry her to the bed.

There was no ceremony. He fell on top of her, the pair of them collapsing together, and then they were kissing again. His hand slid up her bare thigh, fingers biting into the sensitive flesh.

She tugged at his shirt to loosen it and reached for his trouser button, then lost her breath along with the use of her hands when he slid a finger under the band of her knickers and found her heat.

He groaned into her mouth before tugging at her bottom lip with his teeth.

His eyes were hooded and dilated, his ragged breaths hot on her face as his thumb found her sen-sitive nub, and the finger that had slipped under her knickers slid inside her.

Sensation fizzed and pulsed and Aislin writhed against him, needing more, the pleasure from his hand intense but not enough. The fire inside her blazed too hot, had burned through any inhibitions and sanity she'd had left.

She needed more. She needed *everything*.

Fumbling wildly, she found the band of his trousers again and tugged at them, desperate to free him, as desperate for his touch as she was to touch him.

And his touch showed his own manic need for her.

He muttered something she didn't understand and bit at her neck, then strong fingers were digging into her thighs and her knickers were being pulled down. She squirmed and twisted to help, wriggling them to her calves, and then kicked them away with a flick of her ankle while she finally, oh, *finally*, unbuttoned his trousers. There was not a jot of shyness as she yanked his trousers and briefs down to his hips and released him, only fevered desperation. Immediately she took him in her hand and thrilled to find him fully, hugely aroused.

She had a vague awareness of him groping for protection, and Dante's head lifting from her neck so his teeth could rip foil, and then he was sheathing himself...

And then he dove into her.

The relief was immediate and she cried out from the sheer bliss of it.

Again, there was no ceremony. Again, none was needed.

He thrust in and out of her with a driving possession that sent her senses soaring. She had never known pleasure like it and it was all-consuming.

Dante could hardly believe how hot and tight she felt and, *Dio*, how damn welcoming.

Never had he needed to be inside a woman so badly that it was like insanity had taken him over.

He pounded into her with all the madness gripping him and she matched every thrust, legs wrapped tightly around his waist, crying her pleasure, urging him on, begging him with muffled words, nails scratching through the shirt he still wore; pleading, pleading, until her neck arched, her grip around him tightened and her entire body jerked in a spasm that pushed him over the edge, and he plunged into her as deeply as it was possible to go...

And that was the moment Dante experienced an orgasm so powerful he almost blacked out.

How long that last thrust went on for, he couldn't say.

How long they lay there, Dante still inside her, still holding each other tightly, he couldn't say either.

It could have been for ever before he finally raised his head from the side of her neck to look at her.

The dazed, unanchored feeling he was experiencing was right there in her eyes.

He kissed her. Her arm slipped around his neck and she kissed him back, long and deep, razing her fingers over the nape of his neck.

And then she broke the kiss, sighed and burrowed her face in his shoulder with a jerky laugh. 'Well... that was something.'

Rubbing his chin over the top of her soft hair, a laugh escaped his own throat. 'I was thinking more along the lines of mind-blowing.'

'That works.'

Their mouths found each other again for another deep fusion that this time Dante was the one to break. 'I need to get rid of the condom,' he told her.

Her arm didn't relinquish its hold around his neck. 'One more kiss.'

He obliged, then removed her arm and disentangled himself from the woman who had given him more pleasure in one short interlude than he had experienced in the whole of his lifetime.

He could hardly credit he still had all his clothes on. All they'd managed to strip off Aislin was her knickers.

Dio, she had been so wet and ready for him...

The legs he walked on to the bathroom felt as if they belonged to someone else. There was a heavy fuzziness in his limbs but also a fizzing he could not explain.

He stepped back into the room to find Aislin scrambling off the bed, as dishevelled a sight as he had ever seen. The hair that had been professionally smoothed and styled was all tousled, her make-up smudged, her lips plumper than ever, bruised from his kisses.

His only-just-sated loins twitched back into awareness.

Her mouth curved into a half-smile and her eyes found his, a wariness ringing from them. 'Is this the point where we dissect what just happened?'

He leaned against the wall and folded his arms across his chest. 'Do you want to dissect it?'

She shook her head quickly and covered her mouth. Her shoulders rose up and down a number of times.

'Are you okay?'

She shook her head again, nodded then gave it another shake. She sat back on the bed. 'I don't know. To be honest, I feel a little dazed. Did that really just happen?'

He laughed, not from humour but from his own incredulity at what had exploded between them. '*Sì*. It did.'

'Dante...'

'What?' he asked.

She chewed on her lips and stared at the carpet.

He crossed the room and crouched down before her. Placing a finger under her chin to lift it, he stared into her eyes, trying to read what was in them.

Aislin swallowed hard, fighting the erratic beats of her heart, fighting the drumming in her head, but mostly fighting the crazy emotions whooshing through her body.

She had never known it could be like that.

She wanted to hook her arms around his neck, feel all those wonderful feelings for a second time and see if it was as mind-blowing as the first.

'I don't normally behave like that,' she confessed.

Now that the fire between them had been, if not quenched, then at least dampened, good old-fashioned embarrassment was snaking its way through her.

They'd both been so desperate for Dante to be inside her they hadn't even got round to taking their clothes off!

'I never thought you did,' he said gently. 'And, even if you did, there is nothing wrong with it and nothing to be ashamed of. We're both adults. We're both single.'

She managed a bluster of laughter. 'No, we're not, we're engaged.'

His returning smile didn't quite meet his eyes. 'Even less reason to be ashamed.'

'I don't want to be just another notch on your bedpost.'

His chest rose and he took a deep breath before sliding his hand around her neck and delving his fingers into her hair. 'Aislin, you could never be a notch on a man's bedpost.'

Her laugh was morose. 'You reckon? Look,' she continued, not giving him time to respond, 'I'm not saying I want anything more than this. You and I are never going to be love's young dream; we're just too different, never mind the family thing and all the complications that brings, and the fact neither of us wants a relationship, but I have to tell you… I've never had an affair before.' Suddenly realising the absurdity of the situation, she put her forehead to his and gave a genuine laugh. 'What I'm trying to tell you in my round-about way is that I don't know the etiquette for this or how I'm expected to behave now that we've actually done the deed.'

Dante brushed his lips over hers. 'If there is accepted etiquette then no one has told me.'

'How do your lovers normally behave after you've made love?'

'Don't think about them. They are not you. You wouldn't be here if you were.'

She winced.

'Aislin, stop comparing yourself to other women.'

'But I've seen pictures of your other lovers. They're all so…glamourous!'

'Maybe, but none of them has turned me on the way you do.'

Her cheeks pinked and a spark flared in her eyes. 'Really? You're not just saying that?'

He traced a finger over her soft lips. 'You do something to me, *dolcezza*, and I am not going to apologise or feel regrets, because what we shared was incredible.'

The spark deepened into a glow and she skimmed

his finger with her pink tongue. 'It was, wasn't it? I think that's what's thrown me. I didn't know it could *be* so good.'

And neither had he.

Feeling a fresh stiffening in his trousers, Dante groaned and clasped her cheeks in his hands. 'I want to make love to you again.'

She slid her arm around his neck, pupils dilating. 'What's stopping you?'

'The time.'

'What…?' She jerked out of his hold to look at her watch and gave a squeal of dismay. 'Dante, we're going to be late! The champagne reception's about to start.'

'That's what I meant about the time,' he said with pained dryness. He stood up and winced at the ache that had set off again in his loins.

Aislin jumped to her feet and caught sight of her reflection in the full-length mirror by the bathroom door. 'Look at the state of me!'

Her unkempt hair could just about be tamed with a brush, and she could redo her make-up, but her dress was all crumpled.

'Do they have a laundry service here?' She flew to the wardrobe and wrenched the door open. 'I'm going to have to wear the evening dress I got for tomorrow night's wedding reception.'

She could scream with frustration. Tomorrow night's dress was much flashier than the one she had selected for tonight, which she had chosen figuring she should ease herself into this world gently. The only solace she could find was that, having seen Cristina's glamorous dress, tomorrow night's dress would be more fitting.

'What are you talking about?'

'I bought outfits to match the itinerary but I didn't make any allowances for the clothes being crumpled up by having sex in them.' She thought quickly as she pulled out the dress she'd bought for the wedding reception. 'How do people in your world cope with all these outfits? Why can't they just have an outfit for the wedding ceremony that they keep on for the evening party like normal people?'

'Do that, then.'

'But you said everyone will change into party wear for the evening bash.'

'No one will care if you keep the same outfit on.'

'I guarantee you, every woman will be examining my outfits as carefully as their own. I've supposedly bagged Sicily's most eligible bachelor so they're going to be extra curious about me. The clothes I wear will reflect on you.'

'I'll give the personal shopper I hired for you a call and ask her to send more dresses over.'

She pulled a face, torn between not wanting him to waste more money on her and not wanting to show him up by wearing the same evening dress twice. Aislin wanted to fit into this world for the weekend for his sake.

'I'll call her now,' he said while she stood there arguing with herself, strolling over to stand behind her and wrap his arms around her stomach. 'And don't feel guilty.' He kissed the top of her head. 'I'm the one responsible for ruining your dress and, unless you want us to be seriously late, I suggest you take your new outfit and lock yourself in the bathroom before I ruin that one too.'

* * *

When Aislin emerged from the bathroom thirty minutes later, Dante let out a whistle.

'Wait a minute before you say anything,' she ordered then hurried to her suitcase and removed a pair of jade-green high heels. She slipped her feet into them and did a twirl. 'Now you can tell me, how do I look?'

'You look like someone who had better leave this room right now before I throw you on the bed and make love to you again.' He wasn't joking.

Aislin looked ravishing. She'd showered and changed into a beautiful emerald-green silk dress that had a Roman toga appeal to it. High-necked and sleeveless, it gathered at her slender waist, where it was encircled by a thick silk band covered in hundreds of tiny crystals. Falling to her knees, it had elegance and just the right touch of glamour. In the time she'd spent in the bathroom, she'd also reapplied her make-up, her eyes now rimmed with dark kohl, giving a smoky effect. She'd cured the problem of her hair by sweeping it into a messy knot at the nape of her neck. The loose tendrils falling down the side of her face were, he was certain, unintentional. On her ears were huge hooped rose-gold earrings that suited her colouring beautifully.

'I shall assume you mean that as a compliment… *Do* you mean it as a compliment?'

'Yes. Get out.'

They'd made love but it hadn't made a dent in his hunger for her.

When he joined her a few moments later he found her backed against the wall by the door.

Their eyes met.

He wanted to haul her into his arms and ravish every part of her so badly that, right then, he was prepared to say to hell with the wedding celebrations and Riccardo D'Amore, throw her over his shoulder and carry her back inside.

She held a hand out to him.

He stared down at it. Her short but shapely nails were bare of any varnish or the ornate things he guessed every other female guest here would have done to theirs.

A pang of guilt cut through him.

He'd plucked this minnow from a small town and taken her into this city of sharks he inhabited. Even if Riccardo failed to be convinced that Dante was a changed man who was nothing like his deceased father, he had a duty to take care of his minnow and keep her safe from the predators who would eat her alive.

He would not let her out of his sight.

CHAPTER TEN

UNIFORMED STAFF WAITED at the bottom of the stairs to lead the guests through the castle to the champagne reception outside.

Her hand firmly clasped in Dante's, Aislin gazed in awe at the enormous rooms with their high frescoed ceilings and ogled the furnishings that were a mix of old and new, gaudy and stylish. She guessed the generations who had lived here had simply replaced curtains and carpets when the old ones were worn with the latest trends and without sympathy with what was already there. The lack of internal uniformity turned what could easily have been an imposing monument into something more relaxed.

She tried to compose her features into something more relaxed too.

Beneath the beautiful dress she wore with its expensive price tag, she was painfully aware she was just plain old Aislin O'Reilly, a small-town Irish girl whose most glamorous wedding invite to date had been in a three-star Dublin hotel.

A hugely obese man stood on the patio area by the wide double doors that led out to the beautiful gardens, holding court and greeting the guests as they were brought outside.

'Is that Cristina's father?' Aislin asked in an undertone.

'No. That's Riccardo.'

'I thought Cristina's father was hosting this reception?'

'He is but Riccardo cannot resist muscling in and taking over. He has to be in charge even when he isn't.'

'And you want to do a business deal with him?'

'No, I want to do a business deal with his son.' He squeezed her hand, indicating this whispered conversation was over because now they were being taken to him.

Riccardo greeted her politely enough with the traditional Sicilian embrace and kisses, but then took hold of her hand and peered down to examine her ring.

'You are to be married,' he said in heavily accented English when he finally released her, and focussed his little piggy eyes on Dante. 'Congratulations.'

From the tone of his voice, Aislin guessed he already had suspicions about the authenticity of their relationship.

'Thank you,' Dante replied smoothly.

Riccardo patted his perspiring forehead with a handkerchief. He looked as if he was about to say something else when a tiny middle-aged woman with short hair, wearing a trouser suit, joined them.

Immediately, his whole demeanour softened.

'My wife, Mimi,' Riccardo said, before addressing his wife in Italian.

Mimi fixed keen eyes on Aislin before embracing

her and kissing her cheeks. 'No English,' she said, waving her hands as if in apology.

'No Sicilian,' Aislin replied with a grin. Although Sicilians mostly spoke their own dialect which to her untrained ear sounded just like Italian, her studies had taught her that Sicilians were proud of their island and proud to call themselves Sicilian.

Dante spoke a few more words and then he led Aislin away from the D'Amores to join the glamorous guests milling around over the immaculate lawn.

'Don't leave me,' she whispered, squeezing his fingers in her anxiety.

'I won't. Relax.'

And then she found herself thrust into the heart of the crowd which ranged in age from small toddlers right up to a wizened old man with an oxygen tank attached to his wheelchair.

Names were thrown at her, embraces and kisses exchanged and an ever-replenished stream of champagne and fruit juices carried by model-pretty staff was readily available.

When Dante introduced her as his fiancée, virtually everyone found it impossible to hide their shock. As he'd predicted, everyone was keen to look at her engagement ring, and the women especially made appropriate cooing noises.

But she also noticed the whispers between them and the side glances, and felt herself being weighed up and judged. Not all the judgements were favourable. One woman in particular, a beautiful sloe-eyed brunette called Katrina, gave her the chills. Aislin knew she was prone to an overactive imagination but the Medusa had had a friendlier stare than Katrina.

Dante kept her hand in his protectively throughout, as if he were an anchor keeping her rooted through her navigations in this mega-rich world.

It took half an hour of awkward social chit-chat before people stopped feeling the need to circulate quite so extensively and formed small groups. And that was when she received her first real line of questioning.

'How did you two meet?' asked a tall, willowy blonde called Sabine who had mercifully kind eyes and a small child clinging to her legs. Aislin was pretty sure she recognised her and thought she might have once graced the covers of the glossy magazines her old treacherous housemate had liked to buy. Sabine's husband, a squat French media tycoon, had excused himself for a cigarette.

With the Medusa woman finally out of her eyeline, Aislin lowered her guard. 'I broke into his father's cottage and tried to attack him with a showerhead,' she answered with a grin.

Clearly thinking she was joking, Sabine laughed. 'That's one way to make an impression.'

'She certainly got my attention,' Dante drawled, thinking Aislin had pitched her answer just right.

'I can see that. And why did you break into his father's cottage?'

'Ah, well, this is where it becomes a little tricky to explain.' She took a small sip of the champagne she was nursing. 'We share a sister.'

Sabine's eyebrows shot up so high they almost met her hairline.

Dante listened to Aislin explain in that humorous, lyrical way of hers the bare facts of their circumstances. She managed to convey it all without laying blame on anyone and by making it seem, without saying the actual words, that it had been inevitable that they would fall in love.

If he didn't know the truth, he would have been convinced himself.

Sabine turned her attention to him. 'Have you met Orla?'

'Not yet,' he told her smoothly, not adding that he had no intention of meeting her.

A tightness cramped in his guts. He'd given a deliberately non-committal answer to Aislin's invitation to Finn's party. He should have given a firm no.

When this weekend was over his life would return to normal and he would forget all about this sister he'd never known existed and had managed perfectly well without. He would have given her enough money from his own funds that he need not feel any more needless guilt.

And he would forget about Aislin too. If she ever became in desperate need of money, she had the ring. She could sell it and find it worth more than the money Orla would get from Aislin's pure-hearted generosity.

They would all be taken care of and he would carry on with his life.

For this weekend, though, he would take full advantage of the time they had together.

His vow to keep his hands off her and keep things platonic between them had been broken—and, *Dio*, *how* it had been broken—and he had no intention of denying himself more of the exquisite joy he'd found with her.

Dante pulled his gaze away from his Irish fox, now talking with real animation to Sabine about Italian medieval history. Dante had known Sabine for years. He'd steered Aislin to her as, of all the women there, she was the most likely to take her under her wing and not treat her as a rival.

He sensed Riccardo's stare on them and the curiosity behind it. Everyone here was curious about Aislin.

He thought of Lola and the women who had come before her. Forget discussions of medieval history, they would have been too threatened by Sabine's beauty to delve any deeper than a fake tribute to her outfit. They would have been friendly enough but their claws would have been primed, ready to strike at the first sign of weakness, anything to make a perceived potential rival feel small. Aislin had none of that cattiness.

She had a temper on her, though. *Dio*, she had fire in her soul that matched the russet of her flame-like hair.

A huge brass gong was brought out to the grounds, its clang ringing through the still spring air.

Dante breathed a sigh of relief. That was the champagne reception done with. Now it was time for dinner.

In a few hours he would make their excuses and take Aislin back to bed.

The dinner was held in the sumptuous banquet room and the food they were served was delicious and befitting a castle of this magnificence.

Close to a hundred people were seated around a horseshoe-shaped table and it made Aislin's brain hurt to think double the number would be arriving tomorrow for the wedding itself. As Dante's guest, she was on the special insider list of guests which consisted of close family and the closest of friends chosen to spend the whole weekend with the happy couple.

A waiter appeared at her shoulder with a fresh cocktail for her. When they had first filled everyone's wine glasses, Dante had discreetly asked if she could be served something different. Feeling it would totally lower the tone if she had a beer, she'd asked the waiter to come up with something for her. The result was a colourful fruity cocktail that tasted divine. Thankfully, Katrina the Medusa was at the furthest end of the table to her and out of her eyeline, enabling Aislin to relax.

Dante was more relaxed than she'd known him too.

Making love had changed the tone of their relationship. The desire that bound them in its grip had revealed itself in glorious colour. There was nothing left to hide.

Over the seemingly ordinary words they exchanged throughout the meal ran an undercurrent, a seduction, every catch of his eye making her pulse jump, a heady promise in the air of what was to come when this meal was over. Electricity zinged between them. She could feel it as clearly as the beats of her heart. The heat of his thigh pressed against hers lasered through the material of her dress, the effect the same as if she were naked.

She yearned to see him naked.

How many courses had they had? Five or six? She'd lost count.

Lifting her glass to her lips, she took a long drink and put it back down with a trembling hand.

Dear God, she was shaking.

She managed to breathe a little easier a moment

later when the efficient serving staff filed back in and laid individual hot chocolate puddings before them all.

Aislin cut into hers and watched the thick chocolate goo spill out.

That chocolate goo was her, she realised helplessly.

Inside she was melting for him.

It was the most delicious dessert she'd ever tasted but she struggled to swallow even a small mouthful.

'It's not like you to leave food,' Dante murmured when she put her spoon down and pushed her plate aside.

She looked into his eyes and searched desperately for a witty retort.

No retort came, only the truth. 'This is your fault.'

He leaned closer so his warm breath whispered against her earlobe, 'What is?'

She turned her face slightly so the tip of her nose brushed his cheek and inhaled his musky skin. 'That I've lost my appetite for food.'

'Do you have an appetite for something else?'

It took all her strength not to dart her tongue out and lick him.

She clenched the insides of her thighs, as if that action would be anywhere near enough to reduce the heat swirling and pulsing in her pelvis. Every cell in her body danced with awareness...

'Enjoying the dinner?'

In the flash of a moment Aislin was pulled back to earth.

She turned her head to Riccardo D'Amore, who stood behind them, well aware she was blushing like a teenager.

She forced her attention away from Dante's hot

body and the things he was doing to her to the here and now.

Riccardo had made a beeline for them during this sumptuous meal, giving them an excellent opportunity to seal the validity of their relationship in his mind and for her to charm him for Dante's sake.

Unfortunately, she didn't have a clue how to charm *anyone*, and reminded herself that Dante only wanted her to be her. Which was just as well, seeing as she didn't know how to be anyone else.

She would have to blag it.

For Dante's sake she would blag it to the best of her ability.

'Yes, thank you,' she answered cheerfully. 'The food is divine and there's so much of it! I'm just sorry I stuffed my face in the earlier courses because I'm too full to manage another bite.'

Dante put aside his irritation at the interruption and listened with the utmost bemusement at the chatter falling from Aislin's lips. Turning to Riccardo, he was further bemused to see something close to adoration spread over his jowly face.

'The food please you?' Riccardo asked, moving his bulk between them.

Dante could have stuck his spoon in him for forcing Aislin's thigh to part from his.

A rush of discomfort zapped through him to acknowledge that, far from welcoming Riccardo's interest in them, which was the whole reason he was paying Aislin such an obscene amount of money, he was having to bite his tongue to stop himself from telling Riccardo to get lost and leave them alone.

'It's better than any restaurant,' she enthused. 'And the cocktails are to die for. Have you tried one?'

'No.'

'Here.' She handed her cocktail glass to him. 'Try that. I haven't used the straw, you're safe.'

Dante did not think his bemusement could grow any more than to see Riccardo D'Amore complying with Aislin's order.

He took a sip and pulled an appreciative face. *'Molto bella.'*

She obviously got the gist of his approval for she beamed. 'I don't know what it's called—the waiter made it for me.'

He grinned in reply then looked from Aislin to Dante. 'You share sister?'

Needles made a sudden sharp crawl up Dante's spine.

So this was why Riccardo had come to them. The Sicilian gossip mill was on excellent form that evening.

Aislin answered for them with a proud nod and reached into her little clutch bag. 'Her name's Orla. Do you want to see a picture?' She scrolled through her phone and thrust it at him. 'That's Orla.'

Riccardo looked from the picture to Dante, his eyes as black as night. 'She look like your father.' The gist was clear—here was proof of Salvatore Moncada's amorous, immoral ways from beyond the grave.

Dante inclined his head in acknowledgement. The needles had made their way to his scalp.

Aislin took her phone back and scrolled again. 'That's Finn, Orla's son. He's an angel.'

Riccardo smiled. 'A beautiful boy.'

'He is!' she agreed with enthusiasm. 'And he's as bright as a button. He's got cerebral palsy, but he never lets it get him down, and he's always so happy. It's such a shame Dante's missed out on the first three years of his life but obviously that's not his fault, considering he didn't know Orla or Finn existed until recently, but that's all changing—he's buying them a house and is going to help as much as he can. I know he's going to make a fantastic uncle.'

'And father?' he asked pointedly after a beat that was probably caused by him struggling to keep up with Aislin's lyrical flow of chatter.

'One day,' she replied before Dante could get a word in. 'We want to enjoy married life first before having children.'

She made it sound so natural. So real.

He should be proud that she was sticking so closely to the script they'd created but all he felt was those damned needles digging into him.

Oblivious to Dante's darkening mood, Riccardo said, 'You know when you marry?'

'We only got engaged last week.' Aislin spoke if she were confiding something of tremendous importance. 'We're thinking the end of summer—that should give us time to plan it all. We've already decided we want a big white wedding and there is so much to do for it... Well, you would know all that; I bet this weekend's celebrations took months to prepare.' She fixed him with a look that conveyed she held Riccardo responsible for all the planning that had taken place and that she thought he was amazing for having done so.

'It took lot of planning, *sì*.' He nodded, puffing up like a peacock spreading its plumes.

'We'll have to pick your brains about it.'

'It would be my pleasure.'

She beamed again.

Riccardo finally gave his attention to Dante. Switching to their own language, he said, 'I'm impressed. When you get bored of her, send her to me. I have a nephew who would love her. It's time he settled down.'

'Aislin is not a chattel to be passed around.' Dante clenched the stem of his glass to prevent himself from jumping to his feet and knocking Riccardo off his.

The older man stared at him levelly but with a sneer forming on the side of his face. 'I'm glad to hear you say that but I will believe it when I see it. You've treated all your women before her like chattels. But then, they always treated themselves like a commodity too. This one is different. Look after her.'

Then he leaned down, kissed both of Aislin's cheeks and shuffled back to his seat.

Dante drained his wine and fought the swelling urge growing like a tempest inside him to smash the glass on the table.

Sensing danger, Aislin placed a tentative hand on Dante's thigh. She propped her elbow on the table to rest her chin on her free hand and gaze at him. The tension she'd sensed in him on his roof terrace the night before had returned.

'What did Riccardo say to you?' she murmured.

'Nothing important,' he dismissed with a quick smile.

'Then why have you got a face like thunder? Did your plan backfire? Did he not like me?'

'He liked you.' He gave a muted laugh. 'He said

that, when I get bored of you, to pass you on to him so he can marry you off to his nephew.'

Her nose wrinkled. 'Ew.'

She didn't get the chance to question Dante any further for a chill snaked up her spine and the willowy figure of Katrina appeared, talons holding her champagne flute tightly.

'If it isn't the happy couple,' she purred, sliding into the space Riccardo had vacated.

'Do you want something, Katrina?' Dante posed his question politely but there was an edge to his voice.

'I'm just concerned for your fiancée.' She fixed hostile eyes on Aislin. 'It's so hard to be an outsider at an event like this. Are you finding it very difficult?'

Aislin tried not to let her intimidation at the underlying malice behind the seemingly kind question show. 'Everyone has been very welcoming.'

'That's Sicilian hospitality. No one would *dream* of saying anything cruel to your face.'

'No, they would rather make petty remarks to make them feel small,' Dante cut in, his contempt undisguised. He got to his feet and took Aislin's hand. 'Go back to Giovanni, Katrina, and leave Aislin out of your games. *Buona notte.*'

Confused at this short confrontation, Aislin let him lead her out of the banquet room, her mind racing at the why of what had just happened.

CHAPTER ELEVEN

AISLIN WAITED UNTIL they walked the deserted corridor towards their room before asking, 'What was that about?'

His features were taut. 'Katrina playing mind games.'

'Why would she do that?'

'She's a bitch.'

'Is she an ex-lover of yours?'

'No.'

'Does she want to be your lover?'

He unlocked their door. 'Yes.'

For a moment Aislin thought she was going to be sick. 'Is that why she hates me?'

Dante saw the colour fade from Aislin's face and sighed as he shut the door. 'She hates any beautiful woman. Katrina used to be a model. She married an Italian film producer thirty years older than her, thinking it would turn her into a star, but she has no talent. She's bored and stuck in a loveless marriage and gets her kicks from sleeping around. She's a predator. This is the world I live in, *dolcezza*. It's filled with people who care only for their own pleasure and advancement.'

Having Aislin on the receiving end of the bitchy comments that usually passed him by...

The protectiveness he'd felt towards her...

He tugged his jacket and tie off and threw them on the armchair in the corner of the room.

Riccardo's observation about Dante's past lovers had been accurate. His experience of women being all the same was because he had deliberately gone for women of the same mould as each other. He had seen in them what he had wanted to see and it had suited them to play along with it.

Katrina was of that mould. The only thing that had stopped him taking her as a lover was her marital status.

He cradled Aislin's cheeks in his hands and gazed into the striking grey eyes.

She was everything Katrina and the lovers of his past weren't.

Aislin was beautiful inside and out.

He brought his mouth to hers and inhaled the sweetness of her breath before claiming her with his kiss.

It was the mind-blow he needed.

Her scent, her arms locking around his waist and the receptive parting of her lips all worked together to drive out the demons Riccardo's words had dredged in him.

Dragging his fingers across her face to burrow into the knot of her hair, he fought his body's wild response to devour her as quickly as possible.

This time he was going to take it slow.

This time they were going to do it properly.

Splaying his fingers, he found the pins holding her hair in place and pulled them out.

Her russet locks fell in a messy tumble over her shoulders. He rubbed his nose into it and inhaled the scent of raspberries.

As he found her lips again, a distant thought told him he would never again see or taste his favourite fruit without thinking of Aislin and remembering the colour of her lips and the smell of her hair.

Her hold around his waist tightened and she pressed herself so closely to him not even a sliver could come between them.

Dante rubbed his hands down her arms and took her hands in his. He led her to the bed and sat her down, then gently parted her legs to kneel before her.

Like this, they were of equal height.

Gazing into the eyes he felt certain he could pick from a thousand others of a similar shade, he unbuttoned his shirt and shrugged it off, letting it fall to the floor beside him.

Her eyes widened and pulsed.

She reached a trembling hand and placed it to his chest.

He closed his eyes at the sensation her touch released in him.

Aislin could feel the thuds of his heart against her palm and felt the strangest urge to cry.

That was Dante's heart beating so heavily for her. His smooth brown skin covered in dark hair that was softer than she had imagined, his brown nipples, his defined pecs, his taut abdomen.

This was him.

He was beautiful.

Slowly she caressed her fingers over him, soaking it all in with her touch and her eyes. She leaned closer and inhaled the musky scent of his skin and the overlaying spicy cologne. It was a dreamy combination that dived straight into her veins.

Then she continued with her fingertip exploration, dancing lightly down to the belt of his trousers.

Lifting her eyes to stare into his, the hunger gazing back at her knocked the air from her lungs.

She drank his potent hunger in, then leaned forward to press the lightest of kisses to his slightly parted mouth. Aislin closed her eyes and breathed in the scents she found. Coffee, liqueur and Dante himself all coiled like an invisible vapour to join the traces of his skin already committed to her memory and snaking deep in her bloodstream.

She tugged at his belt and kissed his neck. She tasted something indefinable. Dante.

When she finally had the belt undone she found the button of his trousers. As before, she struggled to undo it but there was no rush. Whereas earlier their pent-up desire had erupted and taken them on a soaring supercharged roller coaster, now there was a feeling of calm, as if they had all the time in the world to do all the things they had both dreamed of and fulfil all their unspoken desires.

These were desires that only a week ago had not existed in her.

A week ago, she might as well have been dead from the waist down. Sex and intimacy had had no meaning to her.

The tilting of her world and her awakening to desire no longer frightened her. Dante's reputation no longer frightened her. Even the whispered thought that she would never have these feelings for anyone else didn't frighten her.

If all they had was this weekend then it would be enough.

He leaned forward and brushed his cheek beside hers. His hand rested on hers and together they undid his button and pulled his zip down.

Then he kissed her neck and rose to his feet.

His chest rose sharply as he gazed down at her before removing his trousers and underwear to stand before her, fully, magnificently naked, erect in all senses of the word.

Her thundering heart twisted and her core pulsed and contracted.

Dante was beautiful. Every part of him.

'I want to see you,' he said thickly.

Keeping her eyes on his, she unbuttoned her dress at the neck and removed the crystal-studded belt. Then she lifted her bottom to ease the skirt of the dress up to her waist and pulled it up and off over her head.

She flung it away, uncaring where it landed.

All she cared about at that moment was Dante.

When she next looked at him, what she found sent a rush of emotion ripping through her. His jaw was clenched, his eyes hooded. His breathing was as heavy as the thuds of her heart.

If she'd had any fears about being naked before him that look would have blown them away.

But she had no fears. They had already been blown away.

She reached her hands behind her back and unclasped her bra.

The relief in her breasts to be freed from the lacy restriction was a pleasure in itself, but only a fleeting pleasure, because the ache in them suddenly came into sharp focus. They felt so *tight* and heavier than she had ever known them to be.

But the look in his eyes now was exhilarating.

Slowly she lifted her bottom again, this time to pinch her knickers and pull them down, shaking them off with her feet so that she was as naked as he, and the anticipation of what came next reverberated through her very being.

For the first time in his life Dante was scared to touch a woman, afraid that to touch would be to lose his head a second time.

Every inch of him strained towards her, every inch of his flesh attuned to her frequency. His heart beat so loud and so hard his chest hurt from the blows.

Naked, she was more beautiful than anything his feeble imagination had conjured.

Milky-white skin that looked as if it had never seen the sun set against the almost violent contrast of the deep russet of her pubis. Plump, wholly natural breasts topped with taut nipples the colour of raspberries...

Bellissimo.

Using all the restraint he could gather, he stepped towards the bed and placed a knee between her thighs, then gently eased her down so she lay flat.

He hovered over her for a long moment with his hands placed on either side of her head and did nothing but stare at her beautiful face.

She gazed back.

And then he crushed her lips with his mouth and the rush of desire broke free to consume him.

He kissed her everywhere. He explored her beautiful milky body with his mouth and his hands. He discovered all her tastes and scents, devoured her breasts with his mouth and discovered a flick of his tongue over the raspberry nipples made her gasp. Lower down and he discovered a new heady taste and scent, and discovered a flick of his tongue over her swollen nub made her cry out. When he kept his face there and slid a finger inside her...*Dio*, he had never known such wet heat was possible...he learned even more of her secrets.

And then she learned his.

One minute she was on her back, the next she'd wriggled out from under him and had *him* pressed down on the bed, and then she was covering his body with her mouth and touch, making the same explorations. He could feel the wonder and delight in her movements and for the first time in his life felt as if *he* were being made love to.

Aislin had passion in her pores and fire in her soul, he thought dazedly, and when he was finally sheathed and sliding inside her his last coherent thought was that she was the perfect fit for him.

Aislin's mind had gone, slipped away. All that was left of her were nerve endings.

Dante's cheek was crushed against hers, his body crushed on top of her, driving in and out of her, and the *pleasure*...

It was like nothing she had known before.

She had thought their first time could never be beaten but this...

This was everything.

If the good Lord should come for her now, she would go with rapture in her soul.

The tempo of his love-making increased and she adjusted with it, and as she did so the pleasure heightened.

Words tumbled out of her mouth, an incoherent jumble of cries for more, pleas for this never to end, never end, never end...

And then the words were sucked out of her as the pleasure reached its peak and exploded. She cried out at the same moment Dante released an animalistic roar that penetrated through her skin.

Waves of release crashed through her and she clawed at him, sobbing into his damp cheek pressed so tightly to hers, riding the glorious surges for as long as she could until her entire body felt saturated with their flow.

It was a long time before she could breathe with any semblance of normality.

Blood pounded in her head, pounded in every part of her satiated body.

Eventually Dante lifted his head and kissed her with a tenderness that filled her heart before gently moving off her.

She watched him walk to the bathroom and was suddenly overcome with another urge to cry.

Where the tears came from, she couldn't begin to think, and she blinked them away, burrowing under the covers, not wanting Dante to see.

But it had been beautiful.

When he slipped under the covers beside her and hauled her into his arms, she had to bite her tongue to stop words she would regret in the morning from being spilt.

There, in the darkness, lying with Dante in a jumble of limbs, the urge to say that she loved him almost overwhelmed her.

Aislin crept out of bed and slipped Dante's discarded shirt on. It smelled of him.

She gazed at his peaceful sleeping form with a lump in her throat. An arm was thrown over his head, the sheets tangled around his waist, his breathing deep and regular.

She took her own deep breath and wrenched her eyes away from him to pad to the coffee machine on the table at the end of the room. Once it was made, she took the cup and her phone out onto the secluded balcony, leaving Dante to sleep. The Lord knew he needed it.

There had not been much in the way of slumber that night.

She should be shattered herself but instead she felt wired.

And scared.

She took a sip of the coffee and stared over the balustrade, desperate to shut her thoughts down before they could gain traction.

The only sound was the early-morning bird call. It was so early she doubted even the children were awake.

There was a chill in the early-morning air but the brightening sky was cloudless and promised warmth. The sea in the near distance—she hadn't realised how close to the shoreline they were—had hardly a ripple in it.

She gazed wistfully at it, wishing for the same calm to replace the ripples of tension within her, then scolded herself for even acknowledging it.

She'd known what she was doing last night when she had made love with Dante. These feelings were nothing but a side effect of the heady hormones that had taken her in their grip.

But you never had these side effects with Patrick...
She dismissed that thought immediately. Compared

to Dante, Patrick had been a child, and the girl whose head had been turned by the university jock didn't exist any more.

Dante had awoken the woman inside her. And, unlike with Patrick, she had gone into this affair with her eyes open. Dante had no power to hurt her.

The jealousy she'd felt when she'd fleetingly suspected Katrina of being one of his ex-lovers had been an irrational reflex. Nothing more than that.

The warmth that had filled her at his protectiveness towards her then was nothing but a reflex too.

Needing to take her mind off him, she put her coffee on the table and called her sister. Finn's needs meant Orla had to get up early to care for him.

'What are you doing up at this god-awful time?'

Her sister's rude greeting soothed her.

This was familiar territory.

'I'm standing on a balcony looking over the Mediterranean Sea.'

'Is it raining?'

'There isn't a cloud in the sky. How's Finn?'

'Watching television. He's only asked about you twice since he got up. Have you spoken to Dante yet about his party?'

There was such hope in her sister's voice that Aislin's heart twisted. Poor Orla, let down by so many people: their mother, Orla's father, Finn's father, whom Aislin believed must have let her down in some way for her to have kept the pregnancy from him... All this heartache and still Orla longed for a relationship with the brother she'd never met.

Aislin would do anything to protect her sister and

Finn and it was with a sizeable lump in her throat that she confirmed Dante was hoping to make the party.

She had to trust him on this...

It came to her that she *did* trust him on this. She trusted him enough to let him into her sister's and nephew's lives. Trusted that he wouldn't let them down and hurt them like everyone else had.

It wasn't just the intimacy Aislin had shared with him, or their moonlit talk where they had opened up properly, but a combination of it all.

Orla's happiness at this was infectious, lightening Aislin's mood right until, a few minutes later, she asked, 'Are you still coming home Monday?'

Aislin's heart made a sudden wrench.

'If I can get a flight.' She hadn't even looked at the flight schedule.

Whatever flight she got back, she still only had one night left with Dante.

How quickly things turned on their head.

The slide of the patio door made Aislin turn *her* head.

While Orla started to go into detail about the wheelchair-friendly car she was thinking of buying, Dante, who'd thrown a pair of shorts on, came to stand behind her. He wrapped his muscular arms around her waist and placed a kiss on the top of her head.

Her wrenching heart broke off into a thundering run.

'What colour are you thinking of?' she asked inanely, then missed the answer because Dante had pressed his groin into the small of her back.

He was already fully aroused.

Aislin strove to keep a grip on the conversation but it was a losing battle. Dante slid a hand up her—his—shirt. A large hand found her breasts and squeezed, the other tugged at her hair to tilt her head back, exposing her neck for him to raze his tongue over.

The heat he ignited was instantaneous.

And then he spread his hand down her belly to her bare pubis.

She already knew she was ready for him.

When he slid a finger inside her, he knew it too, and gave a muffled groan into her hair.

'What was that?' Orla asked.

'Room service,' she lied, straining to keep her voice even, but too aware that Dante was tugging his shorts down.

He rested his length between her buttocks and ground into her.

Her entire abdomen melted into lava.

Then came the sound of teeth ripping foil.

'I'd better go,' she said, aware her voice must sound shaky but no longer having any control of it.

Dante pressed her forward and gripped her hips.

'I'll call you back later. Love you, bye.'

Then she disconnected the call at the same moment Dante entered her.

His love-making was fast and furious, an elemental force that released something new, something primal, in her.

When it was over and she stood gripping the balustrade, weak-legged and throbbing from the carnal pleasure he had unleashed, he gently pulled her hair back again and twisted her head to kiss her.

'What are you doing to me, *dolcezza*?' he asked with a groan into her mouth.

She laughed weakly. 'What are you doing to *me*, more like?'

His own laughter was shaky. 'I have no idea how I'm going to get through this day without dragging you off somewhere to make love to you.'

He disappeared back into the room to add to the growing number of condoms in the bin. Aislin picked up her phone, dropped from her fingers without her remembering, and wondered how the heck she was going to get through the rest of her *life* without making love to him.

CHAPTER TWELVE

DANTE DROVE THE short route to the cathedral. Normally he loved to be behind the wheel. When it came to getting from A to B in his busy daily life, he preferred to be chauffeured. Time was a premium. Being driven meant he could get on with work.

As this was a weekend for pleasure he'd decided to drive himself but now regretted the decision. He had to concentrate hard, and fight his eyes from staring at Aislin beside him, ravishing in an off-the-shoulder figure-hugging navy blue dress.

His awareness for her had become a burning infection in him. It consumed him.

When they'd joined the other guests for breakfast, he'd had to remind himself that holding her hand was for show.

But that had been a lie to himself.

It had been such a natural thing for him to do that he hadn't even realised he was holding it until they'd entered the banquet room and he'd been forced to let it go.

Once they'd finished breakfast, she'd gone up to their room, ordering him to give her an hour before joining her so she could get ready for the wedding in peace.

He'd known exactly what she meant. After their escapade on the patio, which his loins still burned to remember, they'd taken a shower together and got so carried away they'd come within a breath of not using a condom.

To while the time away, he'd played snooker in the games room with Alessio's youngest brother, Guido, a grumpy fifteen-year-old. They'd made excellent company for each other: the morose teenager who wanted to be roaming the streets with his mates and the disgruntled thirty-four-year-old man who wanted to be getting naked with his Irish fox.

When the hour had passed he'd gone up to the room and, the moment he'd crossed the threshold, she'd hurried out of the bathroom, hair straighteners in hand and only a towel wrapped around her.

'If you touch me, I swear I'll kick your ankles.' And then she'd hurried back in and locked the door.

Thirty minutes later she had opened the door a crack. 'Get to the other side of the room,' she'd ordered, and waited until he'd complied before stepping out.

She'd held her palms out in a warning. 'I mean it, Moncada. Don't touch me. It's taken me an hour to get my hair right.'

She was fully dressed, her hair loose and in sleek waves around her bare shoulders.

She'd been right to warn him to keep his distance.

If she'd been within arm's reach he would have had her in his hold quicker than she could blink. And they both knew what would have happened then.

He'd already ruined one of her outfits. The replacement dress for the evening reception was en route from Palermo. There was no time to get a replacement dress for the wedding itself.

He figured he had five, maybe six hours until he could make love to her again. There was a three-hour window between the wedding breakfast and the evening reception. That was plenty of time to make love again, maybe twice, and still have time to shower and change.

Dio, he was planning when he could make love to her again?

'Talk to me. Distract me,' he ordered.

'What? Why?'

'Because, *dolcezza*, me driving with a rock-hard erection is going to get us killed. I need a distraction. Tell me something interesting about European medieval history.'

She giggled softly. 'It's all interesting.'

'Narrow it down. Tell me something about Sicily I don't know.'

'Do you know much about how Sicily became a part of the Crown of Aragon?'

'When we were ruled by Spain?'

'That's the one.'

'Educate me.'

For the next ten minutes he relaxed and listened as she told him about a period in his island's history that was familiar to him only on a distant level, bringing it to life in that wonderful lyrical way she had.

'If you're set against being a teacher, have you thought of being a historian?' he asked. 'You could work in a museum giving tours and educating the public.'

'But that would take me away from home,' she pointed out. 'There are no museums near to where we live so to do that would mean having to move away from Orla and Finn.'

'I'm sure they would miss you but Orla will be able to afford professional help rather than rely on you.'

'I would miss them too much,' she stated simply.

'Then get them to move with you. It's time you started living your life for yourself. You've put it on hold for long enough.'

Parking at the cathedral was limited but he found a space easily enough. As he held Aislin's hand to help her out, a figure in the distance caught his attention.

He swore.

Aislin followed his gaze and saw a couple heading their way. The elderly man had a walking stick and a shock of pure white hair that brought to mind Albert Einstein. The much younger, pencil-thin woman holding his arm had dark hair coiffured within an inch of its life and wore a chic silver lace dress and billowing green silk cape. She guessed they were grandfather and granddaughter.

Then she looked back at Dante and saw the distaste curdling his face and felt suddenly sure it was because of the woman he was staring at.

Nausea sparked in her guts, violent and immediate.

Katrina might not be one of his ex-lovers but the odds were that another guest or two would be.

'Who's that?' she asked as casually as she could manage.

'My mother.'

'*What?*'

'That woman is my mother.'

That woman spotted them staring and raised a hand in their direction to wave enthusiastically.

Dante raised a hand in return. He didn't wave it.

'That's your mother? You're kidding me! Seriously?' Aislin, all nausea gone as quickly as it had come, now had the worry that her eyes were going to pop out. Holy moly, that was his *mother*?

She didn't look like any mother of a thirty-four-year-old man Aislin had ever met.

'She could be your sister.'

'Be sure to tell her that. She might love you as much as she loves her plastic surgeon.'

'He must be a very expensive plastic surgeon. Her face is amazing.' Aislin lowered her voice as the couple inched closer to them, their speed hindered by the man's struggle to walk. 'And is that your grandfather?'

'That man, I am guessing, is her latest future ex-husband.'

About to snigger, she noticed Dante's face had become blank.

The snigger died on her lips.

In all their many conversations, Dante had said little about his mother other than that she'd moved to the Italian mainland when Dante had been small... without her only child.

She slipped her hand into his, suddenly feeling protective of him.

As Immacolata came into clearer vision, walking effortlessly on heels that had to be twice the three inches Aislin had braved, her curiosity intensified.

Probably around the same height as Aislin without the heels, that was the only similarity between the two women. Immacolata was as dark as her son, although Aislin would bet the colouring now came from a bottle. Up close, she looked older than first impressions, but still nowhere near old enough to have an adult child. Elegant and beautiful, her startling blue eyes were bright with mischief.

'Dante!' she cried, releasing her partner's arm to embrace her son and kiss his cheeks.

'Mother,' Dante replied returning her greeting coolly. 'Are you going to introduce us?'

'Dante, this is Giuseppe, a good friend of Riccardo D'Amore and a very dear friend of mine. His wife has recently departed, rest her soul.' She made the sign of the cross in a tremendous show of piety. 'Giuseppe, this is Dante.'

He didn't think his mother had acknowledged him as her son since he'd turned eighteen. It would have made people question her own age too closely.

Giuseppe bowed his head and accepted Dante's dutiful embrace. He was so ancient a gust of wind could have knocked him off his feet.

'Helping him get over her death, are you?' he asked his mother in an undertone.

'I do my best,' she said with a demureness that would have made him laugh if it had come from anyone but the woman who had carried and given birth to him. 'He's almost worth as much as you are, darling.'

'Where's Pierre?' Pierre was husband number five.

'Pierre's history.'

'What did he do?'

'Bored me.' She winked at Aislin, who was watching their exchange with a furrowed brow, and then said, 'Who is this beauty?'

'This is Aislin,' he replied, then switched to English. 'Aislin, this is my *mother*, Immacolata.'

His mother gave the slightest of winces as he stressed her relationship to him. She didn't speak English but some words translated into every language.

It gave him a perverse if fleeting dose of satisfaction.

Aislin allowed herself to be enveloped in his mother's cloud of perfume and said, 'It's wonderful to meet you.'

His mother smiled, not understanding a word she'd said. However, she noticed Aislin's hand and grabbed it, examining the ring on her finger.

Then she turned accusing eyes to Dante. 'Did you give her this ring?'

'Yes.'

'You're getting married? You didn't tell me.'

'One, it is a very recent engagement, and two, you didn't bother to tell me you were marrying Pierre or Stavros until after you'd married them.'

As the crowd by the cathedral was growing, Dante thought it past time to cut the conversation short and reclaimed Aislin's hand to join the congregation.

Once they were seated and waiting for the bride to make her grand entrance, both of them making a bee-line for the back of the cathedral, Aislin immediately whispered, 'What did I miss?'

He filled her in briefly.

'So she's dumped your stepdad for a richer widower?' she summarised.

'They don't call her the Black Widow for nothing,'

he said shortly. 'Pierre is her fifth husband and about to become considerably poorer, like all the husbands before him, my father included.'

The orchestra began to play the tune to mark the bride's arrival and the congregation rose to its feet.

After Cristina had made the long walk down the aisle and they'd sat back down for the priest to begin his sermon, Aislin asked quietly, 'How old were you when your mother left?' The woman on her other side was dealing with a fractious baby, its noise enough to cover any illicit conversation.

'Seven.'

'Did she leave because she found out about my mother being pregnant by your father?'

'I don't know why she left.'

Her heart clenched for the abandoned boy. 'Have you never asked?'

'No. She left. End of story.'

'Do I have to worry about her scratching my eyes out when she discovers who I am? And she *will* discover it. Someone is bound to tell her.'

'She's more likely to be curious about you.' He closed his eyes and took a long inhale. 'To be fair to my mother, she's not a cruel woman. She wouldn't blame you for your mother's sin.'

'*My* mother's sin?' Her eyes turned to lasers. 'My mother was nineteen when your father seduced her.'

He sighed. 'I didn't mean to put the finger of blame on her. I didn't know she was that young.'

She was silent for a moment. 'To be fair to your father, from what our mother told us, she knew he was married.'

He asked one of the many questions he'd been denying to himself that he was curious about. 'Do you know how they met?'

'She was on holiday with some girlfriends here in Sicily. Your father knew the owner of their hotel. He saw my mum sunbathing by the pool and it was lust at first sight.' Her eyes hardened. 'It was supposed to be a holiday romance but they were careless. They agreed she would raise Orla and his only contribution would be financial. It suited them both. Poor Orla, she wanted so badly to know him, but was never allowed.'

The priest finished his sermon and invited the congregation to their feet to sing a hymn. The words were in Latin but Aislin knew the tune and happily joined in.

Mass had been a huge part of her childhood and this ceremony, although conducted in a different language, had the same feel to it.

Four rows in front of them, she could see Immacolata Whatever-Her-Surname-Currently-Was belting the hymn out with the best of them.

'Did you see much of your mother after she left?' she asked when they were again invited to sit back down.

'Some. She moved to Florence. I would stay with her for weekends and some holidays.'

Aislin thought of her father. Their relationship had been similar but she had no memory of living with him so had never missed him as a permanent presence. 'You must have missed her.'

He shrugged. 'I would have missed my father more if he'd left.'

'I'm sorry.' She squeezed his fingers, thinking how hard it must be for him. Here she was rabbiting on about their families and the past when he was still dealing with his grief at losing his father and coping with the secrets and lies that had been revealed. 'Do you think she knew that you would miss your father more and that's why she left you with him?'

'I think she was thinking only of herself. Mothers are supposed to nurture. Mine is only interested in nurturing her fingernails. It goes against her grain. It always did.'

She gave him a rueful smile. 'My mother's not really the nurturing type either, in case you hadn't realised.'

No, Dante thought. Aislin was the nurturer in the O'Reilly family.

Little wonder she was so fiercely protective of her sister and nephew. For Aislin, her little family meant everything.

A memory came to him, one he hadn't thought of in a long time, from when a decade ago he'd suffered a nasty bout of flu. For two weeks he'd hardly been able to lift his head up. When his mother had learned of this she had come swanning in to check up on him. She'd stood at the threshold of his bedroom door with a mask covering her fully made-up face and even in his weakened state he'd been disdainful at the distance she'd kept.

For the first time he appreciated that she'd made the effort to see him and satisfy herself that he wasn't about to die. She'd stayed in his home, uninvited, for five days, never getting any closer to him than the bedroom door, but she had stayed until he was over the worst of it and then flown back to whichever husband she'd been married to.

In her own way she did care for him.

If he were in an accident that left him in a coma he was quite sure she would be at his bedside—no germs to worry about from a car accident—and that she would stay until the danger had passed.

When his father had suffered his fatal heart attack she'd flown straight over to be with Dante.

Had she known about Orla? Had she conspired with his father to keep it secret from him?

The pounding increased, the familiar churning in his guts swirling with the poison of all the secrets and lies.

The congregation rose, again, to its feet. Another hymn was sung and then it was time for the exchange of vows.

The noises in his head were loud enough to block their words out and he was glad of it. Love and fidelity were empty promises. Tying yourself into a union where the only guarantee was disappointment, because that was what family amounted to. Disappointment.

Aislin's view of the bride and groom was restricted but Alessio's and Cristina's unwavering voices rang clear and true through the great walls of the cathedral. The solemnity of the occasion suddenly clutched at her and she felt something move and shift within her. The lump she'd found in her throat that morning when she'd watched Dante sleeping came back and she became aware all over again of his fingers clasped through hers.

A week ago, she would have laughed if anyone had suggested she would feel so moved to witness a couple pledge their lives to each other, but there was something so affirming about the moment, the faith

Alessio and Cristina had in each other and the love they shared, that Aislin had to keep her face forward, suddenly afraid to look at Dante.

Would she one day be told by Orla that Dante had surprised even himself by falling in love with someone and that he was going to be married for real?

The slice to her heart at this thought almost made her gasp from the pain.

It took a few moments for her to loosen her grip on Dante's hand.

She was just being sentimental. Weddings did that to people. It was natural to be caught up in the romance and joy of these occasions. When a new day started the feelings would be nothing but a memory.

In two days, Dante would be nothing but a memory too, albeit a memory that was going to be on the fringe of her life for the rest of her existence.

'Do you think they'll last?' she asked him as they filed out with the rest of the congregation to the cathedral grounds for the photographs.

He nodded. 'They both come from families where marriage is sacrosanct. Even if they make each other miserable they'll stay together.'

'Not all marriages end in misery,' she said wistfully.

'No, they all end in death or divorce.'

And then their conversation was cut off as the photographer took control and began ordering everyone into position.

Aislin fixed a smile to her face and joined the heaving crowd.

The happy couple were photographed on their own first, then immediate family were brought in, then extended family. Finally she and Dante were called in with the other friends to take their position.

Dante placed his arm around her waist and held her close and, as they all smiled for the camera, all she could think was that this picture would be the only physical evidence left of her time with him.

CHAPTER THIRTEEN

'CAN YOU DO the buttons up for me, please?'

Dante, who'd been trimming his beard, left the bathroom and stood behind her.

Aislin's face when they'd walked into their room and she'd seen the replacement dress hanging on the wardrobe had been a picture in itself.

She'd put her forefinger and thumb together. 'I came this close to choosing this dress.'

'So I heard. What stopped you?'

'I thought I would look a fool in it.'

'You could never look a fool.' And then, because it had been a good six hours since he'd last made love to her, he'd taken her to bed.

Losing himself in her eager, welcoming body had been enough to dislodge the bitterness the wedding had brought out in him.

He felt himself stiffen to remember all the things they had done to each other.

Catching his eye in the reflection of the mirror they were stood in front of, Aislin gave him her best school-teacher look. 'Just the buttons, Moncada.'

He saluted then set to work on the tiny gold buttons that would keep the dress in place.

Done, he stayed where he was, content to gaze at her. 'You're beautiful.'

Her cheeks pinked and she smiled. 'So are you.'

'I'm glad we ruined your first dress.'

'So am I.'

The replacement dress was strapless and skimmed the top of her cleavage. Dark cream with embellished gold embroidery, it hugged her waist and flared at her hips, falling to her calves at the front and to her ankles at the back. The personal shopper had matched it with cream high heels.

As their love-making had ruined her hair again, she'd twisted it into another knot. Like the night before, the knot was messy but striking, and suited her perfectly. Like the night before, he wouldn't have her any other way. He liked that she'd never been one to perfect hairdos over and over until she could create them with her eyes closed.

'We should go before I give in to temptation and ruin this dress too.'

She hooked her arms around his neck and pressed her lips lightly to his. 'When we get back to the room later, I will help you ruin it.'

He groaned and forced his legs back, away from her.

Feeling giddy and full of fizz, as if she could jump up and defy gravity to fly, Aislin held his hand tightly to keep her grounded on their walk to the ballroom, where the evening reception party was being held.

She would not allow herself to think that this was their last night together or dissect why his cynical comments about marriage had struck like a blow.

This was a night for celebration and their last opportunity to convince Riccardo D'Amore that they were in love.

She would not allow herself to acknowledge the wrench in her heart or what it meant.

As they walked through the banquet room, tonight transformed into a second bar, a man striding towards them caught her eye and stopped her in her tracks. As tall as Dante and almost as handsome, there was something about him...

'Who's that?' The whispered question was hardly out of her mouth when the man spotted Dante.

He greeted him with a huge embrace and kisses to his cheeks. They exchanged a few words before he waved an apologetic hand and hurried off.

'Who was that?' she repeated.

Dante stared at her with narrowed eyes. 'Tonino Valente. Why do you ask?'

'There's something familiar about him.' She screwed up her eyes, trying to think where she'd seen him before.

'He owns the castle. Riccardo is throwing his weight around and keeping all the staff on their toes. Tonino's flown in to troubleshoot.'

'How do you know him?'

'His father and my father were friends. His father owned a hotel chain... I would not be surprised if it was one of his hotels that your mother stayed at when she met my father.'

And just like that it came to her why he looked so familiar and she clamped a hand over her mouth.

'What's wrong?' he asked.

She swallowed and, without thinking, said, 'He reminds me of Finn.'

'Orla's son?'

She nodded. 'Orla came to Sicily six months before her accident. She wanted to meet your father but lost her nerve. That's all she told me about her time here but a month later she discovered she was pregnant. She always refused to say who the father was and I assumed it was a work colleague or something. She always promised she would tell him after the birth... Oh, how could I have been so blind? The dates fit!'

And then, suddenly realising who she was spilling her spiralling thoughts to, grabbed Dante's hand and pressed it to her chest to stare at him earnestly. 'You can't say anything. I might be completely wrong—I probably *am* completely wrong—so promise me you'll keep your mouth shut. Orla would *kill* me if she knew I'd been speculating like this.'

He didn't say anything.

'*Please*, Dante,' she begged. 'Don't say anything to Orla. Or to Tonino. My imagination's just gone a little haywire, that's all. I should have kept my thoughts to myself.'

Yes, she should have, Dante thought grimly. If she didn't learn to control them better, then one day Aislin's overactive imagination and unfiltered mouth would get her into trouble. The thought of Tonino Valente being Finn's father was ludicrous.

But her wild speculation wasn't the cause of the needles driving through his skin.

He'd seen the way she'd looked at Tonino and then, when she had asked about him, he'd experienced something hot and rancid in his guts he had never felt before.

It had been a feeling he suspected felt much like jealousy would feel.

Dante had never been jealous of anyone or anything in his life.

But what else accounted for the burst of relief when she'd explained why Tonino had caught her attention?

He stared at Aislin with the feeling of a man standing in quicksand.

Barely a week with her, only a couple of days as lovers, and he'd had a moment where he had wanted to rip the head off an old friend's neck.

Her eyes were pleading with him. 'Please, Dante, promise you won't say anything.'

As he had no intention of meeting Orla, it was the easiest promise he would ever make. The stab of guilt he felt when making it was as ludicrous as Aislin's speculation.

He had made no promises about meeting his father's secret love-child or her son. He'd been non-committal at best regarding the invitation to Finn's party, and after this day and the virulent feelings that had almost choked him at seeing his mother, the lies and deceptions of his life brought back to the forefront where his time with Aislin had calmed them, he was relieved he'd made no specific promises.

Dante never wanted to be part of a family unit again and that included one with his secret sister who, he knew, was as great a liar as their father.

He rationalised that all these heated, irrational, jealous feelings and all the needles digging into him had been dredged up by what Aislin represented: their shared sister and his father's lies.

They were nothing to do with Aislin herself. He

liked her company. His struggle to keep his hands off her was due to their time together coming with a pre-determined limit heightening the effect.

And, as he thought all this, a modicum of calm settled back into him.

This was a heightened situation. That was all.

He would enjoy the time he had left with Aislin and then say goodbye to her without a second thought.

As great as she was, she was everything he didn't want. This was a woman who had put her life on hold for three years to nurture and care for her sister and nephew during a period in which she should have been making the most of her youth and freedom. She'd done it because she loved them. For Aislin, family meant everything, where for him, family meant nothing.

His feelings for her were nothing extraordinary.

Aislin pushed all thoughts about Tonino Valente away, recognising that her imagination had briefly got the better of her, and instead concentrated on the wedding reception.

She'd been to many weddings in her life but this one topped the lot. The ballroom had been transformed into a sparkly wonderland complete with a champagne fountain that had to break all world records, a chocolate fountain that no one above the age of ten could get near, a cocktail bar, an ever-replenished array of canapés served by an army of waiting staff...all of it set to music pumping out courtesy of a world-famous DJ who had recently hit number one in every continent with his remix of a classic eighties tune.

The atmosphere was pumping as much as the music and she had a whale of a time, drinking lager from a bottle—Dante assured her that propriety should be damned—and chatting to Sabine and her husband, Francois, who after a few drinks loosened up and became excellent company too. Other guests joined them, dipping in and out of the conversation.

All Aislin's feelings of inadequacy had gone. Not even Katrina's malicious presence bothered her. She felt nothing but pity for the beautiful woman trapped in a hell of her own making.

The only fly in the ointment was Dante.

Something was bugging him, she was certain of it. It was nothing she could put her finger on, as outwardly he was his usual sociable self, but she detected an undercurrent to his mood.

Aislin was catching her breath at their table after a vigorous dance with Sabine when Riccardo D'Amore came over to them.

'You drink beer?' he asked her, his brow creased.

She nodded cheerfully. 'Champagne gives me a headache.'

'No cocktail?'

'Not tonight. Too many and I'll get drunk, and then I'll probably fall over and make a fool of myself, so it's safer for me to stick to beer.'

Dante doubted Riccardo had understood half of what she'd just told him in that rapid-fire delivery, but he beamed nonetheless.

And then he turned to Dante. 'Are you free Monday morning?' he asked in their own language.

'That depends why you're asking.'

'I've been having a rethink about that deal you made with Alessio. I think I was a little hasty in my involvement. Alessio has a good head on his shoulders.'

That was as close to an apology as Dante would get but he didn't expect a full one. Riccardo was a proud man. He did not like to admit his mistakes.

'What are you saying?' He wanted it spelt out.

'That I was wrong to interfere. I have spoken to him and he is still of the opinion that the deal with you is the best one on the table. The contracts are still drawn up. He goes on his honeymoon Monday afternoon but can spare a few minutes to sign it before he leaves. That is, if the deal is something you still wish to go ahead with?'

Hiding his euphoria at his plan succeeding so perfectly, Dante pretended to consider the question. 'I have meetings all day Monday. My lawyer will be with me. If Alessio can bring the contract and his lawyers to me for eleven a.m., I should have a window to fit him in then.'

Dante had his pride too. He wanted this deal—he wouldn't have offered Aislin such a large amount of money if it wasn't so important to him—but he would not roll over and demean himself by snatching Riccardo's olive branch without making the man sweat a little. It was the least he deserved. Alessio too, for allowing his father to browbeat him into pulling out of the deal in the first place.

'You are still willing to go ahead?'

'If he can get to me for eleven, then yes.'

'He will be there. Where will you be?'

'Madrid. I fly there tomorrow evening.' His tone left no doubt—Riccardo and Alessio could take it or leave it.

Riccardo pulled his handkerchief out of his top

pocket and patted his perspiring forehead. 'He will be there.'

Dante finally allowed himself a smile and extended his hand. 'Then we have a deal.'

Riccardo clasped it in his clammy paw. 'We have a deal.'

When Aislin opened her eyes the next morning there was a cramping weight in her chest so heavy that it took a few moments before she could breathe with any ease. Dante's arm was draped over her belly, his knee nudging against her thigh, sleeping deeply.

His mood had much improved once the deal with the D'Amores was confirmed as back on. He'd joined her on the packed dance floor and neither had complained that the mass of bodies forced them to hold each other closely.

The euphoric mood had extended to the bedroom. Little in the way of sleep had been found in their bed that night, even less than the night before.

Aislin hadn't wanted to fall sleep. She hadn't wanted to miss a single moment.

But nature had taken its course and she'd been pulled into slumber as the first glimpse of sunlight broke through the join in the heavy curtains.

Hot tears bit into her retinas and she blinked vigorously to contain them.

Her chest *hurt*. Her stomach hurt too, filled with knots being pulled into a giant tangle of pain.

Dante shifted closer and stretched. His arousal replaced his knee against her thigh.

She mustn't cry.

They still had a few hours left.

And maybe…

He slid on top of her and covered her mouth with his.

Maybe Dante wasn't ready to say goodbye yet either.

Breakfast was served in the dining room. The guests who had spent the weekend celebrating with the happy couple were all accounted for, present in body if not in spirit. An awful lot of heads were being clutched and painkillers being swapped like sweets. Only the children had retained their manic spirits but, where they had spent the weekend being indulged, this morning they were shushed.

Aislin couldn't work out why she felt so bad, considering she'd paced her alcohol intake and made sure to drink plenty of water.

Dante didn't look much better either but insisted with a brisk smile that he felt fine. His appetite was as healthy as always.

Although she had little appetite of her own, Aislin took her time, picking at the croissants, chewing slowly, refilling her coffee and orange juice numerous times; anything to drag this last meal out.

Yet, though she tried her hardest to make the time pass as slowly as was humanly possible, she found it hard to look at him. Every time she met his eyes her heart would swell and she would find herself biting her tongue from the plea it longed to shoot out.

Is this really it?

Was it really possible that in the space of a week she had gone from thinking she would never get involved with another man, especially not this one, to feeling her insides would rip to shreds if she never felt his arms around her again?

He was nothing like the man she had imagined.

Just as Dante pushed his chair back, ready to leave the dining room, Riccardo D'Amore and his wife stopped at their table.

'Good morning,' he said in English, smiling, no sign of a headache or any ill-effects from the night before.

'Morning,' Aislin replied as cheerfully as she could manage.

'We like you to come to house for dinner.' He spoke carefully.

'Me and Dante?' She did her best to hide her surprise.

'*Sì*. It will be great pleasure for us. You come... *mercoledì*?'

She glanced at Dante. His lips were curved upwards but the expression in his eyes gave nothing away.

'Mercoledi?' she repeated uncertainly.

'Wednesday,' Dante murmured.

'Right. Wednesday.' Her heart made a sudden leap. She could stay until Wednesday. That was totally doable. Orla could cope a few more days without her and Aislin could have an extra four days with Dante!

Feeling a whole heap lighter inside, she grinned with the whole of her face. 'I don't have anything planned for Wednesday. Have you anything in your diary?' she directed at Dante.

He shook his head.

'It's a date.'

Riccardo translated for his wife, who showed her pleasure by beaming as widely as her husband.

Back in their room, Aislin began to pack her things in her super-posh suitcase, practically dancing a jig with happiness.

Four more nights with Dante! Perfect. She'd give Orla a call in a few minutes and let her know...

'Do you want the balance of the money transferred to Orla?' Dante asked, breaking through her happy thoughts.

'Yes, please.' She bounded over to him and threw her arms around his neck. 'You must be delighted your plan has worked out so well.'

Expecting a kiss, she was disappointed when he kept his gaze focused over the top of her head. 'It is good that he saw reason. The deal with me will make the D'Amores far more money than the deal with my competitor would have.'

'Well, I for one am thrilled it's all worked out for you.'

He gave a tight smile and unhooked her arms from his neck. 'I'll transfer the money now.' He stepped away and removed his phone from his jacket pocket.

'I'll call Orla and let her know to expect it, and let her know I won't be back until Thursday.'

'Thursday?'

'The D'Amore dinner's on Wednesday,' she reminded him.

He perched on the armchair and gave his attention to his phone. 'There will not be a dinner.'

Her stomach dropped like a brick. 'But we said we were going.'

He raised a hefty shoulder nonchalantly.

'Surely you don't want to upset him this late in the day?'

He shrugged again. His fingers were busy working on his phone. 'The contract will be signed tomorrow.'

'Is there not a grace period for him to change his mind?'

'No. Once it is signed, then that's it.'

'So you lied about going to his house for dinner?'

'You agreed to it, not me.'

She stared at him, willing him to look up from his phone so she could see what was in his eyes.

'You said you were free,' she pointed out evenly. The crushing weight was expanding but she refused to acknowledge it. Her overactive imagination could be leading her on a path that was something out of nothing. Dante had made no secret to her of his dislike for Riccardo and, after the way Riccardo had treated him, she understood why he would be reluctant to accept his hospitality.

He probably thought, too, that he would be putting her out. After all, she had told him only the day before that she could never move from her home because she would miss Orla and Finn too much.

He was being considerate.

'It is not important,' he said. 'I will let him know after the contract is signed that we won't be attending.'

'I don't mind going. You're going to have to work with him…'

'No, I will be working with his son.'

'But his feelings will be hurt.'

'I will let him down gently. It was not my company they desired but yours.'

'Honestly, Dante, I don't mind staying a few extra days. It's the least I can do for you.'

He grimaced. 'I'm flying to Madrid tonight and have back-to-back meetings for the next two days.'

'I've never been to Madrid.'

'It's a beautiful city and I recommend you visit it one day.'

One day?

'Dante… Don't you like the idea of us having a few more days together?'

'It would be fun if I had the time, but I don't.'

Fun?

'Have I done something to upset you?'

'No. You've played your part very well… *Va bene*.' His tone lifted a notch. 'The money has been transferred. I will charter a flight back to Ireland for you this afternoon. I would lend you my jet but I need it to get to Madrid. I'll have a car waiting at the airport to drive you home.' He finally looked up from his phone.

The blankness in the eyes, normally so full of expression and life, was enough to make her blood freeze.

'Have you finished packing? We need to go.'

CHAPTER FOURTEEN

DANTE DROVE THE car out of the castle grounds and took the route straight to the airport.

He would drop Aislin there then go home and get himself organised for his flight to Madrid.

He stretched his mind to the coming week and the business he needed to take care of. Now that the deal with the D'Amores was back on, he would need to re-schedule appointments and get systems up and running. There was a lot of work in the weeks and months ahead.

Aislin's phone rang, cutting through the silence.

They hadn't exchanged a word since getting into his car.

She'd been her usual bright, bubbly self when say-ing goodbye to everyone but he had sensed the mel-ancholy beneath it and had the strangest feeling he had hurt her.

It had been good of her to offer to stay with him and attend the dinner with Riccardo but he had put her out enough.

It was time to say goodbye. Their job was done.

There was no reason for him to prolong their time together, something he had told himself with resolute firmness when he had showered that morning before breakfast.

He'd enjoyed some great times with her, but now it was over, exactly as had been agreed right at the very start of it all. His feelings on the matter had only hardened.

'Are you not going to answer that?' he asked when she ignored her phone.

'It'll be Orla.'

'Then why not answer it?'

'Because I know what she's going to ask and I don't have an answer for her.'

'What do you think she wants?'

'I know what she wants. She wants to know if she can meet you before Finn's party.'

His hands tightened on the steering wheel but his heart lifted to see the airport on the horizon.

He put his foot on the accelerator.

Almost there.

A few more minutes and she would be out of his car and out of his life for good, and he would never have to think about the O'Reillys again.

'Fine,' she said through what sounded like gritted teeth.

Nothing more was said until he pulled into the airport's drop-off.

He switched the engine off, twisted in his seat to face her and found himself looking at the back of her head.

'There is a member of the airport staff in the departure lounge waiting for you,' he said. 'She'll have your name on a board, so you can't miss her. She will see you're looked after and get you where you need to go.'

She didn't answer.

'Aislin?'

Her head moved round slowly and then the grey eyes he'd found so striking in that very first glance fixed on him, and what he saw in them was powerful enough to make his heart thump and twist.

Then she blinked and the hurt he'd seen was gone.

'Get your phone out,' she said briskly. 'I'll give you Orla's number and you can call her when the DNA test's done.'

Blood surged in his head. 'Aislin—'

'Will you give me your number too, so I can pass it on to her?' she continued, as if he hadn't tried to speak. 'Even if you don't want to meet before the party it would be good for the two of you to talk.'

He took a deep breath and rested his pounding head back. 'No.'

'No…? What do you mean?'

He'd hoped she would leave without the need for this conversation but she had boxed him in. Non-committal answers were not going to satisfy her now. 'I'm not going to meet Orla.'

'Not meet her…?' She looked as confused as if he'd told her the sky was really a giant mushroom. 'But why would you not want to meet her? She's your sister. Sure, she can be annoying, but she's a lovely person—'

'Orla is not my sister.' Something crawled inside him. It twisted in his veins and bound to his bones, pulsing rabidly under his skin.

'Not this again. She *is* your sister.'

'No, *dolcezza*, she is not.' It was a fight to keep his tone even. 'The test will prove she shares my DNA but that does not make her my sister. I understand that this is not what you have hoped for, but she is a stranger to me, and I have no wish to allow a stranger into my life.'

'You'll have to meet her at Finn's party. You won't be able to avoid her there.'

'I'm not coming to Finn's party.'

'But you said...'

'I said to give me the details. I made no promises.'

'Dante, *please* come. Give them a chance...'

'No!'

Suddenly furious at her refusal to listen, furious at the emotions she dredged up in him, furious that even now when they were saying goodbye there was an ache deep inside him to haul her into his arms, even furious at the shocked widening of her eyes, he slammed his hands on the steering wheel.

Everything he'd been suppressing in the hope of being rid of her without a scene spilled out like venom.

'This is not about chances. I do not want them in my life. I am *sick* of family and all the lies and deceptions that come with them. Sick of it. What does Orla want from me? My money? She has a million euros of it. She has lived her life for twenty-seven years without me, why want me now? My father... Damn him to hell!'

With a roar that erupted from nowhere, he punched the wheel hard enough to bruise. 'All my adult life I have bailed him out. I kept a roof over his head when he blew everything my grandparents and their parents before them built. I helped him whenever he needed me. I loved him, and all that's left is this monstrous lie, and don't let me start talking about my self-obsessed

mother, who bores of everything and everyone, even
her own child.

'I look at my extended family and see nothing but
misery; siblings hating and bitching about siblings,
spouses cheating, hypocritical parents moralising, all
pretending that their lives are great, when underneath
it's all rotten. I don't want any of it. I am not a gambling man but, even if I were, I know the odds would
not be in my favour of anything good coming from
a sister who I already know is a liar like our father.
Whoever the father of her child is, he has a right to
know, but she keeps it a secret from him when she
knows the damage such secrets cause.'

Aislin had shrunk back during his diatribe, but
now she leaned forward, bright red colour slashing
her cheeks. 'If you knew Orla you would know she
would only keep such a thing secret for good reason.'

'I have only your word for that.'

'Is my word not good enough? Hasn't the time
we've spent together this past week proven that I'm a
woman of my word?'

'I take no one at their word,' he bit back.

'And I thought *I* was distrustful...' Aislin shook her
head and tried to control the tempest raging within her.

Bad enough he should be so cynical about Orla but
to be so cynical about *her*, after everything they had
shared... That hurt more than she had dreamed possible, more than his offhand refusal that she stay the
extra days as she had offered.

He'd had his fun with her and, now their time was
up, he was happy to discard her as if nothing had
happened.

'You know, sir, you're not the only one who has

been hurt and let down—it happens to everyone. My
mother left the country when I was nineteen and I
don't think she's ever coming back. She left me to
deal with the fallout after Orla's accident—and, while
we're talking about Orla, need I remind you that she
is the one who has spent her life with a father who
is only a name and a mother who couldn't be bothered to visit her when she was close to death or meet
her seriously ill grandson? You don't see Orla feeling
sorry for herself.'

Warming to her theme, she straightened her shoulders. 'My good-for-nothing ex cheated on me when
my sister and nephew were hovering between life and
death in that godforsaken hospital. I honestly thought
I would never trust anyone apart from my sister again.
I came this close…' she put her thumb and forefinger
together, right in his stony face '…to trusting you. I
thought you were an exaggerated version of him but
then I got to know you and I *stupidly* allowed myself
to believe you were one of the good guys, but you're
not. You're worse. You let me believe you would come
to Finn's party…'

'You let yourself believe that.'

'Stop with the lies and excuses!' The angst and
panic that had been clawing at her suddenly exploded.
'You're nothing but a liar and I cannot believe I was
so blind and so *stupid*!' She slammed her clenched
fists onto her lap in her rage. 'Orla and Finn think
you're going to be a part of their lives. You're the one
who gave me the false hope to let them believe that.
You've made a liar of me, and now I'm going to have
to hurt them with the truth when I would rather cut a
limb off than see them hurt.

'You've tricked Riccardo into believing you're now all family orientated, when you'd rather puke on your own shoes than have a family, and you have the nerve to call *Orla* a liar? You're the biggest liar of all. You're just another selfish bastard but you have the money to throw at your problems and make them go away. Ooh, I need to fake an engagement...let's pay someone. Ooh, a sister I've never met...have some money. Ooh, a seriously ill nephew...have some money. Job done, because obviously that's all they would ever want from you, and it's a good thing that's all you have to offer because you're not fit to lick my sister's boots.'

A sharp rapping on the window brought them both up short.

Dante punched the button to open the window and a uniformed attendant immediately stuck his head in, blabbering rapidly. Aislin didn't need to speak the language to know they were being told to move.

'Don't worry, I'm going.' She pulled the engagement ring from her finger and threw it on the car floor, unwilling to look at his lying face one more time. 'Have a nice life, *sir*.'

Then she grabbed her handbag, jumped out of the car and slammed the door shut behind her.

The roar of his engine and squealing tyres rang in her ears as she walked into the departure gate.

Only when the member of staff who held Aislin's name on a board asked where her luggage was did she remember she'd left it in the boot of Dante's car.

The chartered plane hurtled down the runway and lifted into the air.

Aislin kept her gaze fixed on the English magazine she'd brought. She would not watch Sicily disappear from view.

She would not think of the man she was leaving behind.

She would never think of him again.

In a few hours she would be back with the two people she loved the most in the world.

She would pick her life up where she'd left it but now she would allow herself to think of her own needs too.

She would make something of her life.

And she would never think of Sicily again.

Dante's mother was already seated in a corner of the restaurant when he entered it, a large glass of white wine in her hand. She rose to her feet with a big smile and embraced him tightly.

'This is an unexpected pleasure,' she said, sitting back down. 'Is your Irish beauty not joining us?'

He took his own seat with a grimace. 'Aislin's in Ireland.'

His mother looked at him shrewdly. 'Trouble in paradise?'

'It's over,' he said shortly, then attempted a smile. 'Have you looked at the menu?'

A waiter came over to take their order. As soon as he left them, Dante's mother leaned forward. 'What happened?'

He feigned bored ignorance. 'With what?'

'Your Irish beauty.'

'Nothing happened. We just decided marriage was a step too far.'

She cast him that shrewd look again. 'That's a shame. I liked her. You liked her too.'

'Mother...' he said warningly. He'd never discussed his love life with her before and was not about to start now.

The last person he wanted to talk about was Aislin. All he had to do was recall their last conversation and his blood pressure would rise to dangerous levels.

'Okay, so you don't want to talk about her. What do you want to talk about? I assume there has to be a reason you've invited me here—you've never invited me to dinner before.'

He looked at her, feeling strangely discomfited. He'd picked up the tab on every occasion they'd dined out since he'd turned twenty.

Had none of those occasions come from his instigation? 'Haven't I?'

She waved a dismissive hand. 'It doesn't matter. What's on your mind? Or shall I make an educated guess and ask if it's about your sister?'

The nausea that curdled in his guts at this comment was almost as violent as the nausea he'd experienced when she'd mentioned Aislin.

He inhaled slowly then exhaled for even longer.

In the eight days that had passed since Aislin had slammed his car door, he'd failed to find the focus on work he needed. Instead he'd replayed their many conversations, especially those about his father, over and over, a loop playing so frequently he'd feared his head would combust.

He couldn't go on like this. He needed answers and his mother was the only person who could supply them.

'Is she the reason you left my father?'

Her perceptive eyes narrowed a touch then she gave

a sharp nod. 'I left him when I learned he'd got another woman pregnant but she wasn't the reason. I'd wanted to leave him for years—that affair was the excuse I'd been waiting for.'

Dante's glass of wine was brought to the table, along with a basket of freshly baked rolls.

He took a long drink. 'Why did you need an excuse?'

'To justify it to myself. The Irish woman wasn't the first woman he'd cheated on me with. She was just the first with real consequences.'

He took another sip of his wine then asked the question that had plagued him since Aislin had first suggested it might be for different reasons to what he'd always thought. 'Why didn't you take me?'

Her eyes softened. She rested her elbows on the table and folded her hands together under her chin. 'You were the reason I needed to find justification to leave. I knew I could never take you from him. Your father was a terrible husband but he was a wonderful father to you. And you adored him. When you fell over and hurt yourself, it was always him you would go to. When you had those nightmares when you were tiny, it was always him you called for. People thought I was a terrible mother for leaving you behind but I would have been a worse mother if I had taken you with me.'

Dante plucked a roll from the basket and pulled it apart with his fingers, taking a moment to gather his thoughts.

He *had* always instinctively gone to his father when he'd been in pain or fear. From as far back as he could remember he and his father had been as close as a father and son could be.

'Why didn't he tell me about Orla? Why didn't *you* tell me about her? Why all the secrecy?'

She sighed and reached for her wine. 'That was your father's choice and I had to respect his wishes. The mother didn't want him in the child's life. He could have fought for access but decided against it. He thought—and I agreed with him—that you had enough upheaval with me leaving without having to cope with the knowledge of a sister you would in all likelihood never meet. At the time it seemed the rational thing, the kind thing, to do.'

'Why did he never tell me when I was old enough to understand?'

'I don't know. I think, and of course this is only speculation, that he was afraid you would hate him for keeping it from you. You were the only person he ever truly loved. If it was not for you and having to raise you, I think his gambling problem would have got out of control a lot sooner than it did.'

Their first course was bought to them and then, for perhaps the first time in Dante's life, he and his mother really *talked*—about the past, his mother's life, her never-ending quest for a man who could make her happy.

He came to understand the choices she'd made, and that his father had made concerning him, had always been with the best of intentions. Hindsight might have proved those intentions to be faulty but they had done the best they could.

By the time they had finished their desserts and were sipping liqueur coffees he felt closer to her than he ever had before and it was with regret that he asked for the bill.

'Dante...' Tentatively, as if afraid he would shrug it off, she placed her hand on his. He let her. 'I know I have made many mistakes as your mother but can I give you the wisdom of my experience?'

Curious as to what she had to say, he nodded.

'I have married many times for many reasons and, yes, I admit financial security has always played a part in it, but I have always tried to love my husbands.'

He wanted to smile at her earnest way of admitting she was a gold-digger. His mother was nothing if not a character.

But he couldn't smile. All the muscles in his face had frozen.

Dread beat deep and heavy within him.

He knew where she was leading with this.

'Love is an elusive thing,' she said earnestly. 'It is very rare. When you find it, you have to grab hold of it and never let it go.' Her hold on his hand tightened as if to emphasise her point. 'Your Irish beauty... I don't know what has gone wrong between you, but when I watched you with her at the wedding I could feel the love you have for each other.'

'I am not in love with her.' His denial was automatic. He'd been denying it every one of the eight days since she had flown back to Ireland.

Just because he had fought his hands not to call her did not mean anything. Just because he had woken every day with an ache in his heart that he couldn't shift didn't mean anything either.

They had shared an intense few days together that had ended with bilious, hateful words. And then she had gone.

His mother tilted her head.

Was that *pity* he saw in her eyes?

'It was never love,' he said. 'It was a madness. That's all. It's over.'

She didn't say anything further on the subject but he could see exactly what she left unsaid.

That he was lying to himself.

CHAPTER FIFTEEN

THE TINY END-OF-TERRACE house had a run-down feel to it but no sense of neglect. Even through the pouring Irish rain lashing his hire car, Dante could see the well-tended small front garden.

It had been five days since he'd dined with his mother and received the answers he'd sought. Five days of turmoil and dawning reason followed by self-recrimination and loathing.

He'd been a fool. He'd been everything Aislin had accused him of being.

Just the thought of her name made his heart twist.

As the days had passed, the hole that had lived inside him since she'd slammed his car door had widened.

What had started as a small fissure had become a gulf in his chest.

He'd thought speaking to his mother and making peace with his father would heal him, but how could he be healed when every time he closed his eyes Aislin's face appeared?

He had to see her.

Even if she slammed the door in his face, he could not leave things as they were. Their time together had been fleeting but had left its mark, had altered him in a fundamental way.

He could not live the rest of his life without seeing her face and hearing her Irish brogue.

Without getting to his knees and begging her forgiveness.

Without begging for another chance.

Without telling her that he loved her.

Because he did love her. Aislin brought sunshine wherever she went and the time they had spent together had infected him with its beaming radiance. She had switched a light on in him.

If he was condemned to spend the rest of his life without her sunshine, he wanted to be able to look at his reflection and say he had fought for her.

If she rejected him he would find a way to live with it. Whether she liked it or not, he was going to be part of her family now, because that was another gradual realisation his pig-headed brain had come to accept. He wanted to meet his sister and nephew. He wanted to be a part of their lives.

If Aislin loved them enough that she would lay her life down for them then that told him everything he needed to know about them.

A face appeared in the downstairs window.

Dante's heart slammed.

A moment later the front door opened.

A slim, pretty brunette appeared. She didn't move from the doorway, just stared at him.

On weighted legs, barely feeling the torrential rain falling on him, Dante made the short but excruciatingly long walk to his sister.

Staring into her green eyes was like looking in a mirror.

'I knew you'd come,' she said simply. Her voice was deeper than Aislin's but with the same brogue.

'How?' He hadn't known he was going to come until he'd woken that morning. It had been like waking from a long dream.

She smiled.

'Because you're my brother.'

And then she wrapped her arms around his rigid torso and held him so tightly that Dante found himself responding in kind, returning the embrace of this stranger who was not a stranger. His heart squeezed painfully, then expanded with a brand-new emotion filling it.

This was his sister. His *sister*. His blood.

They held each other for a long time before Orla kissed his cheek and led him into her home.

Finn, she told him as she made coffee in the tiniest kitchen Dante had ever been in, was sleeping. She would give him a little longer before waking him.

It was the opening he needed to ask, casually, where Aislin was.

'In Dublin. She's gone for a job interview.' A tinge of anxiety came into Orla's voice. 'But you'll see her next time... Will there be a next time?'

'Yes.' He took a deep breath. 'I'm sorry for letting you think any different. My head has not been in a good place. If the invitation is still open, I would very much like to come to Finn's party.'

'Of course the invitation's still open!' Her relief was instantaneous. 'I'm sure Aislin will be pleased to see you then too.'

The way Orla averted her eyes for the latter sent a weight plunging into his stomach. The look, coupled with her tone, told Dante clearly that he was the last person Aislin wanted to see.

'How is she?' As painful as the knowledge that Aislin despised him was, he needed to know she was okay.

'She's doing grand. Full of plans for the future. We're moving to Dublin—Aislin talked me into it. There's more resources there for Finn, and Aislin will have a better chance of finding a job she can use her degree for. I can never thank you enough for enabling this for us. You've changed our lives.'

Shortly afterwards, Orla carried Finn downstairs and sat him in his wheelchair. Only then did Dante truly understand the nature of his condition.

'Can he not walk?'

'He can but not for any length of time. His muscles are too weak. When we move to Dublin we'll have access to better treatment for him, so he has every chance of leading a near normal life.' Her brightness seemed forced, as if they were words Orla continually repeated to herself in the hope that repetition would make them come true.

He couldn't help himself from saying, 'Aislin helps you with him?'

Her eyes softened. 'If it wasn't for Aislin, neither of us would be here. I'm so happy she's finally getting her life back on track. She gave everything up for us and now it's my turn to support her.'

Many hours later it was with mixed emotions that Dante embraced his sister and nephew goodbye.

The blood bond between them was stronger than

he had imagined it could be, and he marvelled that it was a bond he'd been so set against forming.

But there was despair in him too and it cast a huge shadow over the joy.

Aislin hated him.

She was taking great strides and reclaiming her life for herself.

Whatever feelings she'd had for him had died. Dante had killed them.

The heavy dark raincloud that poured on him as he walked back to his car matched perfectly the dark heaviness in his heart.

The rose-gold engagement ring he'd brought with him burned a hole in his pocket.

Aislin opened the front door carefully and crept into the house.

'What are you sneaking about for?'

She jumped in fright, then laughed when Orla poked her head around the living room door.

'I wasn't sneaking. I was trying to be quiet in case you were asleep.'

'You think I can sleep when you're out on the road in this weather?'

It had been in weather like this that Orla had had her accident.

Aislin's late return to their home was because she had spent the day a three-and-a-half-hour drive away in Dublin at an interview with a publisher that specialised in historical tomes. She wasn't sure if it was for her, as she had told Orla in her message before she'd made the drive home, but it had felt good to get out of the house and away from her studies for a few hours.

Every time she looked at her textbooks she thought of Dante and remembered how he'd been thumbing through one of them when she had gone down the stairs in his cottage.

He'd couriered her luggage to her the day after she'd returned to Ireland.

Argh! She was thinking about him *again*.

Think only of the future. That was what she told herself constantly.

She kicked her boots off and forced a smile. 'Fancy a cup of tea?'

No matter how dreadful she felt inside, she would never let Orla know. Her sister felt bad enough about how Aislin had got the money for them without having to know the details of what had gone on between her and Dante.

It had broken her heart to tell her Dante didn't want to meet her or Finn. Orla had put a brave face on it but she'd been pretty cut up about his decision.

Tonight, however, Orla looked happier than Aislin had seen her in a long time.

'Has something happened?' Aislin asked as she walked into the poky kitchen.

'I would have told you earlier, but I wasn't sure how you'd react, and I didn't want to cause a distraction when you had such a long drive.'

She lifted the kettle. 'Tell me what?'

'We've had a visitor.'

She put the kettle under the tap. 'Oh?'

'Dante.'

The kettle slipped from her fingers and landed with a clang in the sink.

She composed herself quickly. 'Sorry. Butter fingers. He came?' She put it back under the tap and kept a tight grip on it.

'He did!' Orla's voice was full of joy.

Aislin busied herself with making the tea, letting her sister tell her all the details without interruption.

'He apologised for not wanting to see us. He needed time to process it, which is understandable. I mean, I've known about him for years, but my existence came as a bolt from the blue for him. He stayed for *ages*. Hours! I know you think he's a selfish cad, and that we should be grateful he doesn't want anything to do with us, but he's apologised for all that. I liked him very much.'

She pulled the mugs off the mug tree. Luckily Orla was so full of Dante's visit that she didn't notice the rattle Aislin made, bashing them together with her shaking hands.

'I'm glad he's shown a different side of himself to you,' she managed to say through a throat that felt as if a boulder had lodged in it. 'What did Finn think of him?'

'Finn adored him! He's promised him a new wheel-chair for his birthday. I told him I was already planning one for the move but he insisted. He's coming to Finn's party.'

'Great.'

'He asked after you. Oh, I forgot to say, Dante's going to rent a house for us in Dublin until we can move into ours. He's going to arrange everything. We should be gone from here by the end of the week.'

'That soon?'

'Amazing, isn't it?'

She opened the fridge door and removed the milk. 'He's a quick mover.'

So quick he'd made her go from hating him to loving him in the space of a week...

The milk fell from her frozen fingers to the floor, the plastic bottle splitting on impact.

This time she was unable to compose herself.

She stared with horror at the milk spilling all over the floor and then looked into Orla's suddenly scared eyes. Eyes that were the image of Dante's.

'Ash?'

She clamped a hand to her mouth and shook her head.

Her heart pounded so hard she felt sick with the ripples. Panic tore at her throat.

Oh, dear God, she was in love with Dante.

What else explained the agony she had carried every minute of the thirteen days since she'd left Sicily?

Every night she went to bed and said a prayer for the pain in her heart to ease by the morning, but every morning she awoke after a fitful sleep with the pain a little worse.

Her appetite had gone to pot. She drank gallons of tea but could not stomach coffee because the mere smell of it reminded her of Dante.

Even looking at her own sister was painful because she could see the physical similarities between them.

Life had turned on its head for the better for the O'Reillys but Aislin had entered a living form of purgatory.

Orla read the despair on her sister's face, watched it crumble and watched her legs fall beneath her as she collapsed onto the wet floor, all of it happening as if in slow motion, and dived down to wrap her arms around her.

Aislin buried her face in her sister's comforting shoulder and, finally, the tears she'd held back for so long could no longer stay contained.

Orla stroked her back and her hair, trying her hardest to comfort her, letting her sister's hot tears soak through her jumper until there were no tears left to cry.

'Ash?' Orla stepped into the bedroom.

Aislin rolled over and rubbed the sleep from her eyes. Sunlight poured in through the thin curtains.

She must have slept for hours.

All that crying on Orla's shoulder and her over-due confession of her feelings for Dante had gone on until the early hours. The weight of it had exhausted her. She'd fallen asleep the moment her head had hit the pillow.

'What time is it?'

'Ten o'clock.'

So much for sleep being such a great healer. She still felt dreadful.

Sighing, she sat up as Orla perched on the bed beside her and held an envelope to her. 'This was delivered before I got up this morning.'

Aislin took the envelope with only her name scrawled on it. There was something lumpy and weighty in it.

She ripped it open.

A rose-gold pear-diamond ring fell onto the duvet.

Orla gasped.

Aislin could only stare at it as if it were something that could bite her.

'Is there a letter?'

Orla's voice cut through the roaring in her head.

She tried to breathe.

Fingers trembling, Aislin pulled out the note. She squeezed her eyes shut tightly.

Orla elbowed her ribs. 'Read it.'

'I'm scared,' she whispered.

'Read it.'

Filling her lungs, Aislin summoned the courage to open her eyes.

The writing was atrocious. The words, however...

My darling Aislin,
This ring belongs to you to do with as you will.

I'm sorry for hurting you. I'm sorry for abusing your trust. I'm sorry for being a stubborn, distrustful fool. I'm sorry for everything. I hope one day you can find it in your heart to forgive me.

Thank you for taking such good care of our sister and nephew. Live your life for yourself now—I will be here always to share the load. I swear I will never hurt them again.

Whatever you decide to do with your life, be happy. You deserve happiness more than anyone I know.
My love for ever,
Dante x

Aislin had to read the letter a dozen times before the words sank in.

My love for ever...
My love for ever...
My love for ever...

Her heart leapt, and with it she jumped off the bed and flew to her dressing table.

'What are you doing?' Orla asked, bemusement in her voice.

'Looking for my passport… Can you lend me some money?'

'No, but I can give you some.' Orla's grin went from ear to ear. 'Do you want me to book you a flight to Sicily while you get dressed?'

Dante carried the last box out to the corridor, laid it down for his men to take and put in the back of the truck with the other boxes, then stepped back into his father's office.

He was done.

He stared around at the empty space, bittersweet pain raging through him.

He'd flown back from Ireland early that morning knowing he had one more task to complete. He'd undertaken it alone. It had been the hardest job of his life.

The scent of cigars and bourbon had become very faint but he caught a trace and filled his lungs with the scent of his father one last time.

'I love you, Papa,' he whispered.

And then he turned the light out and closed the door of his father's office, knowing he would never step foot in it again.

The box had already been taken when Dante walked back down the corridor.

He didn't know what he was going to do with the house and the rest of its contents but this job was the one that had pressed on his shoulders with the greatest weight.

He checked the time as the flash of a vehicle's head-lights passed the kitchen, his men taking the truck with the contents of his father's office.

Limbs heavy, he climbed the stairs to his childhood bedroom and sat on the bed that had been his for the first twenty years of his life.

Dante's football posters still hung on the walls. He nudged the bin with his foot and found the old ink stain he'd made on the carpet still there.

He looked out of the window at the huge back garden. His father had played football with him on that lawn. And rugby. And golf. Between them, they'd broken so many windows it had been impossible to keep count.

His mother was right—his father had been a wonderful father to him...

A tidal wave of grief punched him in the guts, doubling him over.

Sinking back onto the bed, he covered his face, unable to hold the tears back any longer.

He cried for the father he'd loved so much and who he missed with every fibre of his being.

And he cried for the woman he'd discarded as if she were a book to be thrown when he'd reached the last chapter.

She'd given him the chance of an epilogue. He saw that now. She'd jumped at the chance of extending their time together and he'd thrown it back in her face.

What a blind fool he'd been.

Aislin was moving on with her life and, other than their shared sister and nephew, that life did not involve him. He accepted that. But he'd been unable to leave Ireland without reaching out to her and letting her know how unbearably sorry he was.

The ring belonged to her. His heart did too. He had no one but himself to blame for her own heart despising him.

Through the crowding noise in his head he heard the faint chime of the doorbell.

Dante cradled his skull and took deep breaths.

He didn't want to see anyone. Not tonight.

Tonight he wanted nothing but to be left to grieve.

The bell rang again.

A moment later, a voice called out. 'Dante?'

He froze.

'Hello?' Aislin closed the door behind her and called out to him again. 'Dante?'

He *had* to be there. It felt like she'd searched the whole of Sicily looking for him. She'd started in Palermo, only to find he wasn't there and that none of his staff was prepared to tell her where he was; so she'd driven to the cottage, only to find it in darkness, covered in scaffolding and the doors locked. Back to Palermo she'd gone and this time she'd found Ciro. After much pleading, he'd given in and told her to try Salvatore Moncada's beachside villa.

'Aislin?'

She turned sharply to the sound of his voice and found him descending the stairs slowly, staring at her much like someone who'd seen a ghost.

For a long time she couldn't speak, only gaze at him. She soaked everything in. He looked…untamed. His hair was mussed, the beard he trimmed most days thick and bushy, his eyes bloodshot and puffy. He looked thinner too.

He reached the bottom of the stairs and stopped.

Slowly she stepped towards him, heart pounding, breath ragged, praying she hadn't misinterpreted the meaning behind his letter.

And if she had…

She had nothing to lose in being here. Nothing could be worse than the torture she'd lived through these past two weeks.

But she couldn't speak.

She cleared her throat and still the words wouldn't form.

He extended a hand and took a shuffling step towards her. His throat moved before he croaked, 'Why are you here?'

She cleared her throat again and finally managed to speak. 'I got your letter.'

He just stared at her.

Aislin took the deepest breath of her life. 'Dante… In your letter, you said whatever I do with my life I have to be happy. Dante… If I'm to be happy in my future…' Her voice became a whispered quiver, everything she wanted to say jumbled. 'The days I spent with you were the happiest I've ever known.'

'What are you saying?' he whispered.

A tear leaked down her cheek. 'That since I've left Sicily it's felt as if I don't know how to be happy any more. *You* make me happy.'

The eyes that hadn't left her face or even blinked gave a sudden spark of life.

'Dante, I'm sorry for the cruel things I said to you…'

'No!' Suddenly he was striding towards her, the warm hands whose touch she'd missed more than she'd believed humanly possible cupping her cheeks, fingers

kneading into her skin. 'Don't you dare apologise for speaking the truth. I behaved abominably.'

Dante cursed and gritted his teeth, sliding his hands around her face to delve his fingers into the russet hair he adored so much.

He'd thought he'd hallucinated her. But she was here, beautiful and sweet-smelling and solidly *real*.

He pressed his forehead to hers. 'I was scared... My feelings for you, all the things I was trying to deal with... I *couldn't* deal with any of it. I was a fool. The biggest fool. I told myself you were everything I didn't want when the truth is you are everything I need.'

Her glistening eyes widened and her chin wobbled.

He kissed her gently. 'I've known you such a short time but it feels as if you've been in my heart for ever.'

'You're in my heart too,' she whispered.

'Am I?' He hardly dared to believe... 'I thought you hated me.'

She placed a tender hand to his cheek and brushed her lips to his. 'I told myself I hated you because it was the only way I could cope, but the truth is I'm lost without you. I try to smile and plan for the future but it's all been a lie because I can't eat, I can't sleep... Our time together did something to me. *You've* done something to me. The only future my heart wants is a future with you.'

Suddenly he did dare to believe.

Dante dared to believe that his future could be happy too.

Claiming her mouth with his, he hauled her to him and wrapped his arms tightly around her, kissing the raspberry lips until he had no air left in him.

Breaking away to trace his mouth over her cheeks,

he then buried his nose into her hair and filled his lungs with her wonderful scent.

'I love you,' he whispered.

She nuzzled her nose into his neck. 'I love you too.'

Those four short words were sweeter than the sweetest confectionery. The weight that had compressed him since she'd gone not only lifted from his chest but from his entire body.

His heart beat loud and rapidly, but for the first time in weeks he could *breathe*, and the air he inhaled had never smelled so good.

When he next looked at the beautiful face he had missed so much, her smile infused every cell in his body with the sunlight it had missed without her. Dante made a vow to himself there and then that he would never drive her sunlight from his life again.

It was a vow he kept for the rest of his life.

EPILOGUE

THE CATHEDRAL BOUNCED with the beams of the late-summer sun and, as Aislin approached it, careful of the enormous train of her dress which Orla and Sabine's children held with such care, and with her father's arm to hold on to, she thought back to the first wedding she'd attended in this great baroque building. Looking back, that was the day she had given her heart to Dante, and now here they were, four months later, about to exchange their own vows.

Dante had proposed to her on Finn's birthday. She hadn't had a moment's hesitation in saying yes. The beautiful rose-gold pear-diamond ring had been worn on her finger ever since. She would never remove it again.

He'd moved just as fast in getting her pregnant. Two days after she'd completed her degree, Aislin had taken the pregnancy test. Dante had squeezed her so tightly she'd almost choked.

The man who hadn't wanted anything to do with family had now decided he quite fancied having a football team of children.

Aislin thought a netball team might be more manageable.

Not even Orla's refusal to move to Sicily, despite

Dante's offer to buy her a home there, could mar her happiness. Modern technology and having Dante's private jet on tap meant they could be as involved in each other's lives as they'd always been. The round-the-clock care Dante had arranged for Finn meant Aislin could sleep knowing her beloved sister and nephew were both as well as they could be.

Aislin missed their daily presence but with Dante she had found something else—a piece of her soul.

He completed her. And, when she walked down the long aisle and saw the love reflecting in his eyes, she knew she completed him too.

Together they were the perfect fit.

Together they'd created their own heaven.

* * * * *

Contracted As His
Cinderella Bride
Heidi Rice

Books by Heidi Rice

Harlequin Modern

Vows They Can't Escape
Captive at Her Enemy's Command
Bound by Their Scandalous Baby
Claiming My Untouched Mistress

One Night With Consequences

The Virgin's Shock Baby
Carrying the Sheikh's Baby

Visit the Author Profile page at
millsandboon.com.au for more titles.

USA TODAY bestselling author **Heidi Rice** lives in London, England. She is married with two teenage sons—which gives her rather too much of an insight into the male psyche—and also works as a film journalist. She adores her job, which involves getting swept up in a world of high emotions; sensual excitement; funny, feisty women; sexy, tortured men and glamorous locations where laundry doesn't exist. Once she turns off her computer, she often does chores—usually involving laundry!

DEDICATION

To my editor, Bryony—I couldn't do this
without you!

CHAPTER ONE

'CALLING RIDERS IN the vicinity of the Strand. Got a pick-up at the jeweller's Mallow and Sons. Drop-off in Bloomsbury.'

Alison Jones skidded to a stop at the amber light on Waterloo Bridge to decipher the crackle of the dispatcher's voice on her radio through the driving rain.

Cold water had seeped through her waterproof hours ago as the rush hour had slowed to a crawl in London's West End. She'd been ready to crash headfirst into a bubble bath since six o'clock and lick her wounds from another evening pedalling the mean streets of Soho. But once she'd registered the instruction, she clicked on the call button and shouted into her receiver. 'Rider 524. Got it!'

She still had several instalments to pay on the debt she'd racked up four years ago for her mum's funeral—and next month's rent on her room in the house she shared with a group of other fashion students in Whitechapel wasn't going to pay itself. Plus she'd already reached peak misery for the evening. She certainly couldn't get any wetter.

The dispatcher confirmed her pick-up as she tried to focus through her exhaustion.

'Delivery's a wedding ring,' he shouted. 'Client's name for drop-off is Dominic LeGrand, address is…'

A shiver wracked Ally's body, the address barely registering as the name scraped across her consciousness, triggering a wealth of disturbing memories from the summer she had turned thirteen.

The heady scent of wild grass and roses. The baking heat of the Provence sun warming her skin. Pierre LeGrand's face—so handsome, so charming—his voice deep and paternalistic.

'Call me Papa, Alison.'

Her mother's smile, so untroubled and full of hope.

'Pierre is definitely the one, Ally. He loves me. He'll take care of us now.'

And then the pulse of heat settled low in her abdomen as she pictured Dominic. The memory of Pierre's sixteen-year-old son was as vivid and disturbing as if she'd seen him yesterday, not twelve years ago.

Those sensual lips always quirked in an insolent, *don't-give-a-damn* smile; those chocolate eyes full of resentment and secrets; the mysterious crescent-shaped scar that hooked his left eyebrow; the brutally short dark blond hair that had lightened in the sun and given his brooding beauty a golden glow.

Dominic, who had been beautiful and bad and fascinating, and landed like a fallen angel into that perfect summer bringing with him danger and excitement.

'I can't take the job,' Ally croaked into the receiver, as the memory of her final night in Provence returned, too.

Her mother's face—so sad, so fragile—a purpling bruise marring her cheekbone. The cloying scent of lavender and gin. Her mother's voice—frantic and fearful and slightly slurred.

'Something terrible's happened, baby. Pierre's very angry with me and Dominic. We have to leave.'

A bus horn blared beside her, jerking Ally out of her trance. She shoved the distressing, confusing memories back where they belonged. When she'd buried her mother four years ago, she'd finally stopped reliving the horror of that night as she stood over the grave and felt nothing but relief that Monica Jones was finally at peace.

She couldn't take this job. She didn't want to see Dominic LeGrand again. Especially as Dominic wasn't the reckless, delinquent boy who had starred in all those innocent adolescent fantasies a lifetime ago, but a billionaire property developer now. Hadn't the tabloids dubbed him 'Love-Rat LeGrand' a year ago after one of his supermodel girlfriends had sold her story of their affair for a six-figure sum? The wedding ring had to be for the fairy-tale romance with Mira Somebody Ally had read about a month ago.

'What do you mean you're not taking the job? I just put it through the system.' The dispatcher's voice sliced into Ally's misery. 'Either you do it or I'm pulling you from the roster. Make up your mind.'

Ally breathed in and breathed out, trying to control the panic making the air clog in her lungs.

She *had* to take this job. She didn't have a choice. She couldn't afford to lose the work. Pressing her freezing finger on the radio, she spoke into the receiver. 'Okay, I'll take it. Give me that address again.'

'The wedding's off, Mira. Your hook-up with Andre the ski instructor has seen to that.' Dominic LeGrand kept his voice even; he wasn't sad or upset, he was furious. They'd had a deal. And his so-called fiancée had broken it.

'But I… I told you it was nothing, Dominic.' Tears sheened Mira's eyes, her voice breaking with emotion. Dominic's impatience sharpened his fury. The woman had the emotional maturity of a two-year-old.

'I thought I made it plain before we entered into this arrangement I expected exclusivity. I'm not marrying a woman I can't trust.'

'But I didn't sleep with Andre… I swear,' Mira said. 'I was a little drunk and flirtatious, that was all.' She leaned across his desk, her breasts pressing provocatively against her low-cut gown, her lips pursed into the pout he'd found hot two months ago, when they'd first met. 'I'm not going to lie—I quite like that you're a little jealous,' she added.

The coy flirtatious look on her face was probably supposed to be enticing. It wasn't.

'I'm not jealous, Mira. I'm angry. It's a breach of our agreement. It could jeopardise the Waterfront deal.' Which was the only reason he'd asked her to marry him in the first place.

The Jedah Consortium, who owned the tract of real

estate in Brooklyn he wanted to develop, was made up of conservative businessmen from a string of oil-rich Middle Eastern countries. They'd been wary of doing business with him after Catherine Zalinski's kiss-and-tell article last year had made him look like a man who couldn't control his own libido, let alone the women in his life.

This marriage was supposed to fix that, until pictures of his fiancée kissing her ski instructor had hit the tabloids this afternoon.

'The whole purpose of this marriage was to stop any more unsavoury gossip about my private life,' he added, in case she didn't get it.

'But you left me alone for a whole month.' The pout became more pronounced. 'I waited for you to come to Klosters but you didn't. We haven't slept together in even longer. What did you expect me to do?'

He hadn't had time to go all the way to Klosters to visit her. The fact he hadn't been particularly desperate to ease the sexual drought confirmed something else—this agreement had been ill-advised from the start. He'd grown bored of Mira even sooner than he'd expected, in bed as well as out of it.

'I expected you to keep your mouth off other men. And your legs closed.'

'Dominic, don't say things like that.' The shocked hurt in her eyes looked genuine. Almost. 'It makes me feel cheap.'

He let his gaze coast down the designer dress he'd paid for.

'Mira, the one thing you're not is cheap,' he said wryly.

She stiffened at the insult.

'Find your own way out,' he said. 'We're done here.'

'You... You heartless bastard.'

Mira's hand whipped out so fast, he heard the crack before the pain blazed across his cheekbone.

He leapt out of his chair, holding her wrist before she could strike him again. But the smarting pain where she'd struck him had a bitter memory spinning back of another slap, from the summer he'd finally been invited into his father's world—only to be kicked out again a month later—and the voice of the girl who had defended him.

'You mustn't hit Dominic, you'll hurt him, Papa.'

'Some people deserve to be hurt, ma petite.*'*

'You're right, Mira, I *am* heartless. I'm also a bastard.' He ground out the words, the hollow ache in his chest at the memory of that slap an emotion he'd thought he'd cauterised long ago. How infuriating to find he hadn't...quite. 'I consider that a strength,' he added, releasing Mira's wrist. 'Now get out. Before I have you arrested for assault.'

Mira's face collapsed, her lips trembling. 'I hate you.'

So what? he thought dispassionately, as she swung round and rushed out of his study.

Hearing the front door slam, he walked to the drinks cabinet, swiped the trickle of blood at the corner of his mouth, then poured himself a glass of single malt Scotch.

He only had a week to find himself another wife to secure the deal he needed to take his business to the next level. The business he'd built from nothing after crawling off his father's estate that summer, his ribs feeling as if they were being crushed in a vice, the welts on his back burning.

He'd flagged down a truck, and the driver had taken pity on him, giving him a ride all the way to Paris. As he'd sunk in and out of consciousness on that endless, agonising journey, he had promised himself he would never see or speak to his father again. And that he would build something to prove to his father, and everyone else who had rejected him, had belittled or dismissed him, that they were wrong.

He welcomed the sting as the liquor hit his split lip.

He would find another wife. Preferably one who did exactly what he told her and knew how to keep her legs closed. But tonight he planned to celebrate a lucky escape.

CHAPTER TWO

'GET OUT OF my way, you filthy…' The woman's voice trailed off into a sneer as she shoved Ally and her bike out of the way.

Ally stumbled, rammed into the gatepost, the bike's pedal scrapping against her calf as the woman marched past her and got into a sleek red sports car.

Ally hauled the bike up. She would have shouted after the woman, but she was too tired and too anxious to bother—and anyway the woman wouldn't have heard her in the rain.

The car peeled away from the kerb in a squeal of rubber.

Ally watched the red tail lights disappear round the corner of the Georgian garden square.

Hadn't that been Mira Whatshername? The woman the wedding ring she had in her pack was for?

The woman had looked furious. Maybe there was trouble in paradise? Ally pushed the thought to one side.

So not your business.

She wheeled the bike to the back of the mansion

house, which stood at the end of the square in its own grounds. Taking a fortifying breath, she propped the bike against the back wall and pressed her freezing finger into the brass bell at the trade entrance.

He won't answer the door. He'll have staff to do it. Stop freaking out.

The rain had reached monsoon levels as she'd left Mallow and Sons. It beat down on her now, drenching her. The tiny package she'd collected weighed several tons in the bike bag hooked over her back.

Unfortunately the freezing March rain, and the numbness in all her extremities, not to mention the now throbbing ache in her calf muscle, felt like the least of her worries as the harsh memories continued to mess with her head.

Stepping back from the door, she peered up at the house. Every window was dark, bar one on the floor above. Swallowing heavily, she pressed the bell again, with a bit more conviction. A figure appeared at the window. Tall and broad and indistinct through the deluge. Her heartbeat clattered into her throat.

It's not him, it's not him, it's not him.

The pep talk became a frantic prayer as she detected the sound of footsteps inside the house.

She jerked her bag to her front. She should get the wedding ring out so she could hand it over as soon as the door opened.

She fumbled with the wet fastenings, her heartbeat getting so loud it drowned out the sound of the storm.

A light in the hallway snapped on, casting a yellow glow over the rain-slicked panels, then a large silhouette filled the bevelled glass.

Ally barely had a chance to brace herself before the door swung wide. A tall man filled the space, his face thrown into shadow by the light from the hallway. But Ally's numbed fingers seized on the bike bag when he spoke—his deep, even voice thrusting a knife into the memories lurking in her belly like malevolent beasts.

'Bonsoir.'

The French accent rippled over her skin, sending sickening shivers of heat through her chilled body—and making the ball of shame wedged in her solar plexus swell.

How could he still have the power to do that? When she was a grown woman now, not an impressionable teenager in the throes of puberty?

'You'd better come inside before you drown,' he murmured, standing aside to hold the door open.

The manoeuvre lit the harsh planes and angles of his face. Ally stood locked in place absorbing the face she had once spent hours fantasising about.

Dominic had always been striking, but maturity had turned his boyish masculine beauty into something so intense it was devastating.

The blond buzz cut had darkened into a tawny brown streaked with gold, and was long enough now to curl around the collar of his shirt. Those dark chocolate eyes had no laughter lines yet, but then that would have been a contradiction in terms—because the Dominic she remembered had never laughed. A new bump on the bridge of his nose joined the old scar on his brow, while the shadow of stubble marked him out as a man now instead of a boy.

As Ally's gaze devoured the changes, she registered how much more jaded the too-old look in his eyes had become, and how much more ruthless the cynical curve of those sensual lips.

The inappropriate shivers turned into seismic waves.

'*Vite, garçon*, before we *both* drown.' The snapped command made her realise she'd been staring.

She forced herself to walk past him into the hallway.

Just give him the ring, then this nightmare will be over.

She bent to fumble with her bike bag, wishing she hadn't removed her helmet, but luckily he didn't seem to be looking at her. He had called her a boy, after all.

The drip, drip, drip of the rain coming off her waterproof seemed deafening in the silent hallway as he closed the door.

'You're a girl,' he murmured.

She made the mistake of looking round.

His scarred brow lifted as the chocolate gaze glided over her figure, making the growled acknowledgement disturbingly intimate.

'I'm a woman,' she said. 'Is that a problem?'

'*Non.*' His lips lifted on one side. The cynical half-smile reminded her so forcefully of the boy, she had to stifle a gasp. 'Do I know you?' he asked. 'You look familiar.'

'No,' she said, but the denial came out on a rasp of panic as her hand closed over the jeweller's bag.

Please don't let him recognise me—it will only make this worse.

She yanked the bag out and thrust it towards him. 'Your delivery, Mr LeGrand.'

She kept her head bent as he took the package, snatching her hand away as warm fingertips brushed her palm and the buzz of reaction zipped up her arm.

'You're shivering. Stay and dry off.' It sounded more like a demand than a suggestion, but she shook her head.

'I'm fine,' she said, drawing out her data console. 'Sign in the box,' she added, trying for efficient and impersonal, and getting breathless instead.

He tucked the jeweller's bag under his arm and took the data-recording device, brushing her hand again.

'You're freezing,' he said, sounding annoyed now and impatient. 'You should stay until the storm passes.' He signed his name and handed the device back. 'It's the least I can do after dragging you out in this weather on a fool's errand.'

'A fool's errand? How?' she asked, then wanted to bite off her tongue.

Shut up, Ally, why did you ask him that?

Starting a conversation was the last thing she needed to do. Her heart thumped her chest wall so hard she was amazed she didn't pass out. To her surprise, though, he answered her.

'A fool's errand because I broke off the engagement approximately ten minutes ago...' The cynical tone reminded her again of the boy.

No wonder Mira Something had been furious. She'd just been dumped.

He ripped open the package and drew out the velvet jeweller's box, then flipped it open.

Ally's heart stuttered. The ring was exquisite—a platinum and gold band.

The irony washed through her, as she thought of another ring.

The ring her mother had said his father had offered her all through the summer. A dream that had died that terrible night when Pierre LeGrand had kicked them out, but the loss of which had tortured her mother for the rest of her life.

'Pierre was the only man who ever really loved me and I ruined it all, baby.'

Her mother had blamed herself, but what had she done to make Pierre so angry?

Dominic snapped the ring box closed, dragging Ally back to the present. 'Which makes this a rather expensive waste of money.'

'I'm sorry,' she mumbled, trying to swallow down the volatile emotions starting to choke her. Emotions she didn't want to examine too closely.

'Don't be,' he said. 'The engagement was a mistake. The eighty grand I spent on this ring is collateral damage.'

The offhand remark had the shame and guilt twisting in her gut.

She shoved her data device back into the pocket on

her bike bag, her fingers trembling with the effort it was taking to hold back the raw emotions.

What was happening to her? Why was she making this into a big thing, when it really wasn't? Not any more. Her mother was dead, and so was Pierre. It was all ancient history now.

'I should go. I've got other jobs to get to,' she said. She just wanted to leave. To forget again. It was too painful to go over all those memories. To remember how bright and vivacious her mother had been that summer, and the hollow shell she had become after it.

'Come in and have a drink, warm up,' he said, or rather demanded.

Was he coming on to her? The thought wasn't as horrific as it should have been, which had the knot of shame in her stomach tightening. But then the clammy feel of the soaked and grubby fabric sticking to her skin made her aware of how much like a drowned rat she must look.

This man dated supermodels and heiresses— women with style and grace and effortless sex appeal. Something she had never possessed, even when she hadn't spent the last six hours cycling around London's West End in a monsoon.

'And we can deal with your leg,' he added.

'What?' she mumbled.

'Your leg.' The chocolate gaze dipped. 'It's bleeding.'

She glanced down to see blood seeping out of a gash on her calf, exposed by a rip in her leggings. It must have been caused by her altercation with his fiancée—or rather his ex-fiancée—and she'd been too cold to feel it.

'It's nothing,' she said. 'I have to go.'

But as she turned to leave, he spoke again.

'*Arrêtes*. It's *not* nothing. It's bleeding. It could get infected. You're not going out there until it has been cleaned.'

The emotion started to choke her. She couldn't stay, couldn't accept his kindness—however brusque and domineering.

'I've got work, another job,' she added, frantically. 'I can't stay.'

'I'll pay for your time, damn it, if the problem is money. I don't want an injured cycle messenger on my conscience as well as an eighty-grand ring.'

He was too close, surrounding her in a cloud of spicy cologne and the sweet subtle whiff of whisky. Her pulse points buzzed and throbbed in an erratic rhythm.

But then he hooked a knuckle under her chin, and nudged her chin up.

'Wait a minute. I *do* know you.' His eyes narrowed as he studied her face. For the first time, he was actually seeing her. The intensity of his gaze set off bonfires of sensation all over her chilled skin. She fumbled with the helmet she had hooked over her other arm, desperate to put it on, to stop him recognising her.

But it was too late as the swift spike of memory crossed his face.

'*Monique?*' he murmured.

Tears stung her eyes. 'I'm not Monica. Monica's dead. I'm her daughter.'

'Allycat?' he said, looking as stunned as she felt. *Allycat.*

The nickname reverberated in her head, the one he'd given her all those years ago. The name she had been so proud of. Once.

As if he'd flipped a switch, the adrenaline she'd been running on ever since she'd got the commission drained away, until all that was left was the shame, and anxiety. And the inappropriate heat.

She dragged in tortured breaths, struggling to contain the choking sob rising up her torso. She didn't have the strength to resist him any more. And what would be the point, anyway?

'Breathe, Allycat,' he murmured.

She gulped in air, trying to steady herself, and got a lungful of his scent—spiced with pine and soap.

'Bad night?'

'The worst.' She bit back the harsh laugh at his sanguine tone. And shuddered, the pain in her ribs excruciating as she struggled to hold the sobs at bay.

What exactly are you so upset about? Having Dominic LeGrand pity you isn't the worst thing that's ever happened to you.

'I know the feeling,' he said, the wry smile only making him look more handsome—and more utterly unattainable.

She forced a smile to her lips as she shifted away from him, and scooped up the helmet that had clattered to the floor.

'It was nice seeing you again, Dominic,' she said, although nothing could have been further from the truth. *Nice* had never been a word to describe Dominic LeGrand. 'I really do have to go now, though.'

But as she headed for the door, he stepped in front of her. 'Don't go, Allycat. Come in and dry off and clean up your leg. My offer still stands.'

She lifted her head, forced herself to meet his gaze. But where she'd expected pity, or impatience, all she saw was a pragmatic intensity—as if he were trying to see into her soul. And something else, something she didn't recognise or understand—because it almost looked like desire. But that couldn't be true.

'I can't stay,' she said, hating the tremble in her voice.

She didn't want to feel this weak, this fragile. She hated showing him even an ounce of her vulnerability, because it made her feel even more pathetic.

'Yes, you can.' He didn't budge. 'As I said, I will pay for your time,' he added, the tone rigid with purpose.

'I don't need you to do that. I'm shattered anyway. I'm just going to cycle home.' She needed to leave, before the foolish yearning to stay, and have him care for her, got the better of her.

Mon Dieu, who would have thought that Monique's shy and sheltered daughter would grow into a woman as striking and valiant as Jeanne D'Arc?

'So there are no more jobs tonight?' Dominic asked.

The girl frowned, but, even caught in the lie, her gaze remained direct. 'No, there aren't,' she said, the unapologetic tone equally captivating. 'I lied.'

He let out a rough chuckle. '*Touché*, Allycat.'

He let his gaze wander over the slim coltish figure, vibrating with tension. Her high firm breasts, outlined by her damp cycle gear, rose and fell with her staggered breaths. With her wet hair tied back in a short ponytail, damp chestnut curls clinging to the pale, almost translucent skin of her cheeks, blue-tinged shadows under her eyes, and an oil mark on her chin, she should have looked a mess. But instead she looked like the Maid of Orleans—passionate and determined.

And all the more beautiful for it.

Not unlike her mother. Or what he could remember of her mother.

Monica Jones had been his father's mistress, during that brief summer when his father had acknowledged him. But the truth was it was her daughter, the girl who stood before him now, her wide guileless eyes direct and unbowed despite her obvious misery, whom he remembered with a great deal more clarity.

She'd been a child that summer, ten or eleven maybe, but he still remembered how she had followed him around like a doting puppy. And defended him against his father's abuse. She had stood up to that bastard on his behalf, and because of that he'd felt a strange connection with her. And it seemed that connection hadn't died. Not completely.

Although it had morphed into something a great deal more potent—if the sensation that had zapped up his arm when he had touched her was anything to go by.

She was quite stunning, pure and unsullied—despite her bedraggled appearance. The compulsion to capture her cold cheeks in his palms and warm her unpainted lips with a kiss surprised him, though.

Why should he want her, when she was so unsophisticated? *Un garçon manqué.* A tomboy without an ounce of glamour or allure. Why should he care if she was cold, or wet, or injured? She wasn't his responsibility.

Perhaps it was simply the shock of seeing her again, and the memories she evoked? Maybe it was the compelling contrast she made with the woman he'd just kicked out of his life? Not spoilt, entitled and indulged but fierce and fearless and proud. The most likely explanation, though, for his attraction was that erotic spark that had arched between them the minute she'd stepped into the house.

After all, it had been over a month since he'd made love to a woman, and considerably longer since he'd felt that visceral tug of desire this woman seemed to evoke simply by breathing.

'Then I will order a car to take you and the bike home in due course,' he answered, because he was damned if he'd let her leave before he had at least had a chance to explore why she intrigued him so much. And no way was he letting her cycle home tonight. It was practically a hurricane out there.

A shiver ran through her and he noticed the small puddle forming at her feet.

'There's a bathroom on the first floor. Dry off and help yourself to the clothes in the dresser,' he said. 'I will meet you up there once I have found some medical supplies for that leg.'

The flush on her face brightened. She looked wary and tense, like a feral kitten scared to trust a helping hand.

'You don't have to do that,' she said.

'I know,' he replied. 'Now go. *Vite*.' He shooed her upstairs. 'Before you flood my hallway.'

CHAPTER THREE

'I DISCOVERED WHERE my housekeeper hides the medical supplies,' Ally's host announced as he strolled into the large study on the first floor and placed a red box on the mahogany desk.

Ally swallowed down the lump of anxiety in her throat. She wrapped her arms around her midriff, but remained rooted to her spot by the room's large mullioned windows.

How did Dominic have the ability to suck all the oxygen out of the room simply by walking into it?

At least she was warm and clean and dry now. Unfortunately, the oversized sweatpants and top that smelled of him, which she'd found in the guest bedroom next door—after taking the world's fastest shower in the en-suite wet room—still put her at a huge disadvantage.

In her bare feet, he towered over her, his suit trousers and white shirt perfectly tailored to accentuate his lean, well-muscled body.

'I see you found some dry clothes.' He studied her makeshift outfit in a way that made her feel like a street urchin playing dress-up before a king.

The intense look had her heart thundering harder against her ribs.

'Yes, thank you,' she said.

'Is the leg still bleeding?' The gruff question had goosebumps springing up all over her skin, despite the cosy cotton sweats.

'I don't think so,' she said. 'I took a shower to clean it. I'm sure it's fine.'

'We'll see,' he said, sounding doubtful. He beckoned her with one finger and indicated a large armchair in the corner of the room. 'Sit down so I can inspect it.'

She debated arguing with him again, because goosebumps were rising on the goosebumps now at the thought of getting any closer to him. But she could see by the muscle twitching in his jaw he wasn't going to take no for an answer.

She crossed the room, trying not to limp, and sat in the chair. The sooner they got this over with, the sooner she could start breathing freely again.

To her astonishment he knelt down in front of her. She braced her hands on the arms of the chair as he opened the box, and began to rummage through the array of medical supplies.

How had this happened? How had she ended up playing doctor with Dominic LeGrand? In his billion-pound house? In the intimacy of his study? While wearing his sweats with virtually nothing under them?

The traitorous heat—which had been lodged in her belly ever since the dispatcher had said his name—throbbed and glowed at her core.

But this time, she replayed the pep talk she'd given herself in the shower.

Why should she feel ashamed of her reaction to him? They were both consenting adults. Dominic had always captivated her, even as a delinquent boy, and he was a world-renowned womaniser now. So she was bound to find him a little overwhelming—especially as she was so pathetically inexperienced with men.

Looking after her mother and keeping food on the table and a roof over both their heads hadn't left her any time to date while she was at school. And after her mother died, trying to realise her dream of becoming a fashion designer and stop her finances from slipping into a black hole hadn't increased her opportunities much. In fact, despite a few fumbling encounters, she was still a virgin. Which explained why she had such a violent reaction to someone as overwhelming as Dominic LeGrand.

Having rationalised her attraction, she watched him unobserved as he arranged a bandage and a packet of antiseptic wipes on the side table.

Even when he was on his knees, his head was almost level with hers. The light from the lamp behind her caught the streaks of gold in his tawny hair. She could make out the scar on his brow, the one she'd wondered about often when they were children. How had he got it?

His shoulders flexed, stretching the seams of his shirt, as he reached down to cradle her heel in his palm.

She jumped, sensation sprinting up her leg and

sinking deep into her sex as callused fingers gripped her ankle.

'Does that hurt?' he asked, his chocolate gaze locking on her face.

'No, it's just...' *No man has ever touched me there before.* 'I was just surprised.' *Who knew my ankle was an erogenous zone?*

'Okay.' He frowned, but seemed to take the explanation at face value. 'Let me know if it does hurt.'

She nodded, her whole foot humming as he gripped her heel and used his other hand to lift the leg of her sweatpants past her knee.

He hissed as the gash was revealed. It wasn't too deep, more like a bad scrape where the pedal had dug into the skin, but it was still bleeding a little and there was some bruising visible around the wound.

'Nasty,' he murmured as he grabbed one of the antiseptic wipes with his free hand.

He ripped the small packet open with his teeth.

'Do you know how you did it?' he asked, dabbing at the wound.

'I got in the way of your fiancée while she was leaving,' she said.

His fingers tensed on her heel. 'Mira did this?' he said and she could hear the fury in his voice.

She nodded, wishing she could take the words back.

Why did you bring up his broken engagement?

He'd seemed pragmatic about it downstairs, but how did she know that wasn't all an act? Like the act he had put on as a boy, when his father had referred

to him as 'my bastard son' at the supper table, or the
don't-give-a-damn smile he'd sent her when she had
witnessed Pierre backhand him across the face—and
she'd tried to defend him.

'Some people deserve to be hurt, ma petite.*'*

His father's answer still haunted her.

No one deserved to be hurt, least of all Dominic, who had seemed to her back then—despite that
don't-give-a-damn bravado—like a lost boy, jealously
guarding secrets he refused to share.

What if he was just as hurt about his broken engagement? And his anger now was only there to disguise that hurt?

'I'm sorry,' she said. 'I didn't mean to upset you.'

'Upset me?' The flash of anger was replaced by
an incredulous look. 'What could you have done to
upset me?'

'By bringing up the end of your engagement. I
didn't mean to remind you of it. I'm sure it must be
awful for you. The break-up?'

She was babbling, but she couldn't help it, because
he had settled back onto his heels and was staring at
her as if she'd lost her mind.

'Alison,' he said and she could hear the hint of
condescension. 'In the first place, *you* haven't upset
me. *She* has, by her spoilt, unpleasant behaviour. She
made you bleed…'

'I'm sure it was an accident,' she said, despite the
warm glow at his concern.

'Knowing Mira and her selfish, capricious tem-
perament, I doubt that,' he said. 'And in the second

place, the break-up has not upset me. The engagement was a mistake and the marriage would have been an even bigger one.'

'But you must have loved her once?' she said, then felt like a fool, when the rueful smile widened.

'Must I?' he said. 'Why must I?'

'Because… Because you were going to marry her?' *Wasn't it obvious?*

He tilted his head, and studied her. 'I see you're still as much of a romantic as you were at ten,' he said, with much more than just a hint of condescension.

'I wasn't ten that summer, I was thirteen,' she countered.

'Really?' he said, mocking her now. 'So grown up.'

She shifted in her seat, supremely uncomfortable. It was as if he could see right past the bravado, the pretence of maturity, to the girl she'd been all those years ago when she'd idolised him. But she wasn't that teenager any more, she was twenty-five years old. And maybe she didn't have much relationship experience, but she had enough life experience to make up for it.

'If I was a romantic then,' she said, because maybe she had been, 'I'm certainly not one now.'

'Then why would you believe I was in love with Mira?' he said, as if it were the most ridiculous thing in the world.

'Maybe because you were planning to spend the rest of your life with her.' She wanted to add a 'Duh' but managed to control it. The room was already full to bursting with sarcasm.

'It wasn't a love match,' he said, the pragmatic tone disconcerting as he bent his head and continued tending her leg as he spoke. 'I needed a wife to secure an important business deal and Mira fit the bill. Or so I thought. But even if I hadn't discovered my mistake in time, the marriage was only supposed to last for a few months.'

'Your marriage had a sell-by date?' she asked, shocked by the depth of his cynicism.

'I might have been misguided enough to propose to Mira,' he said, smiling at her as he grabbed the bandage on the side table. 'But I would never be foolish enough to shackle myself to her, or any woman, for life.'

'I see,' she said, although she really didn't.

He'd always been guarded, and wary, even at sixteen. But had he always been this jaded?

One encounter blasted into her brain, when she'd caught him sitting in one of the chateau's walled gardens, inhaling deeply on a cigarette after his father had goaded him at the lunch table, calling him a name in French she hadn't really understood but had known was bad.

'You shouldn't smoke. It's bad for you. Papa will be angry.'

'Go ahead and tell him if you want, Allycat. He won't care.'

He'd had the same mocking smile on his face then as he had now, but she'd seen the sadness in his eyes—and had known his father's insult had hurt him much more than he'd been letting on. There was no sadness in his eyes now, though, just a sort of rueful amusement at her naiveté.

He finished bandaging her leg.

'All done.' He ran his thumbs along her calf, and she shivered as a trail of fire was left by the light caress. 'How does it feel?'

'Good,' she said and then flushed at his husky chuckle.

Had he sensed it wasn't only her leg she was talking about?

A sensual smile curved his lips and her breath clogged in her lungs.

Yes, he did know.

'Bien,' he murmured, then grabbed the arms of the chair, caging her in for a moment as he levered himself to his feet.

Her heartbeat thundered into her throat and some other key parts of her anatomy as he offered her his hand.

'Let's try walking on it,' he said.

She placed her fingers in his palm, but as she got to her feet the warm grip had the sweet spot between her thighs becoming heavy and hot.

She tested her leg as he led her across the room.

'Still good?' he asked, still smiling that knowing smile.

'Yes,' she said. 'Still good.' And couldn't resist smiling back at him.

Maybe it was dangerous to flirt with him—if that was what they were doing. But she'd never had much of a chance to flirt with anyone before. And certainly not someone as gorgeous as he was.

And let's not forget the massive crush you had on him once upon a time, her subconscious added, helpfully.

'How about that drink?' he asked as he let her hand go, to walk to the liquor cabinet in the bookshelves.

She ought to say no. But she was feeling languid and a little giddy. Maybe it was the fire crackling in the hearth, or the sound of the rain still beating down outside, or the cosy feel of the sweats she'd borrowed, or the glimmer of appreciation in his hot chocolate eyes—which was probably all in her imagination. Or maybe it was the fact he had tended her leg.

When was the last time anyone had taken care of her?

Whatever the reason, she couldn't seem to conjure the ability to be careful or cautious for once. She'd denied herself so many things in the last twelve years—why should she deny herself a chance to have a drink with a man who had always fascinated her?

'Were you serious about ordering me a cab home?' she asked. Because she couldn't drink if she was going to have to cycle all the way to East London.

'Of course,' he said.

'Then thank you, I'd love a drink.'

'What would you like? I have whisky. Gin. Brandy.' He opened the drinks cabinet and bent to look inside, giving her a far too tempting view of tight male buns confined in designer trousers. 'A spicy Merlot? A refreshing Chablis?'

'Spoken like a true Frenchman,' she teased.

'*C'est vrai.* I am French. I take my wine seriously,' he said, laying on his accent extra thick and making her grin.

'The Merlot sounds good,' she said.

He poured the red wine into a crystal tumbler, his fingers brushing hers as he passed her the glass. The prickle of reaction sprinted up her arm, but it didn't scare her or shame her this time. It excited her.

She took a sip of the wine, and the rich fruity flavours burst on her tongue.

'*Bon?*' he asked.

'Very.'

He leaned his hips against the cabinet and crossed his arms over his chest, making his pectoral muscles flex distractingly against the white linen.

'You're not drinking?' she asked.

'I have already had one whisky tonight. And I want to keep a clear head.'

'Oh?' she said. She wanted to ask why he needed to keep a clear head, but it seemed like a loaded question—especially when he smiled that sensual smile again, as if they were sharing an intimate secret.

She got a little distracted by the astonishing beauty of his face—rugged and masculine—dappled by firelight and the ridged contours of his chest visible through the tailored shirt.

She took another sip of the wine, let the warmth of it spread through her torso. This was definitely better than having to cycle back to Whitechapel in the pouring rain.

Mira Whatsherface's loss was Ally Jones's gain.

'Are you enjoying the view?' The deep mocking voice had her gaze jerking back to his face.

She blinked, blinded by the heat of his smile. Momentarily.

Her cheeks heated.

For goodness' sake, Ally, stop staring at his exceptional chest and make some small talk.

'What's the deal?' she asked.

His scarred eyebrow arched. 'Deal?'

'The deal you were prepared to enter into a loveless short-term marriage for,' she elaborated.

'An extremely important one for my business,' he said, without an ounce of embarrassment or remorse. 'There is a large tract of undeveloped land on the Brooklyn waterfront. It is the only undeveloped parcel of that size in the five boroughs. I intend to reclaim it, and build on it. Homes mostly. Unfortunately it is owned by a group of men who refuse to invest with someone they regard as—how did they put it? "Morally suspect."' He used finger quotes while sending her a wry smile. 'My private life needs to be stable and settled without a whiff of scandal while the project is in its early stages. As soon as I was in a position to engineer a board takeover and buy them out, I planned to end the marriage.'

'So it's all about money?' she said.

His smile quirked as if she had said something particularly amusing. 'Money is important. You of all people should understand that,' he said, and she felt her blush heat. 'But no, it's not all about money.

This is about taking my business to the next level. This project will put LeGrand Nationale in a position to dominate the regeneration market in the United States.'

So it wasn't just about money, it was also about legacy and prestige. Was it any surprise that would be so important to him? When he had been forced to prove himself from a young age, the illegitimate son who had been called a 'bastard' by his own father. She couldn't blame him for his drive and ambition, even though his cynicism made her feel sad.

'But let's not talk about business,' he murmured as he released his arms and walked towards her. His thumb glided down her cheek and her breath caught in her throat, the sizzle of heat darting into her sex. 'Tell me about you. How did you come to be a bike messenger? Has your life been hard, since that summer, Allycat?'

His voice caressed the childhood nickname in a way that inflamed her senses—but his attention was even more potent. She needed to be careful; this was a casual conversation, nothing more.

'Not that hard,' she lied. 'I became a bike courier because it's good money. And I can fit it around my classes. I'm... I'm in college at the moment,' she added, as she found herself staring into his eyes, spotting the strands of gold in the chocolate brown.

'So you are smart as well as beautiful.' His thumb glided across her lips and her mouth opened instinctively on a sigh, the blood rushing in her ears.

'If I asked to kiss you, Alison,' he said, the rasp

of need in his voice both raw and sublime, 'what would you say?'

She nodded without thinking.

Kissing Dominic probably wasn't a good idea, but she was incapable of controlling the euphoria rioting in her blood. The knowledge he wanted her was even more intoxicating than his fresh woodsy scent and the feel of his thumb tracing over the pulse in her neck.

'You must say the word,' he coaxed as he stroked the well of her collarbone.

'Yes.' *Please.*

'Merci.'

The hoarse thank-you was as tortured as the need twisting her belly into tight knots.

Her bottom bumped the wall as he pressed her against it, found the hem of her sweatshirt and slid his hands under it to hold her steady.

Then his lips were on hers, hot and firm and seeking. A groan escaped from her constricted throat and his tongue plunged deep into her mouth.

He explored in masterful, demanding strokes as his fingers dipped beneath the waistband of her sweatpants and cupped her naked bottom.

He ripped his mouth away. 'No panties?' he said, the pupils so dilated his chocolate brown eyes had become black.

'They… They were wet,' she choked out.

'I may have to punish you for that, Alison,' he murmured, the mocking tone so fierce it was only half joking.

Raw need careered through her.

'I want to see more of you,' he said. *'D'accord?'*

She nodded again, having lost the power of speech.

Lifting the hem of her sweatshirt, he tugged it over her head. She shuddered as his gaze glided over the damp sports bra she had donned after her shower.

Could she have been wearing anything less alluring?

But his gaze when it met hers still blazed with arousal. *'Trés belle.'*

Capturing both her wrists in one hand, he lifted her arms above her head, until she was pinned against the wall, her breasts thrust out, begging for attention, her breathing so ragged it sounded deafening.

He covered one straining breast with his free hand and scooped it free of her bra. Exposing her to his gaze.

'Magnifique...' he murmured, then lowered his head and licked across the swollen tip.

She bucked against his hold, shocked by the sensations firing down to her core as he teased and tortured the oversensitive peak with his tongue, his teeth.

She couldn't stop shaking, sobbing. Until he covered the erect nipple with his mouth and suckled.

It was too much and yet not nearly enough. The jut of his erection, so hard and large confined in the suit trousers, pressed against her belly. She wanted to feel it inside her, to take the ache away.

Her breathing guttered out when at last he released her engorged nipple. But the relief was short-lived, as he unhooked the bra and freed her other breast to begin again. Torturing, teasing, tormenting.

She was begging, bucking against his hold when he finally returned his mouth to hers. He held her captive, both wrists shackled above her head. The huge erection notched between her thighs, her bare breasts crushed against his chest. The hard shaft found that sweet spot through their clothing, rubbing, rocking, the waves of sensation building from her core.

The orgasm built so swiftly, she couldn't control it, the shattering wave crashing over her with staggering intensity. Her body arched as the bright light fired from her core and shattered into a million glittering shards.

She was struggling to breathe, her body slumped against his, when his voice rasped against her ear.

'*Dieu*, did you just climax, Alison?'

Her eyelids fluttered open, to find him staring at her with a need so fierce it was terrifying and liberating all at once.

Her thundering heart began to slow. He did not look happy. In fact, he looked stunned. Had she done something wrong?

'Yes…' she said. 'I'm… I'm sorry, I couldn't stop it. Was I supposed to?'

His lips quirked and then, to her astonishment, he dropped his head back and laughed.

She tugged on her arms, tried to wrestle herself free of his hold, humiliation engulfing her.

He was still fully dressed. With her bra hanging from one arm and her nipples raw and swollen where he'd played with them she'd never felt more exposed.

'I should go,' she murmured.

But he didn't release her, as the rough chuckles died. His thumbs pressed into the rampaging pulse at her wrists.

'No way. We're not finished yet. Even if you jumped the gun.'

'I said I was sorry about...' She tried to protest, but he silenced her, the swift kiss both demanding and possessive.

'There was no need to apologise,' he said, his gaze compelling—the humour replaced with something much more potent. 'Do you have any idea how adorable you are?'

The gruff words were quietly spoken, but so achingly sincere her heart punched her ribs.

Cupping her cheek, he swept his gaze over her, the approval she saw making her heartbeat thunder in her ears.

What was happening? Because this felt *too* intimate, *too* emotional. More than sex.

'Please, I...' she began.

'Shh...' He stroked his hand down to her collarbone, the ripple of sensation making her shiver. 'I wish to take you to bed, Alison. How do you feel about that?'

'I... I want you too.' *Very much.*

'Bien.'

He sent her a devilish grin, full of wickedness and intent. Letting her arms drop, he dragged the bra away, leaving her standing before him in only the baggy sweatpants.

'Très, très belle,' he murmured again, his voice

thick with arousal. 'My gym pants have never looked so good.'

She crossed her arms over her breasts, brutally aware of how naked she was, compared to him.

But then he scooped her into his arms.

She grasped his neck as he marched her into the spare bedroom. The room was luxuriously furnished with a large tester bed complemented by an array of antique pieces. He closed the door to the study, so the only light in the room came from the bathroom and the bay window that looked out onto the house's grounds. The low lighting had a little of her anxiety retreating as he laid her on the bed.

Her pulse sped up again though as he unbuttoned his shirt, then stripped it off.

Moonlight flickered over the tanned skin, putting the bunched muscles of his torso into stark relief. He was magnificent. Tall, muscular, lean and powerful. The dark hair that defined flat brown nipples and arrowed down into his trousers through his abs had her lungs seizing. Her throat dried as he released the hook on his suit trousers and kicked off his shoes.

The rigid erection sprang up as he lowered his boxers.

Her gaze met his, her breathing so shallow now it was a miracle she didn't faint as he climbed onto the bed.

'Lose the pants, *ma belle*,' he said.

She wriggled out of the sweatpants and flung them away. He climbed on top of her. His skin felt hot and firm as he pressed her into the mattress and a rough palm coasted up her bare thigh. A hoarse cry escaped her throat.

Their skin touched everywhere. His fingertips electrified her nerve endings as they found the sensitive seam of skin at the top of her thigh, then located the slick heat at her core.

'So wet for me, *ma belle*.' She could hear the hunger in his voice. 'Tell me what you like.'

I don't know.

She trapped the answer in her throat. And flattened her palms against the ridged muscles, stalling for time. She didn't know how to answer that question; no man had ever seen her naked before, let alone touched her, stroked her.

His thumb found the bundle of nerves again and she moaned, jerking her hips towards the intimate torture.

'You like that?' he asked as his thumb circled, not quite touching her again where she needed.

'Yes, yes, please do it again.' She didn't care any more about the naked need in her voice, the raw desperation. She wanted to feel that glorious release once more.

'Can I touch you, too?' she asked.

The deep groan against her neck felt like a benediction. *'Oui.'*

She slid her hand down his chest, feeling the muscles quiver. His whole body shook as she wrapped her fingers around the stiff column of flesh. She had a moment of panic as she gauged his size, his girth and the steely strength beneath the velvet-soft skin. How would anything that large and hard ever fit inside her?

But then his thumb found that devastating spot between her thighs and every thought flew out of her head.

She stroked him as he stroked her. But where his caresses were firm and assured, her movements were jerky and uncertain. Still she took pleasure in his shudder when her thumb found the bead of moisture at the head of his erection. She could feel his passion building as the coil at her core twisted and tightened. Her knees fell open, her hips angling forward, in a wanton display of need she couldn't control. Her fingers gripped his rigid flesh as one blunt finger entered her, sinking into the tight flesh, his thumb still working her into a frenzy.

'You are very tight. It has been a while, yes?' he asked.

She nodded. Because what else could she say? It was a lifetime since she'd felt this good.

He swore softly in French, his hips driving into her hand, the hard flesh getting longer, thicker.

'Come for me again, *ma chérie*,' he demanded, and just like that the wave slammed into her, flinging her over that final peak.

She let out a hoarse moan as she fell to earth, sinking into the glorious oblivion. But as the afterglow settled over her like a glittering cloud, her fingers flexed on the erection. He was still rigid, still huge.

Leaning over her, he fumbled in the bedside

drawer, the rip of foil was loud enough to be heard over her staggered breathing.

Lifting her hand from his erection, he kissed the knuckles. 'I cannot wait any longer,' he murmured, the urgency sending new ripples of longing through her exhausted flesh.

He rolled on the condom, then grasped her hips.

She felt the head of his erection probe, before he thrust deep.

Rending pain seared through her and she choked off a sob.

'Merde!' He reared back.

She bit into her lip to stop the cry of pain. Intense pleasure had turned to shock and discomfort, but far worse than the soreness where his erection was lodged deep inside her was the look of pure horror that shadowed Dominic's face.

He knew.

The thought doused the heat, until all that was left was the chill of his disapproval.

Of course, he knew. Why had she thought he wouldn't notice? A man with his experience, who had probably slept with dozens of women.

She shifted, trying to adjust to the thick length inside her, hoping to regain the desire that had disappeared in a rush. But his fingers flexed on her hips, and he flinched.

'Don't move,' he groaned. 'I don't want to hurt you more.'

'It's okay, it doesn't hurt.'

'Don't lie,' he said, his gaze shadowed now, the

horror replaced with surprise and something that looked like guilt. 'I am your first. Is this not the case?'

She wanted to lie, to take the guilt out of his expression. But how could she, when it was clearly obvious?

'Yes, but it's not a big deal,' she murmured, because it really wasn't. Or at least it shouldn't have been. Up until the moment he had entered her, she'd been delirious with pleasure. He'd brought her to orgasm. Twice. And more than anything she wanted to do the same for him. To see him shatter the way he had made her shatter.

'I must withdraw,' he said.

'No, don't.' She clasped his shoulders. 'Don't stop. I don't want you to stop.' The tearing pain had already lessened, the tendrils of heat building again at her core, the pulsing ache becoming sharp and insistent.

'Damn it, Alison, you don't know what you ask of me. I am not sure I can be gentle.'

The growled admission, grudging and yet gruff with desperation, had her heart contracting.

'I don't need you to be gentle, Dominic. I just need you to treat me like a woman.'

To treat me like your *woman.*

The foolishly romantic thought echoed in her head.

She buried it deep. She hadn't lied when she'd told him her virginity was not a big deal to her. She was twenty-five years old. It was ridiculous she'd waited this long. And yes, it had hurt. But already the full stretched feeling had changed into something closer to pleasure than pain. He filled her up in a way that made her breath hitch, and her clitoris throb with renewed yearning.

'I'm not fragile,' she added, because he was still braced above her, not moving, his face strained with the effort it was taking him to hold still. 'Really I'm not. I know what I want.' *And what I want is you.*

She threaded her fingers into his hair, coaxing him to do what they both needed. He swore softly, but then placed a hand at her cheek, brushing his thumb across her lips.

'D'accord, ma belle,' he murmured, his gaze becoming dark and intense as he glided out of her, then thrust back in, slowly, carefully, sinking in to the hilt.

The head of his penis massaged a spot deep inside her and she gasped, the delicious shudder adding to the heat at her core.

'C'est bien?' he asked, his perfect English having deserted him.

'Yes,' she moaned. 'It's good.'

He established a rhythm—slow at first, and then building—digging at that spot ruthlessly, relentlessly as heat fired over her skin.

The waves of pleasure gathered again with each new thrust of his hips, each new jolt of desire. She clung to him, the only solid object in the storm engulfing her. Every pulse and heartbeat became attuned to the ravages of pleasure he was waging on her body. The steady rhythm became harder, faster, overwhelming, unstoppable.

She couldn't think any more, couldn't make sense

of the sounds and sights around her, all she could do was feel…

Her moans became pants, her sex contracting, massaging the hard length. The brutal pleasure coiled tighter at her core. The edge of desire so sharp she felt buffeted, burned, undone.

Then his thumb found the swollen folds where their bodies joined, triggering a conflagration so fierce and all-consuming she cried out.

Her body arched into his, the shattering orgasm exploding along her nerve-endings, like a shimmering light, splintering and then retreating to splinter again.

She could hear her own sobs, her fingers fisting in his hair, as he finally let her tumble to earth— his shout of fulfilment following her over that high wide edge.

His big body collapsed on top of her, his raw pants matched hers, the musty scent of sex and sweat mingling with the shiver of surrender.

She hugged him, exhausted, spent. Her sex sore, her body limp. She caressed the silky strands at his nape now damp with sweat, and tried not to acknowledge the debilitating wave of emotion threatening to engulf her.

It's just sex. Just for one night. It doesn't mean anything.

But still she couldn't quite ignore the faltering beat of her heart at the realisation that, after twelve years, all her foolish teenage fantasises had finally come true. And it had definitely been worth the wait.

CHAPTER FOUR

BREATHE, DAMN IT. Breathe.

Dominic's hands slipped from Alison's hips as he withdrew. She flinched and the dart of shame stabbed at his chest.

His fingers shook as he imagined the bruising imprint of his thumbs on the soft skin where he'd gripped her as he'd pumped into her.

What the hell had just happened? Because what should have been a smooth, subtle seduction had become something frenzied and frantic.

He'd planned to make love to her tonight as soon as they had been alone together in the study—and he'd seen the arousal in her eyes.

She was beautiful, captivating, she wanted him. And she could solve all his problems.

Figuring out where his housekeeper had hidden the first-aid box downstairs had given him more than enough time to consider the tempting possibilities Alison Jones's reappearance in his life tonight might mean.

He needed a wife and she could be perfect for the role.

Not only did she turn him on to the point of madness, something Mira had never done, but he could offer her a home, and financial security. The fact she was completely unknown to the press with no scandal attached to her was another huge point in her favour. It would be a relatively simple job to set up a new PR narrative to explain their whirlwind romance and wedding. Mira had been out of the country for over a month, he and Alison had known each other as children, they'd met again when she'd delivered something to his home and one thing had led to another.

The only question had been whether she desired him, too. Had he imagined that spark? Because it suited his own ends so perfectly?

But as soon as he'd walked into the study and seen her face flush and her breathing accelerate, he'd known he hadn't imagined anything. And when he had touched her bare foot, and she'd nearly jumped out of the chair, he'd had to swallow a harsh laugh.

Game on.

But why hadn't he questioned her artless responses, the beguiling blush that had spread across her collarbone as soon as he'd started flirting with her?

She'd been as eager as him, that was why. He'd assumed the blush, the innocence were all an accomplished act, an act to disguise the fact she was more than ready to take Mira's place—especially when she had questioned him about the business deal.

He'd been in her situation himself, years ago when he'd been destitute after arriving in Paris with three broken ribs and not a penny to his name, so why would he judge her for taking the easy option? Of snagging a rich man? Hadn't his own mother—and hers—tried to do the same?

But once he'd tasted her, the sophisticated seduction he'd planned had changed into something elemental.

She had tasted like she smelled. Strawberries and chocolate. Sweet and decadent. But more than that, she had tasted of summer, and sunshine, and joy and surrender.

The fanciful thoughts had scattered, becoming dark and earthy and driven as she'd squirmed against his hardening erection, like a cat desperate to be stroked.

Bon Dieu, but he hadn't been able to get enough of her, exploring the recesses of her mouth like a man possessed.

And once he'd freed her breasts, felt her nipples harden and swell against his tongue, he'd been lost in a passion so intense it had been a major battle not to take her right there against the wall of his study.

When his hands had cupped her naked bottom, sensation had hurtled beneath his belt with the speed and accuracy of a heat-seeking missile.

Suddenly, he'd become the desperate boy again, instead of the experienced lover.

He'd had to force himself to slow down, to carry her to the bedroom and strip off his clothes, to draw forth another orgasm—simply to prove he could wait to have her, that he was still the one in control—before he'd plunged into her.

But when she had gasped and stiffened in pain, he'd known instantly—this was no act.

She had been a virgin, for God's sake.

He should have stopped then, but, even while he was frantically trying to assess the repercussions of her innocence, his body had refused to obey him once she'd given him permission to continue—so he'd taken what she'd offered, because he'd been unable to do otherwise.

And now here he was, lying in bed beside her, not knowing what the hell to say to her.

Should he apologise? Explain? She'd said it wasn't a big deal, but somehow it was to him. He'd never been a woman's first lover. Had deliberately avoided that sort of intimacy. And what did he do now about his plan to suggest they marry? Because this could complicate things in ways he did not want, and had not anticipated.

His gut twisted as he felt her shift on the bed beside him. She hadn't spoken, probably because she was as shocked by the intensity of their lovemaking as he was. And appalled by his lack of sophistication.

Or was she? How would she know the power of their connection—or how catastrophically he had lost control—if she had never slept with another man?

She sat up with her back to him, but as she went to stand he flung his arm out and caught her hip. 'Where are you going?' he asked, pleased when the words came out reasonably smoothly despite the rawness in his throat.

She glanced over her shoulder. 'I hope you don't mind if I borrow your sweats? I'll return them tomorrow.'

What?

It took a moment for him to register what she was asking him and why as she bent down to scoop the sweatpants off the floor. But when she tried to stand, he at least had the presence of mind to keep his hand anchored on her hip.

'You're not going anywhere tonight, Allycat,' he said, moving across the bed to band an arm around her waist.

She twisted round again, her face so close he could see the confusion in her eyes. 'Why...why not?' she asked.

Mon Dieu, she was even more innocent than he had assumed.

He kissed her shoulder blade. 'Because I have exhausted you. And it is still raining.' They weren't the main reasons, not even close, but he didn't want to talk about anything else until he had calmed down enough to figure out all the angles.

Perhaps her virginity didn't have to be a bad thing. At least it seemed unlikely that as his wife she would be photographed kissing other men. And perhaps his spectacular loss of control was a one-off. She'd unsettled him the minute she had arrived. They had a history; she knew more about his background than any of the other women he had slept with. And he hadn't been with a woman in six weeks. Maybe he'd had longer dry spells before while he was building his business, but perhaps this need, this desperation, the intensity of their connection were nothing more than chemistry and opportunity.

'I thought I'd just get a cab, like you suggested,' she said.

Why had he suggested the damn cab?

'Alison.' He pulled himself up on the bed, and sat behind her, his legs straddling hers. He wrapped his arms around her waist, and dropped his chin on her shoulder. 'There is no need to leave. I want you to stay.'

The heat surged back into his groin—making the erection swell against her bottom.

She stiffened slightly. 'I don't… I'm a bit sore, I don't think I want to do it again tonight,' she said. And he was caught between a laugh and a groan.

'Ignore that, I have no control over my body's reaction to you.' Wasn't that the truth? 'I have no intention of touching you again tonight,' he said. He lifted the sweatpants out of her hands and then manoeuvred himself off the bed so he could stand and put them on. Grabbing the bathrobe that hung on the back of the bedroom door, he passed it to her.

She scrambled into it. He couldn't make out her expression in the half-light, but he could sense her embarrassment and uncertainty. And suddenly the pulse of reaction in his crotch wasn't nearly as disturbing as the pulse of something around his heart.

She was sweet and adorable and genuine, not

something he usually looked for in a hook-up. But then she wasn't a hook-up; he was hoping she would agree to become much more than that, tomorrow. And for what he had in mind, perhaps her innocence could be a huge advantage.

But until he'd had a chance to consider his plan carefully in light of this new information, he didn't intend to let her out of his house.

For tonight, though, it would be best if he kept her out of his bed. Or he would find it very hard to keep his promise—not to touch her again.

'Are you hungry?' he asked.

She shook her head. 'Just tired.'

'Then come with me,' he said, ignoring the renewed pulse of emotion as she hesitated before taking his hand.

He guided her out of the bedroom and into the study.

'There is another bedroom with an en suite on this floor.' He led her down the darkened hallway and across the landing to open the door to another of the house's six bedrooms. He leant against the doorframe as she stepped into the room.

'Get some sleep. I will see you in the morning.' Once he'd worked out exactly how to proceed.

She stood in the room, looking a little lost. 'But I left my bike outside,' she said.

He huffed out a strained laugh. 'I'll bring it in out of the cold.'

'Okay, thanks,' she murmured. 'For everything.' Then flushed, obviously realising the double meaning.

He had to hold back another harsh laugh.

Damn, but she really was utterly adorable. He grasped the lapels of her robe and tugged her close, but restricted the goodnight kiss to a chaste peck on her forehead. '*Bonne nuit*, Allycat.'

Tomorrow they would talk. But for tonight he needed space and distance; they both did. Their spectacular chemistry did not have to be a bad thing, in fact it could be a very fortuitous thing, and not just for his business.

But first he needed to ensure her innocence hadn't created complications he couldn't control.

CHAPTER FIVE

IT TOOK ALLY a moment to adjust to the dawn light shining through the open shutters of the big bay window when she woke the next day. She pushed herself up on her elbows, the sheet sliding over sensitive skin. It took her a moment more to figure out where she was.

Then the memories came flooding back in a dizzying kaleidoscope of scents and sights and sounds and sensations.

The crackle of the dispatcher's voice shouting out Dominic's name through the rain, the aroma of pine soap and whisky, the rich fruity taste of the Merlot, the flicker of moonlight caressing the muscular planes of Dominic's chest, the rending pain and then the shocking pleasure as he filled her to bursting.

And the confusing thoughts as she'd drifted into sleep afterwards.

She swung her feet to the floor and wrapped the sheet around her naked body, aware of all the places Dominic had caressed with such skill and efficiency the night before. Her breasts, her lips, her sex.

What she'd experienced had been so much more than she had been prepared for. She hadn't expected that level of pleasure, or that level of intimacy. How had he known exactly how and where to touch her? Was this what her mother had always craved, that pure physical connection? Was that why she'd exposed herself so easily? To so many men? After Pierre had discarded her?

A chill rippled over Ally's skin, even though the house's heating was set at the perfect ambient temperature.

Another thought intruded, of how Dominic had kept his composure last night, and she'd lost all of hers.

She walked across the room on unsteady legs and shrugged on the bathrobe he'd given her the night before, inhaling the scent of him, which still clung to the material. Then felt foolish.

She needed to leave. She should have left last night. Seeing him this morning would be awkward and uncomfortable for both of them—the fact of her virginity, and the lies she'd told to conceal it from him, not just an elephant in the room but a ten-ton pachyderm.

It was still early, she thought, assessing the light through the window. Probably only six, if that. She had time to take a quick shower, then hunt up her clothing, find her bike and get out.

But when she dashed into the bathroom, she spotted her reflection in the mirrored wall opposite the shower cubicle.

The sight stole her breath. She hadn't expected

to look different, to feel different, had assumed that was a myth women told each other to make their first time have meaning.

But she did look different. Her hair was rumpled, her skin pink in places where his stubble had rubbed against it.

The stupid wave of emotion took her unawares.

Not a big deal. Not a big deal. Don't make too much of it.

A heavy weight sank into the pit of her stomach. *Don't you dare cry.*

After a quick shower, she ran her fingers through her hair and stared at herself in the bathroom mirror, pressing her thumb against the skin of her cheek— tender from beard burn.

Last night had been an experience, an experience she refused to regret. But it was a new day now, the harsh light of the March dawn after the storm signalling a return to real life.

Tiptoeing down the hall, she slipped into the study, cold now with the fire burnt out. She found her bra on the floor where Dominic had discarded it.

Now all she needed was the wet cycling gear she'd left in the bedroom where they had made love. The door was ajar. She huffed out a shaky breath when she peered into the room to discover it empty, the large bed still rumpled from the night before.

A vision of Dominic's magnificent chest limed by moonlight blasted into her brain. The heavy sensation at her core throbbed.

She shook her head, trying to expel the dazed feeling.

So, so *not the point.*

She found her cycling gear where she'd left it, hanging over the heated towel rail in the bathroom. Dropping the robe, she slipped on the now dry clothing, easing the torn cycling pants over the bandage on her leg.

The memory of his fingers, gentle and efficient as he bandaged her calf, had the heat eddying back through her body. And the emotion squeezing her ribs. She breathed. In, out. And waited for the wave to pass.

But as she left the bathroom, she stumbled to a stop as her gaze connected with the unmade bed—and the pulse of guilt and yearning wrapped around her heart like a vice, the bloodstains on the bedsheet like a banner ad to her naiveté.

Had she really believed she could sleep with Dominic, have him be her first lover and suffer no emotional fallout whatsoever?

But even as she acknowledged the foolishness of that assessment, she refused to regret her decision. How many women could say they had been initiated into sex by their childhood crush—and got three amazing orgasms into the bargain?

Dominic and last night had been a gift. A gift she had deserved after the harsh realities of her life ever since that summer in Provence. Through the many dark days spent watching her mother become addicted to prescription painkillers, and throw herself at men who didn't treat her with respect, or kindness. Seeing her become a shadow of the beautiful woman she'd been that summer when Pierre LeGrand had loved her.

Perhaps it was ironic it was Pierre's son who had given Ally this boon, but why did it have to be significant?

She already knew the gift of great sex wasn't something that could last.

It was the one thing she had discovered while watching her mother sink into despair. That it was far too easy to mistake sex for love—and love, even when it was genuine, was totally unreliable.

It required you to allow your life, your happiness, to be dependent on the whims of others. She'd learned a valuable lesson in the last twelve years: not just that love could destroy you if you let it, but that survival meant relying on yourself and no one else.

The yearning she felt, the sadness that last night was never going to be repeated, was purely physical.

Dominic was a handsome, powerful and overwhelming man—and an experienced lover. And they had a past dating back to the days when she'd still believed in love and romance. Of course she'd been captivated by him.

But she could not allow what had happened last night to have any lasting significance in her life.

Plus she was never going to see him again—if she got a move on.

Once she was back on her bike, delivering pizzas and urgent documents and maybe even someone else's wedding ring—last night would all be a wonderful dream, which she'd be able to pull out of her subconscious and enjoy whenever she needed a pick-me-up or an incentive to get through another day.

She flung the sheets over the bloodstains, and sat down to wrestle her still-damp cycling shoes back on. Then walked back out of the room.

There was no sound coming from the floor below.

Thank God, she hadn't sabotaged her getaway with loads of pointless soul-searching.

She rushed down the wide sweeping staircase, then headed along the hallway towards the back of the house, retracing the steps she'd taken the night before; the cleats of her cycle shoes clattered on the polished wood flooring. She spotted her bike, parked inside the back door, and felt the tight feeling in her chest release—and her lungs deflate a little.

It's all good. A quick getaway is for the best, to save the discomfort of the morning after.

A rueful smile tugged at her lips. Never having had sex before, she didn't know the etiquette for a one-night stand, but even *she* knew the morning after was something best avoided. Especially if you'd effectively tricked your lover into taking your virginity.

But as she stepped past the door to the kitchen, a wry voice rang out.

'Alison, you're awake. I hope you slept well?'

Crap! She was totally busted.

Dominic sat on one of the stools next to a large breakfast bar. The doorway she was now standing in like a dummy led into a huge open-plan kitchen—its state-of-the art appliances and stark metal and glass design in striking contrast to the Georgian majesty of the rest of the house.

But it wasn't the kitchen design that had all her attention.

Her lover looked every inch the master of industry in a sharp two-piece business suit, polished loafers and a starched white shirt. Gold cufflinks peeked out from the sleeves of his jacket and she could spot a dimple in his chin she hadn't noticed the night before thanks to his now clean-shaven jaw.

Apart from the fluorescent lighting shining on his slicked-back hair, which suggested he'd showered fairly recently, too—probably while she was wasting time with all her pointless soul-searching over a couple of bloodstains—he couldn't have looked any more indomitable.

Her lover.

The words reverberated in her chest. Novel and delicious—and also ludicrous. Dominic wasn't her lover. He was a man she'd had one glorious night with.

As usual it was impossible to read his expression. The tenderness from the night before, when he had kissed her goodnight, was gone, replaced by a sensuous but oddly impersonal smile. He'd been in control last night, but he was even more so now.

She wrapped her arms around her waist, feeling naked beneath that searing gaze, despite her muddy cycling gear.

'How are you?' he enquired, his gruff French accent rumbling through the already far too sensitive parts of Ally's anatomy.

'I'm good, thank you,' her reply came out on an unconvincing croak.

Fabulous, Ally—can this actually get any more awkward?

She forced herself to release her arms and jerk a thumb over her shoulder. 'I was just heading off.'

'So I saw,' he said, the wry amusement not helping with her breathing difficulties. He beckoned her towards him. 'Come here. We need to talk.'

Her breathing accelerated.

What about?

She walked into the kitchen, her cleats clinking against the room's expensive slate flooring, her heartbeat gagging her.

He patted the stool next to him. 'Sit down.'

She did as she was told, aware of his gaze gliding over her bandaged leg. The rush of adrenaline, the shot of heat melting her panties, only made her more self-conscious.

'How's the leg?' he asked.

'Great. Listen, I really don't have time to—'

'I have a proposition for you,' he interrupted her, then placed his palm on a sheaf of papers on the breakfast bar next to his mug of coffee, and slid them towards her. 'It should be more than worth your time to hear me out.'

'A proposition?' She glanced at the papers, confused. They looked like legal documents. Was he going to sue her or something? What for?

'Yes, a proposition.' He tucked a knuckle under her chin and forced her gaze back to his. 'Don't look so scared, Allycat. This isn't bad, it's good.'

The amused, assured tone hadn't faltered.

'What's the proposition?' she asked.

'You haven't guessed it already?' he asked, and alongside the amusement she could hear the cynicism, which had made her sad for him the night before. It wasn't making her sad for *him* now, it was making her sad for herself. Had she ever been more clueless and out of her depth?

'No,' she said, because she had no idea what he was talking about and there wasn't much point in trying to disguise it, however much she wished she could.

'I need a wife. And you would be perfect.'

'A…what?' she said, her mouth going slack with shock. But the way her heart was pinging around her chest cavity like a ball trapped in a pinball machine told a different story. 'Did you say a *wife*?'

Because she couldn't possibly have heard *that* right.

'Yes, as I told you yesterday. I have an important deal in Brooklyn that's about to go up in smoke if I don't find a way to persuade the conservative consortium who own the land that my private life is…' he shrugged '…stable. And not about to attract any unwanted scandal. I proposed to Mira to solve the problem, but marriage to someone like her would have created other problems. Trying to persuade anyone I was madly in love with her when I could hardly stand the sight of her would have required a level of acting talent I simply do not possess. You, on the other hand...' His gaze darkened as it drifted over her. The tug of desire became a sharp yank in the hot sweet spot between her thighs.

'I... I don't know what to say,' she said, because she really didn't.

She was still processing her shock. In truth, she ought to be horrified. He was proposing marriage as if it were a business transaction.

She wasn't a romantic, and she'd known he was a deeply cynical man, from the way he'd spoken about his broken engagement with Mira yesterday... And maybe even before that, all those years ago, when he'd seemed so much older than his sixteen years.

But if she was so shocked and horrified by the ruthlessness of his proposal, how exactly did she account for her pinballing heartbeat?

'I guess I'd need more details,' she said, to buy time, until her ricocheting heartbeat wasn't threatening to ping right out of her chest.

'Smart girl,' he said, his gaze still dark with desire, but his tone stark with pragmatism. 'I'd need you to sign a non-disclosure agreement and a pre-nup, on the understanding the marriage will only last as long as I need it to. And then we would divorce. It shouldn't tie up your private life for more than three or four months, six at the most. And I'm willing to offer you a generous settlement if you help me.'

'I don't want your money,' she said, her pride kicking in at last.

'Why not?' he said. 'When you can clearly use it.'

'Because it would make me feel compromised,' she said, finally finding the horror she'd been looking for.

Hadn't his father bought her mother for that one summer? Monica Jones had been Pierre LeGrand's mistress. Maybe Ally would never be gullible enough to misconstrue such an arrangement for love, but she wasn't about to offer herself for sale either. Not after she'd seen what it had done to her mother.

'How would you be compromised?' he asked, sounding genuinely confused.

'Well, because we'd be sleeping together, wouldn't we?' she asked.

He chuckled, and lifted his hand to run his thumb down the side of her face. The flare of desire in his dark chocolate gaze was intense and searing. 'I certainly hope so. Yes.'

She captured his finger, and dragged it away from her face, resisting the urge to give into the fierce rush of need dampening her panties.

'Then, that's why,' she said, not sure where the prickle of disappointment was coming from. 'I refuse to become any man's mistress, the way my mother was. Your father bought and paid for her that summer. I know it was her fault she allowed herself to believe he felt more for her than he did, and that's why it broke her when he kicked us both out. I'd never make a mistake like that. But I still don't want to put myself in that position. With you or anyone else. It's demeaning.'

* * *

Dominic stared at the flushed and wary expression of the woman in front of him, which only made her face—the soft skin of her jaw rouged in places by the ferocity of his kisses the night before—more beautiful.

And wanted to punch a wall.

How could he have screwed up this negotiation, so fundamentally? He was an expert in the art of the deal; he knew how to get exactly what he wanted when hashing out a contract.

But as soon as he'd got everything straight in his head last night, then put in a call to his legal team, his emotions had been more engaged in this process than he would have liked—which was probably why he had made so many fundamental errors.

He couldn't risk Alison walking away from this proposal. He was running out of time and she was the perfect candidate to be his wife. She was smart and sensible and a realist. She'd had to live in the real world, unlike Mira, and, as she'd just stated, despite her inexperience she was not a romantic. And he still wanted her, even dressed in the muddy torn clothing; he would have quite happily lifted her up onto the countertop and started up where they had left off last night. In fact, as soon as he'd spotted her making a beeline for the back door, he had briefly considered trying to seduce her into agreeing to this marriage. The only reason he hadn't was that he knew she had to still be recovering from last night's excesses and he couldn't guarantee he could be gentle with her now any more than he had been able to last night.

And then there was the fact of her virginity. The more he'd thought about that last night, the more it had come to seem like a massive benefit instead of a complication.

One of the biggest problems with marrying Mira had been the thought of how hard it was going to be to persuade anyone he was in love with her. Helping Ally discover the limits of her own pleasure, showing her how much she had been missing, was a project he could get behind one hundred and one per cent— making it a great deal easier to pretend he loved her. Passion was often confused for love, after all.

He'd never slept with a virgin before, because he didn't want the responsibility, but he had never considered what it might be like to initiate a woman as innately passionate and responsive as Ally.

She had no idea how much fun they could have together. Hell, fun was too tame a word for what they could do together. On the basis of what they had shared last night, fun didn't even begin to cover it.

But he couldn't seduce her again until he'd got her to accept this deal. And he could see that what had happened between his pig of a father and her sweet, gentle, hopelessly vulnerable mother was going to be a major stumbling block. He should have figured that out sooner.

Luckily, he was good at thinking on his feet.

'To be clear, Alison,' he said, 'I won't be paying you for the sex. And you're certainly under no obligation to sleep with me. My hope was that you would want to. Last night demonstrated we have a rare chemistry...' Being a virgin, she probably didn't realise that. 'I'd love to explore that in the months ahead, making this a business arrangement with considerable benefits for both of us. But if that makes you feel demeaned, I won't press the point.'

He smiled, determined to put her at ease if it killed him.

'I certainly wouldn't expect you to sleep with me against your will.' That much at least he could be very clear on. 'And the divorce settlement I'm offering...' he placed his palm on the sheaf of papers he'd had his legal team and his accountants up all night preparing '...which includes a generous allowance and all your other expenses during the marriage plus a one-off alimony payment of a million pounds sterling when we part, is compensation for your time and your agreement to act as my devoted wife. But only in public. What we do in private is entirely up to you.'

'A m-million pounds!' she stuttered, her pale skin flushing a deep dark pink. 'Seriously?'

She looked so shell-shocked, he found his lips quirking, despite all the missteps he'd made.

He still had the upper hand in this negotiation. Of course he did. Alison was an innocent. She'd never had another lover, and from the peaks of her nipples thrusting provocatively through the soft cotton of her cycling shirt it was clear she was no more immune to him than he was to her. Plus she could definitely use the money.

'I want you to marry me, Alison,' he said, while

she struggled to close her mouth again. 'It would be a mutually beneficial agreement. I travel quite a lot and if the Waterfront deal goes ahead...' which it would as soon as he had this woman on his arm, because her integrity and honesty were as visible and beguiling as those thrusting nipples '...I'll be living in Manhattan, mostly,' he added. 'While I assume you'd want to continue attending college here? So I wouldn't require too much of your time once we have established the narrative. I would just require you to be available for events my wife would be expected to attend with me.'

He'd thought it all through. This relationship would be run on his terms and his timetable. Them having mostly separate living arrangements made sense. He *would* need to spend the majority of his time in Manhattan once this deal got the green light. And she could continue attending college in London. He didn't want this marriage to impact her life too much as it would only complicate things when they parted. And, in the unlikely event he did get bored with her, he would be able to control the amount of time they spent together.

'The narrative?' she asked. 'What narrative?'

'The narrative of our relationship,' he said. 'It is best to stick as close to the truth as possible. My publicist will work out a press release—but it will be along the lines that we knew each other years ago, got reacquainted when you made a delivery here while Mira was in Klosters and I broke off my engagement with her once I realised I was in love with you.'

'Do you think the press will buy that?' she asked. 'You only broke up with her yesterday.'

'I don't really care if they do or not. The important thing is that the Jedah Consortium believes our marriage is real—which they will once they see us together, all loved up for a few key events a week from now in New York.'

If she agreed to his proposal.

He didn't like that *if*. He wanted this settled. Now.

But she hadn't said a word. She still looked dumbfounded. He forced himself to take a breath. And back off a little, before he spooked her altogether.

Unfortunately, he didn't have the luxury of time. He had a Eurostar to catch in two hours for a meeting in Paris this afternoon, then he was travelling to Rome tomorrow for several days—and from there he would fly to New York to finish the final negotiations on the Waterfront deal. By which time, if he wanted the negotiations to go smoothly, his marriage needed to be finalised.

He waited for her to say something, but she simply stared at him.

'Do you have any questions?' he prompted as he glanced at his watch, unable to hide his impatience.

She nodded, and the tension in his chest eased.

'Could I have time to think about it?'

He had to bite his lip to stop the husky, self-satisfied laugh from bursting out of his mouth. This negotiation was already in the bag. Of course it was; he didn't even know why he had been concerned about it. If the price was right, anyone could be bought. Even a woman as artless and forthright as Alison Jones.

He didn't think less of her for it. Money was important. Something he had learned at an early age— while he and his mother had struggled to survive in the slums of Saint Denis on the outskirts of Paris, on the tiny amount she'd been able to scratch together working two jobs—after having been refused child support from the wealthy man who had discarded her as soon as she'd fallen pregnant.

Alison and her mother had struggled in a similar way after that summer thanks to their association with his father, by the sound of it. He had no idea how bad it had become, but he didn't doubt she had to be fairly desperate to be risking her life each night as a cycle courier simply to pay her rent. Alison, unlike the spoilt debutantes and career women he had dated in the past, had to know what real poverty looked like; he was offering her a route out of that.

'Unfortunately, I need a verbal commitment from you this morning,' he said. 'As I have to catch a train to Paris in…' he checked his watch '…one hour and forty-eight minutes. You can take your time to read through the paperwork and negotiate any changes with my personal assistant, Selene, before you sign. If you want to renegotiate the alimony payment I can be flexi…'

'I don't want any *more* money,' she said, sounding horrified. 'Are you nuts?'

He barked out a laugh, unable to stop his amusement at the absolute horror on her face.

'I'm not a complete mercenary,' she added force-fully.

'Noted,' he said, thinking she didn't seem that mer-cenary to him at all. If she'd pressed he would eas-ily have been persuaded to up the lump sum to two million pounds.

Getting the Waterfront deal was worth a great deal more than that to him.

The pulse of arousal struck him unawares. And he was forced to admit it wasn't just the thought of sign-ing that deal that was driving his enthusiasm. She re-ally did look good enough to eat—her eyes wide with confusion and uncertainty. The desire to capture her strawberry and chocolate taste on his tongue was all but overwhelming.

A week-long cooling-off period wouldn't be a bad thing at all. He needed to get a choke hold on his hun-ger before he made love to her again. Or things had the potential to get out of control, the way they had the first time. He wanted to show her he could savour her, that she was worth savouring.

'Come here, *ma belle*.' Before he could second-guess himself, he snagged her wrist and tugged her into the space between his knees.

Inhaling her scent—strawberries and sin—he un-furled her fingers, which had tightened into a fist. Lifting her palm to his mouth, he bit into the soft flesh beneath her thumb. Her shudder of reaction had the heat swelling in his groin. He lifted his gaze to hers, and smiled at the shocked arousal on her face.

'I want very much to make you my wife, Alison.

And I'm willing to admit my reasons for suggesting it are not all about business—nor are they entirely honourable.' In fact, if the ache in his crotch was anything to go by, he wasn't sure any of them were at the moment. 'I think the months ahead will be beneficial to both of us, in a financial sense. You'd be doing me a big favour and I'm willing to pay handsomely for your time, it's as simple as that. But this marriage could also be very entertaining for both of us, on the evidence of last night.'

He dropped her hand, and got down off the breakfast stool. Capturing her shoulders, he pressed a kiss to her forehead, forcing himself not to press, not to push, not to take what he so desperately wanted. If she agreed to his proposition, there would be more than enough time to enjoy their chemistry to his heart's content in the months to come.

'You have twenty-four hours to read over the paperwork but I need your answer now,' he said. 'What do you say, Alison? Will you marry me?'

It was wrong. She knew that. Wrong to marry for convenience, for a business deal and definitely wrong to marry him for money. Whatever he said, whatever qualifications he put on what he was offering her, a part of her knew she was basically selling herself.

Maybe she wasn't selling her body; that much was true. She believed he wouldn't press her if she told him she didn't want a sexual relationship with him, but they both knew the chances of that were precisely zilch now she'd experienced how wonderful he could make her feel.

She also knew he was right about the comparison to his father and her mother's relationship. It wasn't the same thing at all; she could see that now. In fact, it was exactly the opposite—Dominic was offering her marriage and security with no pretence of love, while his father had offered her mother nothing *but* the pretence of love.

And that was the real temptation, she realised. The offer not of marriage, but of security. She didn't want his one-million-pound divorce settlement and she'd tell his PA as much when they ironed out the details of the contract. Whatever he said, she knew her time wasn't worth that much money; it was absurd. But the chance to live in this beautiful house, to have her expenses paid for the next few months, not to have to worry about the rent or the bills or her college fees. To be able to devote her time and energies exclusively to her studies, to designing the collection she wanted to design, maybe even get some of her designs seen while she was playing his devoted wife at the high-profile events he'd talked about. And to travel to places like New York and Paris, places she'd never seen but always wanted to see. That was another major temptation.

And then there was the fairy tale of being with him at those events. That was a powerful temptation too. Because he fascinated her. He always had. She wanted to find out how he'd become so successful, what had driven him, what drove him still.

And let's not forget the sex.

Six months of sex with Dominic LeGrand was not to be sniffed at. After waiting for twenty-five years to discover what all the fuss was about, last night she'd found out. Big time. She wanted to know more. To know everything. And she couldn't think of a better tutor than a man who could make her spontaneously combust simply by crooking his finger at her and directing her to 'come here' in that demanding tone of voice.

Was it really so wrong to say yes to all of that?

As long as she kept her wits about her, and remembered that this was a temporary arrangement, which had a hard and fast sell-by date.

He was offering her a chance to change her life. Why shouldn't she take it?

Didn't she deserve this chance? After everything she'd been through? And she could help him too, to get his business to the next level.

She wanted to do that. If for no other reason than to say thank you to that rebellious boy who had made her feel special and important, once upon a time.

The buzz of the doorbell made her jump, jerking her out of her thoughts, and the frantic reasoning as she tried to make a decision.

'That will be the car to take me to St Pancras International,' he said. 'I'm sorry to rush you, but I need your answer, Allycat?' The request sounded casual, indifferent even, but she could see the muscle in his jaw flexing and the hooded look in his eyes.

He wanted her to say yes as much as she wanted to

say it, she realised. Even though he was trying hard not to show it.

That tiny glimpse of the boy she'd once known, who guarded his emotions, his needs and desires with the same ferocity she had learned to guard hers, was enough to release the dam forming in her throat.

'Okay, I'm in. Let's get married.'

Relief crossed his face first, almost as if he'd actually been in doubt about her answer.

'Fantastique,' he murmured.

A wide smile spread across his far too handsome features. And it occurred to her it was probably the first genuine smile she'd ever seen on his face.

The inappropriate joy exploded in her chest.

This isn't a real marriage, Ally. It's a fake one. For goodness' sake, get a grip.

Tugging a pen out of his jacket pocket, he scribbled something down on the legal papers on the breakfast bar. 'This is Selene's number. She is my personal assistant. She can arrange to have your belongings moved into this house while I am away. I want you to resign immediately from your job as a courier.'

'Resign?' she asked dumbly.

The smile widened as he gripped her chin between his thumb and forefinger and pressed a kiss to her mouth. 'Yes, my little daredevil. I don't want my wife's life put at risk before I have a chance to consummate our marriage.'

My wife? Consummate? Goodness.

She didn't have a chance to process the information—or the heat flooding through her system as his kiss became carnal—before he had torn his mouth away again.

'Hold that thought,' he said. 'Selene will liaise with my legal team once you sign the pre-nup, and the publicist about a press release. We will be married as soon as you land in New York.' His gaze raked over her figure, making her even more aware of her grubby, torn cycling gear. 'Selene can also arrange someone to buy you the right clothes. As irresistible as I find your current attire, I'm afraid it's not going to work at the sort of events you will have to attend as my wife.'

She didn't need a stylist. She could design and make her own clothes—she wanted to be a fashion designer, after all. But before she could point any of that out, he pulled the jewellery box out of his trouser pocket and flipped it open, to reveal the exquisite ring she'd delivered the night before. Her breathing stopped.

The doorbell buzzed again.

'Arrêtes!' he shouted, loud enough to be heard by his driver, and make her jump.

'As I have no engagement ring I would like you to wear this, to seal our promise.'

She nodded.

Lifting her hand, he threaded the ring onto her finger. It felt heavy, but not as heavy as the weight in her chest when he stroked the knuckle and smiled.

'It fits? *Oui?*' He sounded excited. But not as excited as she suddenly felt.

Excited and a bit dazed if she was honest—because the whole situation felt completely surreal.

Her gaze fixed on his. 'Yes, thank you. It's exquisite,' she said.

The quick grin dazzled her.

'Not as exquisite as you, *ma belle*,' he murmured.
The doorbell rang again and he swore softly. 'I will
see you in New York in a week's time.' Grasping her
trembling fingers, he lifted her hand to his lips and
pressed a kiss into her palm. 'Until then *au revoir*,
Madame LeGrand.'

A startled breath expelled from her lungs as she
watched him stride out of the kitchen to the waiting car.

CHAPTER SIX

I'M GOING TO be married. To Dominic LeGrand.

Ally repeated the information in her head as she stared at the woven strands of platinum and gold that Dominic had slid on her ring finger a week ago. She was still finding it difficult to grasp the reality of her situation though, the events of the past seven days whirring through her head.

She glanced out of the private jet's window as it banked into a turn over Brooklyn, ready for its descent into JFK.

Unfortunately, the sight of a city she had always wanted to explore did nothing to slow down the fleet of butterflies in her belly. That would be the same fleet of butterflies that had been going nuts in her belly ever since she'd agreed to Dominic LeGrand's proposal.

The butterflies whose wings had only got bigger and more manic when she'd moved into his town house later on that first day, her meagre stack of belongings looking overwhelmed by the expensive surroundings. Not unlike their owner, she thought with a huff of breath.

She'd signed the marriage contract the next day after a negotiation with his efficient and ridiculously friendly and accommodating UK assistant, Selene Hartley—who had been more than willing to have the one-million-pound alimony payment cut from the settlement. Given that the first payment of the allowance Dominic had stipulated in the contract had wiped out all her outstanding debts and paid the rest of her college fees, she felt that was more than fair.

The week that followed had been spent getting used to her new surroundings—not easy when there were six bedrooms and an espresso machine that could dumbfound a NASA technician—and designing and making a wardrobe fit for a queen, or rather Dominic LeGrand's high-society wife, which was a lot more exclusive. With her college closed for the Easter break, she'd used the full seven days to work on her collection. She'd set up a workshop in one of the mansion's spare bedrooms with the help of Dominic's housekeeper, Charlotte, and, after sourcing some stunning materials from a series of exclusive fabric retailers with the rest of that first allowance payment, she'd spent most days and every evening sketching and pinning and sewing. Working on the designs had helped to ground her, in between the daunting tasks of attending a doctor's appointment to get a prescription for the pill and being ferried in a limousine to a series of exclusive beauty salons and spas arranged by Selene.

In the last seven days she'd been buffed and

plucked and moisturised in places she hadn't even known existed.

The plane descended, dropping through the late afternoon sunshine, the green and gold LeGrand Nationale logo glinting on its wing.

Her newly trimmed and painted fingernails grasped the padded leather of the seat in a death grip as her stomach plunged.

Instead of parking at the passenger terminals, the jet rumbled towards a private hangar at the end of the runway, not unlike the one she had been driven to—in a limousine, of course—that morning in Heathrow.

She ran her palms down the tailored jacket of the silk trouser suit she'd finished the night before as she tried to stay focussed on her ring and her new job.

Of being Dominic LeGrand's wife.

Because this was a job, a job she was being well paid for, and she needed to remember that.

But as she waited for the jet's crew to finish the landing procedure—the butterflies began having a fit.

What on earth was she doing here? In this rarefied world. For goodness' sake, she'd never been on a budget airline before now—let alone a private jet.

The butterflies dive-bombed into her belly as she examined her suit for the five billionth time. Had she made a major error designing and making her own wardrobe for this trip? She had her own unique style, one she'd developed and explored during her two years of fashion college, and had enjoyed turning into reality during the long hours spent working at her sewing machine in the last week to help calm her nerves. But what if the clothes she'd designed were all wrong? She might have her own style, but it was an urban, edgy, East London style. How would it be received in the kind of circles Dominic moved in—circles she knew nothing about? What would he do if he found out she'd pocketed the money he'd given her to buy an exclusive wardrobe and made her own clothes? Especially if her designs made him a laughing stock? Would he be angry with her? Furious? Could he sue? Had she already screwed up the biggest opportunity of her life?

The increasingly frantic thoughts clashed with the dive-bombing mutant butterflies in her belly.

'Madame LeGrand?' The hostess smiled down at her, using the name on the travel manifest.

'Yes?' Ally croaked.

'Are you ready to disembark?' the hostess asked in her heavily accented English, the beatific smile not faltering.

Not at all.

As panic closed her throat she forced her fingernails to release their grip on the seat.

'The immigration officials have checked your documents and Monsieur LeGrand waits for you,' the hostess added, sweeping her arm towards the door of the aircraft in a polite indication for Ally to get a move on.

Ally understood; the poor woman had been on her feet for seven hours.

'Right, sorry,' she said, unlocking the seat belt and standing.

She brushed her trembling palms down the sheer blue silk. And made her way to the front of the plane.

As she stepped out onto the outer stairs, she spotted Dominic standing at the bottom busy tapping out a message on his phone with both thumbs. A man with a briefcase stood beside him who had to be the marriage officiant Selene had told her would be there to issue their marriage licence as soon as she arrived. Apparently the marriage itself would be performed tomorrow, as the law in New York required a twenty-four hour wait after the licence was issued. But it wasn't the thought of the formalities that had the dive-bombing butterflies going up in flames.

Even with his head bent, Dominic looked more gorgeous and overwhelming than he had a week ago. She couldn't help noticing how the seams of his shirt stretched over his biceps as she made her way down the gangway on unsteady legs. How could he seem part savage, even in a business suit?

He's going to be your husband. Seriously?

Her heels clicked on the tarmac and Dominic stopped typing.

His dark chocolate gaze coasted over her figure, burning right through the silk. His eyes flared as his gaze finally met hers, and her ribs tightened around her lungs like a vice.

'*Bonjour*, Alison.' The husky accent rippled through her, setting off bursts of sensation—and making her far too aware of the hours spent tenderising her skin in the spas and salons he'd paid for over the last week.

Was that why every inch of her body felt as if it were about to burst into flames too, along with the dive-bombing butterflies?

'How was your flight?' he asked.

'Great,' she rasped as he approached, and she became aware again of exactly how tall he was.

He had to be at least six foot three.

Thank goodness she'd used some of the money he'd given her to purchase a range of high heels. She was hardly a small woman, having reached her full height of five foot seven at the age of fifteen, but he dwarfed her, just as he had when they were kids. She'd been considerably shorter as a thirteen-year-old. But had he been this tall as a teenager? He certainly hadn't been this broad. Maybe it was the way he'd filled out that made him so much more intimidating.

Stop staring at his muscles.

She forced herself not to step back, but she couldn't hide the shudder of reaction when he took her hand and brushed a kiss across the knuckles.

'You look exquisite,' he said, the approval heating his dark gaze almost as disconcerting as the sensation now shooting up her arm and reigniting those flaming mutant dive-bombing butterflies in her belly.

'Thank you,' she said, but the praise hadn't helped to mitigate her nerves one bit.

He introduced her to the man standing beside him. The balding young man who had been especially hired from the New York City Clerks' Office verified her identity. After they had signed the forms, he issued their licence and explained he would return to perform the ceremony at Dominic's apartment tomorrow, at which point the marriage certificate could be issued.

'*Bon,*' Dominic murmured, after the clerk had smiled and left. 'Only one more day and we can get all the paperwork out the way.'

Ally shivered, knowing that, whatever the officiant said, this marriage was already binding, at least for her, because she'd made a promise seven days ago. A promise she had no desire to renege on.

She felt suddenly naked beneath Dominic's gaze, and the truth was she almost was. What had possessed her to wear nothing but a bra under the jacket?

You idiot! Ruining the jacket's line is not going to matter if you pass out at his feet before you even get a chance to say I do.

Dominic's lips quirked—the way they had when he'd proposed a week ago, as if he were sharing a private joke with her.

'Why do you look so terrified, my darling almost wife?' His gruff accent lingered on the word 'wife'— both provocative and possessive. 'I promise not to seal our bargain until we are somewhere private.'

The laugh she managed to huff out past her constricted lungs didn't sound as confident as she'd hoped.

'That's good,' she said, tugging her tingling fingers out of his grasp—the thought of him sealing the bargain they'd made a week ago sending a battalion of pheromones hurtling to every one of her erogenous zones along with those blasted butterflies. 'I wouldn't want to get arrested my first ten seconds on US soil.'

He laughed, the rough sound raw enough to stimulate her nerve-endings even more.

'*Touché*, Alison,' he murmured, the admiration in his dark hooded eyes so compelling she found herself basking in his approval. Even though she knew she shouldn't.

It's a job. It's a job. It's a job.

But the reminder couldn't stop the flaming mutant butterflies in her belly from going berserk as his warm arm banded around her waist and he led her across the tarmac to a waiting car—which was a huge black limousine. Of course.

Dominic clicked his seat belt into place, thankful for the physical restraint as the jacket Alison was wearing opened to reveal a seductive hint of purple lace while she strapped herself into the car next to him.

She looked absolutely exquisite, her willowy frame displayed to perfection in the striking blue suit, the shadow of cleavage making it hard for him to concentrate on anything other than the desire to get her back to his apartment as soon as physically possible.

He'd prepared for her arrival today by convincing himself his physical reaction to her a week ago had been exaggerated thanks to his long sexual drought, and the expediency of ensuring she agree to become his wife.

But as soon as he'd heard her heels on the tarmac,

and looked up from his smartphone, he'd known he'd been kidding himself.

Dressed in grubby Lycra or oversized sweats, Alison Jones had been subtly sexy. Now she was stunning.

Long, slim, and stylish, her figure in the tailored suit looked both toned and athletic while at the same time being supremely feminine. And her striking bone structure, the translucent skin and those bottomless eyes the colour of a fine whisky, only enhanced by the hint of eyeliner and the lush sparkle of lip gloss, made her irresistible.

He wanted to undo the one button holding her jacket together, capture her full breasts in his palms and fasten his lips on the rampaging pulse fluttering in the delicate well of her collarbone.

The driving need to take her to bed as soon as was humanly possible was so strong, in fact, it had the potential to be problematic.

He didn't like being ruled by his desires—as much as he enjoyed sex, he had never had a problem controlling his hunger before now—and becoming addicted to Alison was not supposed to be part of this arrangement.

So stop leering at her and start talking.

He dragged his gaze away from her cleavage as the car left the airport and headed onto the expressway. She had her nose pressed against the window, obviously absorbing every new sight and sound, like a child outside a candy store.

'So you've never been to the States before?' he asked.

Her head swung round. 'I've never been anywhere before,' she said with an unabashed smile. 'Apart from Provence. But I've always wanted to come here. It's so exciting. Like being in a movie.' Her unguarded enthusiasm, like everything else about her, was utterly beguiling.

Her expression sobered suddenly, so much so he could see the nerves. He wondered what on earth she had to be nervous about.

'By the way, could I ask you something about the events we'll be attending while I'm here…?' she asked.

'What about them?'

'Do you think…?' She paused and bit into her lip, sending another shaft of heat straight to his groin.

'What is it?' he demanded, more curtly than he had intended as the lip bite tortured him. Was she doing it deliberately? If only she were, he thought, feeling less and less in control of the situation. But somehow he doubted it. Because… She had been a virgin.

What had seemed like such a boon before he'd married her—PR wise—seemed less so as the hot blood surged to his crotch with very little provocation. Why did the fact of her inexperience make him all the more eager to explore every aspect of her pleasure?

'I just wondered, do you think this outfit will be suitable?' she finally blurted out.

'*Excusez-moi?*' he asked, because it sounded as if she'd just asked him to give her fashion advice.

'This outfit?' She spread her arms wide, making the button strain even more.

He stifled a groan.

'Do you think it would work? For the kinds of events you were talking about…'

Mon Dieu, she *was* asking him for fashion advice.

'Selene gave me an itinerary,' she continued, the words pouring out as her nerves got the better of her. 'So I know what we're doing. But I've never been to the theatre before. Or the opening of an art gallery… So I had to wing it, and rely on some Internet research to figure out what to…' A guilty flush flowed into her cheeks. 'What to bring with me.'

He sat for a moment, trying to wrestle his libido under control and come up with a credible answer. Because it seemed to be important to her. And silently cursed his personal assistant. Why hadn't Selene employed an expert to help Alison with her wardrobe? Surely there were people who could advise you on your clothing? He was fairly sure he'd shelled out a small fortune for such a person for Mira. But it was too late to suggest that now. He didn't want to make her more nervous or unsure of herself.

'Alison, your outfit is stunning,' he said with feeling, giving the flowing lines of the suit another once-over. That at least was certainly not a lie. 'It will do perfectly.'

Who the hell cared if what she was wearing was the norm, or suitable? he decided. She looked incredible in the suit—enough to tie his libido into knots in sixty seconds or less.

'You really think so? You like the suit?' she asked,

and he could hear her insecurity again. 'It's what you had in mind?'

'I *love* the suit. And I didn't have anything particular in mind,' he said, because the truth was what she would be wearing had not featured at all in any of the many, many erotic fantasies he'd entertained about her in the last week. 'Women's fashions are not my forte,' he added, just in case that wasn't entirely obvious. 'But on the basis of this outfit, I'm looking forward to seeing whatever else you've selected for this trip.' Which wasn't truth either, because he'd been looking forward to stripping her out of her new wardrobe a great deal more. But the tentative smile that curved her lips made him glad he'd lied. 'Does that set your mind at rest?' he finished, trying to keep his mind at least nominally out of his pants and on the main reason why she was with him in New York.

Good to know at least one of us is able to do that.

The sheen of pleasure made the amber of her eyes twinkle in the sinking sunlight streaming through the car window, the distinctive hue becoming all the more captivating.

His pulse bumped his own collarbone as the irony of the situation occurred to him.

How exactly had he ended up having to persuade his own fiancée how attractive he found her?

'I'm so glad you like it,' she said, emotion thickening her voice. 'It means a lot to me.'

He steeled himself against the visceral tug of heat in his groin and the unsettling realisation she was genuinely moved by his compliment.

He'd never had a problem complimenting women on their appearance, especially when they looked as exquisite as Alison did in that moment, but there was something about her gratitude that reminded him of the little girl who had followed him around that summer, and how he'd clung to the open adoration in her eyes.

He cut off the thought, determined to forget the lost children they'd been that summer.

He wasn't that reckless, unhappy boy any more, desperate for any sign of approval. And she wasn't that little girl who had showered him with such unguarded affection.

He'd needed her to like him all those years ago—because under the veneer of teenage hostility and indifference, he'd been scared and confused, unable to understand why his father hated him so.

But he certainly did not need Alison—or anyone else—to like him now.

His phone vibrated, breaking the strange spell. He pulled it out of his pocket. And read the text from his business manager.

We have a problem with the Consortium. Mira Kensington just sold her story to the London Post.

He swore viciously under his breath and clicked on the call button.

Stop being a damn sap, LeGrand. Time to focus on what this marriage is actually supposed to achieve, instead of what it isn't.

* * *

'Dominic, is everything okay?' Ally asked as her fiancé swore in French.

'Yes, but I need to take this call,' he said, his tone curt and dismissive.

Everything didn't sound okay as he spoke in hushed tones to whoever was on the other end of the line in a stream of furious French.

After picking up that the conversation had something to do with Mira, she turned back to the window and tried not to listen.

Because thinking about his ex-fiancée would destroy the happy buzz his compliments had triggered.

A happy buzz that had gone some way to controlling her nerves—and all the feelings of inadequacy that had hijacked her during the flight.

Maybe it was pathetic how much she had enjoyed hearing him say he loved her outfit. And she probably ought to be shot for fishing for a compliment so shamelessly, but still his hot, unguarded approval had meant something.

She'd always believed that fanciful little girl had died after the summer in Provence. Because ever since that night she'd been forced to grow up, be a realist, not dream too big or too passionately, because she hadn't wanted to risk having her spirit crushed again. But that little girl hadn't died, she'd just been waiting for an opportunity like this.

Hearing Dominic's praise for her work, and knowing it was genuine, even if their marriage would be fake, had made her feel as if that child was able to believe in herself again… At least a little bit. And that felt liberating and empowering in a way she hadn't felt in a long time.

The car crossed the Brooklyn Bridge into Manhattan. The legendary skyline rose on the other side of the East River, the skyscrapers like silent sentries to the city's wealth and prominence.

As they drove through downtown she gazed in awe at the canyons of steel and glass and the bustle of traffic and people at street level—like London but so much more urgent, and manic, and less restrained. But as she heard Dominic finish his call it was hard for her to stay focussed on the excitement of being in a new city for the first time in her life.

His tension was palpable as he shoved his phone back into his pocket.

She had caught snippets of the conversation. Her French certainly wasn't fluent, but as well as Mira's name being mentioned several times she'd heard the word *'vierge'.*

Virgin.

Had Dominic been talking about her virginity to someone? Because she didn't even know how to feel about that. Embarrassed mostly, but also confused. Why would that be relevant, to anything at all? The only way to find out what was going on, though, was to ask.

The muscle in his cheek was flexing as he stared out of the window, obviously thinking something through.

'Is there a problem?' she asked.

His head turned. He looked as if he was angry, but trying not to show it.

'No,' he said, too dogmatically to be entirely believable. She might know nothing about his business, but she knew when she was being hoodwinked.

'If there's a problem, I might be able to help,' she said.

The hard line of his lips quirked in a reluctant smile. 'Are you serious?'

She nodded. 'Yes, I am.' She had no idea why he found that amusing, but she decided him being amused was better than him being furious. 'The only reason I'm here is to help you get this deal sorted out.' She coughed slightly, as the blush burned in her cheeks. Okay, that was a blatant lie. 'Well, the *main* reason I'm here is to help you get this deal sorted out.'

'Is that so?' he asked, his eyebrows launching up his forehead as he choked out a laugh.

'Well, yes,' she said.

'*Dieu*, Alison. Have I told you yet how damn adorable you are?'

'Maybe,' she said, glad to see him smile. But even gladder she'd caused that smile.

Especially when he picked up her hand, opened her fingers and pressed his lips into her palm.

Her fingers curled around his cheek, heat shooting into her abdomen.

'Damn but I want you so much,' he said. The admission sounded a little tortured—which made her smile even more.

'Well, good,' she said. 'Because so do I.'

'*Bien*,' he murmured, with that hot possessive look in his gaze that was guaranteed to get the mutant butterflies partying in her pants.

He clasped her hand, and squeezed it. 'Okay, if I tell you what the call was about, will you promise not to be offended?'

'Of course,' she said. Confused now. Because he looked pained. And the slash of regret wasn't his usual default. He struck her as a man who made a point of regretting nothing.

'That was my business manager, Etienne Franco, on the phone. The consortium are questioning the validity of our love match because my former fiancée decided to give an exclusive interview to a British tabloid newspaper, which implied you're...' He paused, the muscle in his cheek flexing again. 'How did she put it in the article? "Being paid to service my sexual appetites while posing as my wife."'

Ally cleared her throat, not sure what to say, because although she knew she *should* be offended by Mira's comments, the fact he seemed to be offended enough for both of them had a bubble of pleasure forming in her throat.

'That's a bit unfair,' she said, trying to sound stern while the bubble of pleasure burst, creating a warm glow through her entire body. 'Seeing as she's never even met me—well, not properly,' she corrected, remembering the altercation on the street.

Damn it, why isn't she furious?

'Alison, it's not just unfair of her. It's libellous.

She's basically suggesting you're a prostitute in a national newspaper.' Dominic ground out the words, still so furious with Mira he could barely speak. But the truth was he was just as disgusted with himself. He should have guessed his ex would pull a stunt like this. And he hadn't done a damn thing to prevent it, or protect Alison.

In fact he'd basically set her up for exactly this kind of attack.

An attack that she was uniquely vulnerable to, not just because she appeared to have no sense of guile whatsoever, but because, as he had just discovered, she had been in much harsher financial straits than he had assumed.

As well as Mira's bitchy comments, the *Post* article had included a detailed description of the harsh realities of Alison's life before he had 'plucked her from obscurity'—and it had turned his stomach. The struggles she'd faced in the last twelve years had been a great deal harder than he had imagined. It seemed she and her mother had been living in abject poverty through her teens—ever since the night his father had thrown them off the estate. Alison had been supporting them both since the age of fifteen with a series of part-time jobs. And her debts had only increased after her mother's death from an overdose of prescription painkillers four years ago.

He'd exploited her destitution to feed the rags-to-riches Cinderella narrative his publicist had used to explain their 'fairy-tale romance' but now it had backfired on him spectacularly. Because he'd had no idea how close it was to the truth.

His father had destroyed her life that night... But his father hadn't been the only one responsible for what had happened to Monica and by extension her daughter.

He pushed the bitter memories to one side.

Do not go there. You can't go back and solve what you did.

But, unfortunately, telling himself that didn't make him feel any less responsible. Not just for what had happened that night, but for the trashing of Alison's reputation now.

'I'm going to sue her and the newspaper. I refuse to have you slandered in that way,' he said, because that at least was explainable.

Maybe his marriage to Alison was essentially a business arrangement, but by this time tomorrow she would finally be his wife, so of course he would have to protect her reputation.

'Wouldn't it be better just to ignore it?' Alison asked, her teeth tugging on her bottom lip again, and sending a now incendiary shot of heat to his groin.

'No, it would not.'

'But, Dominic, what about the Waterfront deal?' she said as his furious thoughts galloped ahead of him.

'What about it?' he barked. Why was she being so damn reasonable and accommodating about this outrage?

'Surely getting embroiled in a legal battle with a British tabloid isn't going to be good for that? Especially if they find out our marriage *is* essentially a business arrangement after all.'

I don't care about the damn deal.

He opened his mouth, to say the words that ricocheted through his consciousness. Then closed it again. As his fury and indignation slammed into a brick wall.

What the hell had he just thought? Hell, what had he almost said? Out loud?

He *did* care about the deal. The deal was everything. The deal was why Alison was here. Why *he* was here. The only reason this marriage was happening. And she was right: if he sued Mira and the *London Post* the real reason behind their marriage would come to light.

'The deal will be fine,' he said, even though he wasn't entirely sure.

Calm the hell down and think.

'I told the business manager to point out to the consortium you were a virgin. That you have never slept with another man before you slept with me. Making you the furthest thing from a prostitute.'

The foolish spurt of pride hit him unawares—the way it had when he had told Etienne.

What the heck was that about, too?

Alison's lack of experience was something he could use, to help make their marriage seem more authentic and to help him secure this deal. That was the only reason it was relevant. Why should he care if he was her first?

'Oh,' she said as a delectable blush rioted across her cheeks. And he almost laughed at the irony.

She was embarrassed about her virginity, but not about being dubbed a prostitute in a British tabloid.

'Did you *have* to tell him that?' she said. 'It's so personal.'

'I know, and I apologise, but I wanted to refute Mira's claims in the strongest possible terms.'

To secure this damn deal, which I completely forgot about a minute ago. Mon Dieu, *LeGrand, get a grip.*

'They're not going to put *that* in the papers, are they?' she asked, sounding horrified.

The rough chuckle burst out without warning. After all the fury and recriminations, the agony of knowing he'd failed her—and jeopardised the deal, which was of course much more important—her reaction seemed hopelessly naïve, but also ridiculously endearing. So endearing it managed to achieve several things at once—defuse his temper, restore his sense of humour and, most importantly of all, restore his sense of perspective.

He'd overreacted, not just to Mira's attack, but also to the disturbing news about Alison's circumstances in the last twelve years. That much was obvious.

What had happened on that night twelve years ago had no bearing on their circumstances now. And yes, maybe he was using Alison, but he had been upfront about that and she had made an informed decision to sign the contract. She was on board with all of this. And he was paying her a million pounds for her pains. He hadn't deceived her or seduced her into this situation. She had come of her own free will.

Alison was also correct. Ignoring Mira's attack made sense—the story would die a death more quickly that way. He'd already told Etienne about Alison's unsullied state to refute the claims made in the article with the consortium. And displaying their happy marriage for all to see over the next few days by escorting his new wife to a few high-profile events would hardly be a chore given that he was struggling to keep his hands off her.

The reason he had lost perspective about Mira's article and its fallout was even easier to explain.

An idiotic part of him had panicked that Alison might back out of their arrangement at the eleventh hour—thanks to the frustrating extra twenty-four hours the officiant had insisted they would have to wait before dotting the last of the *i*'s on their deal. Plus he'd waited seven whole days to consummate this damn deal already—while enduring the sort of sweaty erotic dreams every night that hadn't plagued him since he was a boy.

But Alison wasn't going to back out of this deal. And he didn't need to wait any longer to seal their deal, in the only way that mattered.

'No, they won't put it in the papers,' he said. But couldn't resist the urge to run a thumb over her lips. The sooner he fed this hunger, the sooner it would stop messing with his head. 'But why are you embarrassed about it?'

'Probably because I'm twenty-five years old and being a virgin at that age makes me seem sad and like a bit of a freak!'

'Firstly, you're not a virgin any more,' he said, unable to keep the smugness out of his voice. 'And secondly, I don't think it makes you a freak. It simply makes you discerning. You waited, until a man came along who was a good enough lover to give you the spectacular experience you deserved for your first time,' he added, teasing her now—and going the full smug in the process. 'Which isn't sad, it's smart.'

She huffed out a laugh, but the sparkle of amusement in her eyes was like a drug. When, exactly, had making her smile become so addictive?

'Spoken like a guy with an ego the size of Manhattan,' she said, but the embarrassed flush had begun to fade, so he considered her mockery well earned.

'*Touché*, again, Alison,' he said, grinning back at her as the car stopped in front of the loft apartment building he owned in Nolita.

Nolita, short for North of Little Italy, was the thriving neighbourhood that had been up-and-coming in the nineties but had now firmly arrived, with a young, trendy, arthouse crowd moving in to the turn-of-the-century brownstones and rehabbed tenement blocks.

'What a beautiful building—is this where you live?' Alison asked, her enthusiasm making his ribs feel suspiciously tight.

He'd bought the condemned brick and cast-iron building on the corner of Lafayette five years ago for a steal, then proceeded to work a miracle—gutting and then refurbishing the structure to preserve its historic integrity in the elegant arched windows and cast-iron balconies, while at the same time giving it a luxury, high-spec interior. The ten-storey block now housed the offices of LN's US-based operation, and a four-bed, four-bath penthouse loft apartment where he stayed when he was in the city.

'Yes, I own the building. LN's offices take up the first nine floors and then my apartment's on the top,' he said, then realised he was boasting and didn't know why. He'd never felt the need to impress a woman before.

'It's gorgeous,' she said. 'I love the art deco details.'

He got out of the car, not sure why his chest tightened even more at her praise. 'I'm glad you approve.'

He offered his hand and she took it.

The lapels of her suit jacket—the jacket that had been driving him wild as soon as she'd stepped onto American soil—spread as she stepped out of the car, giving him another provocative glimpse of pale flesh and purple lace.

The familiar shot of adrenaline pounded back into his crotch.

The chauffeur stepped to the back of the vehicle to help the doorman with their luggage, leaving them cocooned on the sidewalk, the car door shielding them from passers-by. He couldn't see any photographers, even though Etienne had suggested they might be besieged for the next few days as a result of Mira's story.

But he found himself tugging her into his arms regardless.

He'd waited seven days to get his mouth on Alison again. And now she was as good as his wife, what better way to finally put his idiotic overreaction to bed and get this agreement back where it was always supposed to be?

He placed his hands on her hips, until she stood flush against his body.

'Madame LeGrand,' he murmured. 'Time to start practising your act as the dutiful wife.'

Although it didn't feel like just an act any more.

But then, it wasn't an act, entirely. This was always supposed to be a business arrangement with benefits. So why not start claiming the benefits?

She looked up through long lashes, her amber eyes like those of a doe who had spotted the huntsman taking aim. And it occurred to him how inexperienced she still was. The punch of lust at the thought that she had only ever been his was visceral and basic and impossible to deny—so he didn't even try.

Her virginity had clearly turned him into a caveman. But he could do nothing but run with it now.

She lifted her arms and flattened her palms on his chest—the movement as brave as it was arousing.

'Es-tu prêtes?' he whispered against her neck, his ability to speak English deserting him momentarily as he inhaled the rich, fresh scent of her, that glorious combination of strawberries and chocolate that had driven him wild in London—far too long ago.

Are you ready?

'Very,' she whispered back, her body shivering with reaction as he pressed his lips to the flutter of her pulse beneath her ear.

Plunging his fingers into her hair, he felt her soft

sob against his lips before he angled her head and plundered. But as soon as his tongue tangled with hers, the surge of adrenaline became an unstoppable force.

He thrust deep, setting up an erotic rhythm spurred on by the grinding hunger beneath his belt.

She responded instinctively, her body surrendering to his will, her soft curves yielding to the hard contours as he pressed her back against the car's paintwork.

Had he ever been this desperate before, the need to rip off her clothes and plunge into the tight wet heart of her all but overwhelming? His hand slipped inside the open lapel of her jacket beneath the lacy bra until he was cupping the soft flesh of her breast, rejoicing in the feel of her nipple swelling against his palm.

'Mr LeGrand, do you have anything to say about Mira Kensington's piece in the London papers?'

The shouted question had him rearing back just as a camera flashed in his face.

Alison gasped and stiffened. The shocked arousal in her eyes turning the hot blood now running through his veins to wild fire.

The reporter stepped closer to shove a microphone between them as she scrambled to right her clothing.

The son of a...

'Get away from my fiancée,' he shouted in English, then repeated the command in French with a great deal more emphasis. The man seemed to get the message because he scurried away with his photographer.

Dominic grabbed Alison's hand.

'Let's finish this in private,' he said, realising the mistake of kissing her in public. He wanted to convince the consortium this relationship was real—but having a photograph of him baring her breast on the sidewalk emblazoned on the celebrity blogs would be counterproductive.

An older woman winked at him as he marched past. And a couple of teenage boys whistled from their spot on a nearby wall.

Dieu, *forget the paparazzi—he'd just put on a show for the whole damn neighbourhood.*

Leading Alison to the elevator at the back of the lobby, he stabbed the button. Damn it, he'd been about to take her right there on a public street.

He hadn't been aware of anything, not of the reporter or the photographer, who'd probably taken more than a few pictures, or the people watching, all he'd been aware of was her—the feel of her soft flesh cradling his erection, her fingers massaging his scalp, the drugging taste of her invading his nostrils and overwhelming his senses, the feel of her nipple hardening in his hand.

The elevator arrived quickly and whisked them to the top floor.

As they walked into the apartment her hand flexed in his and he heard her breath catch.

'Wow, what an incredible view,' she said.

He let go of her, and tried to focus. To give her a moment. To give them both a moment—before he dragged her straight from the street into the bedroom.

Iron colonnades broke up the penthouse's vast

open-plan living space. The designer had insisted on lots of rugs and some bespoke pieces of furniture to warm the harsh concrete floors. Several stories higher than the surrounding buildings, the penthouse's leaded glass walls afforded incredible one-hundred-and-eighty-degree views of the neighbourhoods of SoHo and Little Italy. The Empire State stood proud to the north and the new World Trade Center rose like a phoenix from the ashes of Ground Zero to the south.

The breathtaking view was the apartment's signature feature, but he couldn't even see it because all he could focus on was Alison as she spun round in a circle to capture it all, her cheeks reddened from his kisses. He rubbed his chin and encountered the beard scruff he hadn't shaved since that morning— he needed to slow the hell down. Give her some time to adjust.

But as his erection pounded in his pants, the way it had done every night he'd spent in his bed here alone, the only way he could think of to handle the hunger was to feed it.

'Alison, do you want a tour of the apartment or to finish what we just started on the street outside?' he managed.

Maybe his voice sounded rough and raw, and demanding, but he was giving her a choice, damn it.

She blushed deliciously, her gaze settling on the prodigious erection tenting his pants. 'I'm sorry,' she said.

'Don't be sorry.' He took her hand, squeezed it

to reassure her. 'Just tell me you want this as much as me.'

'I do.'

It was all the permission he needed.

Tightening his grip, he led her across the living space towards the master bedroom.

As soon as they were inside, he slammed the door, and unhooked the button on her jacket that had been tormenting him since she'd stepped off the plane. He slid the jacket off her shoulders. The soft flesh of her breasts was pushed up like an offering in the purple lace. He slid his thumbs into the waistband of the suit's trousers, but couldn't seem to find the fastening.

'Take them off. I need you naked,' he demanded, deciding he couldn't waste time searching for it. His hands were starting to shake.

She quivered, and drew a zip down at the side of the trousers. He was glad to see her fingers were as shaky as his.

'Lose the bra, too,' he said, and watched as she freed her breasts from the lacy confinement.

But as he hooked his fingers in the elastic of her panties, ready to drag them off, she pressed a trembling hand to his shirt. 'Please, I need you naked too.'

The surge of desire at the urgency in her voice had his groin throbbing so hard he was scared he might explode too soon.

Don't be insane, you have never done that. Not even as an untried kid.

He shucked his own clothes in record time, then

tumbled her onto the bed. The bed he'd dreamed about having her in far too often in the last week.

But instead of climbing up there with her—and ending this even sooner—he grasped her hips, tugged her closer until she was sitting on the edge and knelt down, his knees sinking into the rug.

The sharp gasp as he hooked one of her legs over his shoulder, exposing her completely to him, only increased the surge of desire.

He pressed his face into her sex, inhaling her intoxicating scent. *Dieu*, but she smelt delicious—not just of strawberries and chocolate, but of heat and desire. He blew against the trimmed triangle of chestnut curls and licked the slick seam.

She moaned, her fingers plunging in his hair. He tasted her, circling, tantalising, listening to her throaty sobs, learning her contours, finding what she liked, and what she loved. Holding her open with his thumbs, he found the hard, swollen nub with his lips and suckled hard.

She cried out, jerking as the spontaneous orgasm ripped through her. His erection hardened to iron. Her juices soaked his tongue as he lapped up the last of her pleasure.

He rose over her.

With her skin flushed, her nipples begging for his attention, her body sated, and her eyes dazed, she was like a banquet laid out before him. The vague thought occurred to him that he might never get enough of her.

But then the need to feast on her overwhelmed him.

* * *

Ally's breath clogged, her sex already tender from Dominic's mouth as he notched the huge head of his erection at her core. And thrust deep.

The tight sheath stretched to receive him this time, the pleasure becoming so intense as he filled her, it was almost pain.

He rocked out, thrust back, ruthlessly stroking the spot he had found a week ago, working her into a frenzy of need. The orgasm exploded from her core this time, in shattering waves of sensation.

The desperate pants, the moaning sobs turned to hoarse cries of agony and then ecstasy as the wave crashed over her.

He grunted, and hot seed exploded inside her.

He groaned and collapsed on top of her.

She held him, her fingers shaking. Her body drifting in afterglow as her lungs seemed to collapse in her chest.

Why was she struggling to breathe? She'd climaxed. The sex was as good if not better than their first time.

He groaned and rolled off her, easing the still large erection out of her with some difficulty.

'I forgot to ask,' he said. 'Are you on the pill?'

The tightness in his voice made the breath thicken in her lungs.

'Yes.'

'Dieu merci,' he whispered, his relief palpable. *Thank God.*

It was one of the stipulations in the contract she'd signed. He'd provided a detailed medical report to prove it would be safe for them to have unprotected sex, but had requested that if she agreed to a sexual relationship with him, she would also arrange oral contraception.

The clause had made sense to her at the time she'd signed it. Neither of them wanted an accident. Risking bringing a child into a situation like theirs would be disastrous—but as she lay beside him, the scent of sex and sweat surrounding them, his question had an odd shaft of melancholy rippling through her tired body.

Because it reinforced the limits of this relationship.

Not that she needed to have them reinforced.

She looked away from him, towards the wall of windows that looked out onto the famous skyline. The sun had started to set, adding a romantic glow to the silhouettes of the Empire State and the Chrysler Building and the cluster of other skyscrapers to the north she couldn't identify.

Get it together, Alison. It's not cynical to be on the pill—it's smart.

She listened to him get off the bed and disappear into the bathroom; the lock clicked.

When he returned a few minutes later, she had managed to drag her exhausted body under the sheets.

He wore a robe, but still the glimpse of washboard abs had the traitorous pheromones skittering back into her tender sex.

But she yawned, as the exhaustion of the flight, and everything that had happened since she had arrived, began to claim her.

'You should get some sleep,' he said, but the suggestion seemed strangely impersonal. 'You can stay in here and I'll pick one of the other bedrooms.'

What? They weren't going to share a bedroom?

A silly wobble of emotion tightened around her throat, but she didn't protest as she watched him gather a few pieces of clothing from the dresser drawers.

'I'll get the staff to reorganise our belongings tomorrow,' he said.

'You don't have to give up your bedroom,' she said, feeling stupidly bereft.

'Not a problem,' he said. Then strode back to the bed, leant down and kissed her forehead. The wobble intensified. 'Make yourself at home,' he added. 'Manny the doorman can order you in any food you want—just dial zero on the interlink. He can also arrange a car and driver if you want to go sightseeing or shopping tomorrow.'

'You won't be here?' she asked, then wanted to bite back the suggestion because it made her sound needy, and clingy. And she'd never been either.

'I'm going to be busy with the deal negotiations until tomorrow night... I'll see you back here at seven when the clerk is due and then to escort you to...' he paused '...whatever event we're supposed to be seen at.'

'The opening of the Claxton Gallery?' she said, because she'd memorised the schedule Selene had given her.

Stupidly she'd been looking forward to spending the next twenty-four hours with him, getting to know

him a little better, because there had been nothing on
the schedule. She realised the foolishness of that sup-
position, though. He was a busy man, and his business came first. He was certainly under no obligation
to entertain her while she was here.

'On the Upper East Side? At eight?' she added,
because his face had gone blank, his gaze dipping
down to the place where her fingers clutched the sheet
over her breasts.

His head lifted. '*Oui*—that.' His smile seemed
tight and a little strained, and she wasn't sure he had
even heard her, but still the wry tilt of his lips helped
the breath to release from her lungs. 'Will you be okay
on your own?' he asked.

'Yes, of course,' she said. 'Terrific.'

But as he left the room, the wobble became a wave.

CHAPTER SEVEN

'HI. IT'S ALISON, isn't it?'

Ally swung round from the lavish buffet laid out against the raw redbrick wall of the stark modernist art gallery to find a beautiful and heavily pregnant woman—her plate already laden with delicacies—smiling at her.

'Yes, it's Alison, although everyone calls me Ally,' she said.

'Everyone except your new husband.' The woman's smile became sweetly conspiratorial. 'It's very hot the way Dominic calls you Alison in that French accent. Sorry, I should introduce myself. My name's Megan De Rossi—I'm Dario De Rossi's wife. De Rossi Corp were one of Dominic's early investors when he moved LN's main offices to New York a few years ago.' She offered her hand. 'Which means I've basically been abandoned too—because my husband and your husband have been talking shop ever since we arrived.'

Ally took Megan's hand, feeling hideously exposed by the woman's relaxed, friendly manner. She'd never felt less like Dominic's wife. Other than their marriage ceremony—which had been dealt with in a few short sentences—they had hardly spoken to each other since yesterday evening.

Not since their mind-blowing session to seal their marriage bargain. When he'd treated her as if she were a particularly sumptuous treat that deserved to be savoured and devoured at the same time—then abandoned her.

The memory of their lovemaking and his abrupt departure had kept her awake in the huge king-size bed most of the night. And she'd been obsessing about it most of the day while she took the car and driver Dominic had insisted she use to do some window-shopping in the fashion boutiques of the East Village.

Dominic had appeared at the same time as the clerk to complete the marraige and escort her to this event as scheduled an hour ago, but since the perfunctory ceremony, he'd barely spoken to her—far too busy typing on his phone.

She'd felt his eyes on her when she'd stood beside him in front of the clerk, but no compliment on her outfit had been forthcoming like the last time. And her enquiries during their ride over about how the deal negotiations were going had elicited one-syllable replies.

During the silent, tense ride in the limo, a thousand and one questions had spun through her mind—had she done something wrong, messed up somehow? But she'd forced herself to bury her insecurities deep.

This deal was important and he was obviously pre-occupied. Not everything was about her.

So she'd remained silent during the ride. And when they'd arrived, she'd been far too affected by his nearness, warm and solid and overwhelming when he had taken her arm and held her close—as any besotted newly-wed would—as they'd run the gauntlet of reporters and press photographers outside the event, to breathe let alone speak.

As soon as they were safely inside, he'd introduced her to a couple of the consortium members who were attending the event—but once the conversation had moved on to the intricacies of the deal, which was clearly still being negotiated, she had known she was surplus to requirements and had excused herself by explaining she was keen to look at the art.

She'd been miserable ever since—feeling like the class geek who had been invited to the birthday party of the most popular girl in school by mistake. Everyone else here seemed to know each other, drinking and chatting and laughing and mingling to their hearts' content. Ally had stood in the corner, and watched them, trying not to go over and over in her head all the things she hadn't had the guts to ask Dominic in the car.

Being a trophy wife was so much tougher than it looked.

'I thought I'd come and join you,' Megan added. 'I hope you don't mind.'

'Not at all,' Ally said, stifling her discomfort. She knew of Megan De Rossi—she was an important influencer on the New York social scene, not just because her husband was a billionaire but because she ran a ground-breaking charity to help women trapped in abusive relationships and she was the daughter of Alexis Whittaker, a famous British It-Girl of yesteryear. What Ally hadn't expected was the other woman's thoughtfulness—having spotted Ally looking like a lost cat, she had come over to rescue her.

'When is your baby due?' Ally asked, hoping to direct the conversation away from the subject of their 'husbands'.

Megan smiled as she stroked a hand over the prodigious baby bump. An odd shaft of envy pierced Ally's chest.

'Not baby, as it turns out, but *babies*.' Megan laughed. 'Dario and I got the shock news four months ago and we're still adjusting to it. I'm actually only six months, even though I'm the size of an elephant. The two of them, both boys, are not due until June.'

'Twin boys!' Ally grinned, she couldn't help it, impressed by the other woman's *sangfroid*. 'Wow, that… That must be exciting…and terrifying.'

'Right on both counts.' Megan grinned back. 'Although the most terrifying thing so far has been explaining to our daughter Issy she's going to have two more younger brothers when she's not that impressed with the one she's got. Our only consolation is that my sister Katie, who is also due in June, discovered she's having a girl.'

'I'm sure your daughter will get over it,' Ally said, feeling stupidly envious now. 'It's so much better to have siblings than not, even if they are brothers!'

'Precisely, although Issy's not convinced.' Megan

popped a delicate mini quiche into her mouth and swallowed. 'But enough about me. I wanted to come over and congratulate you on your marriage. I always knew Dominic would eventually find a woman worth keeping. He certainly seemed to be looking hard enough,' she added with a laugh.

'Thank you, I think.' Ally's heart wrestled with her tonsils at Megan's smile—if she could joke about Dominic like this they must be good friends, although he hadn't mentioned Megan, or anyone else. Embarrassed colour rushed into her cheeks as she realised how little she knew about her brand-new husband's private life.

'And I also wanted to discover where you bought that dress.' Megan's gaze slid over the cocktail dress Ally had spent the afternoon finishing while she'd waited for Dominic to arrive.

An above-the-knee design of aquamarine silk, inspired by a waterfall she'd seen once in a magazine, the dress was all flowing lines and quiet power. The gold band round her biceps had seemed like the perfect finishing touch. But Ally had been second-guessing her decision to wear it as soon as she'd arrived. Was it too revealing? Too funky? Not formal enough?

'It's so original and stylish,' Megan said. 'You look incredible in it.'

The flush of pleasure at Megan De Rossi's heartfelt praise had Ally's ribs contracting. This was exactly the kind of feedback she had hoped for.

'Actually I made it myself,' she said.

Megan's eyes widened, but then she whistled. 'That's even more amazing. You're really talented. I've never seen anything so cool and distinctive.'

Ally's heart squeezed. She'd hoped for a reaction like this, but she hadn't expected it.

'You're nothing like Dominic's other girlfriends— no wonder he decided to marry you,' Megan added, making the blush fire across Ally's chest. 'And that's without even factoring in that super-hot kiss,' Megan finished, her grin becoming decidedly wicked.

Ally's blush went ballistic.

Photos of their kiss on the sidewalk had hit the Internet yesterday. Ally knew because she'd been inundated with messages from her friends in London asking to know what the heck was going on. But she hadn't replied and she'd studiously avoided social media all day.

'I'm sorry,' Megan said, immediately looking contrite. 'I didn't mean to embarrass you. But, honestly, you two looked amazing together. So hot and so much in love, if anyone thought he shouldn't have ditched Mira they certainly won't after seeing that photo. Was that amazing blue suit one of your designs, too?'

'Yes,' Ally croaked, quietly dying inside.

She'd known she would have to lie, but she hadn't realised it would be quite this hard.

She already liked Megan De Rossi. The woman was smart, and witty, and sweet and surprisingly down to earth. And she clearly had exceptional taste. Megan and she might have become friends, if her marriage to Dominic had been real, instead of a subterfuge to secure a property deal.

'Um…' Ally began, not sure what to say, when she was rescued by a tall man in a dark grey designer suit, who swooped down on them like an avenging angel.

'Damn it, what are you doing on your feet? And holding something so heavy, *piccola*.' He whisked the laden plate Megan had been nibbling on out of her hand.

This was Dario De Rossi, Ally realised, in the flesh. She'd seen his picture in magazines, but it didn't do him justice. He was a strikingly handsome man, his Italian heritage evident in the black hair, olive skin, phenomenal bone structure—and his wildly overprotective manner.

'You are carrying two babies. *My* babies. You need to sit down, *piccola*,' he said, cradling his wife's elbow to lead her to a chair.

'And *you* need to stop calling me *piccola* now I'm the size of a house.' Megan rolled her eyes comically but allowed herself to be led. 'Ally, meet Dario—my very own papa bear. Dario, this is Ally, Dominic's new wife.'

Having deposited Megan on one of the white leather couches that lined the stark walls of the art gallery, and handed the plate back to her, Dario offered Ally his hand.

'Ally, it is good to meet you. I have heard much about you from Dominic.'

You have?

Ally shook his hand, wondering what on earth Dominic could have found to say about her, seeing as he hardly knew her. The firm handshake settled her nerves a fraction, until Dario shouted at someone.

'Dominic, over here.' He beckoned over Ally's shoulder, then smiled down at her. 'Your husband has been searching for you, like a besotted newly-wed.'

He has? But he isn't a besotted newly-wed.

Before Ally had a chance to process why Dominic might *really* have been searching for her, a large hand settled on the small of her back, burning the sensitive skin through the silk. She tried not to jump, not to overreact to the sensuous caress as Dominic's palm coasted to her hip and dragged her to his side.

'There you are, Alison,' he murmured in her ear, very much like an attentive lover but she could hear the edge in his voice. Something wasn't right.

'Megan, Dario, this is my *wife*, Alison,' he said, the possessive tone sending an inappropriate shaft of heat to her sex.

Fabulous, Ally, even his temper has the ability to turn you on.

'We've met,' Megan chipped in after swallowing another mouthful from her plate. 'And for once I approve, Dominic. Your bride is amazing,' she added, sending Ally a conspiratorial wink.

'*Merci beaucoup,*' Dominic murmured, dryly.

'Although I'm not sure you deserve her,' Megan added.

'I'm sure I do not,' Dominic replied, the tone deliberately self-deprecating but Ally could still hear that edge, even if Megan couldn't.

She had definitely screwed up somehow. Not acted quite dutiful or besotted enough, maybe?

'I can't believe you didn't at least mention in your press release about the marriage that Ally is a talented fashion designer,' Megan said.

Ally tensed at the innocuous comment as Dominic's hand jerked on her hip. Oh, crap. She hadn't expected Megan to blurt that out.

'By the way, I forgot to ask where your designs retail,' Megan asked her, caressing her baby bump. 'I can't wait to check them out, as soon as I get rid of these two and loose the five hundred extra pounds I've managed to put on.'

'Stop.' Dario cupped her cheek. 'You are not fat. You are pregnant and beautiful.'

'Spoken like a man who isn't carrying around five hundred extra pounds,' Megan said, but covered his hand with hers in a gesture that made Ally's heart leap into her throat.

What must that be like? To have a man be devoted to you? Exciting? Scary? She had no idea.

Dominic's hand had tightened on her waist. Whatever had annoyed him already, he was clearly a lot more annoyed now.

Why hadn't she told him she was making her own wardrobe for this trip?

'What designs?' he said.

His jaw had hardened. Okay, he wasn't just annoyed, he was *really* annoyed. And no wonder—

she'd just potentially exposed what a sham their marriage was to two of his friends. She should have kept her mouth shut about the dress to Megan until she'd had the guts to admit she'd made it herself to Dominic.

'I need to go to the ladies' room,' she said, hoping to escape and defuse the situation. But he held her in place.

'What designs is Megan talking about?' The sharp frown made heat prickle over her skin.

She could feel Megan's and Dario's gazes on the two of them.

'Can we talk about this later?' she whispered. Surely he wasn't going to flip out in front of his friends—wouldn't that blow their cover completely? But he seemed unconcerned by their audience when he placed his free hand on her other hip and tugged her to face him.

'*What* designs, Alison?' he repeated, the tone broaching no more argument or prevarication.

'I... I made some of my own clothes for this trip,' she said.

'You didn't know?' She heard Megan's gasped question, but all Ally's focus was on Dominic now. On his reaction. Because his brows had lowered ominously.

I'm so sorry, I should have told you, but don't make a big deal of it or we'll both be totally busted.

She tried to communicate the desperate plea to him telepathically.

'Which clothes?' he said, not picking up on her frantic telecommunications.

'Well...' Colour burned her cheeks as his gaze roamed over the dress—in much the same way as it had when he'd recited his vows earlier.

'Tell me,' he said, stroking her hips now, making the soft silk feel like sandpaper as it rasped over her skin.

'All of them.'

He swore softly, let go of her hips and grasped her hand. 'We're leaving.'

Panic assailed her as she heard Megan's shouted comment. 'Where are you going?'

'I have to *talk* to my wife.' Dominic threw the comment over his shoulder.

Ally attempted to wave her new friend goodbye, but she was already being whisked through the crowd. People turned to watch as she was marched out of the gallery. Some of the women giggled behind their hands, a few of the men laughed, others simply stared at the spectacle they were making or lifted their phones to record her humiliation.

Ally allowed herself to be led; trying to resist would only make the situation worse. He was furious, obviously. It was the only explanation for the sparkle of heat in his eyes, the tight line of his jaw, the way his hand clasped hers in a firm, unyielding grip.

She should never have designed and made her own clothes, instead of buying them from somewhere expensive and exclusive the way he'd expected her to.

He was a proud man and this marriage was all about appearances. She had miscalculated badly. Very badly.

Stopping on the sidewalk outside the gallery, he whistled through his fingers. The limousine they'd arrived in appeared out of the snarl of traffic like a magic carpet.

'I'm sorry, Dominic, I should have told you, about the clothes,' she whispered, trying to placate him. 'I realise you're probably annoyed that I didn't buy something from a named designer, but I've been studying design for two years and I—'

'Get in.' Dominic opened the door and held it for her. She hesitated.

'Alison. Get. In. The. Damn. Car.' The tone was low, more firm than threatening, but still she felt it ripple down her spine. *'Now.'*

She jumped at the barked command, and slid into the seat. Moments later she was cocooned in the back of the car with him as it peeled away from the kerb. The scent of leather and man, spicy cologne and pine soap invaded her senses; the blare of car horns, the cacophony of sound from the street as New York woke up to the night buzzed in her brain, combining with the sensation careering over her skin.

Why was he so mad at her? And why did it still turn her on?

'Listen, I'm really sorry I wasn't honest with you about my wardrobe. But Megan liked this dress, really, it isn't all bad—'

'Stop apologising about the damn dress. The dress is not the problem. It's stunning, and it's been driving me to distraction ever since I saw you in it. So I'd say Megan's opinion is correct.' The searing confession surprised her so much, the bottom dropped out of her stomach.

'Then… What is the problem?' Because there was clearly a problem and she still had no idea what it was.

He turned to her then, the naked hunger on his face so shocking the heat fired up her torso. 'The problem is, for this to work there has to be trust. You chose not to tell me about the clothes, and in some ways I understand that—you're obviously not as confident about your abilities as you should be.' His hand touched her thigh and she shivered, the sensation both brutal and yet delicious as the calluses trailed up her leg. 'Which is ironic, because the minute I saw you in this outfit tonight, all I wanted to do was rip it off you.'

'I'm not sure that's relevant,' she managed because she'd already started to lose the thread of this conversation, and she was still none the wiser as to why he looked so furious.

He swore suddenly and let her go, to lean back in his seat. 'Then it should be,' he said, staring out of the window.

She wondered if she should apologise again, for not telling him about the clothes, because it had upset him in ways she hadn't thought she could upset him, but she didn't want to keep apologising.

The ride through Manhattan seemed to take an eternity as she waited for him to say something, anything. Her thigh quivered where the imprint of his brief caress still lingered—making her brutally aware of exactly how tangled this situation had become. Because she still wanted him so desperately, even though on several levels he was completely infuriating.

Her need and her anxiety had reached fever pitch when he finally turned back to her.

'Why did you have Selene cut the one-million-pound payment from the divorce settlement?' he said tightly, the searing heat in his eyes accompanied by an emotion that made no sense whatsoever.

Guilt.

That was the problem? She opened her mouth to reply, but then closed it again, because she still didn't understand what she'd done that was so wrong.

'Answer me,' Dominic demanded. He was so angry and frustrated he was finding it hard to speak. He'd trusted her and she'd tricked him.

Hold it together. And don't touch her, damn it, because then you'll never be able to get an answer.

Her eyes had gone wide with confusion. Making the fury boiling under his breastbone threaten to ignite.

He'd only found out about the contract change a half-hour ago, when he'd been scanning an email from Selene while waiting to pick up a glass of champagne for Alison at the event's crowded bar.

He'd been planning to celebrate. And he'd wanted to celebrate with her. The consortium members had been completely charmed by her, as he'd known they would be. She'd put on a convincing show, not least by excusing herself when his introductions had led on to a discussion about zoning issues on the project. One of the businessmen had laughed and congratulated him on his marriage and his beautiful wife, pointing out, 'Only a real wife would feel comfortable making it abundantly clear she found her husband's talk of business boring. My wife is exactly the same.'

The consortium members had agreed to sign the first phase of the deal tomorrow morning. His decision to marry Alison had been the right move.

But then he'd read Selene's outline of the marriage-contract negotiations, and the excitement had died. His assistant hadn't bothered to mention the change Alison had requested before now, because he'd given Selene *carte blanche* to negotiate the terms, telling her to refer anything problematic to his legal and financial teams. He hadn't wanted to be too closely involved. He'd been having enough trouble forgetting about Alison while he'd waited for her to arrive in New York. And, of course, his legal and financial teams had been more than happy to strike the lump-sum payment at the end of the marriage from the contract, because it would save LN a million pounds.

But he wasn't happy. He was furious about the unnecessary change.

The whole purpose of the payment was to keep his conscience clear. To pay off his responsibility after the marriage ended, not just towards the woman whose virginity he had taken, however unintentionally, and then exploited, but also towards the little girl who had been left destitute after that summer.

By refusing that payment, she had turned the tables

on him. Made him responsible again. And guilt was not an emotion he enjoyed.

'I just… I didn't want the money,' she said. 'It was too much. You're already giving me so much.'

It was exactly the sort of naïve, artless statement he should have expected. He tried to bank his fury. But he could do nothing to hide his frustration.

'We agreed on the money the morning you agreed to this marriage. And then you deliberately reneged on that understanding. And you chose not to mention it before we actually went through with the ceremony. Why?'

'I didn't think you'd mind,' she said, still confused, which only spurred his temper more.

'Of course I mind,' he said. 'I always pay my debts. It's an important principle of the way I do business.' And something he'd stuck to throughout his career, even when it had meant going hungry. Because he had promised himself the night he had crawled off his father's estate he would never, ever be beholden to anyone again. That no one would ever have the power to control him in that way. And now this woman had managed to undermine that essential tenet to the way he lived his life—without even trying.

'Why did you even wish to change that part of the agreement?' he said. He had offered her a million pounds; why hadn't she taken it? Because he knew exactly how much she could use the money.

Her blush was visible even in the dark interior of the car.

'It's too much, Dominic.'

'No. It. Isn't.' He spat the words out. 'You're going to live as my wife for the next six months—do you really think I want to leave you destitute again when we divorce?' And why was it already so damn hard to say that word?

She looked shocked, which only infuriated him more. He couldn't let this pass.

The car drew up at the Lafayette apartment. He unbuckled them both and hauled Alison out of the car. She still hadn't said anything, but it was probably better they had this discussion in private. He didn't want to risk another display for the paparazzi out on the sidewalk.

He marched into the lobby, ignored Manny the doorman's jaunty evening greeting and stabbed the elevator button.

Unfortunately a couple of his staff arrived behind them, and joined them in the lift.

Her fingers flexed on his, but he didn't release his grip as he replied to his staff members' innocuous comments about the weather—even as the adrenaline raced through his bloodstream. How could he still be so aroused, when he was almost choking on his indignation?

At last the two employees stepped out of the lift and they arrived a few moments later at the penthouse apartment. He dragged her through the doors as soon as they swished open. Once they were safe in the privacy of his apartment he released her hand.

'I want to know why you pulled this stunt,' he said. 'And then we're going to have to renegotiate the contract or it's not going to work for me.'

CHAPTER EIGHT

Was it wrong to notice how hot Dominic was when he was mad?

Ally tried to corral her wayward thoughts and stick to the problem at hand.

And it was a problem. She should have told him she'd decided not to accept the pay-off. That much was obvious. But she really hadn't thought it would be a deal breaker. And she had to wonder why it was.

But she was going to have to give him an answer first. An answer that would expose all her insecurities. Which was probably why she hadn't told him in the first place.

But the truth was, she'd already told him the reason; he just hadn't been listening. So now she would have to tell him again.

'I couldn't get past what happened to my mother with your father. Accepting your money felt like I was making the same mistake. She persuaded herself she loved him. But I'm not sure she ever really did. What she loved was the security his money provided. I don't want to sell myself short the way she did.'

'This deal, this marriage, hasn't got a damn thing to do with what happened all those years ago. We already established that.' The edge in his voice sharpened.

'Yes, it does. I won't compromise myself like that. I can't.'

'So you expect me to compromise my integrity instead,' he shot back.

'What?' she asked, because she was confused now as well as heartsore. She hadn't meant to cause an argument. And she certainly didn't want to infuriate him. But she couldn't budge on this. She'd tried and she just couldn't; her pride wouldn't allow her to accept the money. 'I don't… I don't understand.'

'Really?' he said, thrusting his fingers through his hair. 'Then let me explain. You don't want to be like your mother, but you're happy to make me into my father. To have me exploit you the way my father exploited her and hundreds of other women. The way he exploited my own mother. If you don't want to be like her, what makes you think I want to be like him?'

It didn't make any sense. This had nothing to do with his father. Far from it. But from his tortured expression it was obvious it mattered to him.

'But you're not exploiting me, Dominic,' she said, as patiently and gently as she could—she needed to defuse this situation and make him see sense. 'I want to be here. I signed that contract and went through with the ceremony earlier in full knowledge of the facts. I just don't want the money. It's too much.

You're not responsible for what happened to my mother. They were the grown-ups, not you.'

'*Mon Dieu.* How do you know what I am responsible for when you don't even know what happened that night?'

The growled admission struck her like a blow. Bringing back the memories she had never really confronted. And the words her mother had whispered before dragging her out of bed in the middle of the night, her cheek bruised and her eyes wet with tears, returned.

'*Something terrible's happened, baby. Pierre's very angry with me and Dominic. We have to leave.*'

'What are you saying, Dominic?' A horrible thought curdled in the pit of her stomach. Had something happened between her mother and Dominic? The thought had never even occurred to her. Because it would be ludicrous and paranoid—but a stifling coating of jealousy joined the snakes writhing in her belly, regardless.

Which only disturbed her more. Imagine being jealous of a dead woman. A woman who was her own mother.

He swore and turned away from her, striding to the open-plan kitchen and pulling a beer out of the fridge. He snapped off the cap against the countertop and gulped down half the bottle.

She followed him, her insides churning. A part of her had always wondered what had happened to turn Pierre against her mother. But it couldn't be this, could it?

'Did Pierre catch you together?' she asked.

Had her mother seduced a sixteen-year-old boy? The thought was so appalling she knew she would never be able to get past it. She had clung to that last modicum of respect for her mother for so long—through the drug addiction, the endless affairs with increasingly inappropriate men. But this would destroy the last of it. And be worse than anything she'd been forced to witness her mother do in the years after that night.

'Is that why he hit her?' she asked. 'Why he kicked us out? Did you and my mother have a relationship?'

But as she steeled herself against hearing the worst, Dominic choked on the beer and the bottle slammed down on the countertop.

'What the…? Are you…? How do you say it in English?' he said, the frustration hitting boiling point. 'Are you insane?' he managed. 'Of course I didn't have a relationship with *Monique*.'

The stabbing pain in Ally's belly unlocked. *Oh, thank God.* Her mother hadn't done the unthinkable and seduced a child.

'I was only sixteen and your mother was in her thirties, stunningly beautiful and in love with my father. Even I was never that precocious,' he said, sounding so shocked she felt pretty foolish for even thinking it might have been a possibility, let alone actually asking him. But she was still glad she had. She never wanted that ugly picture in her head ever again. And now at least it was gone… But if that wasn't what had caused his father to hit her mother, what had? And why would Dominic feel responsible?

'But you were there, when Pierre hit her?' she asked. He must have been. Because her mother had mentioned him and he had just implied as much. 'Do you know why he hurt her? Why he turned on her?'

His gaze became shuttered, but not before she caught the flash of something that looked like regret.

He braced his hands against the countertop and dropped his head. She could see the tension in the rigid line of his shoulder blades, and hear the deep sigh as his chest released.

'There was no reason,' he said, but she could hear the bitterness that he couldn't disguise. 'My father never needed a reason. His temper was volatile and easily roused. I think your mother made some innocuous comment about their engagement. And he exploded.'

'I see.' Ally's chest deflated, his agonised words, the description of what he'd witnessed, having the hideous ring of truth. 'So he *had* offered her marriage?' she whispered.

Dominic's head lifted, and he nodded. 'Of course, it was how my father liked to operate. Dangle the carrot and then apply the stick.'

Ally's heart shrank in her chest.

Dominic gulped down the last of the beer. And dumped the empty bottle in the trash. He looked exhausted. As exhausted as she felt. She noticed the scar bisecting his left eyebrow, the scar she'd wondered about often as a child.

He liked to dangle the carrot, then apply the stick.

His statement stirred the memories again, of all the altercations she'd witnessed between father and son that summer. The bullying, the insults, the constant, endless attempts by Pierre to let his son know he was a bastard, that he wasn't enough.

As a child she'd been in awe of Pierre, the way her mother had. Because he'd always been so charming to her, she'd never been able to figure out why he was so mean to Dominic. But now she could see, Pierre had treated her like a pet that summer, not a daughter. And a tool, his praise for her just one more stick to beat Dominic with, to let him know that even his mistress's child had a greater place in Pierre's affections than his illegitimate son.

'I'm sorry,' she said. 'For bringing it up, for making you relive that summer and those events.'

His eyes met hers, the confusion in them as compelling as the wariness. Dominic, she thought, was not a man comfortable with displays of emotion, or affection—no wonder this evening had exhausted him.

But even so she refused to hold back. Reaching across the breakfast bar, she placed her palm on his cheek, trying to soothe the bone-deep exhaustion she could see in his eyes.

'And I'm sorry for thinking, even for a moment, you were to blame for the horrid way my mother and I were treated at the end of that summer, when it was always, always him.'

* * *

Dominic tensed, and jerked his head back, away from the soft stroke of her fingers.

The compassion and understanding in her eyes horrified him almost as much as the desire to lean into the caress. To take whatever solace she offered.

She dropped her hand, and tensed, as if his rejection were a physical blow.

But he didn't deserve her sympathy, or her apology. She didn't know the full extent of what had happened that night—that his father wasn't the only one to blame.

But he had absolutely no intention of telling her.

It was ancient history now. And it had no bearing on who they were now. And on their marriage.

One thing was clear, though: despite everything that had happened to Alison, and however much she might think she was as cynical and pragmatic about this relationship as he was because of those struggles—she wasn't. Some of that hopeful, generous, open-hearted child still remained. Or she would never have believed his explanation about that night so easily, been so ready to absolve him. And she certainly would not have refused to take the one million pounds he'd offered her.

Walking round the breakfast bar, he cupped her chin, pulled her head up. 'I don't want to talk about the past again. It is dead and has been for a long time.'

It was a brutal thing to say, especially when he saw the humiliating colour fire into her cheeks. But he had to be cruel to be kind now, or she would invest too much of herself in this relationship.

'You must take the money,' he said again. 'For this arrangement to work.'

She tugged her chin out of his hand, looked down at her clasped hands, the knuckles white with strain.

He waited for her to accept the inevitable. She had to know he was giving her an ultimatum.

When she lifted her head all he could see in her eyes was an aching sadness—and even though he didn't feel particularly triumphant, he thought he had won.

But then she shook her head and to his astonishment she said, 'I can't, Dominic. I just can't. If that means we have to part, then I'll understand.'

He was so shocked, the riot of emotions flowing through him so strong and so new—panic, fear, regret, but most of all loss—he had no idea how to process them, let alone how to combat them.

'Non,' he said. Placing his hands on her cheeks, he drew her face towards his. Before he could think better of the impulse, he covered her mouth with his. He wasn't going to lose her; he couldn't.

She opened for him and he plunged his tongue into the recesses of her mouth. Taking, demanding, possessing her—refusing to accept her stubbornness, her intransigence.

The deal. The deal required she stay. That was the reason he felt so desperate. The reason the yearning was so intense. It had to be.

Her instant and unequivocal surrender was like a drug. Sex would fix this problem.

The blood rushed to his groin as he lifted her into his arms and carried her towards his old bedroom. The one she'd chosen the day before.

This is madness. She knows this is madness. We don't have to end this over something so foolish. As long as I can prove she still wants me too. That's all that really matters here.

He placed her on her feet, held her waist and looked into amber eyes, dark with arousal. 'We can fix this in the morning,' he said, his voice hoarse. He would figure out a way if it killed him. 'But for now I want to do what we do best.'

It wasn't really a question but she nodded anyway. And his heart leapt in his chest.

This isn't over. Not yet.

Yes, I want you. I want this. I don't want to leave.

The heat plunged low in Ally's abdomen, rebounding in her sex.

Just take me to bed and let's forget, for tonight at least.

She shuddered, her body alive with too much sensation, as his hands skimmed over her bottom and lifted her dress. He dragged her into his embrace, until the thick evidence of his desire rubbed against the soft, liquid warmth flooding between her thighs.

She didn't see how they could fix this. But for now all she wanted to do was feel, because it might be her last chance.

His thumbs edged under the legs of her panties. He cupped her bottom in hard hands.

'I can't go slowly. Is that okay?' he asked, his voice full of an urgency that only made her more desperate.

'Yes,' she said, her sex already clutching and releasing, desperate to feel that thick length inside her, one last time.

'Bien.' He found the hammering pulse in her neck with firm lips.

She clung to him, trying to dispel the fear, and the sadness.

She jumped at the sound of rending fabric as he ripped away her panties, and her senses soared. The turmoil of emotions forgotten, as giddy shock became giddy excitement.

He turned her round and bent her over the bed.

Her thighs quivered as she heard him release himself from his pants. Large hands positioned her, skimming over her hips, brushing her bottom, then the huge head of his erection notched at the slick seam of her sex.

She jerked, shocked by the need coursing through her like wild fire as he impaled her in one slow thrust.

'Always so wet for me, Madame LeGrand,' he said, but the tone sounded rough, and raw.

She groaned as he filled her to the hilt, the penetration from this angle so deep what had been overwhelming before became devastating.

He began to rock, out and back, going deeper, taking more. She gripped the coverlet, trying to anchor herself for the heavy thrusts, trying to control the depth of penetration. Her muscles contracted, pushing her towards that high wide ledge, but his movements only became more frantic, the pleasure refusing to subside.

His thumb found her swollen clitoris, sending her soaring, shattering, flying again. Her shocked sobs matched his deep guttural groans.

One large callused palm found her breast, ripping away the silk of her dress, the confining lace of her bra, until hot skin found hot skin. Freed, the stiff peak engorged under his relentless caresses, driving her even higher as he sank deeper and deeper inside her.

The sound of sex, graphic and basic, the cries of pleasure and passion, filled the room, the sensations dazzling and disorientating.

She crashed over one final time and fell to earth. He grew even larger inside her, the hot seed pumping into her as he shouted out his fulfilment.

She collapsed onto the bed.

The shaking began as he eased out of her.

'Are you okay?' he said, his gruff voice rippling through her in the darkness.

'Yes,' she said, because she was, even though the thought of having to leave him tomorrow was crucifying her.

She rolled over and sat up, gathering the torn bodice of her dress, feeling suddenly defenceless. Scared to look at him. Scared not to.

'I damaged your beautiful gown,' he said. 'Can it be repaired?'

'It's okay,' she said. 'I can make another. I like to

do it,' she added, because he looked a little dazed. She knew the feeling. How could the sex be so powerful, so overwhelming, so right, when everything else seemed so wrong?

He nodded. 'We will talk tomorrow morning. And work this disagreement out,' he said.

The sadness settled back over her body, dispelling the golden glow of the orgasms he'd given her. But she nodded. Prepared to pretend she believed it.

'I'll see you in the morning,' he said.

'Yes,' she said.

She wanted to snag his wrist, to ask him to stay, to sleep with her, to hold her, just this once, but she knew that indulgence would only make tomorrow harder.

So instead she watched him leave the room. Then dropped back on the bed and blinked furiously, to stop the tears she wanted to shed from falling.

Their marriage had been legal for approximately three hours. And already it felt so much more real than it should. Which was why she couldn't give in and accept the money.

She had to preserve her independence, and this was the only way she could think of to do it, because it would be far, far too easy to surrender everything to this man. Not just her body, but also her soul.

While all the time knowing he would never be willing to surrender more than his body in return.

CHAPTER NINE

FEVERISH THOUGHTS CIRCLED Ally's brain as she showered and dressed the next morning. It was past nine
o'clock when she stepped into the apartment's living
room feeling as if she were about to step into the abyss.

Dominic sat at the breakfast bar eating a bagel and
scrolling through what she suspected were market re-
ports on his phone.

He put the bagel down and wiped his mouth when
he spotted her.

'*Bonjour*, Alison.'

She drew in a breath and forced herself to walk
towards him. Even dressed in jeans and a T-shirt,
his feet bare and his damp hair slicked back from his
forehead, he looked indomitable and unreachable.

Her heart sank. She'd gone over all the possible
solutions she could think of to their problem and she
couldn't see one. She couldn't take the money, and
Dominic would not accept her refusal.

'Don't look so worried,' he murmured as he held
out his hand. 'I have an idea that will satisfy me and
I hope will also satisfy you.'

She placed her fingers in his palm, felt the familiar frisson of electricity as he grasped her hand and directed her to the stool next to him.

'I still can't accept the money,' she said, scared that his solution would involve going over the same ground as yesterday.

'And I cannot accept leaving you destitute when we part.'

She wouldn't be destitute, but it was pointless arguing about it once more.

'Then we're at an impasse.' She blinked furiously, pathetically close to tears, again. Why was she about to cry?

His intransigence, his unwillingness to bend on a point that was so important to her, surely proved this arrangement had always been doomed to failure.

'Not necessarily.' His lips curved in a persuasive smile. 'How about, rather than giving you a million pounds at the end of this marriage, I invest in your business instead?'

'What business?' she asked, completely nonplussed.

'Your fashion design business, of course,' he said.

'But I don't have a fashion design business.'

'This is exactly the point. You don't have one, but you should.' His gaze slid over the short dress she had put on, ready to return to London on the next plane. He touched the flounced neckline. 'This is one of your designs, is it not?'

She nodded, brutally aware of the approval in his eyes.

'You are extremely talented. Even I can see this and I know nothing about fashion. Megan De Rossi does and she agrees with me. She asked where your designs were retailing yesterday at the gallery, is this not so?'

'That was just a casual comment,' she said. 'She was being kind and friendly.'

'No, she wasn't, because I phoned her an hour ago and asked her if she would be willing to throw her support behind your brand.'

'You did…*what*?' Ally jumped off the stool. 'Dominic, how could you?' She covered her face with her hands, wishing the beautiful concrete floor of his apartment would crack open and swallow her whole.

His fingers curled around her wrists and he drew her hands away from her face. He peered at her, the smile so confident now it was verging on smug. 'Don't you want to hear what she said?'

'No! I don't.' She yanked her hands free, not sure whether she wanted to shout at him or simply curl up in a ball and weep. 'She's your friend, and you put her on the spot. I have no doubt she was polite.' She stepped away from him.

How would she ever survive the humiliation?

Megan De Rossi had been wonderful. And for that bright beautiful moment when the other woman had admired her design yesterday, Ally had felt as if she belonged, truly belonged. But it had all been an illusion. An illusion that Dominic had shattered with careless disregard for her feelings.

'You've exposed me to ridicule, Dominic. Can't you see that? I haven't even finished fashion college yet. I've got months of work left before my final year show. And then, if none of the fashion houses are interested, it could be years before I manage to get an internship. They're hugely competitive and I don't even know if I've got what it takes to—'

'Megan wants to invest,' he interrupted her, his smile not smug so much as sympathetic.

'What?' What on earth was he talking about now?

'Megan De Rossi wants to invest in your brand, *ma belle*,' he said again, chuckling as he grasped both her wrists again and tugged her struggling body back towards him, until she was positioned between his thighs. 'She loves your designs. She says you have huge potential. I told her I was considering bankrolling your collection. I asked her for her advice, whether she thought it would be a good investment. I didn't want to suggest something that would not succeed. She not only said it would be a fabulous investment, she said she wanted to invest, too.'

'She…she didn't.' Ally's body went limp, the shock making her knees tremble. Megan De Rossi had liked her designs enough to invest in them? It didn't even seem possible, let alone plausible. This was huge. It was beyond huge. It was… Everything.

'She did,' he said. Resting his hand on her neck, he rubbed his thumb across her collarbone where her pulse was pounding like a jackhammer. 'Why are you so surprised?'

'Because…' The tears that she had refused to shed yesterday made her throat raw, and her eyes sting. 'Because it's… It's like a dream come true.'

Dominic tucked a knuckle under her chin, the glitter of unshed tears destroying him. He'd wanted to find a solution to the problem of the money; it seemed he'd found much more than that.

How could he not have realised how insecure she was? Because she'd been so brave and bold and determined up to now—that was why. But underneath that was a woman who had had to fight for every chance, every opportunity, and drag herself through God only knew what to make her dream a reality. Well, she didn't have to drag herself any more. He was going to make sure she soared.

'So, if I said I was going to invest in your start-up, you would accept?'

He saw the dazed hope in her face fade a little. 'But I don't know anything about business. All I know is how to design and make clothes.'

He nodded. This much he could help her with. 'Luckily for you, I know a lot about business,' he said. 'The idea is we would be partners in this venture.' Like a real husband and wife, he thought, but didn't say; he didn't want to spook her, any more than he wanted to spook himself. 'I'll give you all the financial and business support you need. Rent premises in London for your workshop, pay for the salaries of your staff…'

'Staff?' Her eyes went so large he had to resist a laugh.

'Yes, staff. A business manager, a personal assistant, a publicist, and those are just the basics. I would assume a fledgling fashion brand would also need creative staff.'

'But... Isn't that going to be very expensive?' she said and he could already hear her insecurities putting the brakes on her dream.

But he wasn't going to allow it. This was the way he could give her something of value from their marriage. Something that would endure long after their liaison was over. Something that would ensure she would never be destitute again. And he would not have to feel responsible.

'You have to invest money to make money, Alison—that's the way business works.'

'But how will I pay you back?' she asked. And he had to bite his tongue.

He mustn't become frustrated with her, not again. Her insecurity—like his driving ambition—had stemmed from the scars inflicted on both of them that summer. *He* knew she could do this, but she did not, and until she did he would have to be her mentor, her supporter. Gently nudging her in the right direction until each new success showed her how much she could achieve. Confidence didn't happen overnight—confidence had to be built, brick by tortuous brick. He'd discovered that when building his own business, so now he could show her while she built hers.

'You won't pay me back,' he said, but before she could protest he held up his hand. 'Wait, let me explain. The money isn't a gift, or a pay-off, like the alimony payment I was proposing. I intend to get a handsome return on my money, eventually, once the brand is established. We'll make a formal agreement and, for my investment, I want a fifty per cent share of the profits.'

'But what will I be giving to the business that entitles *me* to fifty per cent?' she said, the frown on her face so adorable he wanted to kiss it. 'I haven't got any money to invest in it.'

She really was clueless about how business worked. Why did that make the thought of going into business with her all the more exciting?

'Your contribution is your time and your talent,' he said. 'I'm afraid I'm going to be far too busy with the Waterfront project here to be anything more than a silent partner. And I know absolutely nothing about fashion.'

'But what if I fail?' she said, and his heart cracked at the tremble of uncertainty.

He stifled the foolish feeling of empathy. This was business, just like their marriage, there was no place for sentiment—but even so he kept his voice gentle. 'If you fail, I write the investment off as an expense and reduce my tax burden. Either way, it is a win-win for me financially.'

But she wasn't going to fail. She had the talent, according to Megan, to be a success. The only thing holding her back would be lack of business expertise—

which he could supply her with—and her own fear of failure.

And if there was one thing he could show her how to do, it was how to conquer that fear.

'So, what do you say? Do you want to go into business with me, Madame LeGrand?'

She pressed a hand over her breast, as if she were trying to stop her heart jumping out of her chest. He knew how she felt, because he'd felt the same way when he'd signed his first deal with the precious stake he'd earned working round the clock as a cycle courier in Paris.

'I'm terrified,' she said, her honesty so captivating he struggled not to kiss her.

'Only terrified?' he asked.

'And also excited,' she admitted. Hope sparked in her eyes, and found an answering spark in his heart.

'So is that a yes?' he asked, needing the clarification.

'Yes—yes, it is!' she said.

'Magnifique!'

She laughed and grasped his shoulders as he wrapped his arms around her waist and spun her round in a circle.

'Congratulations, Madame LeGrand,' he said as he finally put her down, absorbing the delicious echo in his groin as her body pressed against his.

'Thank you. Thank you for suggesting this,' she said, her face alight with exhilaration. 'It's a brilliant solution.'

'Yes, I know,' he said, and she laughed again, the sound sweet and carefree.

He slanted his mouth across hers, his pulse pounding in his ears when her eager response turned the kiss from hungry to ravenous in a heartbeat.

He scooped her into his arms.

'Dominic, what are you doing?' she asked, breathlessly as he carried her back into the bedroom.

'Celebrating,' he said, although he thought that much was obvious.

It wasn't till much later though, as he headed down to his offices to get the legal team involved in setting up the new business, while Alison called Megan to talk about coming on board as an investor, that it occurred to him he wasn't even sure what made him smile the most.

The hum in his groin from the celebratory sex they'd just shared; the thought that the first stage of the Waterfront deal would be signed later today; the realisation he would be able to keep his fake wife, without any regrets; or the thought of the months ahead, when he would be able to help Alison blossom and grow into the woman she was always meant to be—both in bed and in business.

Now they had established trust and secure boundaries to their relationship—ensuring there would be no more messy heart-to-hearts about their feelings or about things that had happened so long ago they no longer mattered—their marriage could progress as originally planned.

They would live separate lives—with Alison busy

working on her business in London, while he was engaged in the Waterfront deal in Manhattan.

As he bounded down the emergency stairs to his ninth-floor office, the thought was so enticing, he might even have been whistling.

CHAPTER TEN

'CAN YOU GET them to rethink, Muhammad? We need that Indian silk. It's a key component of the whole collection.' Ally spoke rapidly, her nerves fraying as she opened the gate to the London town house. The smattering of rain permeated the thin sweater she wore. Deciding to walk home this evening hadn't been the smartest idea, but she had wanted some fresh air after a week of eighteen hour days finishing off the designs. Panic constricted around her throat—and now the signature feature of every one might be missing.

She'd fallen in love with the stunning craftsmanship of the embroidered fabric offered by a charitable workshop in Mumbai. She'd been in negotiations with them for weeks—and everything had been going so well, they were due to sign the contracts an hour ago, when she'd got a call from her supplier, Muhammad Patel, with some very bad news.

'They're saying another buyer has promised them a better investment,' her supplier replied. 'I'm sorry, Ally, you've been great and I know they were really torn. Rohana was full of apologies when she told me,' he said, mentioning the workshop's owner who Ally had been dealing with. 'But the other buyer's got more clout in the marketplace.'

Which was code for another designer with an actual name had stepped in and offered, if not more money, then more exposure.

'I understand,' she interrupted him, because she did. 'And please tell Rohana not to feel bad about this. They've got to make the right choice for their business.'

She shoved the phone into her bag, her anxiety threatening to choke her. What had she expected? She didn't have a pedigree, just a rich husband willing to invest in a pipe dream. It had been two months since her deal with Dominic, since she'd started playing businesswoman and pretending to be a fashion designer, and she didn't feel any more secure now than she had then.

Dominic had been wonderful, but he was busy, and she didn't want to bother him about the minutiae of her business problems on the few days a month when she got to see him. After the almost-end to their arrangement a day into the marriage, she'd been determined to stick to her end of the bargain—and to enjoy every second of time she had with him.

The sex had been awesome. The way he could make her body feel was a revelation—the familiar heat blasted through her at the memory of their last merry meeting in Paris a week ago, when he'd had to attend the opening of a rail project his company had financed and he'd wanted her there.

She had become addicted to his texts. Usually a curt two lines telling her where and when he needed her to be. She'd travelled all over the globe in the last two months. To Rio, to Cannes, to Paris and Hong Kong and even Niagara Falls. Whenever he'd summoned her, she'd gone. She'd become an expert at smiling for the cameras, and addicted to the stolen hours they had alone together, before and after the balls and galas, the charity banquets and high-profile sporting events he needed his wife to be seen at.

They spoke often about her growing business. His advice and encouragement had proved invaluable and he seemed genuinely interested in her progress.

But the wall he had erected after the almost-collapse of their marriage remained. It had cost her not to try to breach that wall again, to talk about more than just sex or business, because the yearning to know him better, to understand every little thing about him, remained too. He fascinated her, he always had and that would never change. But she'd forced herself to be content with the companionship—and the spectacular sex—and to remember the deal they'd made. That this relationship had a sell-by date—a sell-by date she'd agreed to.

Plus she adored being with him, and she didn't want to ruin their time together with pointless yearning for something more, when she already had so much.

Just as it was pointless to wish she could get his advice about this latest disaster. He always had a solution, and was willing to share his phenomenal expertise—but she didn't see how he could help her with this.

She was an upstart, a newbie, in this business. She'd wanted to succeed, not just for herself, but also to repay him for his confidence in her. But renting a studio in Holborn, hiring a business manager and a personal assistant and a brilliant seamstress, didn't suddenly make her a fashion designer. What it made her was a fraud—no wonder Rohana hadn't wanted her beautiful fabrics gracing the Allycat Collection.

Ally closed the back door and dumped her bag on the hall stand.

She rubbed her belly, the dull ache from the period that had started that morning just one more thing to drag her spirits down into her boots.

She slipped off the wet shoes, and took a moment to knead her arches, which were sore after twelve hours spent on her feet directing traffic at the studio.

As she stood in the hallway where they'd first met again all those weeks ago, another wave of melancholy blindsided her.

Dominic had never returned to their London home... *Her* London home. Since that first night and the following morning.

She totally understood that. His life, his work, was in New York.

But as she stood staring into the empty hallway, she missed him. Terribly. Why not admit it? She missed him a little bit more every time she had to fly back to London without him.

How wonderful would it be to have him here tonight? To have that broad shoulder to lean on. That glorious body to explore, so she didn't have to think about how she was going to drag herself back up after this latest knock-down.

She tried to shake off the loneliness and longing, as she had so many times before, and headed towards the kitchen.

Get over yourself, Jones. You're just knackered. And scared.

As she approached the kitchen she picked up the muted hum of the TV playing a news channel.

She stopped. Hesitated.

Had Charlotte, the housekeeper, left the set on? Before she'd left for the evening?

Edging open the kitchen door, she gasped.

'Dominic?'

The wave of emotion almost floored her.

Was she having an out-of-body experience? Because she'd imagined him in her home, *their* home, so many times in the last couple of months? Had she somehow conjured him up because she needed him here?

He seemed real and solid enough though, as he turned from the countertop. Dressed in faded denim and a T-shirt, his feet bare and his hair mussed, he looked so different from how she usually saw him— which was either formally dressed or gloriously naked.

'At last you're home. Where have you been?' he said, in his usual direct way, the slight frown making her heart tick into her throat. 'It's past ten o'clock— you should have finished work hours ago.'

Yup, that was her husband: pushy and overprotective.

He stalked towards her, then cradled her cheek, his gaze gliding over her face, his expression intense and observant. *'Tu as l'air fatiguée.'*

You look exhausted.

She leaned into his callused palm despite the less than complimentary comment. Joy enveloped her as she breathed in his scent. Spicy cologne and clean pine soap. A scent she often dreamed about on the nights she spent alone.

She covered his hand. 'I didn't know you were coming to London,' she said, not making any effort to keep the pleasure out of her voice. 'It's so wonderful to see you.'

She smothered the tiny voice, warning her not to get sentimental, or over-invested. Just this once, she wanted to rejoice in the unexpected gift of spending an evening home alone with her husband.

'I've got a meeting in Mayfair tomorrow,' he said. 'And some news about the business that I wanted to deliver in person.'

News? About his business? She couldn't imagine what it could be, but it was so good to have him standing in front of her, warm and solid and frowning. And even more wonderful to know that when something happened in his working life, she was the one he wanted to tell about it.

It was comforting to know that even if their marriage had considerable limitations they had managed to become friends as well as lovers in the last two months.

'What's the news?' she said, then grimaced as a cramp tightened across her abdomen.

He swore softly, then clasped her shoulders. 'What's wrong? Are you ill?'

'No, I'm… I'm fine,' she said, stupidly pleased by his concern.

'Don't lie,' he said, lifting her chin. 'I can see the pain in your eyes.'

'It's nothing,' she said, but the cramp chose that precise moment to tighten like a vice and a small groan escaped her lips.

'That's it!' He tugged his smartphone out of his back pocket. 'I'm calling an ambulance.'

She laughed and grasped his wrist as he lifted the phone to his ear. 'Dominic, don't. Really, that's not necessary, it's just…' She hesitated, a flush heating her skin.

'It's just what?' he demanded, his frown deepening.

'It's period pain,' she said, realising how ridiculous it was to be embarrassed to talk to her husband about something so natural. 'It started this morning. It's always sore the first twelve hours or so.'

His arm dropped, as he tucked the phone back into his pocket, but the frown remained. She wondered if he was one of those men who freaked out about women's menstrual cycles. Weird she didn't even know that, when they'd been married for two months. But then being on the pill meant she'd been able to time her periods so they didn't fall on the nights they spent together.

'Have you taken any painkillers?' He slid a warm hand around her neck, his thumb stroking the pulse-point below her ear.

'Not yet,' she said.

He pressed a kiss to her forehead. 'Then let's fix that, first,' he said with his usual confidence.

No surprise there, then. Dominic *wasn't* one of those guys who was freaked out by periods. But then why would he be? He'd dated loads of women before her.

She stifled the ungenerous thought. And the prickle of envy that came with it. He was with *her* now, in *their* kitchen. That was what mattered.

Crossing to the kitchen counter, he opened and closed the drawers.

'They're in the drawer on the far right,' she said, realising she had moved things around some since he'd lived here.

He poured her a glass of water and watched while she took a pill. Then handed her another. 'Take two,' he said. 'I didn't like the sound of that groan.'

She dutifully obeyed then handed him back the glass.

'Is there anything else that will help?' he asked. 'A massage? A heat pack? Food? Wine? Sex?'

'*Sex?* You wish!' She smiled at the urgent, solicitous tone. 'That's the absolute last thing I want,' she said, protesting maybe a bit too much as a familiar heat flushed her skin.

Who knew? The thought of making love to her husband while she was having her period wasn't nearly as icky as she might once have assumed. But he didn't need to know that, she decided. It would be nice just to absorb him tonight and the novelty of having him in their home, and take some much-needed comfort from their friendship to bolster her flagging ego. Her period was the perfect excuse not to jump each other the first chance they got.

'Well, hey, it was worth a try,' he said, smiling sheepishly as he put the box of pills and the water glass on the countertop.

Nope, definitely not a guy freaked out by periods.

'So what's your news?' she said, trying to get comfortable on the kitchen stool as her belly tightened again. 'Is it the Waterfront deal?'

'Nope,' he said. 'But I'm not telling you until we've got you comfortable. I don't want you freaking out on me.'

Freaking out? Why would she freak out? Her tired mind shot straight to a worst-case scenario. Was he about to tell her he didn't need his fake wife any more?

'*Arrêtes...* Stop it.' His smile widened as he clasped her chin. 'I can see you're panicking already. Relax, it's good news, I swear. You're going to be pleased when you get used to the idea.'

Get used to the idea. Okay, that didn't sound that good either. How could something to do with his business affect her, other than their marriage? But then he kissed her on the nose, the gesture so sweet, her heart butted her tonsils so hard she had trouble breathing, let alone thinking.

* * *

Dominic forced himself to release her, aware of the emotion glittering in her eyes. And ignored the tight feeling in his chest.

He'd dealt with this feeling many times before. His heart felt too full, too big every time he gave her advice and her eyes lit up with understanding, every time he gave her a compliment and she blushed, every time they made love and he watched her respond without holding an ounce of herself back until she shattered. And every time he left her bed and the desire to keep her, to hold her, to stay with her just a little longer threatened to overwhelm him.

This time was no different from any of those. He couldn't allow himself to get sentimental about what they had, or too attached.

It would only complicate this relationship more. And it was already complicated enough. But as she looked at him, the gratitude plain on her face, he couldn't seem to make himself regret his concern at the bruised smudges under her eyes. She needed a decent meal, and for the painkillers to kick in before he told her his news.

He knew it was going to freak her out, because according to Megan she'd already resisted this development, which was why he'd flown across an ocean to persuade her.

That was her insecurity talking. She needed a nudge now, and he intended to give it to her. But only once she'd stopped looking so fragile.

The sweet smile, and the explanation—that she

was struggling with period pain—had been a relief. So much so that when her smile had disappeared, he'd felt the loss of it right down to his soul.

And he had a bad feeling he knew the cause. She had assumed he was going to suggest they end the marriage.

Which was insane. Why would he end an arrangement that was working so well?

He'd been in complete control of when and where and how often they met. And the sex had been phenomenal—hot, raw and wildly exciting. So much so that he'd got into the habit of accepting invitations to events he would never usually have bothered attending—simply so he would have an excuse to get his hands on her hot, sweet, responsive body again.

Which had to explain why each time they were together, each time he took her to his bed, he'd found it harder and harder not to demand she stay.

It was probably a good thing she was on her period and not in the mood this evening. He needed to put a few brakes on his libido.

Too much of a good thing was turning him into a fool.

'Have you eaten?' he asked. 'It should get the painkillers working faster.'

'Not since breakfast.'

He swore under his breath. 'No wonder you look so pale.'

He returned to the counter where he'd begun to assemble a sandwich from the supplies he'd found in the fridge.

'What do you want on your sandwich?' he asked. 'There's three different types of ham, Emmental and provolone cheese, *de la salade*, *des avocats et des tomates*?'

'Anything and everything,' she said and he glanced over his shoulder. 'I'm starving.'

'What's so funny?' he asked, even though her spontaneous smile had tugged on the weight in his chest.

She propped herself back on the stool, the flush of pleasure on her cheeks only making her more captivating. 'I'm just looking forward to sitting here and watching the big bad billionaire make me a sandwich.'

He raised an eyebrow at the amused and incredulous tone. 'You think I don't know how to make a sandwich? I worked twelve-hour shifts making sandwiches in a bistro on the Ile de France for six weeks after busting my ankle on the bike the summer after I arrived in Paris.'

'You broke your ankle?' Her face fell comically. 'How? Were you badly hurt?'

The concern shadowing her eyes had the weight in his chest dropping down into his stomach. Not good. 'Long story,' he murmured.

She got the message and didn't press, and the moment passed. Thankfully.

They ate their sandwiches with a Cabernet he had found in the cellar. And she asked him about four more times to tell her his news. He resisted, until he had her resting in the living room on the sofa. Sitting beside her, he picked up her feet and put them in his lap, because the urge to touch her never went away, period or no period.

She sighed, and a deep shudder went through her as he dug into the arch of her foot with his thumb.

'Good?' he asked, pleased as he felt the tight muscle release—even if her soft moan wasn't making him feel particularly relaxed.

'Spectacular,' she murmured, the flushed smile the only reward he needed.

'How is the pain?'

'Gone,' she said. 'Now will you tell me what your business news is?'

He assessed her to make sure she wasn't lying, but she looked comfortable and sated, and as relaxed as he was going to get her.

He worked the muscles in her feet a moment more. Realising he was a little nervous himself. He had been sure this was a good thing, that she needed this push, but he hoped he hadn't miscalculated.

'Dominic, please,' she said. 'What's happening with your business?'

'It's not my business, it's yours. Or rather ours.'

'What about it?' she said, her foot tensing right back up again.

'I've arranged for you to show the Allycat Collection at a Fashion Week prelim event for new designers in July in TriBeCa. Megan suggested it. It's basically a competition to win a spot at the week itself in September.'

'You did what?' She jerked her feet out of his lap,

her face going so pale she looked as if she were about to pass out. 'You can't be serious? I'm not ready for this. The collection's not ready. July is only a few weeks away.'

'It's a month and a half away,' he said.

'Oh, God.' She swung her feet to the floor and bent over, clutching her stomach as if she were about to be sick. 'I haven't even made any of the prototypes yet,' she moaned.

'Megan told me the designs are incredible and the make-up and fitting stage shouldn't take more than a month. Plus you only need a small sample for this show.'

'You've been talking to Megan behind my back?' She was still clutching her stomach, the horrified expression making the weight in his abdomen swell.

He'd known she would be against the idea at first, which was precisely why he'd taken this step without consulting her. She was still letting her insecurities rule her decision-making process.

'Megan only brought the opportunity up in passing because she couldn't understand why you hadn't thought of entering. I contacted the organisers on my own.'

'You don't know what you've done.' She stood up, pressing a hand to her forehead. 'Maybe I could back out.'

He stood and placed his hands on her shoulders, turned her round to face him. 'We're not backing out,' he said. 'Whatever you need to make this happen, you have my full support.'

He hadn't meant to upset her and it made his stomach hurt too, to see her in this much distress; he hadn't realised she was still this insecure. Everything she'd told him about the business, and everything he'd gleaned from Megan, had been overwhelmingly positive. Apparently, she'd been holding out on him.

But that didn't alter the fact this was a great opportunity. Even if she didn't win the competition, it would give her visibility and experience. So far, she'd stayed in her comfort zone. You couldn't make things happen in business if you did that.

'I can't do it,' she said, the panic and devastation clear in her voice. 'I don't even have the proper materials any more. The fabric I had planned to use as the signature feature of my collection just got poached by another designer.'

He held her shoulders and pulled her into his arms. Damn, she was shaking. She wasn't just freaking out now, she was having a full-on panic attack.

He cradled her face in his hands, pulled her gaze to his. 'Can you get a replacement?'

'It took me two months to find this one. And I don't have that time. Not if I'm going to show a collection that doesn't even exist in six weeks.'

At least she was admitting the show would happen. He took that as a positive step.

Reaching into his back pocket, he pulled out his phone. 'Who's the supplier?'

'It's a Mumbai co-operative. They work with girls and women who have been abused or made homeless. Their workmanship is exquisite and the fabrics they make stunning. But they need exposure, exposure I can't give them. It was naïve of me to think I could when I'm...'

'This show will give them exposure, no?'

'Yes, but...' Flags of colour appeared on her pale cheeks, but her eyes remained dark with fear. 'Not the exposure they need, if it's a disaster.'

His frustration flared—why hadn't she told him about this problem when she'd arrived? But he banked it. She was scared. He understood scared. But he had her back. That was what he'd promised her two months ago. Now it was time to deliver.

'What's the name of the co-operative?' he asked.

'The Dharavi Collective.'

He keyed in Selene Hartley's number and lifted the phone to his ear. 'Selene, there is a fabric workshop in Mumbai called the Dharavi Collective. Allycat Designs would like to secure exclusive use of their fabrics for the next year. We will beat any price they have been offered by a rival brand and would also like to put the full weight of LN India behind them to get funding and exposure for their charitable work.'

After Selene had asked him a few further questions about the negotiation, he ended the call.

'If they have already signed with your rivals we can negotiate with them for a licence to use the material.'

Alison blinked, looking shell-shocked. 'I didn't know you had offices in India.'

'LeGrand Nationale is an international company,' he said. 'I've been to India many times. It's a fasci-

nating, beautiful country, full of talent and initiative.
And projects such as this collective. Why wouldn't I
have offices there?'

'Yes, why wouldn't you?' she said. But her chin
dropped to her chest and her shoulders slumped and
he knew they were not out of the woods yet.

The fabric situation was only a symptom of a much
bigger roadblock. Alison's fear of failure.

He tucked a knuckle under her chin. 'You must
talk to me, Alison. I can't help, if you don't tell me
what the problem is.'

'I just...' She sighed. 'I'm not sure I'm good
enough. Everything's happening too fast. I'm scared
to make a mistake, to let anyone down. If the show
fails, the—'

'No, no, no.' He gripped her face, pressed a kiss
to her forehead, to stop the rambling irrational fears.
'This is nonsense, Alison.' The heavy weight twisted
into a knot. 'You won't fail, but, even if you did, it
is not the end, it is just an opportunity. A beginning.
There are many ways we can ensure the collective
will be okay, but that's not the real fear that is holding you back, am I right?'

She sucked in a jerky breath, and he watched her
step back from the cliff edge, but then she nodded.
Because however panicked she was, she was not stupid.

'Yes, the real fear is that I'll fail. That I'll take everyone down with me. But I don't know how to stop
worrying about it. How to get past it.'

'You never stop worrying, that's not how it works,'

he said. 'I have over five thousand employees world-wide. People who depend on me to feed and clothe and house themselves and their families. And that responsibility weighs on me constantly. But every day I take new risks. Sometimes there is a reward, other times a punishment. And if the risk doesn't pay off, if I fail, I try to bear the brunt of the punishment, to protect the people who work for me. But without the risk and the reward, my business would die anyway, do you see?'

'But it's easier for you to take those risks,' she said, although he could see he was getting through, because the colour had come back into her cheeks. 'You're good at it. You know when a risk is worth taking and how to survive the punishment.'

'Precisely, so next time you must let me help. Not bottle up your fear.'

His phone buzzed. He pulled it out of his pocket and read the text from Selene. Then smiled.

Problem solved.

Clicking on the link Selene had sent through, he passed the phone to his wife. 'Your new fabric supplier Rohana has a message for you.'

He watched over Alison's shoulder as the message played. An excited woman, gesticulating madly at the screen, told Alison how pleased they were to be working with her on the collection and how they couldn't wait to send the first batch of materials.

Alison sniffed as she passed him back the phone. 'I don't believe it. You fixed a problem I've been wrestling with for weeks in a two-minute phone call.' Her grin was tentative but there, which was all he cared about. They had weathered this storm, just like the last one. She would do the show, despite her misgivings, and it would be a triumph, because just like the Dharavi Collective she was brilliant at what she did, even if she was the last one to believe it.

He nodded. 'Of course.'

She choked out a laugh. 'I guess being married to a twenty-eight-year-old billionaire has it uses,' she said. 'Even if I keep tripping over his enormous ego.'

He laughed. Slinging an arm around her shoulder, he placed a kiss on the top of her head, to resist the powerful urge to kiss the teasing smile off her lips. Because that would be bound to start something they would not be able to finish.

'Actually I'm not that precocious,' he murmured. 'I turned twenty-nine while we were in Paris.'

He only realised his mistake when she whipped round and stared at him, her eyes huge with shock.

'It was your birthday while we were in Paris? Why didn't you say something? We should have celebrated. I should have bought you a present. Baked you a cake. Something. Perhaps we could celebrate it now?'

The weight in his stomach twisted back into a knot as he noticed the sheen of hope and excitement.

'Forget I mentioned it,' he said. 'I don't celebrate it,' he added.

'Why not?' she said.

'Because I never have,' he replied.

'*Never?* Not even when you were a child?' She sounded horrified.

'My mother didn't consider my birth something to celebrate,' he said. 'Getting pregnant was what ended her affair with my father.'

He'd always tried not to let it bother him. Marking his birthday each year would have been painful for his mother. It had made him feel left out when other children had talked about their birthdays, but he'd forced himself not to care. They hadn't had money for gifts anyway, so what would have been the point? In truth, he'd only found out about his birth date by accident, after discovering his birth certificate—with his father's name on it—in one of his mother's drawers.

'But, Dominic, that's awful.'

'What you don't have, you don't miss,' he said, suddenly wanting to cut off the conversation. Why had he confided so much?

'Are you sure you don't want to start celebrating it?' Alison said. 'I make a mean chocolate cake.'

'Yes, I'm sure.'

He steeled himself against the shadow of hurt in her eyes. And the brutal pang of longing. What would be the point of celebrating his birthday this year, when there would be no one here to celebrate with him next year?

CHAPTER ELEVEN

Can you come to Rome tomorrow night? Selene will make all the arrangements if you can spare the time before the show. D

ALLY READ THE text that had popped up on her smartphone five minutes ago for the twentieth time. Or was it the thirtieth time? She was looking for hidden meaning, or additional information. Or some sign that things had changed in their relationship, if only a little bit, since their night together in London.

But Dominic's text was exactly the same as all the others she'd received over the past three months requesting her presence by his side—polite, pragmatic and distant.

The giddy jump in her pulse was familiar, but the strange feeling of disappointment not so much.

Why had she expected there to be something more this time? It had been three whole weeks since his visit to London—and they had both been extremely busy.

Three weeks since she'd woken up to find him gone again, and had been stupidly crestfallen.

They'd had a wonderful evening, after he'd given her a heart-to-heart about her business, persuaded her to do the runway show in TriBeCa and fixed her problem with the Dharavi Collection…

And confided in her why he didn't celebrate his birthday.

But as they'd sat on the couch together watching an old black and white movie on the large flat-screen TV she never used, a series of unanswered questions had tormented her. How had he survived as a child with so little love? How selfish was his mother, that she hadn't wanted to celebrate her son's birth? Had she made him feel guilty just for being born? It had made Ally feel desperately sad for him. But it had made her even sadder to know he didn't want to celebrate it with her.

He'd shut down as soon as he'd told her, closed himself off again and made it clear she couldn't go there. So she hadn't.

Still she'd hoped he might be there in the morning. So she could get up the guts to ask him a few of the questions that still burned inside her, but of course he hadn't been.

She clicked on the phone's reply bar but her fingers stalled as she tried to formulate a response to the businesslike text—a reply that didn't sound too needy, or too clingy, or too over-emotional.

This was an invitation she'd been waiting for and hoping to receive every day for the past three weeks, ever since that morning—she didn't want to spoil it with expectations that were unlikely to be fulfilled.

Eventually she settled on a simple reply.

Looking forward to it. I could do with a break from all the chaos here. A

But as soon as she'd sent the text, she added another line.

I've never been to Rome.

She didn't want him to know how much she was looking forward to seeing him.

What mattered wasn't what Dominic put in a text, but that he had asked her to be with him and she was going to see him again, tomorrow night.

Twenty-four hours later she was feeling considerably less positive as she stood in the empty penthouse suite of a five-star hotel overlooking the Palazzo Poli.

Decorated in glorious Baroque flourishes to match the building outside, with an imposing four-poster bed in the main bedchamber, the suite of rooms was spectacular. She'd been whisked by limousine from Fiumicino airport and then greeted in Dominic's suite two hours ago by one of his assistants and a small army of beauty professionals. Ally had brought her own gown for the evening—one of the early prototypes she and her seamstress had been working on for the past two weeks. But even after being prepped by the team of beauticians and a hair stylist for an hour, she didn't feel any more secure.

Why hadn't Dominic met her at the airport? It was nearly six o'clock and she'd been ready for over an hour; all she'd received so far was a text to say he would be late—but no explanation as to why.

Rome's nightlife buzzed with vitality a hundred feet below as she stood on the suite's ornate balcony. The scene was awe-inspiring—or should have been. The water tumbled over the iconic Roman stonework of the Trevi Fountain, given an enchanting glow by the nightlights. The fountain was the imposing centrepiece of a square choked with tourists and a few courting couples.

But, unlike the many other new sights and sounds she'd seen since marrying Dominic, the scene below her failed to inspire the usual excitement or exhilaration. Because, for the first time, he wasn't here to share it with her.

Her gaze landed on one of the couples in the square, fooling around on the side of the fountain. The girl stood with her back to the water and threw in a coin over her shoulder. Her boyfriend locked his arms round her waist and swung her in a circle. The noise of the crowd and the free-flowing water drowned out the sound but she was sure she could hear the girl's carefree giggle floating on the warm Roman evening.

The sight pierced her heart—reminding her of the time when Dominic had lifted her and spun her around in his arms when they'd agreed to become business partners. She'd felt so young and happy in that moment, convinced that, whatever the limitations of their marriage, she was doing the right thing, but now she wasn't so sure. Had she become too dependent on Dominic, on his strength and support? She'd tried so hard to remember that end-date, that this relationship was essentially a business arrangement with some spectacular benefits. But why didn't it feel like that any more? And where had this yearning come from to know more about him, to have him give her more?

She heard the suite door open and close behind her.

A low voice rippled down her spine. 'Alison, *bonsoir*—sorry I am late.'

Swinging round, she felt her heart leap into her throat. The swell of emotion so strong and elemental at the sight of him—strong and indomitable in the tailored tuxedo—it flooded through her body like a tsunami.

And suddenly she knew the answer to the question she had been so careful not to ask herself until now.

The reason she wanted more, she needed more, was that she had fallen hopelessly in love with her husband.

'Bonsoir,' she said, her voice coming out on a panicked whisper as she pressed shaking palms into the red velvet of her gown.

Oh, Ally, what have you done?

'You look exquisite,' he murmured.

She forced a smile to her lips, despite her fear. 'So do you.'

In a tuxedo Dominic was completely devastating. But that wasn't the reason her heartrate was accelerating like a racing car on the starting grid at Brands Hatch.

He gripped her fingers and pulled her into his embrace. Something dark and dangerous flared in his rich chocolate eyes and he pressed his lips to her neck, making the sensitive skin sizzle and burn.

'I wish we didn't have to go to this damn event now,' he murmured as his hands stroked her bottom.

She felt the instinctive shudder of need—and wished they didn't have to attend it either. Her panties were already damp at the prospect of his lovemaking. She wanted the security of hard, sweaty sex, of feeling him deep inside her, to take the fear and panic away. At least for a little while. Until she knew what to do with this revelation. Because she instinctively knew Dominic was far from ready to hear it.

But surely he would be, given time. He'd already been like a real husband in so many respects, offering her support and encouragement, pushing her to be the best she could be in business. Giving her ecstasy and security in equal measure. And she hoped she'd given him the same. If only he would let her give him her love this could be a good marriage, a strong marriage, a lasting one.

'Do we have to go?' she asked.

He let out a strained chuckle and lifted his head. 'Unfortunately, yes. It is a charity event. If we do not show it will reflect very badly on our public image.' He smiled, the sensual smile that always drove her wild—full of a boyish charm she had come to adore.

'Especially as everyone will guess what we were doing instead.'

She blushed as his teasing ignited the hot spot between her thighs.

'Plus we don't want to waste an opportunity for you to get exposure for this dress.' His hand remained fastened to her side as he led her across the suite to pick up the stole she'd left on the chaise longue. 'Is it one of the designs for the show?'

He wrapped the stole around her bare shoulders and then lifted the tendrils of hair that hung down her neck.

'Yes,' she said, hearing the strained chuckle at her shiver of reaction.

'It is beautiful,' he said, the desire flaring in his eyes as he escorted her to the penthouse suite's private elevator.

She held onto him as they stepped into the gilded lift. The fear and panic coalescing in her stomach into a wellspring of hope as he murmured: 'You are going to be a sensation in three weeks' time.'

And for the first time, she believed it. If she could conquer that fear, surely she could conquer this one, too, and find a way to tell him, eventually, how much more she wanted from this marriage.

They arrived at the elegant forecourt of the Teatro dell'Opera di Roma less than fifteen minutes later for a production of Verdi's *Otello*.

Ally absorbed the stunning grandeur of the nineteenth-century auditorium as they were escorted into the royal box—red velvet upholstery and curtains added another layer of luxury to the intricate gold plasterwork. She dipped her head back, letting her gaze travel past the five tiers of viewing galleries at the other side of the stage until it reached the rotunda decorated with nymphs and cherubs cavorting across a heavenly sky.

While Dominic thanked the young usher who had brought them to their seats and gave him a generous tip, Ally scanned the programme. She didn't understand much of it because it was all written in Italian, until her gaze snagged on the name of the charity, which was in French. How odd. *Fondation pour les Garçons Perdus.*

'That's interesting,' she said as Dominic took the seat beside her. 'The charity this event is supporting is French.'

'Is it?' he said, undoing the button on his tuxedo, but tension had rippled across his jaw.

'I think so. The name is French. Doesn't that mean Foundation for Lost Boys?' She showed him the programme, pointing to the French wording.

'Yes, I guess so,' he said, but then he took the programme from her hand and placed it on the table in front of them. 'Come here,' he said, and gripped her hand as the lights dimmed.

'Dominic, what are you doing?' she gasped as he tugged her out of her seat.

As applause rained down from the different tiers, the opening bars of the opera rang around the auditorium—stark and dramatic—and the curtain lifted,

she found herself pulled into Dominic's lap. His callused palm sent giddy arousal sinking into her sex as
it stroked her thigh under her gown.

'I want you too much,' he growled as his hand
sank into her hair, sending the pins holding the elaborate do flying.

Before she could protest, or even get her bearings,
his mouth was on her—firm, seeking, demanding.
His tongue drove the hunger as he forced her to strad-
dle him, her damp panties connecting with the thick
ridge in his pants.

He was fully erect, hard and long. The feel of his
need was like a match lighting the fire inside her. As
he sucked on her tongue, drawing her deeper into the
erotic fog, his hand travelled to the juncture of her
thighs and the heel of his palm pressed against the
aching bundle of nerves.

She bucked, the contact too sweet, too brutal.

'Dominic?' She dragged her head back. 'We can't,
we'll be arrested. People can see us.' She moaned
against his ear as his hand continued to tantalise the
swelling spot between her legs. The music and the
deep male voices from the stage reached a crescendo,
drowning out her ragged pants as the battle raged inside her.

'No one is watching,' he said, the urgency in his
voice matching her own.

But even cocooned in darkness, she felt exposed,
raw, her heart sinking into her abdomen, her need too
visceral, too demanding.

'Stand up,' he commanded, then grasped her waist

to lift her off his lap. He stood and dragged her to the side of the booth, giving them a semblance of privacy, hidden behind the heavy velvet curtain she'd been admiring only moments before.

'I want to be inside you,' he said.

She nodded, her heart ramming her throat at the urgency in his voice.

She could have sworn she could hear the sibilant hum of his zip releasing above the cacophony of sound coming from the stage. His hands stole under the layers of velvet and taffeta in her dress; her back butted the wall as he boosted her into his arms.

'Wrap your legs around my waist,' he urged, the thick head of his penis probing past the gusset of her panties and finding the slick folds of her yearning sex.

She did as he told her, disorientated. How could she survive this need? This desperation?

She clung to him as he thrust heavily inside her.

She groaned, the fullness immense. He paused, but only for a moment, to give her time to adjust to the brutal pleasure. Then he started to move. Slow at first, but then faster, harder, rocking out, thrusting deep. Her pants became sobs, his groans became grunts, until all she could hear, all she could feel was the devastating wave washing through her like a tsunami. She tumbled over, but he didn't stop, didn't even slow down, dragging her back into the maelstrom.

The dark need grew again, becoming huge, becoming overwhelming, the coil at her core twisting, as he dug ruthlessly at the spot inside her he knew would destroy her control… The pleasure became pain, so sharp, too sharp. She clung on, grasping his shoulders, and rode the whirlwind only he could create.

'*Encore.*'

The guttural French demand echoed in her head. *Again.*

She plunged over the edge, her cry muffled against his shoulder as he plunged into her one last time and then followed.

Her galloping heartbeat slowed, but her wits remained scattered in the heady wave of afterglow. His fingers tensed on her hips, the ache immense as he eased out of her.

He held her arm as she tried to steady herself, her legs like limp noodles, as he placed her on her feet.

She must look a mess, her dress creased, her breathing uneven, her hair falling down on one side.

'*Pardon,*' he said, the word so rigid and filled with self-disgust she flinched. 'I don't know what happened to me.'

She lifted a hand to his cheek, caressed his stiff jaw, hearing the self-recriminations, the fury with himself, and wanted to weep. 'It's okay, Dominic, I was desperate, too. It's been a long three weeks.'

And I love you.

The declaration echoed in her mind, but she held onto the words. It was too soon, not the right moment, to burden him with more, when he already seemed to be burdened with so much she didn't understand.

His phone buzzed. He lifted it out of his pocket and she could see the screen.

A woman's face appeared by the call sign, next to the name 'Marlena'.

Who's Marlena?

'I must take this,' he said, then stepped away from her.

He spoke furiously into the phone in a stream of fluent Italian.

He spoke Italian?

Whoever Marlena was, she had his full attention as the call continued, none of which she understood.

It could only have lasted a few minutes, but it felt like hours as she watched the emotions cross his face in the shadows of the booth, for once unguarded and unrestrained. Concern, panic, desperation, was that what his love really looked like?

Desdemona's melodic soprano from the stage couldn't drown out the discordant beats of her heart as he ended the call.

'I must leave,' he said.

He lifted her fingers to buzz a kiss across the knuckles but his detachment, his distance, felt like a physical blow. He wasn't here with her any more, he was with Marlena.

'Wait, Dominic.' She held onto his hand, refusing to let him discard her so easily when her sex was still aching from his lovemaking.

She knew he'd kept things from her. She knew he had never wanted her to see past the barriers he put around his heart. And she'd respected that because she'd thought she had to, until he was ready. Until they were *both* ready to take the next step.

But she had never thought, not even for a moment, that this marriage had been a complete sham—a cover for something else.

All this time, while she had been convinced he wasn't ready to love, had he been giving what she yearned for to someone else?

'Who's Marlena?' she asked, her voice dull.

His scarred brow rose in surprise, but then she saw the guilt flicker across his face.

'She does not concern you,' he said. 'Stay and enjoy the rest of the show.' The suggestion came out as a command. Cold and final.

As he strode out of the box without a backward glance, her heart—which had been so full, so joyous, so hopeful only moments before—shattered.

Dominic was still shaking as he climbed into the SUV and barked an instruction at his driver.

A new message appeared on his phone in Italian from Marlena Romano.

Dominic, there is no need to leave the event. We have alerted the police to Enzo's disappearance and will inform you as soon as we have any news.

He typed a reply in Italian—not easy with his fingers still trembling from the feel of his wife, coming apart in his arms. And the look of devastation on her face afterwards.

Not a problem, Marlena. I am on my way.

He had caught Enzo, a ten-year-old street kid, trying to pick his pocket that afternoon, while he had been waiting outside the hotel for the car that was due to take him to the airport and Alison.

He'd been so preoccupied with thoughts of his wife and how much he wanted to see her again, to hold her, to find out how her show was progressing, that the nimble-fingered young thief had almost got away with his wallet.

But as soon as he'd grabbed the child's bony wrist, heard the boy's cry of distress and seen the angry defiance in his jaded eyes, it had been like looking into a mirror. And all the reasons why he shouldn't be quite so eager to see Alison again had come tumbling back to him.

Marlena was right, of course. It wasn't an efficient use of his celebrity to leave an event that had been planned for months to help fund the Lost Boys charity he had set up in Rome and a collection of other European cities, to help street kids like himself, both boys and girls—children who had no hope and no chance and no opportunities. To give them the support and encouragement they needed to succeed and tap all that wasted talent and potential before it was too late.

All he would be doing was getting in the way. Marlena and her staff were highly trained and extremely capable and once the police located Enzo, and returned him, the staff would be better placed to convince the boy to take the chance the home could offer him.

But when he had received Marlena's call he hadn't been thinking straight. The truth was he hadn't been thinking at all.

He'd needed a way out, an excuse to escape from the emotions threatening to choke him as he'd looked at his wife's dishevelled appearance, and the dazed shock in her eyes, and felt like an animal.

How could his hunger, his need, have got so spectacularly out of control that he'd taken her against a wall during a public event? When was it ever going to end? Because the more he had her, the more wild he became.

And the driving hunger for sex wasn't even the worst of how delusional he was.

He'd seen the way Alison had gazed at him when he strode into the hotel suite earlier that evening. Her eyes soft with longing.

They only had a few more months of their marriage left, and already he had let it get so far out of hand he couldn't even control his hunger for her, let alone the greed to have more of her than he could ever deserve.

That would have to end tonight. He would speak to Marlena, gauge the situation with Enzo, wait for word from the police and stay away from Alison until she had gone back to London. And he wouldn't contact her again, until he was finally back in control of his senses.

The car sped past the Coliseum on its way out of Rome towards the suburbs.

The arc lights illuminated the ancient building's

broken façade and for the first time, instead of seeing the epic majesty of the place, and everything the
people who had built it had achieved, all he saw was
a ruin, the brutal bloodshed once celebrated within
its walls a symbol of the hollow shame inside him.

CHAPTER TWELVE

ALLY WATCHED THE black SUV stop in front of a large mansion block in the outskirts of the city.

Dominic got out of the car and headed past the children's play equipment in the building's front garden, the bars of a climbing frame glinting in the moonlight. Confusion accelerated the hammer thuds of her heartbeat.

She wasn't even sure what had possessed her to follow him. She'd left the opera in a daze, the pain of his betrayal so huge it was almost choking her.

The questions running through her mind telling her what a fool she'd been.

Why had she assumed their marriage would be exclusive? After all, he'd never put that stipulation in any of the paperwork he'd made her sign. Why had it never even occurred to her to ask? Because she'd never asked him about anything? She'd never insisted or demanded a single thing. She'd trusted him implicitly, right from the first.

But as the young cab driver had sped through the streets of Rome following the SUV with the skill and precision of Jason Bourne in a chase scene—and telling her in broken English how much he'd always wanted a fare like this one—the open wound in her chest had made it brutally clear that stupidity and naiveté weren't her only flaws. She still loved him, despite her suspicions.

'*Scusa, signorina?* You go in?' the cab driver asked from the front of the car.

Did she want to go in? Indecision added to the trauma.

The building Dominic had disappeared into looked like a school. Or maybe a children's home.

Did his mistress work here? What if she'd made a terrible mistake and he wasn't seeing another woman? Perhaps she should return to the hotel as he'd requested, wait for him to come back?

But even as the desperate hope that she had been wrong, or misguided, that she'd jumped to the wrong conclusion, bubbled inside her, the voice in her head that had persuaded her to follow him in the first place refused to be silent.

Was this really about whether or not Dominic had been seeing another woman? Or was it much more fundamental than that?

He'd shut her out, from so much of his life, his past, his future, and yet he had become such an important part of hers. He'd refused to let her in. Hidden behind the business arrangement they'd made long after it had stopped being just about business and become so much more for her.

She'd fallen in love with him weeks ago, maybe

even months ago, and she'd been in denial about that, too. But she wasn't in denial any more.

Whatever this place was, whoever Marlena was, they were significant in Dominic's life and yet she knew nothing about them. Good grief, she hadn't even known her husband spoke fluent Italian.

He'd talked about trust once before, when they'd consolidated their marriage bargain—but she'd always trusted him. It was him who had never trusted her...

Opening her purse with trembling fingers, she pulled out two twenty-euro notes and passed them to the driver. *'Grazie, mille.'*

'Grazie, signorina. You want I wait?' he asked as he took the money.

Yes. Just in case I don't get up the guts to follow him into that building.

She stifled the plea. She'd been enough of a coward already. Letting him set the boundaries of this relationship. She didn't want to be bound by that contract any more. She wanted a real marriage. Or no marriage at all. She couldn't live like this, or she would be exactly what she'd always strived to avoid. A shadow of who she could be, a woman like her mother, chasing dreams and not facing reality.

'No, *grazie,*' she said and forced herself to step out of the car.

She took a deep breath, which did nothing to calm her racing heartbeat, or close the hole that had opened up in her belly. And walked up the path to the building's main entrance as the cab drove away.

As she rang the bell she read the sign on the door: *Fondazione per Ragazzi Perduti.*

It was an Italian translation of the charity named in the opera programme—the charity Dominic had pretended to know nothing about.

The bitter truth stabbed at her stomach like a rusty blade. So he'd lied about that too.

The door opened, and a middle-aged woman in jeans and a jumper stood in front of her, her warm caramel eyes widening in surprise.

Marlena.

Ally recognised her immediately; she was striking, even though she looked considerably older than she had in the picture on Dominic's phone Ally had glimpsed a half-hour ago.

Ally almost smiled at the shock on the woman's face. This situation would have been comical if it weren't so tragic.

'Signora LeGrand?' she said, and Ally realised she must have recognised her from the press photos, but as Ally nodded, unable to speak round the boulder of misery in her throat, the woman didn't look remotely guilty or abashed.

A tiny portion of the pain faded. So Marlena wasn't Dominic's lover. She had been wrong about that. But the relief she ought to have felt didn't come.

Why had Dominic deliberately let her assume the worst? Exactly how much contempt did he have for her and their marriage? And how much more pathetic could he make her feel? When she had chased him across Rome simply to have the truth confirmed.

'*Buena sera,*' the woman said, her expression changing from surprise to concern. 'Come,' she said, gesturing for Ally to step into the lobby of the building. 'Dominic is here—you are looking for him, yes?'

The lobby was warm and bright, modern and colourful. Framed children's paintings covered the walls. There was a chalkboard pinned with a series of flyers and messages in Italian. She could hear rap music playing and see what looked like a rec room through a glass partition, where a group of teenagers lounged, some watching a football game on a large flat-screen TV, others competing with each other on a computer console.

'I told him he did not need to come,' Marlena said from behind her, her English perfect. 'Enzo absconded earlier, but the police have found him. I am so sorry your evening has been interrupted.'

'Enzo? Who's Enzo?' she said, blankly.

'Enzo is the homeless boy Dominic caught trying to pick his pocket this afternoon.' The woman smiled, but her puzzled expression said it all; clearly she had expected Dominic to mention this boy to Ally.

'Dominic brought him to us earlier. He is one of the many children Dominic has helped with his patronage of *la fondazione,*' the woman added.

Her explanation was drowned out by the pounding in Ally's ears when Dominic appeared from a door at the back of the lobby, staring at his phone as he spoke in a stream of Italian. The only word she understood was '*polizia*'.

'Dominic?' Marlena interrupted him and his head jerked up. 'Your wife has arrived.'

His whole body stiffened, and Ally felt the rusty blade in her stomach twist.

'Alison, why are you here?' he said, the edge in his voice sharpening the knife. She wasn't wanted here, in this part of his life, that much was obvious.

'I… I came to find you,' she managed to get out as he marched towards her.

'Come.' His fingers closed over her bare arm like an iron band. 'We should leave.' He said his good-byes to Marlena, but didn't give her a chance to do the same before he had escorted her out of the building.

'Get in the car,' he said as he opened the door to the large black SUV.

She slid into the seat, and stared out of the window as she heard him get in behind her. Her stomach felt as if it were a ship in a storm, being tossed on the undulating waves of her emotions. She couldn't speak, couldn't even think as the car pulled away from the kerb.

'I cannot believe you followed me here,' he said, sounding both angry and incredulous. 'When I asked you to stay at the opera.'

She ought to say something, in her own defence, but as she gazed into the night she decided for once she had nothing to apologise for. If he hadn't wanted her there, he shouldn't have left her with the impression he was running off to see another woman.

'I'd appreciate it if you didn't do that again.' He bit

off the words in staccato bursts of temper. 'I prefer not to be humiliated in front of people who work for me.'

Wouldn't we all prefer that? she thought bitterly.

Silence descended over the dark interior of the car as they made their way back through the city. The tension became like a living breathing thing as she refused to look at him. But finally the one thing that had always failed her in the past began to burn in her gullet like a comet, choking off everything else—the heartache, the pain, the humiliation, the embarrassment, the confusion and panic—until all that was left was the rage.

The rage that she had learned to bury deep, during the years spent watching her mother die.

The car pulled up at the kerb, but, instead of waiting for Dominic to get out and walk around the car to open her door, Ally got out on her own and marched towards the hotel entrance.

She heard him shout something behind her, but she kept on going, the rage cleansing, empowering, enlightening. It flowed through her veins now, burning through everything in its wake like a fireball.

He caught up with her in the lobby, grasped her arm to swing her round to face him. 'Where the hell do you think you are going?' he said—looking wary now as well as angry.

Good.

'To our suite, to pack my bag and go home.' She yanked her elbow free.

Everything she could say, everything she wanted to say, everything she should have said weeks, maybe even months ago careered around her head like dodgem cars in a cheap arcade as she stormed into the elevator and stabbed the button. She'd left him standing in the lobby. He shook his head, as if he were dazed, and then charged after her, but he was too late, the doors closing before he could get his hand inside.

'*Arrêtes*, Alison, we must talk,' he shouted, obviously expecting her to hit the 'open door' button. She didn't.

Everything that needed to be said was still lodged in her solar plexus.

The elevator arrived at their floor. She scrambled in her purse to find the key card, desperate to get into the suite and lock him out.

He'd broken her heart deliberately. It was the only thing her tired brain could grasp hold of. He'd known how she was coming to feel about him, and he'd hurt her, crushed her because he could.

She found the card, but as the green light flashed on the door, the emergency exit slammed open. He must have run up the stairs rather than waiting for the elevator. His footsteps raced down the corridor.

She rushed inside, swung round to slam the door closed just as his palm slapped against the wood. He pushed it open and she scrambled back into the room.

'Get out. I don't want you in here,' she said, the tears streaking down her face.

'*Ma belle*, stop—don't cry...you mustn't cry.'

He reached out to cradle her cheek, his anger replaced by devastation.

But she slapped his hand away. 'Why mustn't I?' she said around the choking sobs now.

'Because I am not worth it,' he said.

Did he really believe that? It seemed that he did from the shame and regret burning in his eyes. But she didn't care, she wasn't going to let him off that easily.

'Why did you do it? Why did you let me believe Marlena was your mistress? Why won't you let me into your life? Why does everything have to be a secret?'

'Because you would hate me more, if you knew what was inside here.'

He pressed a hand to his heart, the need and desire in his eyes almost as painful as the shame.

She backed up until there was nowhere else to go.

'Let me love you. Let me take away the pain?' he said.

He was talking about sex, she understood that, when she wanted so much more, but she couldn't say no to him as he found the zip on the back of her dress and pulled it down. She pushed his jacket off his shoulders, yanked at the buttons on his shirt; the fight to get naked became a battle.

He kicked off his shoes, she unhooked her bra, he unzipped his trousers, shoved them down, the rampant erection bouncing up to tempt her, to mock her.

Within seconds they were naked, panting, the feral need to mate, to forget, gripping them both the way it had in the opera booth. He turned her to the wall, spread her legs and placed his palm above her head as he notched the thick head of penis at her entrance and thrust in from behind.

The visceral wave of pleasure as he ground into her stole her breath and her resistance and the whole of her heart.

Their frantic mating was over in seconds, the glorious peak slamming into her with the force and fury of a freight train as he emptied himself inside her for the second time that night.

They sank to the carpet together, their breathing ragged, the sweat drying on their skin. But as she turned in his arms, to hold his head, to look into his eyes—they hadn't settled anything, they'd only made it more complicated—her gaze snagged on the cheval mirror at the other side of the room. At first all she saw was the tangle of limbs, her pale skin starkly white against his tanned body. Then her heart seized.

A criss-cross of white scars marred the smooth skin of his back. The marks ranged from his shoulder blades right down to the lighter skin of his backside.

What had happened to him? Who could have done such a thing?

'Some people deserve to be hurt, ma petite.'

And suddenly she knew exactly who. And the words he had whispered before they'd fallen on each other—to try and erase the hurt with sex—came back, too.

'Because I am not worth it.'

Sharp pain dug into her stomach, her gasp of distress ringing off the room's luxury furnishings.

His body went rigid and he heaved himself off her. Their gazes locked.

Shame flickered across his face, making the knife in her gut plunge deeper.

All the questions, came tumbling back, but she had answers to them all now.

So this was why they'd always made love in the dark or the semi-darkness…why he always left her in the morning…why he hadn't shared a bedroom with her…why he locked the door so she couldn't join him in the bathroom. It was another secret he'd guarded for three months.

He reached behind him to drag on the shirt that had fallen off his shoulder. To cover the scars.

She grasped his wrist, felt the warm blood pulsing through him, and her heart broke inside for the boy he'd been. 'Don't hide them from me, Dominic, you don't need to,' she whispered, naked, vulnerable, but unafraid.

She'd had no idea his father had been such a monster, but how could she not have known, when all the signs had always been there?

'Your back… The scars…' She choked the words out and saw the muscle in his cheek flex as he looked away. 'Did Pierre do that?'

His eyes darkened, his expression becoming strained and tense.

'I'm so sorry.' She allowed all the compassion she felt for that boy to show in her face.

'Why are you sorry? You didn't do it,' he said, his

voice clipped and wary. 'It was a long time ago and I deserved it.'

'Dominic, how can you possibly believe that?'

Dominic pressed his thumb to her lips. He didn't want to talk about that time in his life, or that night. Why the heck did she think he'd gone to so much trouble to stop her seeing the scars? But he hated seeing the sheen of moisture in her eyes, the compassion he didn't deserve.

Somehow, she had sneaked under his skin. Made him care when he didn't want to care. Made him want more than he should. And more than he would ever be able to reciprocate.

She was so young and vulnerable, so honest and open, so brave and strong, but she had no idea who he really was. He had hoped to keep this from her, had clung to the delusion that if she never discovered the truth, they could end their marriage with dignity. But this relationship had never played out on the terms he'd tried to insist upon. He'd become captivated, enchanted by her and invested in a future he had no right to expect.

And by trying to protect her he'd only hurt her more.

'I'm not that screwed-up kid any more, and my father has been dead for a long time,' he said, determined to take that misty look out of her eyes.

'I know, but why did you hide...?'

'Shh, Alison.' He stroked his thumb across her

lips—wishing he could kiss her into silence. But knowing he had to stop being a coward, and tell her the truth.

She blinked, those amber eyes glossy with tears. 'Did you get those scars that night? Because you were protecting my mother?'

'No.' If only that were true. 'She was protecting me, that's why he hit her, why he threw you both out. I snapped, sick of the insults. I thought I could best him, thought I could finally make him pay for what he'd done to my mother, by abandoning her and me. But I was wrong. I was a stupid child, hyped up on my own bitterness and resentment. She found him using his belt on me and she tried to stop him.'

'Oh, Dominic...' Her eyes widened, the compassion so fierce, he had to fist his fingers to stop from taking what he wanted from her. 'I'm so sorry...'

'You misunderstand me, Alison. I was young and foolish and full of bravado and I was spoiling for a fight with him. And you and your mother paid the price.'

'You can't blame yourself for your father's violence, surely you must see that,' she said. 'You didn't do anything wrong.'

Hadn't he? It certainly hadn't felt right when he had been crawling through the grounds, puking into the underbrush as he'd struggled to breathe through three broken ribs and stave off unconsciousness before he got to the road.

'Maybe.' He wanted to believe the faith in her eyes;

he'd lived with the guilt of that night ever since he'd found out how destitute she and her mother had been. But that wasn't the biggest problem. 'The point is I'm not that boy any more. I look after number one now. Always. I can't give you what you need.'

He brushed her short curls back from her cheek, pressed his lips to the soft skin. She shuddered with reaction, her wide amber eyes darkening on cue.

He forced himself to drop his hand, the rough chuckle strained.

'Yes, you can. You already have. I love you, Dominic,' she said, with such yearning, such honesty. 'So much.'

The guilt gripped his insides.

This was his own fault. He'd stepped over a line three weeks ago in London, maybe even before that. Every time they made love, he wanted to absorb more of her kindness, her care, her tenderness—and Alison's romantic nature, her sweet, compassionate heart had done the rest.

'You can't love me,' he said, forcing his voice to remain firm, despite the riot of emotions churning in his stomach. 'You don't know me.'

He found his boxers and put them on. Then handed her his shirt and turned his back, waiting for her to cover herself. He threaded his fingers through his hair, his hand shaking. He couldn't look at her, couldn't see the pale skin, the marks he'd left on it from their lovemaking, and tell her the truth.

'You cannot love me, Allycat,' he said, his voice breaking on the words. 'No one can.'

* * *

'Why not?' Ally asked.

Dominic lifted his head, his chocolate eyes full of the secrets that he'd worked so hard to hide. And suddenly she understood, who he had been protecting all this time—with his insistence on them living separate lives, in separate countries. Why he had never wanted to stay overnight, why he had hidden the scars, denied their significance, even denied her feelings for him.

He hadn't been protecting himself, he had been protecting her.

'Why, Dominic?' she asked again. 'Why can't I love you?'

He shook his head, looked past her, but the light had left his eyes, becoming flat and wary. 'I am sorry I hurt you,' he said with a finality that chilled her. 'That was not my intention, even if it was inevitable. I will have my lawyers finalise the divorce.'

But as he turned to go, to walk out of her life, she rushed after him and grasped his arm.

'Dominic, stop.'

He glanced down at her fingers, but she refused to remove them. She curled her hand around his forearm instead and gathered every ounce of her courage to say the one thing she knew he would not want to hear. The one thing he had denied for so long, the thing that had been inculcated in him as a young boy by a woman who had never wanted to celebrate his birth and a man who had acknowledged him on a whim one summer and then discarded him in the cruellest way imaginable.

'You're not worthless,' she said.

He tugged his arm free, the amused frown a defence.

'I know I'm not. LN is worth upwards of five billion dollars on the open market,' he said.

'You're not worthless,' she said again.

'I know that,' he replied. But he backed up a step, and her heart broke for him all over again.

The arrogance, the control, the desperate need not to accept her love. Not to need it. It had all been a defence, all along. Because he'd loved his mother and tried to gain his father's respect and they had both thrown his need back in his face.

Of course he didn't trust her feelings, because he didn't trust his own.

This marriage *had* always been more than a business arrangement. His desire to cherish and protect her. His insistence that he invest in her business. His encouragement and concern. And she'd let her own insecurities blind her to that truth. She hadn't challenged him…she hadn't even put up a fight. But she was going to fight now.

'You're not worthless,' she said again. 'Whatever she made you think, whatever he told you. You're not.'

He shook his head, but she could see the arrogance falling away. She'd struck right at the heart of his insecurities but she couldn't let up now. However painful it was for him, however big a risk it was for her, she had to see this through.

'I *do* love you. And it's not because you're incredible in bed, or one of the richest guys on the planet. Or because you've supported my business, supported me.' She let out a weak laugh as the confused frown descended on his face.

No one had ever loved him for who he was. But she did. And she intended for him to know it and believe it. Then they would see.

'Why, then?' he asked, as if he genuinely didn't know. And she had the opening she needed.

'It's because you let me follow you around like a puppy that summer and you never once complained. It's because you blamed yourself for what happened to my mother, to me, when it was never your fault.'

'But you suffered so much,' he said.

'And so did you,' she said, realising so much of that valiant boy—who had wanted payback for his own mother and had taken on a monster to do it— still existed, even if he couldn't see it. 'It's because when I rang your bell all those months ago, you insisted on tending my leg.'

'I was planning to seduce you,' he qualified again. 'I needed a wife.'

She grinned. 'Do you hear me complaining?'

'You were innocent,' he said, his eyes dark with the heat and intensity she had come to adore. 'However much you enjoyed it,' he added, cupping her cheek.

She felt the sizzle of heat, and the connection that had always been there, ever since that summer, arc between them.

She covered his hand, leant into the caress. 'I loved

that you were so scared of exploiting that innocence, even though it really wasn't a big deal to me,' she said, loving his concerned frown even more.

Honestly, men! What was the big deal with virginity?

'And because you fought to give me security and stability in this marriage,' she added, the swelling in her chest making her heart beat in hard, heavy thuds. 'Even though it was supposed to be fake.'

'It never felt fake, even when I wanted it to,' he murmured, cupping her other cheek, and touching her forehead with his.

At last, she'd broken through that shield he erected to protect himself from rejection. The shield that had made him believe he didn't deserve to be loved. That he didn't deserve her.

The connection was so sure, so solid, she could hear it in his ragged breathing. How ridiculous that they'd both denied the importance of that connection for so long.

'It's because you're the kind of man who wants to give children like Enzo the helping hand you never had,' she continued. 'And because you pulled out all the stops to help me achieve my dream, even when I was busy sabotaging it with self-doubt.' She sighed. 'And because you gave me a foot rub to try and ease my pain.'

'That's such a small thing,' he murmured, his voice barely a whisper as she held his waist and he caressed her neck, his fingers threading into her hair.

'Well, it was a really excellent foot rub,' she said,

smiling at him. 'So not *that* small.' Then she sobered. 'It's the small things that matter, Dominic. As much as, if not more than, the big things.' She drew back, so she could look into his eyes. The small things they'd both been denied by living separate lives when they deserved to be together.

'Now do you believe I love you?' she asked quietly.

He nodded. 'But do you love me enough to stay with me?' he asked, the yearning, the longing that she'd thought was hers alone clear in his voice.

She sucked in a deep breath. Knowing it would be so easy to just say yes. She already had so much more than she'd thought she'd have. But she couldn't chicken out. Her cowardice—and his—had brought them to this point. Now they both needed to be brave. He'd been brave enough to admit how unsure he was about love. She needed to be brave enough to demand what she needed.

'I want to stay, but I have conditions.'

His eyebrow arched. 'Conditions? What kind of conditions? Are we going to have to renegotiate the contract again?'

She laughed, the breath releasing in a rush. Maybe this was going to be much easier than she had assumed. 'No, we're going to have to tear it up.'

'I see,' he said.

'I don't want a time limit on our marriage. I want… I want us to be a real couple in every sense of the word. I don't want to limit my feelings for you. And I want us to live together. Either in London or New York, or wherever works.'

He nodded. 'I'm sure we can work something out,' he said, and her heart leapt into her throat.

'I want to be able to tell you I love you. And know that it doesn't scare you, or threaten you or—'

'It doesn't,' he said, interrupting her. 'It humbles me.'

'Really?' she asked, letting the last of her insecurities show.

'*Dieu*, Alison. How could it not?' he said. He stroked her cheek. 'You're so tough and smart and sweet. How could I not fall in love with you?'

'You don't have to say that to make me stay, Dominic,' she said, wanting to take the words at face value, but knowing she couldn't. Hadn't her mother believed them for all the wrong reasons? At least she wasn't going to make that mistake. 'Love is a gift, not an obligation,' she said, because she suspected he had no idea what love was. Who had ever loved him, but her? 'It's enough that you want to give this relationship a chance. A real chance. You don't have to love me back. Not yet.'

'That's very generous of you,' he said, but his lips curved in a rueful smile and she felt the bubble of hope break open inside her chest, spreading warmth and light where only minutes ago there had been despair. 'Unfortunately, it's too late for that,' he whispered against her lips, the soft glow of happiness joined by the sharp pulse of heat. 'Because I already do.'

Dominic let his mouth take hers, claiming his wife in a kiss that touched his very soul. He was still scared, still terrified really. He wasn't convinced he was as worthy as she believed him to be. Was still sure he didn't deserve her. But after almost losing her, he was damned if he would let that hold him back from claiming her ever again.

She was his wife now, in every sense of the word. Damn the contract, damn his father, damn the fear that had held him back from admitting how he really felt for so long.

Yes, it was a huge risk. But Alison Jones, his Cinderella bride, was worth every ounce of effort it was going to take for him to prove, to himself as much as her, that he deserved to be her husband.

EPILOGUE

Fifteen months later

'SOCIAL MEDIA IS going mad, Ally. And listen to that applause. It's another triumph for the Allycat brand.' Megan De Rossi gave Ally a high-five as the last model strutted onto the catwalk and the wave of noise hit the backstage area. 'Consider New York Fashion Week well and truly conquered,' Megan added, tears forming in her eyes. 'You did it—they adore you.'

'*We* did it,' Ally said, beaming back at her. 'They adore *us*.'

All the hard work, the long hours, the endless worries about everything from a model's sprained ankle yesterday to those first days over a year ago when Dominic had secured her partnership with the Dharavi Collective had paid off. It had been a long hard road to this point—and there would be more bumps along the way—but her brand was due to launch at the end of the month in Europe at Paris Fashion Week and she was already clothing A-list movie stars, Grammy-winning pop stars and a string of influential celebrity vloggers. And now this, another triumph in TriBeCa after that nail-biting baptism of fire a year ago now, when she'd done that first prelim show Dominic had pushed her into.

She could still remember the sweat and tears of that first shaky step onto the fashion industry's world stage. Her nerves had reached fever pitch that evening but she'd pushed through them, and Dominic had been beside her at every step. Offering not just support and encouragement, but also his strength and determination. And the rewards had been immense, not just in that first tentative triumph—although she hadn't won a spot at New York Fashion Week that year, the exposure had started a word-of-mouth buzz about her designs that had led to orders and other opportunities—but also inside herself. Because after that night, she'd discovered that Dominic was right, that risk in business was the same as the risk she'd taken in her private life on him, on them... That risk wasn't something to be afraid of, not if you embraced it and put your all into it, because with risk came rewards, rewards beyond her wildest dreams.

'Come on, you need to take a bow,' Rohana, who was here with some of the women from her collective, shouted above the applause as she and Megan linked arms with Ally to lead her onto the catwalk.

As her team roared their support from the wings, she walked down the narrow runway with the two women who had been an integral part of making her brand such a success.

The cheers reached epic proportions, camera phones flashing, the media spotlights trained on her as the crowd rose to their feet.

But as she waved, and smiled, and bowed, she scanned the crowd. She could see Dario, Megan's husband, standing in the front row with their daughter Issy—who had been given special dispensation to attend the show without her brothers—and Katie, Megan's sister, with her husband, Jared, who had their toddler daughter, Carmen, in his arms. But where was Dominic? She needed him here, because this was his triumph as much as hers.

'Be still my beating heart,' whispered Rohana. 'Your man is a fine sight to see.'

It was all the warning she had before Dominic leapt up on stage.

He strode towards her—the dark blue business suit doing nothing to disguise the ripple of muscle in his big body. The crowd went wild, beginning a chant of 'Kiss her' as he approached—which had become a feature of all her shows since that sidewalk kiss all those months ago in Nolita had made them an Internet sensation.

How far we've come, she thought as he reached her. Gripping her round the waist, he swung her round in a circle, then put her down and cradled her face in his palms.

'Congratulations, Allycat,' he said, then his lips were on hers. The kiss was driven, hungry, joyous, igniting all the needs that would never die.

Her hands found his waist as she clung to him and

kissed him back, her tongue tangling with his, and let the love pour through her.

This man, this marriage, meant everything to her. Without it, without him, without love, even wowing New York Fashion Week wouldn't mean as much.

It was several hours later before they were finally alone together, in the limousine heading back to their Manhattan apartment. The apartment they rarely used since Dominic had made the decision to move permanently to London.

Ally clung to his hand, wishing she could just be beamed up now to their bedroom and they could finally celebrate the brand's latest success in style.

'Happy?' he murmured as he pressed her fingers to his lips.

'Ecstatic,' she said.

'*Bien*, because I have a suggestion,' he said.

'What is it?' she asked, loving the mischievous glint in his eyes. She certainly hoped his suggestion involved them both getting naked as soon as possible.

But then he surprised her.

'That we both take the next week off. It is way past time we had a honeymoon. Can you do it?' he asked.

'Absolutely,' she said without hesitation, because she couldn't think of anything more wonderful. It would mean rearranging her schedule, postponing the interviews she had lined up, getting her team to handle the European launch, but they'd already done a ton of advance publicity, and she trusted them.

'Where would you like to go?' he said. 'Name anywhere in the world and I will take you.'

'Honestly? I can choose anywhere?' she said, knowing there was only one place she wanted to go. And one person she wanted to be with.

Over the past year, her wanderlust had been sated a hundred times over. Ever since that night in Rome, when they had committed to making this a real marriage, life had been a roller coaster as she'd set up her business and his had continued to expand. They'd worked overtime to make this marriage work but it had meant shoehorning snippets of quality time in between all their other commitments. Each moment they'd spent alone together had been precious and wonderful and important...

But a whole week felt like a banquet, a banquet she didn't want to squander on sightseeing, or shopping, or elaborate meals in fancy hotels.

'Of course,' he said. 'Wherever you want to go, it is your choice.'

'Okay, then I want to go home to London, shut the doors, turn off our phones and the Internet, tell everyone we've gone to Outer Mongolia and just stay there, with you, for a week. I want us to watch slushy movies together, cook all our favourite foods, have sex in every room and finally get around to celebrating all the birthdays of yours that we've missed.'

They'd celebrated his thirtieth birthday that summer and the memory of the particularly inventive way he'd found to devour the chocolate cake she'd baked him still made her blush.

Even so, she held her breath, wondering if he would object. Dominic was an active, driven over-achiever; getting him to sit still for long was never easy. But instead of objecting, he threw back his head and laughed. The sound was deep, and sexy and—was that relief she could hear?

Reaching across the seat to cup her cheek and pull her towards him, he whispered across her mouth. 'I like your thinking, Madame LeGrand. But I'm not sure we have enough bedrooms—there are twenty-nine birthdays to catch up on, after all.' Running a hand under her dress, he found the melting heart of her. 'But do not worry,' he added as his mouth de-scended to seal the deal. 'I can improvise.'

Happiness burst like a firework in her chest—not least because she knew exactly how good her hus-band was at improvising.

* * * * *

A Cinderella For The Greek
Julia James

Books by Julia James

Harlequin Modern

A Tycoon to Be Reckoned With
Captivated by the Greek
The Forbidden Touch of Sanguardo
Securing the Greek's Legacy
Painted the Other Woman
The Dark Side of Desire
From Dirt to Diamonds
Forbidden or For Bedding?
Penniless and Purchased
The Greek's Million-Dollar Baby Bargain
Greek Tycoon, Waitress Wife
The Italian's Rags-to-Riches Wife
Bedded, or Wedded?

Visit the Author Profile page at
millsandboon.com.au for more titles.

Julia James lives in England and adores the peaceful, verdant countryside and the wild shores of Cornwall. She also loves the Mediterranean—so rich in myth and history, with its sunbaked landscapes and olive groves, ancient ruins and azure seas. "The perfect setting for romance!" she says. "Rivaled only by the lush tropical heat of the Caribbean—palms swaying by a silver sand beach lapped by turquoise waters...what more could lovers want?"

DEDICATION

To my younger self.

CHAPTER ONE

Max Vasilikos lowered his tall frame into the leather chair by the desk and relaxed back into it, his long legs stretching out in front of him.

'OK, what have you got for me?'

His UK agent handed him a set of glossy brochures. 'I think there are some good contenders here, Mr Vasilikos,' he said hopefully to this most demanding of clients.

Max's dark eyes glanced briefly, and then he found his gaze lingering on only one of the properties.

An English country house, in warm honey-coloured stone, with wisteria tumbling over the porch, surrounded by verdant gardens and sheltering woodland, with a glimpse of a lake beyond the lawn. Bathed in sunshine, the whole place had an appeal that held his gaze, making him want to see the real thing.

He picked up the brochure and shifted his gaze to his agent.

'This one,' he said decisively.

Ellen paused in the hallway. She could hear her stepmother's sharp voice coming from the drawing room.

'This is exactly what I've been hoping for! And I will *not* have that wretched girl trying to spoil it—again!'

'We've just *got* to hurry up and sell this place!'

The second voice came from Ellen's stepsister Chloe, petulant and displeased.

Ellen's mouth tightened. She was all too aware of the source of their displeasure. When Pauline had married Ellen's widowed father she and her daughter Chloe had had only one aim—to spend his money on the luxury lifestyle they craved for themselves. Now all that was left, after years of their lavish spending, was the house they had jointly inherited with Ellen after her father's sudden death last year from a heart attack—and they couldn't wait to sell it. That it was Ellen's home, and had been in her family for generations, bothered them not in the slightest.

Their hostility towards her was nothing new. From the moment they'd invaded her life Pauline and her daughter had treated Ellen with complete contempt. How could Ellen—tall and ungainly, clumping around 'like an elephant', as they always described her—possibly compare with slender, petite and oh-so-pretty Chloe?

She clumped down the rest of the stairs deliberately now, to drown out their voices. It sounded, she thought grimly, as if her stepmother had hopes of a potential purchaser for Haughton. Despite knowing she would need to resort to legal action against her stepdaughter in order to force a sale through, Pauline obdurately kept the house on the market, and relentlessly went on at Ellen to try to wear down her resistance and force her to agree to sell up.

But Ellen's heart had steeled in that first winter without her father, when her stepmother and Chloe had been disporting themselves expensively in the Caribbean. She would make it as difficult as she could for Pauline to sell her beloved home—the home Ellen had been happy in until the terrible day her mother had been killed in a car crash, sending her father spiralling into a grieving tailspin of loneliness that had made him so dangerously vulnerable to entrapment by Pauline's avaricious ambitions.

As Ellen walked into the drawing room two pairs of ice-blue eyes went to her, their joint expressions openly hostile.

'What kept you?' Pauline demanded immediately. 'Chloe texted you an hour ago saying that we needed to talk to you.'

'I was taking lacrosse practice,' Ellen returned, keeping her tone even. She sat down heavily on an armchair.

'You've got mud on your face,' Chloe informed her sneeringly.

Her gaze was not just hostile, but contemptuous. Ellen could see why. Her stepsister was wearing one of her countless designer outfits—a pair of immaculately cut trousers with a cashmere knit top—her nails were newly manicured and varnished, her freshly cut and styled ash-blonde hair and make-up perfect.

A familiar silent sigh went through Ellen. Chloe was everything she was not! Petite, with a heart-shaped

446 A CINDERELLA FOR THE GREEK

face, and so, *so* slim! The contrast with her own appearance—she was still wearing the coaching tracksuit from the nearby private girls' school where she taught Games and Geography, with her thick, unmanageable hair gripped back in a bushy ponytail and her face devoid of any make-up except the streak of mud on her cheek that Chloe had so kindly pointed out!—was total.

'The estate agents phoned this afternoon,' Pauline opened, her gimlet eyes on Ellen. 'There's been another expression of interest—'

'And we don't want *you* ruining things!' broke in Chloe waspishly, throwing a dagger look at her step-sister. 'Especially with this guy,' she continued.

There was a note in her voice that caught Ellen's attention. So, too, did the discernibly smug expression in Pauline's eyes.

'Max Vasilikos is looking for a new addition to his portfolio—he thinks Haughton might be it.' Pauline elucidated.

Ellen looked blank, and Chloe made a derisive noise. 'Oh, for heaven's sake, don't expect *her* to know who Max Vasilikos is,' she said. 'Max Vasilikos,' she spelt out to Ellen, 'is a stinking rich property tycoon. He's also just had an affair with Tyla Brentley—you *must* have heard of her, at least?'

Ellen had, as a matter of fact. She was an English actress who'd found fame in Hollywood in a hugely successful romantic blockbuster, and the pupils at her school were full of her. But as for this Max Vasilikos... Apart from surmising that with a name like that he must be of Greek origin—well, 'stinking rich' property tycoons were nothing to do with her.

And they would be nothing to do with Haughton either, please God! A cold shiver went down her spine. Someone like this Max Vasilikos would sell it on for a huge profit to a Russian oligarch or a Middle Eastern sheikh who would spend a week or two in it, at best, every year or so. And it would languish, unloved and unlived-in...

Pauline was speaking again. 'Max Vasilikos is sufficiently interested to come and view the property himself. As a courtesy I have invited him to lunch with us.'

That smug expression was in her eyes again. Ellen just looked at her. 'Does he understand the ownership structure of Haughton and that I am unwilling to sell my share?' she asked bluntly.

Pauline waved a hand to brush aside this unpalatable detail. 'What *I* understand, Ellen,' she said bitingly, 'is that if—*if*—he expresses an interest, we will be very, very fortunate. I do *not*,' she emphasised, 'want *you* rocking the boat. Moreover—' she glared at her stepdaughter '—if nothing I can say will make you see sense about selling up, perhaps Max Vasilikos can.'

There was an explosive, choking half-laugh from Chloe. 'Oh, Mummy, don't,' she jeered. 'You simply *can't* inflict *her* on him!'

Ellen felt the jibe, flinching inwardly and yet knowing it for nothing but the truth. No man—let alone one who dated film stars—could look at her with anything but complete indifference to her appearance. She had nothing to attract a man in her looks. Knew it…accepted it. At least, though, she wasn't cruel like her stepsister.

Pauline had turned to Chloe. 'Nevertheless, that's just what we are going to have to do,' she continued. 'Ellen *has* to be there.' Her gaze went back to her stepdaughter. 'We'll present a united front.'

Ellen stared. United? A more fractured family was hard to imagine. But, although it would be gruelling to endure, it would at least, she realised grimly, give her the opportunity to make it clear to this Max Vasilikos just how unwilling she was to sell her share of her home.

With reluctant acquiescence she got to her feet. She needed a shower, and she was hungry, too. She headed for the kitchen. It was the part of the house she liked best now—the former servants' quarters, and the perfect place for keeping out of Pauline and Chloe's way. Cooking was not a priority for either woman.

She'd moved her bedroom to one of the back rooms as well, overlooking the courtyard at the rear of the house, and adapted an adjacent room for her own sitting room. She ventured into the front part of the house as little as possible—but now, as she headed back across the hall to the green baize door that led to the servants' quarters, she felt her heart squeeze as she gazed around her at the sweeping staircase, the huge stone fireplace, the massive oak doorway, the dark wood panelling and the ancient flagstones beneath her feet.

How she loved this house. Loved it with a strong, deep devotion. She would never willingly relinquish it. *Never!*

Max Vasilikos slowed the powerful car as the road curved between high hedges. He was deep in Hampshire countryside bright with early spring sunshine, and almost at his destination. He was eager to arrive—keen to see for himself whether the place that had so immediately appealed to him in the estate agency's photos would live up to his hopes. And not just from an investment perspective. The encircling woods and gardens, the mellow stonework, the pleasing proportions and styling of the house all seemed—*homely*. That was the word that formed in his mind.

In fact... *It's a house I could see myself in—*

The thought was in his head before he could stop it, and that in itself was cause for surprise. He'd always been perfectly happy to live a globetrotting life, staying in hotels or serviced apartments, ready to board a plane at any moment.

But then, he'd never known a home of his own. His eyes shadowed. His mother had always been ashamed of his illegitimacy, and that was why, Max thought bleakly, she'd married his stepfather—to try and disguise her child's fatherless status.

But the very last thing his stepfather had wanted was to accept his wife's bastard into his family. All he'd wanted was a wife to be a skivvy, an unpaid drudge to work in his restaurant in a little tourist town on a resort island in the Aegean. Max had spent his childhood and teenage years helping her, keeping the *taverna* going while his stepfather played host to his customers, snapping his fingers at Max to wait at tables while his mother cooked endlessly.

The day his mother had died—of exhaustion as much as the lung disease that had claimed her—Max had walked out, never to return. He'd taken the ferry to Athens, his eyes burning not just with grief for his mother's death, but with a fierce, angry determination to make his own way in the world. And make it a glittering way. Nothing would stop him. He would overcome all obstacles, with determination driving him ever onwards.

Five years of slog in the construction industry and finally he'd saved enough from his wages to make his first property purchase—a derelict farmhouse that, with the sweat of his brow, he'd restored and sold to a German second-home-owner, making enough profit to buy two more properties. And so it had begun. The Vasilikos property empire had snowballed into the global enterprise it now was. His tightened mouth twisted into a caustic smile of ruthless satisfaction. It even included his stepfather's *taverna*—picked up for a song when his stepfather's idleness had bankrupted him.

Max's expression changed abruptly as his sat-nav indicated that he'd arrived at his destination. Manoeuvring between two large, imposing stone gate pillars, he headed slowly along a lengthy drive flanked by woodland and massed rhododendrons that in turn gave way to a gravelled carriage sweep alongside the frontage of the house. He slowed down, taking in the vista in front of him, feeling satisfaction shaping inside him.

The photos hadn't deceived—everything they'd promised was here. The house was nestled into its landscaped grounds, the mellow stonework a warm honey colour, and sunshine glanced off the mullioned windows. The stone porch with its gnarled oak door was flanked by twisted wisteria, bare at this time of year, but with the promise of the show to come. Already in bloom, however, were ranks of golden daffodils, marching thickly along the herbaceous borders on either side of the porch.

Max's sense of satisfaction deepened. It looked good—more than good. Not too large, not too grand, but elegant and gracious, and steeped in the long centuries of its existence. An English country house, yes, built for landowners and gentry, but also inviting, its scale domestic and pleasing. More than a grand house—a *home*.

Could it become my home? Could I see myself living here?

He frowned slightly. Why was he thinking such things?

Have I reached the age where I'm starting to think of settling down? Is that it?

Settling down? That was something he'd never thought of with any woman—certainly not with Tyla. She was like him: rootless, working all over the world.

Maybe that's why we suited each other—we had that in common.

Well, even if that had been true enough at the time,

it hadn't been sufficient to stop him ending things with her. Her absorption in her own beauty and desirability had become tiresome in the end—and now she was busy beguiling her latest leading man, a Hollywood A-lister. Max wished her well with it.

So maybe I need a new relationship? Maybe I'm in search of novelty? Something different—?

He gave himself a mental shake. He wasn't here to ponder his private life. He was here to make a simple business decision—whether to buy this property or not for his extensive portfolio.

Engaging gear again, he crunched forward over the gravel, taking the car around to the back of the house. He drew to a halt and got out of the car, again liking what he saw. The rear façade, built as servants' quarters, might not have the elegance of the front section of the house, but the open cobbled courtyard was attractive, bordered by outhouses on two sides and prettied up with tubs of flowers, and a wooden bench positioned in the sunshine by the kitchen door.

His approval rating of the house went up yet another notch. He strolled towards the door, to ask if it was okay to leave his car there, but just as he was about to knock it was yanked open, and someone hefting a large wooden basket and a bulging plastic bin bag cannoned straight into him.

A Greek expletive escaped him and he stepped back, taking in whoever had barged so heavily into him. She was female, he could see, and though she might be categorised as 'young' she had little else that he could see to recommend her to his sex. She was big, bulky, with a mop of dark bushy hair yanked back off her face into some kind of ponytail. She wore a pair of round glasses on her nose and her complexion was reddening unbecomingly. The dark purple tracksuit she wore was hideous, and she looked distinctly over-weight, Max decided.

Despite her unprepossessing appearance, not for a moment did Max neglect his manners.

'I'm so sorry,' he said smoothly. 'I was seeking to enquire whether I might leave my car here.' He paused. 'I *am* expected. Max Vasilikos to see Mrs Mountford.'

The reddening female dragged her eyes from him and stared at his car, then back at him. Her cheeks flushed redder than ever. She shifted the weight of the basket on her hip but did not answer him.

'So, *is* it all right to leave my car here?' Max prompted.

With visible effort the woman nodded. She might have mumbled something as well, but whatever it was it was indistinct.

He gave a swift, courtesy-only smile. 'Good,' he said, dismissing her from his notice, and turned away to head around the house to the front entrance, his gaze sweeping out over the gardens as he walked. Even this early in the spring he could see that they would be beautiful as summer arrived.

Again he felt that unexpected sense of approval that was nothing to do with whether or not this place would be a profitable investment to make. He walked up to the front door—a massive, studded oak construction—hoping the interior of the house would match the charms of the exterior.

The door opened in front of him—clearly his arrival had been communicated. The female standing there could not, Max thought, have been more different from the one who'd cannoned into him at the kitchen door. She was petite, ultra-slender and immaculately styled, from her chic ash-blonde hair and perfect make-up to her well-tailored outfit whose pale blue hue matched the colour of her eyes. The fragrance of an expensive perfume wafted from her as she smiled warmly at him.

'Mr Vasilikos—do come in!'

She stood back as Max walked in, taking in a large hall with a flagged stone floor, a cavernous fireplace, and a broad flight of stairs leading upwards. It suited the house, Max thought.

'I'm Chloe Mountford. I'm *so* glad you could come.' The daughter of the house—as he assumed she must be—was gliding towards one of the sets of double doors opening off the hall, and she threw them open with a dramatic gesture as he followed after her.

'Mummy, it's Mr Vasilikos,' she announced.

Mummy? Max reminded himself that it was common in English upper crust circles for adult children to use such a juvenile form of address for their parents. Then he walked into the room. It was a double aspect drawing room, with another large but more ornate marble fireplace and a lot of furniture. The decor was pale grey and light blue, and it was clear to his experienced eyes that a top-class interior designer had been let loose in there.

He found himself conscious of a feeling of disappointment—it was all just *too* perfect and calculatedly tasteful—and wondered what the original decor would have looked like. The effect now was like something out of a highly glossy upmarket magazine.

I couldn't live in this. It's far too overdone. I'd have to change it—

The thought was in his head automatically, and he frowned slightly. He was getting ahead of himself again.

'Mr Vasilikos, how lovely to meet you.'

The slim, elegant woman greeting him from one of the upholstered sofas by the fire, holding out a diamond-ringed hand to him, was extremely well preserved and, like her daughter, had clearly lavished money on her clothes and her appearance. A double rope of pearls adorned her neck which, Max suspected, had benefitted from the attentions of a plastic surgeon at some time.

'Mrs Mountford.' Max greeted the widowed owner, his handshake firm and brief, then sat himself down where she indicated, at the far end of the sofa opposite, away from the fire. Chloe Mountford settled herself prettily on a third sofa, facing the fire, at the end closest to Max.

'I'm delighted to welcome you to Haughton,' Mrs Mountford was saying now, in a smiling, gracious tone.

Max smiled politely in response as her daughter took up the conversational baton.

'Thank you for taking the time from what I'm sure must be a dreadfully busy schedule. Are you in England long this visit, Mr Vasilikos?' she asked brightly.

'My plans are fluid at the moment,' Max returned evenly. He found himself wondering whether Chloe Mountford was likely to make a play for him. He hoped not. The current fashion might be for ultra-thin figures, but they were not to his taste. Nor, of course, were women at the other extreme.

His mind flickered back to the female who'd cannoned into him at the back door. Being overweight wasn't a good look either—especially when a woman was badly dressed and plain to boot. A flicker of pity went through him for any woman so sadly unattractive. Then Chloe Mountford was speaking again.

'There speaks the globetrotting tycoon!' she said with a light laugh.

She turned her head expectantly as a door set almost invisibly into the papered wall opened abruptly and a bulky frame carrying a loaded coffee tray reversed into the room. It belonged, Max could see instantly, to the very female he'd just been mentally pitying for her lack of physical appeal.

The unlovely tracksuit had been swapped for a grey skirt and a white blouse, the trainers replaced with sturdy lace-up flats, but her hair was still caught back in a style-less bush, and the spectacles were still perched on her nose. She made her way heavily into the room, looking decidedly awkward, Max could see.

'Ah, Ellen, there you are!' exclaimed Pauline Mountford as the coffee tray was set down on the low table by the fireside. Then his hostess was addressing him directly. 'Mr Vasilikos, this is my stepdaughter, Ellen.'

Max found his assumptions that the hefty female was some kind of maid rearranging themselves. Stepdaughter? He'd been unaware of that—but then, of course, knowing the details of the family who owned Haughton was hardly relevant to his decision whether to purchase it or not.

'How do you do?' he murmured as he politely got to his feet.

He saw her face redden as she sat herself down heavily on the sofa beside Chloe Mountford. Max's glance, as he seated himself again, went between the two young women sitting on the same sofa, took in the difference between the two females graphically. They could hardly be a greater contrast to each other—one so petite and beautifully groomed, the other so large and badly presented. Clearly nothing more than stepsisters, indeed.

'Mr Vasilikos,' the stepdaughter returned briefly, with the slightest nod of her head. Then she looked across at her stepmother. 'Would you like me to pour? Or do *you* want to be mother?' she said.

Max heard the bite in her voice as she addressed the owner of the house and found himself sharpening his scrutiny.

'Please do pour, Ellen, dear,' said Mrs Mountford, ignoring the distinctly baiting note in her stepdaughter's tone of voice.

'Cream and sugar, Mr Vasilikos?' she asked, looking straight at him.

There was a gritty quality to her voice, as if she

found the exchange difficult. Her colour was still heightened, but subsiding. Her skin tone, distinctly less pale than her stepsister's carefully made up features, definitely looked better when she wasn't colouring up, Max decided. In fact, now he came to realise it, she had what might almost be described as a healthy glow about her—as if she spent most of her time outside. Not like the delicate hothouse plant her stepsister looked to be.

'Just black, please,' he answered. He didn't particularly want coffee, let alone polite chit-chat, but it was a ritual to be got through, he acknowledged, before he could expect a tour of the property that he was interested in.

He watched Pauline Mountford's sadly unlovely stepdaughter pour the coffee from a silver jug into a porcelain cup and hand it to him. He took it with a murmur of thanks, his fingers inadvertently making contact with hers, and she grabbed her hand back as if the slight touch had been an unpleasant electric shock. Then she ferociously busied herself pouring the other three cups of coffee, handing them to her stepmother and sister, before sitting back with her own and stirring it rapidly.

Max sat back, crossing one leg over the other, and took a contemplative sip of his coffee. Time to get the conversation going where he wanted it to go.

'So,' he opened, with a courteous smile of interest at Pauline Mountford, 'what makes you wish to part with such a beautiful property?'

Personally, he might think the decor too overdone, but it was obviously to his hostess's taste, and there was no point in alienating her. Decor could easily be changed—it was the house itself he was interested in.

And he *was* interested—most decidedly so. That same feeling that had struck him from the first was strengthening all the time. Again, he wondered why.

Maybe it's coming from the house itself?

The fanciful idea was in his head before he could stop it, making its mark.

As he'd spoken he'd seen Pauline Mountford's stepdaughter's coffee cup jerk in her grip and her expression darken. But his hostess was replying.

'Oh, sadly there are too many memories here! Since my husband died I find them too painful. I know I must be brave and make a new life for myself now.' She gave a resigned sigh, a catch audible in her voice. 'It will be a wrench, though...' She shook her head sadly.

'Poor Mummy.' Her daughter reached her hand across and patted her mother's arm, her voice warm with sympathy. Chloe Mountford looked at him. 'This last year's been just dreadful,' she said.

'I'm sorry for your loss,' Max murmured. 'But I can understand your reasons for wishing to sell.'

A sharp clunk came from the sofa opposite, and his eyes flicked to see his hostess's stepdaughter had dropped her coffee cup on to its saucer. Her expression, he could tell, was tight. His focus sharpened. Beneath his swift glance in her direction he saw her cheeks redden again. Then she reached for the silver coffee pot and busied herself pouring another cup. She did not speak, but the tightness in her face was unabated, even as the colour started to ebb. She took a single gulp from the refilled cup, then abruptly got to her feet.

'I must go and see about lunch,' she said brusquely, pushing past the furniture to get to the service door.

As she left Pauline Mountford leant towards him slightly. 'Poor Ellen took my husband's death very hard,' she confided in a low voice. 'She was quite devoted to him.' A little frown formed on her well-preserved and, he suspected, well-Botoxed forehead. 'Possibly too much so...' She sighed.

Then her expression changed and she brightened.

'I'm sure you would like to see the rest of the house before lunch. Chloe will be delighted to take you on the grand tour!' she gave a light laugh.

Her daughter got to her feet and Max did likewise. He *was* keen to see the house—and not keen to hear any more about the personal circumstances of the Mountford family, which were of no interest to him whatsoever. Chloe Mountford might be too thin, and her stepsister just the opposite, but he found neither attractive. All that attracted him here was the house itself.

It was an attraction that the 'grand tour' only intensified. By the time he reached the upper floor, with its array of bedrooms opening off a long, spacious landing, and stood in the window embrasure of the master bedroom, gazing with satisfaction over the gardens to let his gaze rest on the reed-edged lake beyond, its glassy waters flanked by sheltering woodland, his mind was made up.

Haughton Court would be his. He was determined on it.

CHAPTER TWO

ELLEN MADE IT to the kitchen, her heart knocking. Having *anyone* arrive to look over her home, thinking he was going to buy it, was bad enough—but…oh, dear Lord…that it was such a man as Max Vasilikos! She felt her cheeks flame again, just as they'd flamed—horribly, hideously—in that first punishingly embarrassing moment of all but sending him flying at the back door.

She had been gawping like an idiot at the devastating male standing in front of her. Six foot plus, broad-shouldered, muscled, and just ludicrously good-looking, with classic 'tall dark stranger' looks and olive skin tones. Sable hair and charcoal eyes, a sculpted mouth, incised cheekbones and a jaw cut from the smoothest marble…

The impact he'd made had hit her all over again when she'd taken in the coffee. At least by then she'd been a fraction more prepared—prepared, too, for what she'd known would be the inevitable pitying glance he'd cast at her as she took her place beside Chloe.

She felt her throat tighten painfully. She knew exactly what he'd seen, and why he'd pitied her. She and Chloe couldn't have made a bigger contrast, sitting beside each other. Hadn't she seen that same expression countless times over the years, whenever male eyes had looked between the two of them? Chloe the svelte, lovely blonde—she the heavy, ungainly frump.

She wrenched her mind away from the image. She had more to concern her than her lack of looks. Somehow she was going to have to find an opportunity to lay it on the line for Max Vasilikos about his buying her home. Oh, Pauline and Chloe might trot out all that sickeningly hypocritical garbage about 'painful memories', but the truth was they couldn't wait to cash in on the sale of the last asset they could get their greedy hands on.

Well, she would defy them to the last.

They'll have to force it from me in a court of law, and I'll fight them every inch of the way. I'll make it the most protracted and expensive legal wrangle I can.

A man like Max Vasilikos—an investment purchaser who just wanted a quick sale and a quick profit—wouldn't want that kind of delay. So long as she insisted that she wouldn't sell, that he'd have to wait out a legal battle with Pauline and Chloe, she would be able to fend him off. He'd find somewhere else to buy—leave Haughton alone.

As she checked the chicken that was roasting, and started to chop up vegetables, that was the only hope she could hang on to.

He'll never persuade me to agree to sell to him. Never!

There was nothing Max could say or do that would make her change her mind. Oh, he might be the kind of man who could turn females to jelly with a single glance of his dark, dark eyes, but—her mouth twisted—with looks like hers she knew only too painfully she was the last female on the planet that a man like Max Vasilikos would bother to turn the charm on for.

'Sherry, Mr Vasilikos? Or would you prefer something stronger?' Pauline's light voice enquired.

'Dry sherry, thank you,' he replied.

He was back in the drawing room, his tour of the house complete, his mind made up. This was a house he wanted to own.

And to keep for his own use.

That was the most insistent aspect of his decision to purchase this place. Its prominence in his mind still surprised him, but he was increasingly getting used to its presence. The idea of having this place for himself—*to* himself. Mentally he let the prospect play inside his head, and it continued to play as he sipped at the proffered sherry, his eyes working around the elegant drawing room.

All the other rooms that Chloe had shown him bore the same mark of a top interior designer. Beautiful, but to his mind not authentic. Only the masculine preserve of the library had given any sense of the house as it must once have been, before it had been expensively made over. The worn leather chairs, the old-fashioned patterned carpets and the book-lined walls had a charm that the oh-so-tasteful other rooms lacked. Clearly the late Edward Mountford had prevented his wife from letting the designer into his domain, and Max could not but agree with that decision.

He realised his hostess was murmuring something to him and forced his attention back from the pleasurable meanderings of the way he would decorate this room, and all the others, once the house was his to do with as he pleased.

He was not kept making anodyne conversation with his hostess and her daughter for long, however. After a few minutes the service door opened again and Pauline Mountford's stepdaughter walked in with her solid tread.

'Lunch is ready,' she announced bluntly.

She crossed to the double doors, throwing them open to the hall beyond. Despite her solidity she held herself well, Max noticed—shoulders back, straight spine, as if she were strong beneath the excess weight she must be carrying, if the way the sleeves of her ill-fitting blouse were straining over her arms was anything to go by. He frowned. It seemed wrong to him that his hostess and her daughter should be so elegantly attired, and yet Ellen Mountford—presumably, he realised, the daughter of the late owner—looked so very *in*elegant.

But then, sadly, he knew that so many women who felt themselves to be overweight virtually gave up on trying to make anything of what looks they had.

His gaze assessed her as he followed her into the

dining room, her stepsister and stepmother coming in behind him.

She's got good legs, he found himself thinking. Shapely calves, at any rate. Well, that was something, at least! His eyes went to her thick mop of hair, whose style did nothing for her—it wouldn't have done anything for Helen of Troy, to his mind! A decent haircut would surely improve her?

As he took his seat at the end of the table, where she indicated, his eyes flicked over her face. The glasses, he decided, were too small for her, making her jaw look big and her eyes look small. And that was a shame, he realised, because her eyes were a warm sherry colour, with amber lights. He frowned again. Her lashes might be long—what he could see of them through her spectacle lenses—but that overgrown monobrow was *hideous*! Why on earth didn't she do something about it? Do something about the rest of her?

It wouldn't take that much, surely, to make her look better? Plus, of course, decent clothes that concealed her excess weight as much as possible. Best of all, however, would be for her to shift that weight. She should take more exercise, maybe.

And not eat so much...

Because as they settled into lunch it was clear to Max that he and Ellen Mountford were the only ones tucking in. That was a shame, because the roast chicken was delicious—the traditional 'Sunday lunch' that the English loved so much and did so well. But neither Pauline Mountford nor her daughter did anything more than pick at their food.

Max found himself annoyed. Didn't they realise that being too thin was as undesirable as the opposite? His eyes flickered to Ellen Mountford again. *Was* she overweight? Her blouse might be straining over her arms, but her jawline was firm, and there was no jowliness or softening under the chin.

She must have noticed him glancing at her, for suddenly he saw again that tide of unlovely colour washing up into her face. *That* most certainly did nothing for her. He drew his glance away. Why was he thinking about how to improve the appearance of Ellen Mountford? She was of no interest to him—how could she possibly be?

'What are your plans for the contents of the house?' he asked his hostess. 'Will you take the paintings with you when you sell?'

A sound that might have been a choke came from Ellen Mountford, and Max's eyes flicked back to her. The red tide had vanished, and now there was the same tightness in her face as he'd seen when her stepmother had mentioned her bereavement.

'Very possibly not,' Pauline Mountford was answering him. 'They do rather go with the house, do you not think? Of course,' she added pointedly, 'they would all need to be independently valued.'

Max's eyes swept the walls. He had no objection to having the artwork—or, indeed, any of the original furniture. The pieces that had been acquired via the interior designer were, however, dispensable. His gaze rested on an empty space on the wall behind Chloe Mountford, where the wallpaper was slightly darker.

'Sold,' said Ellen Mountford tersely. The look on her face had tightened some more.

Chloe Mountford gave a little laugh. 'It was a gruesome still life of a dead stag. Mummy and I hated it!'

Max gave a polite smile, but his gaze was on Chloe's stepsister. She didn't seem pleased about the loss of the dead stag painting. Then his attention was recalled by his hostess.

'Do tell us, Mr Vasilikos, where will you be off to next? Your work must take you all over the world, I imagine.' She smiled encouragingly at him as she sipped at her wine.

'The Caribbean,' he replied. 'I am developing a resort there on one of the lesser known islands.'

Chloe's pale blue eyes lit up. 'I *adore* the Caribbean!' she exclaimed enthusiastically. 'Mummy and I spent Christmas in Barbados last winter. We stayed at Sunset Bay, of course. There really isn't anything to compare, is there?' she invited, after naming the most prestigious resort on the island.

'It's superb in what it does,' Max agreed. The famous high-profile hotel was nothing like the resort *he* was developing, and the remote island was nothing like fashionable Barbados.

'Do tell us more,' invited Chloe. 'When will the grand opening be? I'm sure Mummy and I would *love* to be amongst the very first guests.'

Max could see Ellen Mountford's expression hardening yet again with clear displeasure. He wondered at it. Out of nowhere, memory shafted like an arrow. His stepfather had been perpetually displeased by anything he'd ever said—so much that he'd learnt to keep his mouth shut when his stepfather was around.

He dragged his mind away from the unhappy memory, back to the present. 'Its style will be very different from Sunset Bay,' he said. 'The idea is for it to be highly eco-friendly, focussing on being self-sustaining. Rainwater showers and no air conditioning,' he elucidated, with a slight smile.

'Oh, dear…' Pauline shook her head regretfully. 'I don't think that would suit me. Too much heat is very trying, I find.'

'It won't be for everyone, I agree,' Max acknowledged tactfully. He turned towards Ellen. 'What do *you* think—would it attract you? Wood-built lodges open to the fresh air and meals cooked on open fires in the evenings?' He found himself unexpectedly wanting to draw her into the conversation, to hear her views. They would be different from her hothouse stepsister's, he was sure.

'Sounds like glamping,' she blurted in her abrupt manner.

Max's eyebrows drew together. 'Glamping?' he echoed, mystified.

'Glamorous camping. I believe that's the contraction it's for,' she elucidated shortly. 'Upmarket camping for people who like the idea of going back to nature but not the primitive reality of it.'

Max gave a wry smile. 'Hmm…that might be a good description for my resort,' he acknowledged.

A tinkling laugh came from Chloe. 'I'd say "glamorous camping" is a contradiction in terms! It would be luxury for Ellen, though—she runs camps for London kids. A million miles from upmarket. Totally basic.'

She gave a dramatic shudder, and Max heard the note of dismissal in her voice.

'Adventure breaks,' Ellen said shortly. 'The children enjoy it. They think it's exciting. Some of them have never been into the countryside.'

'Ellen's "good works"!' Pauline said lightly. 'I'm sure it's very uplifting.'

'And muddy!' trilled Chloe with a little laugh, and sought to catch Max's eye to get his agreement.

But Max's attention was on Ellen. It was unexpected to hear that she ran such breaks for deprived inner-city children, given her own privileged background. He realised that he was paying her more attention.

'Do you hold them here?' he asked interestedly.

If so, it was something he might keep on with—adding it to the extensive list of charitable enterprises that were his personal payback for the good fortune that had enabled him to attain the wealth he had.

'They're held at my school, nearby. We set up camp on the playing fields,' came the answer. 'That way the children can use the sports pavilion, including the showers, and have use of the swimming pool as well. So they get the fun of camping, plus the run of the facilities of a private school.'

As she spoke for the first time Max saw something light up in Ellen Mountford's eyes, changing her expression. Instead of the stony, closed look that alternated only with the tomato-red flaring of her cheeks when he paid her attention there was actually some animation, some enthusiasm. It made a significant difference to her features, he realised with surprise. They seemed lighter, somehow, less heavy, and not even those wretched spectacles could hide that.

Then, as if aware of his regard, he saw her face close down again and she grabbed at her wine glass, that telltale colour washing up into her face, destroying the transformation he'd started to glimpse. For some reason it annoyed him. He opened his mouth to make a reply, to ask another question, see whether he could get back that momentary animation, draw her out again. But his hostess was speaking now, and he had to turn his attention to her.

'After lunch,' said Pauline Mountford, 'I'm sure you would like to see the gardens here. It's a little early in the season as yet, but in a week or two the rhododendrons along the drive will start their annual show,' she told him smilingly. 'They are a blaze of colour!'

'Rhododendrons...' Max mused, more for something to say than anything else. 'Rose tree—that's the literal translation from the Greek.'

'How fascinating!' said Chloe. 'Do they come from Greece, then?'

'No. They come from the Himalayas.' Her stepsister's contradiction was immediate. 'The Victorians introduced them to England. Unfortunately they've taken over in some places, where they are invasive pests. '

Max saw her eyes flicker to Pauline and her daughter, her expression back to stony again.

Chloe, though, continued as if her stepsister had not spoken. 'And then a little later on in early summer we have the azaleas—they are absolutely gorgeous when they are fully out in May. Masses and masses of them! Mummy had the most beautiful walk created, that winds right through their midst—'

There was an abrupt clatter of silverware from her stepsister.

'No, she did *not*. The azalea walk has been there far longer. It was *my* mother who created it!'

The glare from behind Ellen Mountford's spectacle lenses was like a dagger, skewering the hapless Chloe as Max turned his head abruptly at the brusque interjection. Then his hostess's stepdaughter scraped back her chair and got to her feet.

'If you've all finished—?' she said, and started to grab at the plates and pile them on the tray on the sideboard. She marched out with them.

As she disappeared Pauline Mountford gave a resigned sigh. 'Oh, dear,' she said. 'I do apologise for that.' She glanced at her daughter, who promptly took up the cue.

'Ellen can be so very…*sensitive*,' she murmured sadly. 'I should have known better.' She gave a little sigh of regret.

'We do our best,' her mother confirmed with another sad sigh. 'But, well…' She trailed off and gave a little shake of her head.

It *was* tricky, Max allowed, for his hostess and her daughter to have to smooth over the prickly behaviour of their step-relation, in which he was not interested, so he moved the conversation back to the topic he *was* interested in, asking how far Haughton was from the sea.

Chloe Mountford was just telling him that it would make an ideal base for Cowes Week, if sailing was an interest of his, when her stepsister made another entrance, bearing another tray weighed down with a large apple pie, a jug of custard and a bowl of cream, which she set down on the table heavily. She did not resume her place.

'I'll leave you to it,' she announced shortly. 'Coffee will be in the drawing room.'

Then she was gone, disappearing back through the service door.

'So, Mr Vasilikos, what do you make of Haughton?'

Pauline Mountford's enquiry was perfectly phrased, and accompanied by a charming smile. She was sitting in a graceful pose on the sofa in the drawing room, where they had repaired for the coffee that Ellen Mountford had so tersely informed them would be awaiting them.

Max had been the only one to partake of the apple pie—no surprise—but he was glad he had. It had been delicious—sweet pastry made with a very light touch indeed, and juicy apples spiced with cinnamon and nutmeg. Whoever had made it could certainly cook.

Had the graceless Ellen made it? If so, then whatever her lack of beauty she could certainly boast of *one* key asset to draw a man to her side. His thoughts ran on. But perhaps being a good cook was not to her personal advantage—not if she overindulged in her own creations.

He gave a little shake of his head. There he was,

thinking about that woman again. *Why?* She was nothing to him, and would remain so. He relaxed back a fraction in his seat. His hostess was clearly fishing for whether he wanted to buy this place or not. Well, why not give her his good news right now? He'd made his decision—and every passing moment only confirmed it. It might have been a decision made on impulse, but it was a strong impulse—the strongest he'd ever had—and he was used to making decisions on the spot. His instinct had never failed him yet—and it would not fail him now.

'Charming,' he said decisively, stretching out his legs towards the fire in a fashion that was already proprietorial. 'I believe...' he bestowed a smile on her '...that we will be able to reach an agreement in the region of your asking price—which is a realistic one—subject, of course, to the usual considerations of purchase: a full structural survey and so forth.'

He saw her eyes light up, and from the corner of his eye he was sure that her daughter's had done the same.

'Oh, that is *excellent*!' came Pauline's gracious response.

'Marvellous!' echoed her daughter.

Enthusiasm was in her voice. And relief too—Max could detect that.

It did not surprise him. Being forced to live here with the perpetually prickly Ellen could hardly be comfortable. He did not blame either mother or daughter for being eager to make new lives for themselves. Or even, he allowed, for having preferred to be abroad this last year. Hadn't he himself hightailed it from his stepfather's *taverna* the moment his poor mother had been finally laid to rest?

He pulled his mind away again. He did not want to remember his miserable childhood and downtrodden mother. Nor was he interested in the tense convolutions of the Mountford family either.

He set down his empty cup. 'Before I leave,' he said, 'I'll take a look around the gardens and the outbuildings to the rear. No, don't get up—' This to Chloe, who had started to stand. He smiled. 'My footwear is more suitable for the outdoors than yours,' he explained, glancing at her stylish high heels and not adding that he preferred to keep his own pace, and would rather not have her endless panegyrics about the charms of a property he had already decided would be his.

Though it was only prudent to check out the areas he had not yet seen, he did not envisage there being anything so dreadful as to make him change his mind.

He strode from the room, and as he shut the door behind him he heard animated conversation break out behind him. To his ears it sounded...*jubilant*. Well, his own mood was just as buoyant. Satisfaction filled him, and a warm, proprietorial sense of well-being. He glanced around the hallway—soon to be *his* hallway.

He paused in his stride. A family had lived here for generations. Emotion kicked in him. It was an emotion he had never felt before, and one that startled him with its presence—shocked him even more with his certainty about it. The words were in his head, shaping themselves, taking hold. Taking root.

And now it will be my home—for my family.

The family of his own that he'd never had…the family he *would* have.

A pang stabbed at him. If his poor mother had survived longer how he would have loved to bring her here—make a home for her here, safe from the harshness of her life, cosseting her in the luxury he could now afford to bestow upon her.

But I'll do that for your grandchildren—give them the happy upbringing you could not give me—and I'll feel you smile and be glad! I've come a long way—a long, long way—and now I've found the place I want to call my home. I'll find the right woman for me and bring her here.

Who that woman would be he didn't know, but she was out there somewhere. He just had to find her. Find her and bring her here.

Home.

He started to walk forward again, heading for the baize door that led through to the back section of the house. He would check it out, then go out into the courtyard area, take a look at the outbuildings before making his way around to the gardens and exploring them.

He was just walking down the passageway towards the back door when a voice from the open doorway to what he could see was a large stone-flagged kitchen stopped him.

'Mr Vasilikos! I need to speak to you!'

He halted, turning his head. Ellen Mountford was standing there and her face was stony. Very stony indeed. Annoyance tensed him. He did not want this.

He wanted to get outside and complete his inspection of the place.

'What about?' he replied with steely politeness.

'It's very important.'

She backed away, indicating that he should step into the kitchen.

Impatiently Max strode in, taking in an impression of a large room with old-fashioned wooden cupboards, a long scrubbed wooden table, a flagstone floor and a vast old-fashioned range cooker along one wall. The warmth from the oven enveloped him, and there was, he realised, a cosy, comfortable, lived-in feel to the space. No top interior designer had been let loose in here, that was for sure—and he was glad of it.

He turned his attention to Ellen Mountford. She'd taken up a position on the far side of the kitchen table and her hands were pressed down over the back of a chair. Tension was in every line of her body, and her expression was both stony and determined.

He frowned. *Now what?*

'There's something you have to know!'

The words burst from her, and he realised with a deepening of his frown that she was in a state of extreme agitation and nervousness.

He levelled his gaze at her. She seemed to be steeling herself after her dramatic outburst. 'And that is…?' he prompted.

He watched her take a gulping breath. Her cheeks seemed pale now—as pale as chalk. Not a trace of the colour that had so unflatteringly rushed there whenever he'd looked at her before.

'Mr Vasilikos, there's no easy way to tell you this, and for that I'm sorry, but you've had a completely wasted journey. Whatever my stepmother has led you to believe, Haughton is not for sale. And it never will be!'

CHAPTER THREE

MAX STILLED. THEN deliberately he let his gaze rest on her. 'Perhaps,' he said, and he made no effort to make his voice sound anything less than the way he intended it to sound—quelling—'you might like to explain what you mean by that.'

Ellen swallowed, had to force herself to speak. To say what she *had* to say. 'I own a third of Haughton and I have no wish to sell.'

Somehow she'd got the words out—but her heart was thumping like a hammer inside her. Ever since she'd rushed from the dining room, emotions storming, she'd been trying to nerve herself to find Max Vasilikos, get him away from Pauline and Chloe and tell him what she had to tell him. And now she'd done it—and he was not, it was obvious, taking it kindly.

His expression had steeled, and the dark brows were snapping together now. For a moment Ellen quailed. Up till now Max Vasilikos had, she realised belatedly, been playing the role of courteous, amenable guest. Now he was very different. A tough, powerful businessman who was hearing something he did not want to hear.

As she'd delivered her bombshell something had flickered in Max's mind at what she'd said, but it wasn't relevant for the moment.

His gaze rested on her. 'Why not?'

He saw her swallow again.

'What relevance does that question have?'

Max's expression changed. A moment ago it had looked formidable. Now there was a cynical cast to it. 'Perhaps you are holding out for a higher price,' he said.

Ellen's lips pressed together. 'I don't wish to sell Haughton—and I shan't.'

He looked at her for a moment. He looked neither quelling nor cynical. He seemed to be studying her, but she suddenly had the feeling that he'd retreated behind a mask.

'You do realise, do you not, that as only part-owner of this property if any of the other part-owners wish to sell they have the legal right to force such a sale?'

There was no colour in her face. Her cheekbones had whitened. Something moved in her eyes. Some deep emotion. He saw her jaw tense, her knuckles whiten over the chair-back.

'That would take months. I'd drag it out as long as I could. No purchaser would want that kind of costly delay.'

She would make that delay as long as possible, fight as hard as possible. *I won't roll over and give in!*

She felt sick with tension. Max Vasilikos's gaze rested on her implacably. Then, abruptly, his expression changed. His long lashes dipped down over his deep, dark and entirely inscrutable eyes.

'Well, be that as it may, Miss Mountford, I intend to view the rest of the property while I am here.'

She saw his glance go around the kitchen again, in an approving fashion.

'This is very pleasing,' he said. 'It's been left in its original state and is all the better for it.'

Ellen blinked. To go from defying him to agreeing with him confused her completely. 'My stepmother wasn't interested in doing up the kitchen quarters,' she said.

Max's eyes glinted. 'A lucky escape, then,' he said dryly.

There was a distinctly conspiratorial note to his voice, and Ellen's confusion deepened.

'You don't like the decor in the main house?' she heard herself saying, astonished. Surely property developers *loved* that full-blown interior-designed look?

Max smiled. 'Taste is subjective, and your stepmother's tastes are not mine. I prefer something less... contrived.'

'She's had it photographed for a posh interiors magazine!' Ellen exclaimed derisively, before she could stop herself.

'Yes, it would be ideal for such a publication,' he returned lightly. 'Tell me, is there anything left of the original furnishings and furniture?'

A bleak, empty look filled Ellen's face. 'Some of it was put up in the attics,' she said.

Any antiques or *objets d'art* of value that Pauline had not cared for had been sold—like the painting from the dining room and others she'd needed to dispose of so she and Chloe could go jaunting off on their expensive holidays.

'That's good to hear.' He nodded, making a mental note to have the attic contents checked at some point. There were art valuations to get done, too, before the final sales contract was signed.

For signed it would be. His eyes rested now on the female who was so obdurately standing in the way of his intentions. Whatever her reasons, he would set them aside. Somehow she would be brought to heel. In all his years of negotiation, one thing he'd learnt for sure—there was always a way to get a deal signed and sealed. *Always.*

He wanted this place. Wanted it badly. More than he had ever thought to want any property... He wanted to make a home here.

He smiled again at the woman who thought so unwisely—so futilely!—to balk him of what he wanted. 'Well, I shall continue on my way, Miss Mountford. I'll see myself out—'

And he was gone, striding from the kitchen and down to the back door.

Ellen watched him go, her heart thumping heavily still, a feeling of sickness inside her. She heard the back door close as he went out. Words burned in her head, emotions churning.

Please let him leave! Leave and—and never come back!

Let him buy somewhere else—anywhere else. But leave me my home...oh, leave me my home!

* * *

Max stood in the shade of a tall beech tree overlooking the lake and took in the vista. It was good—all good. Everything about this place was good. He'd explored the outbuildings, realised they'd need work, but nothing too much, and mentally designated some of the old stables for his cars. He might keep some as stabling, too. He didn't ride, but maybe his children would like ponies one day.

He gave a half-laugh. Here he was, imagining children here before he'd even found the woman who would give them to him. Well, he'd have plenty of volunteers, that was for sure—not that he was keen on any of his current acquaintance. And his time with Tyla had been enjoyable, but their ways had parted. No, the woman he would bring here as his bride would be quite, quite different from the self-absorbed, vanity-driven film star bent on storming Hollywood. His chosen bride would be someone who would love this place as he would come to love it—love *him*, love their children…

He shook his head to clear his thoughts—he was running ahead of himself! First he had to buy this place. He frowned. The tripartite ownership structure should have been disclosed to him at the outset, not be delivered by bombshell. His frown deepened.

Well, that was a problem to ponder for later. Right now, he wanted to finish exploring the grounds beyond the formal gardens surrounding the house. He could see that a pathway ran through the long, unmown grass beside the sheltering woodland, around the perimeter of the reed-edged lake. He would walk along it and take a look at what he could see was a little folly on the far side.

My kids would love playing there—and we'd have picnics there in the summer. Maybe barbecues in the evening. Maybe swimming in the lake? I'll get a pool put in as well, of course—probably indoors, with a glass roof, given the English climate...

His thoughts ran on as he emerged from the shelter of the woodland. Then abruptly they cleared. He stared. There was someone over by the folly, leaning against the stonework. He watched as she straightened, and then set off along the path towards him. She was in running gear, he could see that from this distance, but not who it was. He frowned. If neighbours had got into the habit of using the place as a running track he'd better know about it—

Slowly he walked forward on an interception course. But as the runner approached him he felt the breath leave his body. Incredulity scissored through him.

It couldn't be! It just *couldn't*!

It could *not* be the sad, overweight, badly dressed frumpy female he'd pitied—impossible for it to be Ellen Mountford. Just *impossible*.

But it *was* her.

As the figure drew closer, its long, loping gait effortless and confident, his eyes were nailed to it. Tall, long-legged, with dark hair streaming behind like a flag, and a body...a body that was a total knockout—

It was impossible to tear his stunned gaze from her. From her strong, lithe body, perfectly contoured in a sports bra that moulded generous breasts, exposing not an inch of fat over bare, taut-waisted abs, with matching running shorts that hugged sleek hips, exposing the full length of her honed, toned quads.

Thee mou, she wasn't fat—she was *fit*. In both senses of the word! Fit and fabulous!

Every thought about her completely rearranged itself in his head. He could not take his eyes from her. He was in shock—and also something very different from shock. Something that sent the blood surging in his body.

Thanks to the sight of hers...

Greek words escaped his lips. Something about not believing his eyes, his senses, and something that was extreme appreciation of her fantastic physique. Then another thought was uppermost. *How did she hide that body from me?* At not one single point had there been the slightest indication of what she was hiding—and he hadn't noticed. Not for a moment, not for an instant! How had she done it?

But he knew—she'd done it by disguising that fantastic, honed, sleek, fit body of hers in those appalling clothes. In that unspeakable purple tracksuit that had turned her into some kind of inflated dummy, and that shapeless, ill-fitting grey skirt and even more shapeless and ill-fitting white blouse whose tightness of sleeve had had nothing whatsoever to do with her arms being fat—but had simply been because her biceps and triceps were honed, compacted muscle. He could see that now, as she approached more closely.

He stepped out from amongst the trees. 'Hello, there,' he said.

His greeting was affable, and pleasantly voiced, and it stopped her dead in her tracks as if a concrete block had dropped down in front of her from the sky.

Something that was partly a shriek of shock, partly a gasp of air escaped from Ellen. She stared, aghast— Max Vasilikos was the last person she wanted to see!

The emotional stress of the day, the agitation from having had to commandeer him and tell him she would never agree to sell her share of Haughton, had overset her so much that the moment he'd closed the back door behind him she'd headed upstairs to change into her running gear. She'd had to get out of the house. Had to work off the stress and tension and the biting anxiety. A long, hard run would help.

She'd set off on the long route, down the drive and looping back through the woods, then into a field and back into the grounds, taking a breather by the folly before setting off around the lake, hoping against hope that by the time she got back to the house he and his flash car would have gone.

Instead here he was, appearing in front of her out of nowhere like the demon king in a pantomime!

A demon king in whose eyes was an expression that sent a wave of excruciating colour flooding through her.

She was agonisingly aware of her skimpy, revealing attire. Mercilessly revealing her muscular body. She lifted her chin, desperately fighting back her reaction. She would *not* be put out of countenance by him seeing her like this any more than she had been when he'd seen her plonked beside Chloe, and the dreadful contrast she'd made to her stepsister. It was a comparison that was hitting him again—she could see it as his eyes swept over her appraisingly.

'I could see you were totally different from Chloe—but not like *this*!' he exclaimed. 'You couldn't be more unalike—even sharing a surname, you'd never be taken for sisters in a thousand years.'

He shook his head in disbelief. Missing completely the sudden look of pain at his words in her eyes. Then he was speaking again.

'I'm sorry—I shouldn't be delaying you. Your muscles will seize up.' He started to walk forward in the direction of the house, his pace rapid, with long strides. 'Look,' he went on, 'keep going—but slow down to a jog so we can talk.'

He moved to one side of the path. She started up again, conscious that her heart was pounding far more quickly than the exertion of her run required. She found herself blinking. The casual cruelty of what he'd just said reverberated in her, but she must not let it show. With an effort, and still burningly conscious of her skimpy attire and perspiring body, of her hair held back only by a wide sweatband, of being bereft of the glasses she'd been wearing over lunch, she loped beside him.

'What about?' she returned. The thought came to her that maybe she could use this wretched encounter to convince him that there really was no point in his staying any longer—that buying Haughton was off the menu for him.

'I'm making an offer for this place,' he said, glancing at her. 'It will be near the asking price...' He trailed off.

Dismay lanced through her. 'I still don't want to sell my share,' she replied grittily.

'Your third...' Max didn't take his eyes from her '...will be well over a million pounds...'

'I don't care what it is. Mr Vasilikos—please understand—my share is not for sale at any price. I don't want to sell.'

'Why not?' His brows snapped together.

'What do you mean, why not?' she riposted. 'My reasons are my own—I don't want to sell.' She turned her face, making herself look at him. 'That's all there is to it. And I'll make it as hard as I possibly can for you to complete a sale. I'll fight it to the bitter end!'

Vehemence broke through in her voice and she could see it register with him. His eyebrows rose, and she knew he was about to say something—but she didn't want to hear. Didn't want to do anything but get away from him. Get back to the house, the sanctuary of her bedroom. Throw herself down on the bed and weep and weep. For what she feared most in the world would come true if this man went through with his threat!

She couldn't bear it—she just couldn't. She couldn't bear to lose her home. The place she loved most in all the world. *She couldn't bear it.*

With a burst of speed she shot forward, leaving him behind. Leaving behind Max Vasilikos, the man who wanted to wrench her home from her.

As he watched her power forward, accelerating away, Max let her go. But when she disappeared from sight across the lawns that crossed the front of the house his thoughts were full.

Why was Ellen Mountford so set on making difficulties for him? And why were his eyes following her fantastic figure until she was totally beyond his view? And why was he then regretting that she was beyond it?

The question was suddenly stronger in his head, knocking aside his concern about an easy purchase of the place he intended to buy, whatever obstacles one of its owners might put in his path.

When he reached the house Max went in search of his hostess. She was in the drawing room with her daughter, and both greeted him effusively, starting to ask him about his tour of the outbuildings and the grounds.

But he cut immediately to the chase.

'Why was I not informed of the ownership structure of this property?' he asked.

His voice was level, but there was a note in it that anyone who'd ever been in commercial negotiations with him would have taken as a warning not to try and outmanoeuvre him or prevaricate.

'Your stepdaughter apprised me of the facts after lunch,' he went on.

He kept his level gaze on Pauline. Beside her on the sofa, Chloe Mountford gave a little choke. An angry one. But her mother threw her a silencing look. Then she turned her face towards Max. She gave a little sigh.

'Oh, dear, what has the poor girl told you, Mr Vasilikos?' There was a note of apprehension in her voice.

'That she does not wish to sell her share,' he replied

bluntly. 'And that she is prepared to force you to resort to legal measures to make her do so. Which will, as you must be aware, be both costly and time-consuming.'

Pauline Mountford's be-ringed fingers wound into each other. 'I'm so sorry, Mr Vasilikos, that you have been exposed to…well, to this, unfortunate development. I had hoped we could reach a happy conclusion between ourselves and—'

Max cut across her, his tone decisive. 'I make no bones that I want to buy this place,' he said. 'But I don't want problems and I don't want delays.'

'We don't either!' agreed Chloe promptly. 'Mummy, we've just *got* to stop Ellen ruining everything.'

He looked at the pair of them. 'Do you know what is behind her reluctance to sell?'

Pauline sighed again, her face shadowing. 'I believe,' she said slowly, 'that she is a very *unhappy* young woman. Poor Ellen has always found it very… *difficult*…to have us here.'

'She's hated us from the start,' Chloe said tightly. 'She's never made us welcome.'

Pauline sighed once more. 'Alas, I'm afraid it's true. She was at a difficult age when Edward married me. And I fear it is all too common, sadly, for a daughter who has previously had the undivided attention of her father not to allow that he might seek to find happiness with someone else. I did my best…' she sighed again '…and so did poor little Chloe—you did, darling, didn't you? You made every effort to be friends, wanted her so much to be your new sister! But, well… I do not wish to speak ill of Ellen, but nothing—absolutely nothing that we did—could please her. She was, I fear, set on resenting us. It upset her father dreadfully. Too late, he realised how much he'd spoiled her, made her possessive and clinging. *He* could control her a little, though not a great deal, but now that he is gone...' A little sob escaped her. 'Well, she has become as you see her.'

'She never goes *anywhere*!' Chloe exclaimed. 'She just buries herself here all year round.'

Pauline nodded. 'Sadly, that is true. She has her little teaching job at her old school—which in itself surely cannot be advisable, for it keeps her horizons from widening—but that is all she has. She has no social life—she rejects all my attempts to...to involve her!' She levelled her eyes at Max. 'I want nothing but the best for her. If Haughton holds too many memories for *me* to bear, for her I am sure it is much, much worse. Doting on her father as she did was not emotionally healthy for a young woman...'

Max frowned. 'Did she not want her father to include you in his will? Neither you nor her stepsister?' he asked.

Was that the root of the matter? That Ellen Mountford had wanted everything her father had left to go to *her*, cutting out his second wife and stepdaughter completely?

'That may be so, alas,' confirmed Pauline. 'My poor Edward quite thought of Chloe as his own daughter—she took his name, as you know. Perhaps that led to some...well, perhaps some jealousy on Ellen's part? Possessive as she was about her father...'

Memory stung in Max's head. His mother might

have taken his stepfather's name, but he—the name-less, fatherless bastard she had borne—had never been permitted to.

Pauline was speaking again, and he drew his mind back to the present.

'You must not think, Mr Vasilikos, that Edward has been in any way unfair to Ellen. Oh, he might have taken steps to ensure that Chloe and myself were taken care of financially, by way of including us in the ownership of this house, but Ellen was left every-thing else. And my husband...' she gave a sigh '...was a very wealthy man, with a substantial stock portfolio and other assets.' She took a little breath. 'Our share of this house, Mr Vasilikos, is all we have, Chloe and I, so I'm sure you will understand why, as well as find-ing being here without Edward too painful, we must sell. And,' she pointed out, 'of course Ellen's share of the sale price will be handsome.'

Max absorbed the information, keeping his expres-sion impassive. What Pauline Mountford said rang all too true. That open bristling that he had seen from Ellen Mountford in her stepmother's company—

He got to his feet. There was nothing more to be achieved here right now. 'Well, I will leave it with you. See what you can do to change Ellen's mind and attitude.'

He smiled down at them—the courteous, imper-sonal smile he used to keep others well-disposed to-wards him for his own benefit.

Ten minutes later he was heading off down the drive, his glance going to either side, taking in one last sweep of the place. For now. His expression tightencd. Whatever was necessary to induce Ellen Mountford to abandon her objection to selling her share of this place would, he determined as he turned out through the drawn-back iron gates on to the road, be done.

With or without her co-operation.

CHAPTER FOUR

MAX HEARD OUT his legal advisor, then drummed his fingers on the polished surface of his mahogany desk. Forcing a sale would indeed be time-consuming, and he wanted to take possession without delay—before summer was over. Which meant getting Ellen Mountford to drop her objections.

He gave a rasp of exasperation, swivelling moodily in his leather chair, his dark eyes baleful. There had been no good news from Pauline Mountford, and he strongly suspected there would not be. If Ellen was as entrenched in her hostile view of her stepmother as she seemed to be, then Pauline was doubtless the last person capable of changing her stepdaughter's mind.

But *he* might be able to.

An idea was forming in his head—he could feel it. An idea to make her *want* to sell up.

Chloe Mountford's voice echoed in his memory. *'She never goes anywhere—she just buries herself here all year round!'*

His eyes glinted. Maybe that was the key that would start to unlock the problem.

Impulsively he summoned his PA. 'Tell me, have

I got any particularly glitzy social events coming up soon here in London?' he asked her.

Five minutes later he had his answer—and had made his decision. He sat back in his chair, long legs extended, a smile of satisfaction playing around his mouth. Oh, yes, he'd made his decision, all right. And Ellen herself had given him the way to convince her of it.

That mention she'd made of her surprising involvement in a charity for giving city children a countryside holiday under canvas. That would do nicely. Very nicely. His plan would help him lever Ellen Mountford out of his way—he was sure of it.

And as he settled down to work again, in a much better frame of mind, he became aware that he was sure of something else as well. That, of all things, he was looking forward to seeing her again—and making an end, once and for all, to all that nonsense of hers about looking the unappealing way she did.

I've seen her real body—her goddess body!—and now I want to see her face look just as good as her figure.

The smile played around his mouth once more, and the gleam in his eyes was speculative. Anticipatory.

And for a moment—just a moment—the prospect of finding a way to remove Ellen Mountford's objections to selling him the house he wanted to buy was not uppermost in his mind.

How good could she look? How good could she really look?

The glint came into his eye again. He wanted to find out.

* * *

Ellen turned off the ignition and got out. Her car needed a service, but she couldn't afford it. Her salary was wiped out simply paying for the essentials at Haughton—from council tax to electricity bills—and, of course, for the *in*essentials. Such as the weekly deliveries of hothouse flowers from the local florist, and Pauline and Chloe's regular visits to the local county town for their endless hair and beauty appointments. Their other extravagances—replenishing their wardrobes, their lavish social life and their foreign jaunts to luxury destinations and five-star hotels—were all funded by the stripping out of anything of value still left in the house, from paintings to *objets d'art*.

She hefted out a pile of schoolbooks, becoming aware of the sound of a vehicle approaching along the drive. As the sleek, powerful car turned into the courtyard dismay flooded through her. She'd hoped so much that Max Vasilikos had decided to buy somewhere else and abandoned his attentions to Haughton. Pauline and Chloe had finally lapsed into giving her the silent treatment, after having harangued her repeatedly about her stubbornness in refusing to do what they wanted her to do. Now they had taken themselves off again on yet another pricey jaunt, to a five-star hotel in Marbella while Ellen was just about to begin her school holidays.

Their departure had given Ellen cause for hope that Max Vasilikos had withdrawn his offer—in vain, it seemed. She watched him approach with a sinking heart—and also a quite different reaction that she tried to quash and failed utterly to do so. She gulped silently as he walked up to her, his handmade suit sheathing his powerful frame like a smooth, sleek glove. The dark eyes in his strong-featured face were levelled down at her. She felt her pulse leap.

It's just because I don't want him here. I don't want him going on at me to sell Haughton to him!

That was the reason for the sudden quickening of her breathing—the *only* reason she told herself urgently. The only reason she would allow…could possibly allow—

'Good afternoon, Miss Mountford,' he said. His voice was deep, and there was a hint of a curve at the corner of his sculpted mouth.

'What are you doing back here again?' she demanded. It was safer to sound antagonistic. Much safer.

Safer than standing here gazing gormlessly at him in all his incredible masculinity and gorgeousness. Feeling my heart thumping like an idiot and going red as a beetroot again!

Her hostile demand met with no bristling. Just the opposite. 'I wanted to see the rhododendrons,' Max returned blandly. 'They are indeed magnificent.' He paused, smiling his courteous social smile. 'Aren't you going to invite me in?' he said.

She glowered at him from behind her spectacles, her thick eyebrows forming that monobrow as she did so, and she was once again, he noted with displeasure, wearing the unspeakable baggy tracksuit that totally concealed her glorious body. Mentally, he earmarked it for the bonfire.

'Would it stop you if I didn't?' she glowered again.

'I doubt it,' he said, and then reached forward to remove half of the tottering tower of schoolbooks from her arms. 'After you,' he said, nodding at the kitchen door.

She cast him a burning look, refusing to say thank you for relieving her of much of her burden, and stomped indoors, dumping her load on the kitchen table. He deposited his share next to it.

'I hope you don't have to get all these marked for tomorrow,' he observed.

She shook her head. 'By the start of next term,' she said shortly.

'You've broken up?' enquired Max in a conversational tone. He knew perfectly well she had, as he'd had her term dates checked, and had timed his visit here accordingly.

'Today,' she said. She looked across at him. He seemed taller than ever in the kitchen, large though the space was. But then, she knew a man like Max Vasilikos could effortlessly dominate any space he occupied. 'You've wasted your journey,' she said bluntly. 'Pauline and Chloe left for Marbella yesterday.'

'Did they?' he returned carelessly. 'I'm not here to see them.'

Ellen lifted her eyes to him, glaring. 'Mr Vasilikos, *please* don't go on at me any more! Can't you just accept I don't want to sell Haughton?'

'I'm not here to talk about Haughton. I'm here to help your charity.'

Astonishment showed in her face and he went on smoothly.

'I'm confident I can increase your funding, enabling you to run camps more frequently. A national children's charity I support—for advantageous tax reasons—takes on new projects regularly. Yours I'm sure would be ideal for it.'

She was staring at him with an expression of extreme suspicion. 'Why would you do that?' she demanded. 'Do you think it will change my mind about not selling Haughton?'

'Of course not,' he returned equably. 'My only concern is the deprived children. Is that not yours, too?' he countered, with precise gentleness and a bland look in his eye.

She took a breath. 'Well, if you can get us more funding we won't say no,' she managed to get out. There was something about the way he was casting a long look at her that threatened to bring the colour rushing to her cheeks.

'Good,' Max said. Then blithely went on. 'The thing is, though, you'll need to come up to London with me today—make a personal presentation. Time is very short—they have to spend the last of this year's money before the end of the financial year coming up.'

He was hustling her, he knew, and it was deliberate—he wanted to give her no excuse to get out of this.

'What?' Consternation filled Ellen's voice. 'Impossible!'

'No, it's quite all right—it won't inconvenience me at all,' said Max in a smooth voice, deliberately misunderstanding the cause of her objection. He glanced at his watch. 'You go off and get ready while I take another stroll around the gardens—admire those rhodo-dendrons!' He smiled at her, completely ignoring the fact that her mouth was opening to object yet again. 'I'll give you twenty minutes,' he said blandly, and was gone.

Ellen stared after him, open-mouthed. Consternation was tumbling around inside her—shot through with aftershock. Slowly she gathered her composure back, by dint of piling her marking neatly into class rows. Did Max Vasilikos *really* imagine she'd waltz off with him to London for the day, to pitch for more funding for her camping project?

More money would be really helpful right now. We could double the numbers at the half-term session— buy more tents and sleeping bags. Run another week in the summer holidays...

The problem was, though, she thought, as she descended to earth with a bump, that in order to get her hands on the funding she'd have to sit next to Max Vasilikos all the way to London, enclosed in his car. Would she be a captive audience for his determination to wrest Haughton from her?

But the reverse will be true, too. If he goes on at me, then he'll also have to listen to me telling him I'm never going to agree to sell. Never!

Yes, that was the way to think—and *not* about the way the image of Max Vasilikos, seen again now in all its devastating reality, was busy burning itself into her retinas and making her heart beat faster. Because what possible point was there in her pulse quickening? If even ordinary men looked right past her, wanting only to look at Chloe, then to a man like Max Vasilikos, who romanced film stars, she must be completely invisible.

In a way, that actually made it easier. Easier for her to change into something more suitable for London—the well-worn dark grey suit and white blouse that she donned for parents' evenings and school functions, and sturdy, comfortable lace-ups, before confining her unruly hair into a lumpy bun—and then heading back out into the courtyard.

Max Vasilikos was already behind the wheel of his monstrous beast of a car, and he leant across to open the passenger door. She got into the low-slung seat awkwardly, feeling suddenly that despite being invisible to him, as she knew she was, *he* was very, very visible to her.

And very close.

With a shake of her head, to clear her stupid thoughts, she fastened her seat belt as he set off with a throaty growl of the engine. Oh, Lord, was she insane to head off with him like this? All the way to London in the all too close confines of his car? She sat back tensely, fingers clutching the handbag in her lap.

'So, tell me more about this charity of yours,' Max invited as he turned out of the drive on to the narrow country lane beyond. He wanted to set her at ease, not have her sitting there tense as a board.

Gratefully Ellen answered, explaining how she and a fellow teacher had started it two years ago. She also told him about their hopes for expansion, which more funding would definitely enable.

Max continued to ask questions that drew her out

more, and as she talked he could see she was gradually starting to relax. The enthusiasm he'd seen so briefly over lunch the other day was coming through again, and she was becoming animated as she spoke. He moved the subject on from the practicalities of the venture to some of its underlying issues.

'How do you find the children respond to the camping?' he asked.

'Usually very well,' she replied. 'They all have to do chores, share the work, and most discover grit and strength in themselves—a determination to achieve goals that will, we hope, enable them to transfer those lessons to their future and make something of themselves, despite their disadvantaged and often troubled backgrounds.'

She became aware that Max was looking at her, a revealing expression on his face.

'Reminds me of myself,' he said. 'When my mother died I had to make my own way in the world—and it definitely took grit and strength and determination. Starting with nothing and building myself up from scratch.'

She glanced at him curiously. 'You weren't born to all this, then?' she asked, indicating the luxury car they were sitting in.

He gave a short, humourless laugh. 'I worked five years on building sites to make enough to buy a ruin that I then spent two years restoring myself and selling on. I took the profit to do the same again and again, until I'd bootstrapped my way up to where I am now,' he told her. His sideways glance was caustic, but there was a trace of mordant humour in it. 'Does that improve your opinion of me at all?' he posed.

She swallowed. She would have to give him his due—anything else would be unfair, however unwelcome he was in her life. 'I respect you for all the hard work you've obviously had to put in to make yourself rich. My only objection to you, Mr Vasilikos, is that you want to buy Haughton and I don't want to sell it to you.'

Belatedly she realised that she herself had brought the subject back to what she did *not* want to discuss—selling her home. But to her relief he did not respond in kind.

'Tell me, how old were you when your mother died?' he asked instead.

Her eyes widened and she stared at him, wondering why he was asking such a personal, intrusive question. Then something he'd said chimed in her head. '*When my mother died...*'

'Fifteen,' she answered. 'She was killed in a head-on car crash.'

'I was the same age when mine died,' Max said.

His voice was neutral, but it did not deceive Ellen.

'She died of lung disease.' There was a slight pause. 'It's not a good age to lose a parent,' he said.

'When *is*?' returned Ellen quietly. It was strange to think of this man, from so utterly different a world from her, having that same tragedy in her life as she did. To think that they, who were so utterly, glaringly unalike, had that in common.

'Indeed.'

He was silent a moment, manoeuvring the car effortlessly around a tight bend, accelerating out of it. When he spoke again it was to return to the subject of the charity and what financial constraints further funding might alleviate.

Ellen was relieved—talking about such deeply felt emotional issues with this man was...*strange*. Yet even though he'd changed the subject, reverted to his smooth, urbane social manner, she felt a curious sense of having somehow touched a chord in him, drawn by the mutual personal tragedy in their lives.

They joined the motorway soon after, and Max could let the car really rip, cruising down the fast lane as if merely out for a stroll. His mind cruised too. Ellen Mountford was definitely losing that excruciating self-consciousness that had dominated her reaction to him up till now, and he was glad of it. It helped that they could talk without looking at each other, and that he had the road to focus on. It seemed to take some of the pressure off her. But there was more to it than that, he was aware. That oh-so-brief mention of his mother—and hers—had been like a flicker of real communication between them. Something that could not have happened between two mere social acquaintances.

He frowned. *Do I want that? Do I want any real communication with her? Why should I? She is merely someone standing in the way of what I am determined to achieve—ownership of a house I want to live in myself. And bringing her up to London is merely the means to that end. Nothing more than that.*

His expression lightened. Of course there was one

other reason for bringing Ellen Mountford to London with him. He was all too conscious of that too.

I want to see what she can really look like—when she makes the most of herself instead of the least!

And he would want to know that, he realised, even if she'd had absolutely nothing to do with blocking his way to the house he wanted to possess. Curiosity was mounting within him about Ellen Mountford for herself—not for her house. Across his retinas flickered the recalled image of her in her running gear, showing off that fantastic figure. Which was more than could be said for what she was wearing now—it was no better than the tracksuit. A heavy, badly cut suit and the same ill-fitting white blouse, and those ugly lace-up shoes, which were doing absolutely nothing for her.

A smile flickered about his mouth. What he had in mind for her to wear tonight was quite different...

He dragged his thoughts away and went back into making easy-going conversation with her, taking the opportunity of their passing Windsor Castle to ask something about the British Royal Family. She answered readily enough, and he asked another question to keep her talking.

It dawned on him that she wasn't actually shy at all. Away from her stepmother and stepsister she was noticeably more voluble. Animation lifted her features, lighting up her tawny eyes even behind the concealing lenses of her unflattering glasses, and helping to detract from that damn monobrow of hers which made her look as if she was always frowning. Now that he was seeing her again, he realised, it was clear that actually she didn't look nearly as morosely forbidding as she had when in the company of her stepmother and sister.

So, if she wasn't shy, why the total lack of personal grooming? Why look as dire as she did, considering that she could look so much better?

The question circled in his head as they approached London and headed for the West End, eventually drawing up at his hotel in Piccadilly. His passenger looked at him in surprise.

'I thought we were going to the charity's headquarters,' she said, 'so I can make my pitch for funding?'

Max smiled at her. 'Not exactly,' he said, getting out of the car.

A doorman was opening her door, and as she got out, seeing Max toss the keys to the valet parker, Ellen was suddenly conscious of her plain, dowdy appearance. Utterly unworthy of such a smart hotel—or for keeping company with a man like Max.

'This way,' he said blandly, ushering her inside and guiding her across the swish lobby towards a bank of lifts.

They whooshed upwards, and when they emerged she saw with a frown that they were on the penthouse floor and Max was leading her into one of the suites. She gazed around, confused, taking in the lavish decor of a vast lounge and huge windows overlooking St James's Park. Max was speaking.

'I have not been entirely comprehensive in what I've told you,' he said, his voice bland. He quirked one eyebrow. 'You don't make your pitch now—you make it tonight.' His smile deepened. 'At the ball.'

Ellen stared. 'Ball?' she echoed blankly.

'Yes,' said Max, in that same smooth, urbane manner. 'The annual fundraising ball the charity always holds at this hotel. You'll be sitting on my table, and so will one of the charity's directors. You can have a little chat then, tell him about the camping holidays and what funds you need to expand them.'

Ellen felt the floor disappear from under her. 'I *cannot* go to a *ball*!' she said. The man was mad—completely mad!

'Ah, well,' said Max, his voice as smooth as cream, his smile as rich as butter, 'in that I have to say you are quite, quite mistaken.'

CHAPTER FIVE

ELLEN TOOK A BREATH. Or tried to. There didn't seem to be any breath left in her body because her lungs seemed to be caught in a vice. Horror drenched her—horror at the very thought of being paraded at a *ball* with Max Vasilikos. Her mortification would be exquisite, unbearable—hideous! As hideous as her appearance would be. She felt the colour drain from her cheeks and there was a sick feeling in her stomach.

Max was continuing to speak, still in that same blandly smooth way. 'If you're worried because you have nothing to wear, don't be. I'll have some suitable gowns delivered and you can make your choice. We'll have lunch first, and then afterwards I'll leave you in the hands of the stylists I've booked—it's all arranged. Now…' His tone changed and he walked to the house phone on the desk at the side of the room. 'Time for that lunch. Would you like a preprandial drink? You look somewhat pale.'

In fact she looked like a dish of curds and whey, he decided, and without waiting for an answer crossed to the drinks cabinet and found a bottle of sherry, pouring her a generous measure.

'Drink up,' he said cheerfully.

She took it with nerveless fingers but did not drink. Instead she made her voice work, though it sounded like creaky hinges. 'Mr Vasilikos, I cannot possibly go through with this! It's very…kind…' she almost choked on the word '…of you, but…but…no, I can't. It's out of the question. Impossible. Unthinkable.' She swallowed. Made herself look at him. 'Unthinkable,' she said again, trying desperately to put a note of finality into her strangled voice.

It did not work. He simply gave her a straight look. She'd reverted, he could see, to having that grim expression on her face she'd had when he'd gone to Haughton to view it. It didn't suit her—beetling her monobrow and pulling heavily at her features.

'Why?' He gave her an encouraging smile. 'You'll enjoy it, I promise you.'

She swallowed again. 'I'm *not*, Mr Vasilikos, a party animal.' There was strain in her voice, as if she were forcing herself to speak. 'I think that's pretty obvious.'

He was undeterred. 'It will do you good,' he said blandly.

A knock on the door diverted him and he went to open it. Lunch had arrived.

'Come and sit down,' invited Max, and gestured to the table once all the food had been laid out for them and the servers had departed.

Involuntarily, Ellen felt hungry suddenly. She also realised she must have gulped down half the sherry, for there was a taste of alcohol in her throat. She'd better eat something now…

I'll eat lunch, then head off to the station and get home. Maybe if I write to the charity director he'll consider my application anyway.

Because doing what Max was so ludicrously suggesting was out of the question—just totally out of the question.

Thank God he hadn't mentioned me going to the ball in front of Chloe. She'd have had a field day, sneering and mocking me. Laughing like a hyena at the thought of me dressed up for an evening with Max Vasilikos!

Cold snaked down her spine as she made a start on her meal. It was delicious, she noticed absently— a seafood terrine with a saffron sauce, and keeping warm an entrée of lamb fillet. Hunger spiked in her and she tucked in. From the other end of the table Max glanced at her. It was good, he realised, to see a woman eating well. Not that it would put any fat on her—he knew that now. Not with a toned, sleek body like hers. Memory leapt in his head at just how toned and sleek her body was, and how it was that he'd discovered the amazing truth about this woman he'd crassly assumed was overweight.

'Did you go running this morning?' he heard himself enquire.

She looked up. 'I run every morning,' she said. 'Plus I use the school gym and the pool. Taking Games lessons also keeps me pretty active.'

'Hockey?' Max asked interestedly.

She shook her head. 'Lacrosse. A much better game!' There was a note of enthusiasm in her voice that even her dismay at Max Vasilikos's absurd notion of taking her to a ball—a *ball*, for heaven's sake!—could not squash.

Well, she wouldn't be going to any ball—with or without him, tonight or any other night—so there was no point worrying about it. She would just put it out of her head, enjoy this delicious lunch, and then head for the station. Maybe she'd look in at the Natural History Museum in South Kensington, get some more ideas for her Geography classes, pick up some learning material for her pupils. Yes, that was what she would do.

Relaxing slightly at the realisation that of *course* Max Vasilikos couldn't make her go to this ridiculous ball of his, she heard him asking, 'Isn't lacrosse somewhat violent?' He frowned.

She shook her head again. 'You're thinking of men's lacrosse. That can be vicious! But then so can men's hockey. Girls play a gentler game. But it's fast and furious for all that. I've always loved it. Nothing to beat it.' There was open enthusiasm in her voice now.

'Were you in the team when you were at school?' Max asked.

It was good to hear her speak without that note of almost panic in her voice that had been there as she'd reacted to his mention of the evening's ball, and he knew it was necessary for him to back off for a while, let her calm down again. Her forbidding expression was ebbing, too, and that *had* to be good.

Besides, it was, he realised, something of a pleasant novelty to be lunching with a female in his private suite and not have her endlessly making doe eyes at him, batting her eyelashes, trying to flirt and get his attention. With Ellen there was no such tedious pre-dictability. Instead it was refreshing to talk to a woman about keeping fit, exercise and sport—all of which he enjoyed robustly himself. And she was clearly in her el-ement on such subjects, knowledgeable and confident.

She nodded, then answered him. 'On the wing—loads of running there.'

He glanced at her speculatively. 'What about Chloe? Was she sporty?'

He knew perfectly well she wouldn't have been, but he wanted to hear what Ellen would say about the step-sister she so glaringly resented. Would she despise her for not being in the team?

A tight look had formed in Ellen's eyes. 'Chloe wasn't in the sporty crowd,' she said.

Max picked his next words with deliberate care. 'It must have been difficult for her, joining a new school after her mother married your father. She must have looked to you to help her fit in.'

Ellen's expression froze. Memory pushed into her head. Vivid and painful.

Chloe, with her long blonde tresses, her supercil-ious air of sophistication and her worldly experience of boys and smoking and alcohol and fashion and music and make-up, had been instantly accepted into a bitchy, cliquey set of girls just like her, effortlessly becoming the meanest of the mean girls, sneering at everyone else. Sneering most of all at her hulking, clumping, games-loving stepsister, who'd so stupidly tried to be-friend her initially, when she'd actually believed that her father's remarriage might bring him happiness instead of misery and ruin.

Max's eyes rested on Ellen, seeing her expression close up. Had he hit home? he wondered. He hoped so—because it was for her own good, after all, getting her to face up to what was keeping her trapped in the bitter, resentful, narrow life she led, refusing to move on from the past.

She has to let go of her resentment against her step-family, stop using her share of their inheritance as a weapon against them. Stop clinging to the past instead of moving into the future. I need to bring her out of herself. Show her the world beyond the narrow confines she's locked herself into—let her embrace it...enjoy it.

And what could be more enjoyable than a ball? A glittering, lavish affair that she might enjoy if only she would give herself a chance to do so! But for now he would not press her. For now he just wanted to keep her in this unselfconscious, relaxed zone. So he didn't wait for an answer to his pointed comment about Chloe, but turned the subject back to an easier topic that she clearly found less uncomfortable.

'What kind of workout routine do you do?' he asked. 'You must use weights, I take it?'

To his surprise she flushed that unflattering red that he'd seen all too frequently on his first visit to Haughton.

'That's pretty obvious, isn't it?' she mumbled, knowing he'd have spotted her developed muscle tone—so mercilessly mocked by Chloe, who jibed at her for being more like a man than a woman—when he'd seen her in running gear. 'But I'm good at them and I enjoy it.'

Was there a defensive note to her voice—defiance, even? If so, Max wondered why. She obviously had a fantastic physique—he'd seen that for himself, and had very much enjoyed doing so! But she was speaking again now, and he drew his mind back from that tantalising vision of her fabulous body when she'd been out running.

'I balance weights with cardio work, obviously, but I'd rather run than cycle. Especially since it's such a joy to run in the grounds at home—' She broke off, a shadow in her eyes. Those glorious early-morning runs she loved to take would become a thing of the past if Haughton were wrenched from her...

'What about rowing?' Max asked, cutting across her anguished thoughts. 'That's a good combo of cardio and strength work. It's my favourite, I admit. Though only on a machine.' He gave a rueful smile. 'When I'm on the water I'd rather swim, sail or windsurf.'

She made herself smile. 'Well, you've got the weather for that in Greece!' she riposted lightly, glad to be away from the subject of her overdeveloped muscles, which so embarrassed her. She knew she was being stupid, feeling self-conscious about it with a man who couldn't care less what she looked like as a woman. Inevitably she was invisible to him in that respect. Much less stressful to blank all that and just talk to him as she'd been doing, about sport and exercise, without any connotations about the impact on her appearance.

'It must be great not to need a wetsuit,' she said enviously.

'Agreed.' Max smiled, glad that he was getting her to relax again.

Deliberately he kept the conversation going along convivial lines, asking her about her experiences in water sport, which seemed to be mainly focussed on school trips to the Solent—definitely wetsuits required. Equally deliberately he waxed lyrical about how enjoyable it was to pursue water sports in warmer climes, recommending several spots he knew well. He wanted to open her mind to the possibilities of enjoying the wider world—once she had freed herself from the self-inflicted confines of her past, stopped clinging to the house he wanted her to let go of.

But with the arrival of the dessert course he steered the conversation back to the reason for her presence here.

As they helped themselves to *tarte au citron* Max was pleased to see Ellen tucking in with obvious enjoyment. *It's a sensual pleasure, enjoying food.* The thought was in his head before he could stop it. And the corollary that went with it. *There are more sensual pleasures than food for her to enjoy...*

The words hovered in his head, but he put them firmly aside. They were inappropriate. All he was doing was introducing her to the delights that could be hers if she embraced the world instead of hiding away from it.

Starting tonight.

He pushed his empty plate away and glanced at his

watch. 'We've time for coffee, then a team of stylists are arriving and I'll leave you to them.' He smiled at Ellen.

Her fork promptly clattered to the plate. She was looking at him, her former ease vanished, her expression now one of panic. Panic that changed to a kind of gritty stoniness. He'd seen that look before, and knew it meant she was locking herself down into herself again.

She began to speak, her voice as tight as her expression as she bit the words out. 'Mr Vasilikos—look, I'm sure you mean well, in your own way, but I really, *really* don't want to go to this ball tonight! It would be...' she swallowed '...horrendous.'

He levelled his gaze at her. 'Why?' he demanded simply.

Ellen felt her hands clench the edge of the table as if it might support her. Then she forced herself to speak. To spell out the brutal truth he seemed oblivious to for reasons she could not fathom. She had to disabuse him of *any* notion that going to a ball would be anything other than unspeakable torment for her.

'Because,' she said, and it dawned on him that she was speaking as if she were talking to a particularly intellectually challenged pupil, 'you said it to me yourself at Haughton, when you saw me running. You said, *"You're nothing like your stepsister Chloe."* You couldn't have made it plainer. And you're absolutely right—I *am* nothing at all like Chloe and I never have been. I accept that completely—I've no illusions about myself, believe me. I know exactly what I look like. *That* is why going to a ball, or anything resembling a ball, or any social gathering of any kind at all is anathema to me. The very thought of dressing up and trying to be…trying to be…trying to be *anything* like Chloe—'

There was a choking sound in her voice and she broke off. She felt as if the blood was curdling in her veins—as if Chloe herself were standing there, her mocking peal of derisive laughter lashing at her at the very *thought* of her going to a ball—and with Max Vasilikos of all men! Her eyes tightened shut again, screwing up in their sockets, and her fingers indented into the wood of the table as she gripped it. Then her eyes flew open again.

'I *know* what I am. What I've always been. What I always will be. I'm pushing six foot tall, I've got size eight feet and I've got muscles that can bench fifty kilos. I'm like some gigantic *elephant* compared with Chloe.'

The misery and the self-loathing in her face was contorting her features. Consuming her. Across the table Max had sat back, gazing at her with a new expression on his face. Abruptly he spoke.

'Tell me, do you think Chloe beautiful?' There was a strange note in his voice. Enlightenment was dawning in him like a tsunami in slow motion. Was *this* what was screwing up Ellen Mountford?

Ellen stared. 'What kind of question is that? Of *course* she is! She's everything I'm not. She's petite and incredibly slim, and she has a heart-shaped face and blue eyes and blonde hair.'

The new expression on Max's face did not change.

'And if I described her,' he said carefully, his eyes not letting her go for an instant, 'as…let's see…like a scrawny chicken, what would you say?' Deliberately he chose as harsh a term as she had used about herself to make his point.

She said nothing. Only stared at him, not understanding. Incapable of understanding, Max realised with dawning comprehension. He shook his head slightly. 'You wouldn't believe me, would you?' His voice changed, becoming incisive, incontrovertible. 'Do you not realise,' he demanded, 'that it is only *you* who thinks you are like an elephant?'

She stared at him. Her face was expressionless. Her voice as she answered him toneless. 'Chloe thinks so too.'

She revels in thinking it. Taunts me endlessly. Is viciously gleeful about it. Goes on and on about it! Has tortured me ever since she and her vulture of a mother smashed my life to pieces—going on and on at me about how big I am, how heavy I am, how clumping and lumping and pathetically, pitifully plain and repulsive I am, how I'm just an embarrassing joke! Someone to laugh at and sneer at and look down on! Elephant Ellen…

Max made a sound in his throat and his dark eyes flashed. 'And has it never dawned on you that Chloe, with her tiny size zero frame, would consider a greyhound to be the size of an elephant?' He took a heavy breath and his eyes bored into her. Something in Greek escaped his lips.

Ellen could only stare at him, her face stricken at

the ugly memory of Chloe's years of merciless cruelty about her appearance.

'I fully appreciate,' he said, now speaking in English, spelling out each word carefully, emphatically, so that they would penetrate her skull, reach deep inside her where they needed to reach, 'that for whatever reason—the fashion industry, the prevalence of eating disorders and God knows what else!—extreme thinness is currently regarded as beautiful. And I fully appreciate,' he went on, not letting Ellen do anything except sit and stare at him with blank eyes full of helpless misery, 'that Chloe happens to fit the current description of what makes for a "fashionable" figure. But—'

He held his hand up now, silencing any retort she might have been likely to make.

'That is entirely and completely irrelevant. Because *you*, Ellen…' He paused, and a new timbre suddenly underlaid his voice, resonating through words that echoed in the sudden shift in his expression. 'You,' he breathed, and his eyes were boring into hers, never letting them go for an instant, an iota, 'have the body of a goddess. A *goddess*, Ellen.'

There was silence—complete silence. Max let his eyes rest on her, saying nothing more. Watching her react. It was like a slow-motion sequence in a movie. Red washed into her face like a tide, then drained out, leaving it white and stark. Her eyes distended, then shut like the shell of a clam.

'Don't,' she said. 'Please don't.'

But he did. 'The body of a goddess,' he repeated.

'Don't tell me you don't—because I've seen it. I've seen damn nearly all of it. And believe me…'

Suddenly his long, long lashes swept down over his dark, dark eyes and Ellen felt a kind of hollowing out in her stomach that had nothing to do with the tide of misery that had been drowning her and everything to do with the hot, humid memory of how she'd been wearing only a sports bra and brief shorts when he'd seen her out running that time.

'I liked what I saw. I liked it, Ellen…' and now there was a huskiness in his voice '…a lot.'

He shifted in his seat, relaxing now, his broad shoulders moulding the back of the chair, a smile starting to curve his mouth. 'I've seen a lot of women with fantastic figures, Ellen—and my time with Tyla Brentley, especially when I was out in LA with her, supplied that amply!—so I promise you, you can trust my judgement on these matters. And you can trust my word, too.'

His expression changed, and so did his voice.

'My word,' he announced, 'is that I will donate five thousand pounds to your city kids charity today if you will agree to the following. To put yourself into the hands of the team of stylists this afternoon and let them do whatever it is they do. When they've done it, if you still don't want to come to the ball tonight I will let you off and double the five thousand pounds. If you *do* want to come, however, I'll triple it.' He gave a brief, slashing smile. 'Deal?' he posed.

Ellen stared back.

Five thousand pounds… Ten—because of course it

would be ten! Of course she wouldn't want to go to the ball tonight. No way on God's earth would she volunteer for such an ordeal, however desperately she was scrubbed at by whatever professional make-up artists and the like he had lined up. Yet even as she made that mental averment she could still hear his voice echoing in her head.

The body of a goddess, Ellen.

She heard it, felt it—felt its power. Its temptation.

'Well?' he prompted.

He was holding his hand out across the table. His large, square, strong hand. Into which slowly—very slowly—her own hand seemed to be placing itself, though her head was still reeling with what he'd said to her.

'Good,' said Max. 'So that's all settled, then.' Satisfaction was blatant in his voice. He sat back, withdrawing his hand, moving it towards the coffee pot and starting to pour. 'Cream?' he asked, with a lift of his eyebrow, and poured it in anyway. With a honed, toned body like hers she could drink cream by the bucketload and it would never turn to fat.

Goddess body sorted. Now all that was needed was to sort out the rest of her appearance. Happy anticipation filled him.

People were doing things to Ellen. She had no idea what, and she didn't care. Even about the painful bits that involved tweezers and razors, hot wax and skin peels. She shut her eyes mostly, and let them get on with it, focussing her mind on what she'd do with the ten thousand pounds she'd get for the charity when they'd finished with her.

There were three of them working on her, stylists, beauticians, hairdressers. Whatever they were, they were chattering away. They were all stick-thin, just like Chloe, all wearing ultra-fashionable clothes and four-inch heels, with sharp hairstyles and loads of make-up—which was par for the course, Ellen reasoned, if one worked in the beauty industry. Their conversation seemed to be about clubs and bands, film stars and fashion brands, about which they were intimately knowledgeable.

They looked about twenty and made her feel like thirty. She hoped they were getting paid generously by Max, considering the impossibility of what they were attempting—making her look good enough to go to a ball. Because of course that was impossible. How could it be otherwise?

Dear God, how Chloe would laugh like a hyena if she could see this. She'd be filming it on her phone, posting it to her bitchy friends on social media, and they'd be squealing with laughter. Elephant Ellen, trying to look glamorous! How hilarious! How beyond pathetic!

Cold ran through her at the thought. Well, she'd be spared Chloe's mockery. Because the moment she had that cheque for ten thousand pounds in her hands she'd wipe off all the gunk the stylists were putting on her, get back into her school suit and head home. Back to the safety of Haughton—blessedly hers alone for the next few weeks while Pauline and Chloe were away. Hers to make the most of…the very, very most…

While she could.

Fear bit at her. Max Vasilikos was powerful, rich and ruthless. He'd clearly set his mind on trying to eject her, and he probably had the financial means to do so. It would cost him—but did he care? Maybe he was one of those men who had to win at any price. Wasn't what he was attempting this evening proof of it? Resorting to trying to flatter her into submission?

Telling me I have the body of a goddess!

She heard his voice again in her head, low and husky.

She silenced it.

She realised that one of the stylists, who was busy painting her nails a dark crimson—or the nail extensions that had been stuck on—was talking to her.

'You are *so* lucky to be going out with Max Vasilikos tonight.' There was open envy in her voice. 'He's just to die for!'

Mortified, Ellen steeled her jaw. 'This isn't a *date*,' she said, horrified at the implication and trying desperately to sound composed. 'It's a charity fundraiser.'

Her protestation was ignored. 'He took Tyla Brentley last year,' the second stylist confirmed, doing something with long pins and a curling tong to Ellen's newly cut, coloured and piled up hair. 'She was a sensation.'

'Her dress was stunning' said the third, applying yet more mascara to Ellen's eyelashes, having already lavished eyeshadow and eyeliner plentifully upon her.

'It was Verensiana, and the shoes were Senda Sorn,' the first rattled off knowledgeably. 'She wore Verensiana to the film awards this year too—he's her *totes* fave designer. She went with Ryan Rendell, of course—they are *so* an item now!' She sighed soulfully, and then her eyes brightened as she smiled encouragingly at Ellen. 'Don't worry—she is, like, so *totally* over Max Vasilikos now. So the coast is completely clear for you.'

Ellen let them babble on, not bothering to try and refute their insanely wrong assumptions. Nails finished, the stylist dried them off with a hairdryer, before standing back with the other two stylists, who'd also finished whatever it was they'd been doing to her.

'OK,' announced the first stylist, 'let's go for the gown!'

Resigned, Ellen got to her feet, as requested, shedding the cotton robe she'd been inserted into after bathing, standing there in underwear that consisted of a low-cut underwired bra that hoicked up her breasts, plus lacy panties and black stockings—a universe away from her usual plain and serviceable underwear. As for the gown that had been selected for her, she had no idea and didn't care. It wouldn't be on for long anyway— just long enough for her to tell Max to hand over the cheque for ten thousand pounds.

But as she watched one of the trio fetch the gown out of the wardrobe she gasped. 'What is *that*?' she breathed.

'Isn't it *fabulous*?' came the answer.

'But it's…it's…'

'Edwardian,' said one of the others confidently. 'You

know—like Victorian, but later. But not flappers like the roaring twenties.' She looked at Ellen. 'Didn't you know it was a costume ball?'

No, Ellen had not known. Had not known anything of the sort.

And right now, as the trio started to help her step into the stiffly draped dark red skirts and draw up the whalebone bodice so that it fitted tightly over her bust, pulling narrow straps over her shoulders to flare outwards in a spray of black feathers, her only conscious thought was that it was going to be hellish getting herself out of the dress again when she changed back into her own clothes. There must be a zillion hooks to undo.

CHAPTER SIX

MAX GAVE HIS bow tie a final twitch. Thank heavens Edwardian male evening dress was not a million miles from modern formal wear. It was very different for women. An anticipatory gleam lit his eye. Oh, he was looking forward to this. He was really, *really* looking forward to it. It would cost him fifteen thousand pounds, but it would be money well spent, he was sure—and not just for the sake of the charity!

Checking his cuffs, he strolled to the drinks cabinet, extracting a chilled bottle of vintage champagne and setting it down by two flutes. The noise at the bedroom door made him turn. It was not the stylists—they'd already gone in a flurry of chatter and on their phones already. Ellen was emerging.

His eyes narrowed. And then—

Yes! He wanted to punch the air in triumph. *Yes, yes, yes!*

He watched her walk into the room in a trail of long skirts. She halted abruptly when she saw him. He saw her face tighten.

'OK,' she said, 'where's this cheque you promised me?'

She spoke brusquely, because Max's eyes were like a hawk's on her, and it made her feel acutely, agonisingly uncomfortable. Even though she hadn't looked at her own reflection yet—she couldn't bear to!—she knew exactly what he was seeing. A big, hulking woman in a ridiculously tightly laced preposterous costume dress, with a tottering hairstyle and a face full of make-up that did absolutely nothing for her—because she had a face for which absolutely nothing could be done and that was all there was to it.

Yet again in her head she heard the peal of Chloe's derisive laughter mocking her...mocking the pathetic attempt to make Elephant Ellen look glamorous.

Well, she didn't care—*wouldn't* care. She only wanted the cheque that Max Vasilikos had promised her, then she was getting out of this ridiculous get-up—zillion hooks or not—and hightailing it to the station and home.

Max smiled his urbane, social smile and reached inside his breast pocket. 'Here you go,' he said, and held the cheque he'd promised out to her.

Awkwardly, Ellen walked over and took it. Then her expression altered and her gaze snapped back to him. 'This is for *fifteen* thousand,' she objected.

'Of course it is,' he agreed affably. 'Because of course you're coming to the ball with me. We're both kitted up—let's have a look at ourselves. See if we look the part.'

He helped himself to her arm with a white-gloved hand—he was wearing evening dress of the same Edwardian era, she realised, but on a man it was a lot less immediately obvious—and turned her towards a huge framed mirror hung above a sideboard.

'Take a look, Ellen,' he instructed softly.

Ellen looked.

And made no response. Could have made no response even if someone had shouted *Fire!* Could only do what she was doing—which was staring. Staring, frozen, at the couple reflected in the mirror. At the tall, superbly elegant and dashing figure of Max Vasilikos—and the tall, superbly elegant and stunning woman at his side.

The dark ruby-red silk gown was wasp-waisted and moulded over her hips to flow in a waterfall of colour the full length of her legs and out into a sweeping train, the body-hugging boned bodice revealed a generous décolletage, and the spray of feathers at each sculpted shoulder matched the similar spray in the aigrette curving around the huge swirled pompadour of her hair.

Curling tendrils played around her face—a face whose eyes were huge beneath winged, arched brows… rich tawny eyes that were thickly lashed and fathoms deep—a face whose cheeks were sculpted as if from marble, whose mouth was as lush and richly hued as damsons.

'Didn't I tell you?' Max said softly to her, because he could see from the expression on her face that something profoundly important and significant was happening to her. She was seeing, for the first time in her life, someone she had never seen before—the strikingly, dramatically beautiful woman that was looking back at her from the glass. 'A goddess,' he murmured.

'Didn't I tell you? In figure and in face...like Artemis the huntress goddess...strong and lithe and so, so beautiful.'

He let his gaze work over her reflection, drinking in face and figure, her beauty fully and finally revealed to him. A frown flickered in his eyes. 'Have you put in contact lenses?' he heard himself ask. What had happened to those wretched unflattering spectacles of hers?

She gave a slight shake of her head, feeling the soft tendrils curling down from her extravagant hairdo wafting softly and sensuously at her jaw.

'I only really need glasses for driving,' she answered. 'But I wear them because—' She stopped, swallowed.

Max said nothing—but he knew. Oh, he knew now why she wore them.

Ellen's eyes slid away. Her voice was heavy, and halting. 'I wear them to tell the world that I know perfectly well how awful I look, and that I accept it and I'm not going to make a pathetic fool of myself trying to look better, not going to try to—'

She broke off. Max finished the painful, self-condemning sentence for her.

'Not going to try to compete with your stepsister,' he said, his voice low.

Ellen nodded. 'Pathetic, I know. But—'

He caught her other arm, turning her to face him. '*No!* Don't think like that!' His expression was vehement, even fierce, as she stared at him. 'Ellen, whatever you've come to think in your head about yourself it's *wrong*!' He took a breath. 'Don't you realise you don't *have* to compete with Chloe? Leave her to enjoy her fashionable thinness! You...' His voice changed. 'Ah, *you* have a quite, quite different beauty.' He lifted a hand to gesture to her reflection. 'How can you possibly deny that now?'

Ellen gazed, her mind still trying to keep on denying what Max was saying to her—what the reflection in the mirror was telling her. That a stunningly beautiful woman was gazing back at her. A woman who was...*her*...

But that was impossible! It *had* to be impossible. It was *Chloe* who was lovely—*Chloe* who possessed the looks that defined beauty.

And if it was *Chloe* who was lovely, then she, Ellen, who was everything that Chloe was not—not petite, not blonde, not thin, not with a heart-shaped face, not blue-eyed, not *Chloe*—could only be the opposite. If it were *Chloe* who was lovely—then she, Ellen, could only be *un*lovely.

That was the logic that had been forced on her—forced on her with every sneering barb from Chloe, every derisive glance, every mocking jibe from her stepsister—for years... Those vulnerable teenage years when Chloe had arrived to poison her life, poison her mind against herself, destroying all her confidence so that she'd never even tried to make something of herself, instead condemning herself as harshly as her stepsister condemned her. Believing in Chloe's contempt of her. Seeing herself only through Chloe's cruel eyes.

But how could the woman gazing out at her from

the mirror with such dramatic beauty possibly be described as unlovely? How could a woman like that be sneered at by Chloe, mocked by her, treated with contempt by her?

Impossible—just impossible. Impossible for Chloe to sneer at a woman such as the one who was gazing back at her now.

Emotion swept through Ellen. She couldn't give a name to it—didn't need to. Needed only to feel it rush through her like a tide, sweeping away everything that had been inside her head for so many years. And now Max was speaking again, adding to the tide sweeping through her.

'You can't deny it, can you?' Max repeated. His eyes were fixed on her reflection still. 'You can't deny your beauty—your own beauty, Ellen. *Yours.* As different from Chloe's as the sun is from the moon.'

He gave a laugh suddenly, of triumph and deep satisfaction.

'We shall drink a toast,' he announced. 'A toast to the goddess revealed.' He drew her away, towards the tray of champagne, opening the bottle with skilled long practice and filling the flutes to hand one to her.

Ellen took it numbly, her eyes wide, as if she was in a dream. A dream she still could not quite believe was reality after all.

Her eyes flickered back to her reflection in the mirror.

Is it really, truly me? Can it be—?

Then Max's gloved hand was touching her wrist, lifting his own foaming glass, and she looked back at

him, still with that bemused expression in her eyes, as
if she dared not believe the truth of her own reflection.
He held her gaze, not letting go for an instant.

'To you,' he said. 'To beautiful Ellen. Beautiful,
stunning Ellen!'

He took a mouthful of champagne and she did too,
feeling the bubbles burst on her tongue, feeling a glow
go through her that had nothing to do with champagne
at all...

He smiled down at her. 'Tonight,' he told her, his
mouth curving into an intimate smile, his lashes dipping over dark eyes lambent with expression, 'every
man will envy me—you'll be a sensation.'

The word echoed in her head. A sudden memory
stung like a wasp in her mind. She lowered her champagne glass, her fingers gripping it hard suddenly.

'Those girls—the stylists—they said you brought
Tyla Brentley here last year—that *she* was a sensation.'

Max heard the sudden panic in her voice, that demon
of self-doubt stabbing at her again. He wanted to kick
it into touch without delay. He gave a deliberately dismissive shrug. 'Of course she was,' he said indiffer-
ently. 'Her fame guaranteed that. And Tyla adores men
gazing at her. It flatters her insatiable vanity.'

Even as he spoke he knew his words were true. He,
too, had once fed that vanity—until he'd realised that
Tyla's self-absorption meant it was impossible for her
to think of anyone but herself. His wealth had been useful to her, coming as it did with the person of a male
whose looks could complement her own, and she had
known with her innate instinct for self-publicity that

she and he together made a couple that would always
draw both eyes and attention, gaining precious press
coverage to help her build her career. Tyla's belief in
herself, in her own charm and beauty, had been total.

The very opposite of Ellen.

She was looking at him doubtfully still, as if she
could not believe his indifference to having once
squired a Hollywood film star. He wanted that doubt
gone—completely—and so raised his champagne glass
to his lips, deliberately letting his gaze wash over her.

'Tyla's got a good body—no doubt about that—
but…' And now he let something else into his gaze
that he knew from long experience had an effect on
all females. 'But I can promise you that she had absolutely nothing on you. If Chloe,' he said 'is a tiny little
Chihuahua…' he made his voice amused, deliberately
exaggerating her stepsister's petiteness '…then Tyla is
a…a gazelle, I guess. But *you*…' Once more his gaze
rested on her, sending her the message he wanted…
needed…her to get. 'You, Ellen, are a lioness!'

He grinned at her, and tilted his champagne glass
to her in tribute.

'And lionesses gobble up little dogs and antelopes
for breakfast!'

He toasted her again, his eyes becoming serious now,
holding hers, sending home his essential message to
her, the reassurance she needed—the reassurance that
he would give her whatever it took. He would make
sure of that. His eyes rested on her, their expression intent. Suddenly it seemed crucially important that Ellen
believed him, and believed in her own newly revealed

beauty. And it was for a reason that had nothing to do with his plans for Haughton. For a reason he was only dimly aware of—and yet it seemed to be forcing itself into his consciousness with an insistence he could not ignore.

I want it for her sake—not for mine. I want it so that she can be happy—happy in her own body, finally. I want that for her.

'Be proud of what you are,' he told her. 'Be happy in your body. Your fantastic body! Strong and lean and lithe—'

She felt gloved fingertips glide down the bare length of her upper arm.

'And with great muscle tone!' he finished approvingly.

Ellen's eyes flickered uncertainly. 'Maybe I need a shawl over my arms,' she ventured. 'I'm too muscular—'

Max rolled his eyes, shaking his head. 'Uh-uh! Remember—think lioness!' He let his gaze liquefy again, knowing the effect it would have, the effect he wanted right now. 'Think Artemis. Think goddess. Think beautiful…' There was a sudden husk in his voice that he had not put there deliberately at all, but which came of its own powerful accord. 'Very, very beautiful.'

The wash of his warm gaze over her was instinctive, and he felt it resonate with a warming of his blood, too, that surged in his body powerfully, unstoppably.

His eyes were holding hers, not letting her go. Ellen felt her breath catch in her breast, felt her heartbeat give

a sudden surge, felt the surface of her skin tighten as if
an electric charge were spreading out through its whole
expanse, radiating out from her quickened heart rate.
She could feel her pupils flare, her lips part—felt faint,
almost, heard drumming in her ears…

The world seemed to slow down all around her.

And then the sound of the suite's doorbell ringing
broke the moment. For a second Max just went on staring, unable to relinquish his gaze on the woman whose
beauty he had revealed to her—and to himself. Then,
with an exclamation in Greek, he dropped his hands,
strode to the door and yanked it open.

As he saw who it was he relaxed immediately. 'Ah,'
he said. 'Come in!'

Ellen turned, dazed, her pulse hectic, still blinking,
breathless from that strange, powerful moment that had
hummed like charged plasma between them. She saw
a neatly suited man walk in, a briefcase handcuffed to
his wrist. She blinked again. What on earth…?

'So,' she heard Max saying as the man set his briefcase on the table, unlocking it, 'what have you brought
us?'

The man opened the lid and Ellen gasped audibly.
It was jewellery, carefully nestled in black velvet lin-
ers, glittering in every hue—diamonds, emeralds, sapphires and rubies.

Rubies…

Ellen's eyes went to them immediately—it was impossible for them not to. She felt her breath draw in
sharply as her gaze fixed on the ruby set, deep and
glowing, a necklace, bracelet, earrings and a ring.

Max saw her focus on the set. Her expression was fixed, and for a second—just a second—he thought he saw something fleeting cross it, like a sudden convulsion. Then it was gone, and he was speaking.

'Ah, yes,' he said. 'Rubies, definitely. Ideal for your gown.'

The jeweller started to lift the pieces. 'As you can see,' he told them, 'their setting is of the period, and original. If I may…?'

He carefully lifted the necklace—a complex design of several loops of different lengths, with pendent rubies from each—and as he placed it around Ellen's throat the necklace occupied a considerable amount of the bare expanse of flesh between her throat and the swell of her breasts. He fastened the necklace, then held up a large hand mirror so she could see herself.

She gazed, her expression strange, and that fleeting look passed across her face again as she lifted her hand to touch the gems.

'Perfect,' said Max, well pleased. 'Let's get the rest of it on so we can see the final effect.'

Ellen still had that strange expression on her face. Max found himself wondering at it. He watched her hold out her wrist as the jeweller fastened the glittering bracelet around it and handed her the earrings. As he lifted the ring he paused, glancing doubtfully at Ellen's large hands.

'It will fit—just,' Ellen said.

She sounded sure of it and took the ring, pausing to glance at the inscription inside, which Max could see but not read, before carefully working the ring over her knuckle. It did, indeed, just fit—as she had forecast. She looked at it on her finger for a moment, the same strange, fixed expression on her face.

Then it was gone. She got to her feet. There was something different about her, Max fancied—some subtle change had come over her. There was an air of resolve about her—confidence, even. But then he was taking in the impact of her appearance, finished to perfection now with the glittering ruby parure that went so superbly with her Edwardian gown and hairstyle.

Beautiful!

That was the woman standing there, with her up-swept hair, gems glittering, her toned, honed body sumptuously adorned with the lustrous ruby silk of her gown. He reached for his champagne glass and drained what was left, prompting Ellen to do likewise. They set their flutes down and Max turned to Ellen, holding out his arm to her.

'Time,' he said, and he gave her a little bow, his eyes glinting with pleasure and anticipation and appreciation, 'to take you to the ball.'

Walking into the hotel's ballroom, its rich red and gold decor a perfect complement to her black and ruby styling, Ellen tightened her hand on Max's sleeve. Being at his side, she thought, her own generous figure seemed completely in proportion. His height easily topped hers by several inches—his wide shoulders and broad chest saw to that. Unconsciously, she seemed to straighten her shoulders further, and her hips moved with regal

ease, her chin held high, as she walked beside Max
with her athletic gait.

She should have felt nervous—but she didn't. Oh,
the glass of champagne had helped, but it was not the
bubbles in the champagne alone that were gliding her
forward, filling her with wonder and elation.

She could see eyes going to her as they made their
entrance, and for the first time in her life she experienced the oh-so-pleasurable thrill of knowing she was
turning heads—for every reason a woman could dream
of. Because she looked—*stunning.*

They both did.

As they walked past a mirror she caught their joint
reflection and could see exactly why people were pausing to look at them. They were both tall, both sleekly
groomed, with stunning looks, male *and* female, between them. Surely even Max and the glamorous Tyla
Brentley could not have turned more heads?

We make a fantastic couple!

The thought was in her head before she could stop
it. Urgently she sought to suppress it, then gave in.
Yes, she and Max *did* make a fantastic couple—but it
was for tonight only, for the purposes of this glittering charity bash. That was what she had to remember.
And one other vital thing.

*He's only doing all this to soften me up—to try and
persuade me to give up Haughton to him.*

But even though she knew it was true she didn't
seem to mind right now. How could she when what
he'd given her this evening was something she had
never thought she would ever possess in all her life?

Freedom from the malign hex that Chloe had put on her so many years ago.

Self-knowledge flooded through her, washing away so much of the blindness that had clouded her image of herself for so long. The blindness that she had allowed her stepsister to inflict on her.

I let Chloe have that power over me. I let her control my mind, my image of myself, my sense of worth.

It seemed so strange to her now, to think of how defiant she'd always been with Pauline and her daughter—and yet they had controlled her at this most basic, potent level. But no longer—never again! A sense of power, of newborn confidence swept through her. Unconsciously she lifted her fingers to the necklace, touching the jewels around her throat. Beautiful jewels to adorn a beautiful woman. A woman worthy of a man like Max Vasilikos.

She looked up at him now, easily a head taller than her, and smiled. He caught her expression and answered it with his own. Long lashes swept down over his eyes and he patted the hand hooked into his.

'Enjoy,' said Max, smiling down at her.

And enjoy she did. That was the amazement of it all.

Time and again her fingers brushed at her necklace, or grazed the gold band around her finger beneath its ruby setting—and every time she did she gave a little smile, half haunting, half joyous.

As Max had promised her, sitting to her left she found one of the host charity's directors, who listened attentively as she told him about the camps she ran, then nodded approvingly and told Ellen he'd be happy to help with her funding.

Glowing, she turned to Max. 'Thank you!' she exclaimed, and it was heartfelt.

And she was not just thanking him for setting her up with this funding, or his cheque for fifteen thousand pounds. It was for lifting Chloe's curse from her shoulders—setting her free from it.

His eyes met hers and, half closed, half veiled, they flickered very slightly. As if he were thinking about something but not telling her. He raised his glass of wine to her.

'Here's to a better future for you,' he murmured.

The corner of his mouth pulled into a quizzical smile, and she answered with one of her own in return, lifting her glass too.

'A better future,' she echoed softly.

At the edge of her consciousness Haughton loomed, still haunted by Pauline and Chloe, the dilemma insoluble. But the house she loved so much, the home that she longed only to be safe, seemed far, far away right now. Real—much more real—was this moment... this extraordinary present she was experiencing. All thanks to Max, the man who had made it possible for her.

For an instant her gaze held his, and she felt bathed and warmed by the deep, dark brown of eyes fringed by thick lashes, flecked with gold. And then for an even briefer instant, so brief she could only wonder whether it had been real, there was a sudden change in them, a sudden, scorching intimacy.

She sheared her gaze away, feeling her heart jolt within her as if an electric shock had just kicked it. As if it were suddenly hard to breathe.

All through the rest of the meal, and the speeches and the fundraising auction afterwards, she could feel the echo of that extraordinary jolt to her heartbeat, flickering in her consciousness as port and liqueurs, coffee and petit fours circulated. Then, on the far side of the grand ballroom an orchestra started up.

'Oh, how lovely!' she exclaimed as the music went into the lilting strains of a slow waltz, ideal for an Edwardian-themed ball.

'It's Lehár!' exclaimed one of the women at their table, delighted.

'So it is!' agreed Ellen, starting to hum the composer's familiar melody—the waltz from *The Merry Widow* operetta.

'Well, I think this calls for audience participation,' said the charity director at her side, as all around them at the other tables guests were getting to their feet to take to the dance floor. 'Will you do me the honour?' he asked Ellen with a smile.

But he was forestalled. Max was standing up.

'I claim the first waltz,' he said, catching Ellen's elbow and guiding her to her feet. His rival conceded gracefully. Max bore Ellen off.

She was in a state of consternation, aware that her heart was racing and that she felt breathless. Taken over.

But then Max has taken me over all day, hasn't he? I've done everything he wanted, all the time!

Well, now she was going to dance with him, and she wasn't getting a choice about it. Except—

'I have *no* idea how to waltz!' she exclaimed. 'And I think the Viennese waltz is different from the English waltz anyway. And I—'

He cut her short. 'Follow my lead,' he instructed, and simply took her into his arms and swept her off.

Into the dance.

Into the irresistible, lilting music that wafted them around the ballroom floor.

She felt her long, heavy silk skirts become as light as a feather, swirling around her legs as Max whirled her around until she was dizzy with it, until all she could do was clutch helplessly at his shoulder, hang on to his hand for dear life as he turned her and guided her and never, never let her go.

'You see? It's easy.' He smiled at her. 'Much easier than you feared.'

And she knew, with a little skip of her heart, that it was not just the waltzing he meant.

It's all been so, so easy. The lifting of the hex. Her transformation tonight. Putting on this gorgeous costume, being swept away in his arms...

Joy filled her—a wonderful sense of carefree elation as if, simply by whirling her around like this, he had whisked away all that oppressed her.

And for tonight he has! I know that I will have to go home tomorrow, back to all the difficulties and the stress and the fear of losing Haughton. But for tonight I will waltz my cares away.

The music ended with a flourish, and the cessation

of the swirling made her head spin instead. But then she was joining with the others in applauding the orchestra, its players in historical costume as well, and their leader was turning and bowing, introducing the next dance they were going to play.

It was a polka, and Ellen's eyes widened again.

Max didn't let her speak. 'Just follow my lead,' he instructed again.

And once more she did. It was just as well, she thought absently, that she was pretty fit, for the dance was vigorous and not a few couples finished panting. But Max wasn't the slightest out of breath, and neither was she.

'Thank goodness for early-morning runs!' she exclaimed.

'It's hot work, this elegant dancing,' Max agreed, running a finger around his distinctly damp collar.

Ellen smiled. 'My father used to say that *his* father, when they went to dances before the war, had to take spare collars with him because they wilted during the night.'

Max laughed. 'Well, I envy you your bare shoulders and arms, I can tell you. Will it cause a scandal if I shed this very hot evening jacket, I wonder?'

'You'll be blackballed instantly!' she warned him with a laugh.

'Oh, well, I'm just a foreigner and a parvenu, so I won't care,' he riposted, and took her back into his arms as the music started up again.

It was a much slower waltz now, and Ellen was relieved. Or at least she was until she felt Max's hand tightening at her waist. It was hard to feel much through the whalebone bodice, but there was something in the way he was imprinting his hold on her that made her breath catch despite the slowness of the music. Made it catch again when she saw the expression in his eyes, looking down at her. She felt colour run out into her cheeks. She tried to stop it, tried to hope that he would take it only for heat, no other reason. She tried to pull her gaze away, but it was hopeless…

'Glad you came to the ball?' he asked, a faint smile ghosting at his mouth.

His long lashes swept down over his eyes and he smiled at her. Were there gold flecks in those eyes? She could only gaze into their depths, captivated and entranced.

Her lips parted in a wide, joyful smile. 'Oh, yes! It's just…*wonderful*! All of it. Every bit!'

A wicked glint gleamed in Max's eyes. 'Even the whalebone in your bodice?' he asked.

'OK,' she allowed. 'Not that.'

'Though it *does* give you the most superb figure,' he said, and now…oh, most definitely…now there were golden flecks in his eyes.

He pulled a little away from her so his eyes could take in the glory of her narrowed waist, the full round-ness of her hips, and then, moving upwards, the gener-ous curvature of her breasts. His gaze lingered…then he dragged them away.

No. The voice inside his head was stern. No, he must not. This evening was about liberating Ellen Mountford from the chains that weighed her down. Freeing her

from the mental burdens that blighted her life, made
her want to hide herself away in her safe place, her
childhood home, where she could moulder away, never
emerging into the world.

Well, she was emerging now, all right. Male eyes
were all over her. Max had seen that the moment he'd
walked into the ballroom. They were on her still, and
he didn't blame them.

Mine are too...

No. The stern voice inside his head came again.
No—he must not permit that. This evening was for
her, not him! Oh, it was for himself too—of course it
was—but only because showing Ellen how wonderful
her life could be once she joined the world, instead of
hiding herself away at Haughton, would mean that he
could acquire what he was set on acquiring. Which was
not Ellen Mountford—it was the house she would not
willingly sell to him.

But you could have her as well...

The siren thought was in his head, as sinuous and
seductive as the slow pulse of the music he was moving to.

Ellen was in his arms, her body so close to his,
her weight pressing in on him as they turned, his arm
around her waist, her rich ruby mouth smiling up at
him. Tempting him...

The music ended and he was glad. He led her back to
their table and immediately the charity director was on
his feet. Ellen was led away, and Max watched her go.
Was there a reluctance in her now? Would she rather
have not danced again but sat with him and watched the

dancers? He didn't know—knew only that there was a kind of growl inside him…a growl that made him reach for the cognac bottle and pour himself a glass.

The two other couples at the table were taking a break as well, and were chatting, drawing him into their conversation. He joined in civilly but his gaze, he knew, kept going back out to the dance floor, searching for Ellen.

I want her.

That was the voice in his head now. Stark, blunt and simple. His jaw set. He could want her all he liked, but fulfilling that want would lead to complications.

The question was—did he care?

And right now, watching her in another man's arms—this woman he'd released from the bondage of her mental chains, freed to revel in the natural beauty that was hers—and feeling that deep, primal growl rising in him again, he knew as the fiery liqueur glazed his throat and fuelled his heated blood that he didn't care at all…

CHAPTER SEVEN

THE WORLD WAS whirling pleasantly around her—oh, so pleasantly! Ellen felt herself swaying slightly, as if she were still dancing, humming a waltz tune, hearing her long silk skirts rustling. The ball was over, midnight long gone, and now she was back up in the penthouse suite. The orchestra was still playing in her head. And everything was wonderful! Oh, just *wonderful*! Her gown was wonderful, her hair was wonderful, the dancing had been wonderful, the evening had been wonderful!

Max had been wonderful...

She gazed at him now, blood singing in her veins. He was twisting open a bottle of water, looking so tall, so strong, so utterly devastating in his Edwardian evening dress, and her eyes just drank him in as the room swirled around her and the music played in her head and on her lips. All she wanted to do, all she longed to do, was to be back in his arms, dancing and dancing...

'Drink this—and drink it all,' Max's deep voice instructed her as he came to her and handed her a large glass of water. 'You'll thank me in the morning, I promise you.'

'I feel fine,' she said. 'Absolutely fine.' Still, she gulped down the water, never taking her gaze from Max—wonderful, *wonderful* Max!

How gorgeous he is—how incredibly handsome and gorgeous and wonderful and devastating and...

Then she yawned—a huge, exhausted yawn. Her eyes blinked.

'Time for bed,' said Max.

But not, alas, with him. He knew that. The champagne, the wine, the liqueurs she'd drunk made that out of the question. Should he regret it? He shouldn't, he knew, but he did all the same.

Maybe it's for the best. That was what he needed to tell himself. Remind himself of all the complications that might arise were he to follow what he knew his body wanted right now...the new-found desire that had swept over him.

I want to celebrate her new-found freedom with her. I want to take the final step of her liberation with her. I want to be the man who does that—

Well, not tonight. Frustration could bite at him all it liked, but that was that. And he—he'd be back in his own bedroom in the hotel suite, heading for a cold shower.

But first he had a real ordeal to get through. One that was going to test him to the limits.

'Hold still!' he instructed her, catching the back of her shoulders to steady her.

It was a mistake, for the warmth of her bare skin

under his palms was an unwise sensation for him to feel
right now. He pulled his hands away as if burnt, made
his fingers drop down to the fastenings of her dress
instead. *Thee mou*, there were a million of them! As
he started the finicky work of undoing them he could
feel the effort of not thinking about what he was doing.

*Don't think about how her beautiful bare back is
emerging...how she's dropped her head, exposing the
tender nape of her neck caressed by tendrils of her
chestnut hair...how easy...how tempting it would be
to lower your mouth and graze that delicate skin with
your lips. No, don't think about any of that—*

He swallowed heavily, dropping his hands away.
'Done!'

She turned, oblivious to the punishing, disciplined
self-control he was exerting, her unfastened bodice
held up only by her hands pressed to her half-exposed
breasts, her feathered shoulder straps collapsing down
her arms as well. A sigh of happiness, of bliss escaped
her, and her eyes were clinging to his.

'This has been,' she announced, 'the most *wonderful* night of my life.'

Her lips were parted, her eyes glowing, her face
lifted up to his. She swayed towards him in the motion
of a dance, with intoxication in her blood, unconscious
invitation in her glorious goddess body.

And he was lost. Totally, completely lost. Could resist her no longer.

His hands fastened on her upper arms and he hauled
her to him. Drew her smiling parted lips to his and took
his fill. He could not resist it—just could not.

Tasting first, he glided his lips across the velvet softness of hers, taking possession of her mouth, tasting her bouquet like a rich, radiant wine. Then, as his kiss deepened, he opened his mouth to hers and she came with him—came with him every iota of the way—moving her mouth on his, opening to him, tasting him, taking her fill of him.

He could feel her full breasts pressing against the cotton of his shirtfront, feel her nipples start to peak, feel desire flare through her, fuelled by the wine in her blood, the champagne in her veins, the music in her head.

Hunger for her leapt in him, seared through him. He knew his body was surging, engorging, knew that desire and need and all that could burn like an inferno between a man and a woman was igniting within him now. Knew that in seconds the conflagration would take hold—unstoppable, unquenchable.

With a groan, he let her go, wrenching his mouth from hers, pulling his hands away, stepping back from her.

There was a dazed expression on her face, the bewilderment of loss in her eyes—her huge, widened eyes—and their pupils were flaring with desire, arousal...

He shook his head. Held up his hands. Stepped further back.

'Goodnight!' he said.

His voice was shaken, he could hear it, and he could feel the heat in his body still, the fullness still there, but he had to beat it back, subdue it. Whatever primal hunger was possessing him, he had to defeat it. To indulge himself now, when far too much wine and champagne was coursing through her, would be unforgivable.

For a second a stricken look was there in her eyes— a look that somehow pierced him like a stiletto blade in his throat—and then, like the sun coming out from a cloud, dazzling in its brightness, she smiled. Her face lit up once more.

'Goodnight!' she breathed. 'Oh, *goodnight*!'

He backed to the door. He did not want to do this. Did not want to leave. But he had to. Had to get back to his room—had to get that cold shower sluicing down over his body...*had* to!

As he reached the door she lifted her hand from one side of her bodice, dangerously exposing yet more of her sweet, succulent flesh, a final torment for him, and then, with another dazzling smile, an insouciant, joyous gesture, she kissed her fingers and blew the kiss to him.

'Thank you!'

They were the last words he heard before he got out through the door and pulled it shut, to keep him safe.

Safe from the only thing in the world he wanted to do right now...

Go right back in and sweep her into his arms.

Ellen was asleep, but someone was making her wake up. A hand was on her shoulder, gently shaking her. She shrugged it off, nestled back down into her pillows, but the hand returned. Someone said something to her, but she didn't know what. It was foreign. Greek?

Greek!

She bolted upright, only just having the presence of mind to clutch her bedclothes to her, her eyes flaring

open. Max Vasilikos, freshly showered—she could
tell from the damp hair feathering his forehead and the
towelling robe that emphasised the Mediterranean tan
of his skin—was sitting on her bed.

'How are you feeling?' he enquired. His voice was
urbane, equable—and amused.

She pushed her hair out of her face. It seemed to
her to be softer than it usually was, and finer, and less
heavy. She blinked, looking around her, dragging her
gaze past the figure of the man sitting at the foot of the
bed, with his dark eyes resting on her speculatively and
a curve at his sculpted mouth that suddenly made her
very, *very* aware of her state of dishevelment.

'Um—fine,' she got out.

Was she fine? she wondered. She blinked. Yes, she
did seem to be OK. Memory came rushing back, tumbling into her head like a series of snapshots. The ball—
that fantastic, gorgeous, wonderful ball! Chatting away
to all those people over dinner. Dancing with Max.

Kissing Max…

Colour flared in her cheeks as memory flooded her,
intense and vivid.

*He kissed me! Max Vasilikos—the man who made
me beautiful and waltzed the night away with me!*

Max saw the colour flare and knew what she was
thinking. It was what he was only too conscious of
himself. His night had not been peaceful. It had been
disturbed by dreams. Dreams in which there had been
no need to tear himself away from the woman he'd
been kissing.

No—don't think about it now! Not when he was sitting on her bed and she was only a metre away from him, her naked body shielded only by the sheet she was clutching to her, her lush hair tumbling wantonly around her shoulders, her smeared mascara making her eyes smoky and deep…

He got to his feet, stepping away from the bed. Well away. 'I've ordered brunch,' he told her. 'So have a wake-up shower and come on through.'

She nodded, and waited till he was well clear of the room before getting up.

It was strange, she thought as she caught her reflection in the mirror of the en-suite bathroom… She was so used to her body, so used to thinking it large and muscular and unattractive. And yet now— Her eyes held her own naked reflection. Saw it for the very first time not through Chloe's eyes, but through someone else's completely.

Max's eyes…

Tall, with sculpted shoulders, taut arms, generous breasts, flat abs, toned glutes, strong quads, long legs. A goddess body?

And her face still held the beauty conjured from it by those skilful magic-making stylists last night. Her fingers lifted uncertainly to her hair. Whatever those chattering women had done to it, it was amazing. Its colour was so much richer, glowing in the lights around the vanity unit, and it felt so light on her head, yet it waved in lush tresses down over her shoulders, softening her face, her jaw, caressing her neck. She touched her mouth with her fingertips—

elongated nails still crimson with varnish—and felt a smile part her mouth.

A goddess indeed...

She heard Max's words in her head, felt his eyes on her, his hand on her spine as they'd waltzed.

The melody played in her head again. Happiness filled her. Whatever her worries, whatever her woes, this...*this* would always be with her now.

He made me beautiful.

He might be trying to take her beloved home from her, but he had given her something she had never thought to have—something that Chloe's cruelty had taken from her, that her own self-doubt, self-criticism had *let* her stepsister take from her.

And Max—wonderful, wonderful Max!—had now restored it to her.

With a smile of wonder and gratitude still playing on her lips she piled her hair up, pinned it loosely, and stepped into the shower unit. Brunch beckoned—and so did the thought of seeing Max again.

Even if only for what was left of the morning.

A pang smote her. She swallowed as the hot water plunged down over her shoulders, rousing her to full wakefulness. Suddenly the thought of leaving him, of returning home to Haughton, seemed like the worst thing in the world.

But the ball is over—and it's time to go home.

For the first time in her life she did not want to.

Max was already seated at the table when Ellen emerged. He was clad, like her, in a white towelling

robe. Seeing him like that seemed suddenly very…
intimate.

Into her head came the memory, vivid and real, of
how he had kissed her.

Oh, she might have been intoxicated—with champagne and wine, with music and wonder—but that
could not dim the searing memory.

Instantly she reproved herself fiercely.

*It was just a kiss! Don't make anything of it! It was
only a kiss. It meant nothing—just a way to say goodnight.*

Yet even as she told herself that she could feel the
colour flare in her face. Busily, she sat herself down,
hoping Max hadn't seen. Didn't know the reason for it.

*It would have meant nothing to him—think how
many women he's kissed in his life! With looks like
his…*

And one of those women—the most recent—had
been a film star. To a man used to kissing film stars—
used to doing a whole lot more than kissing!—bestow-
ing a goodnight kiss on *her* was…well, nothing.

But not to me.

Her eyes flickered a moment. No, it had not been
nothing to her…

*To me his kiss was the ultimate breaking of Chloe's
vicious hex. The one I gave in to—was too cowed to
fight, to deny. I gave her an easy victory. A victory
she revelled in!*

Her expression steeled. But no more. Chloe's cruel
mental domination of her was over. She had to keep
it that way.

She looked across at Max. His eyes were resting on her with an expression in them that was half glinting, half veiled. She met it square-on, refusing to let any self-conscious memory colour her cheeks. Then she looked at the lavish brunch spread out before her. She was instantly hungry.

'Mmm…eggs Benedict. My favourite,' she announced appreciatively.

She took a generous helping and got stuck in. Max was doing likewise—well, he had a big frame to fill, and muscle burned more calories than fat…not that there was a trace of fat about him. He was lean and powerful and devastatingly attractive, and the way the tan of his skin contrasted with the white of his robe, the way there was really quite a lot of chest exposed in the deep vee…

She gulped silently and focussed on her food.

'No sign of a hangover?' Max enquired. She didn't look hungover in the slightest, and she shook her head, making her long wavy tresses resettle on her shoulders and waft around her cheeks. He felt satisfaction go through him. Those stylists had been worth their weight in gold! Even with all the make-up now scrubbed off, the changes they'd made were glaringly noticeable—most of all the taming of her fearsome, frowning monobrow.

She wasn't frowning now at all. 'Nope,' she said. 'All that water you poured into me before I flaked out did the trick!'

'I told you you'd thank me in the morning,' he replied with a glint in his eyes.

She made herself look at him, pausing in her eating. 'I *do* thank you,' she said 'I thank you for...for everything!'

She didn't have to spell it out. He knew. He smiled at her down the length of the table. Then raised his glass of orange juice to her. 'To the new you, Ellen—and may the old one be banished for good!

He took a draught of the juice, setting down the glass. 'Now,' he opened, sounding businesslike, 'what we need to get done today is sorting out your wardrobe. Fabulous though you look in Edwardian costume, it's not for every day,' he finished lightly, with another smile. 'So, when we've eaten it'll be time to go shopping.'

A troubled look shadowed her face. 'I really need to go home,' she said.

Max raised his eyebrows. 'What for? It's not term-time—'

'Yes, but... Well... I really ought to...'

He gave an airy wave of his hand. No way was Ellen going to beetle off back to Haughton and bury herself there again! Not yet—not by a long way! He hadn't done with her...

Deep in his abdomen he felt an oh-so-masculine response kick in. He'd had to relinquish her last night—anything else would have been inexcusable—but the impulse he'd experienced then, the overriding rush of desire, had in no way been attenuated. His mind was made up—the long, sleepless, frustrated hours of the night he'd just spent had given him conviction of that.

A romance is exactly what she needs. It will show

her how wonderful life can be if she just emerges from her shell, tastes all that life can offer now that she knows how beautiful she is. She can start to shed the burden of bitter resentment, knowing that her deep, dark, disturbing jealousy and envy of her stepsister is quite unnecessary.

And with that burden of resentment lifted—well, then she wouldn't need to keep trying to thwart Pauline and Chloe by refusing to sell her share of Haughton. Wouldn't need to keep trying to punish Pauline for marrying her father and Chloe for having the beauty she thought she herself was denied.

'So,' he said decisively, 'it's all settled. There's absolutely no call for you to head off straight away, so we'll definitely go shopping.'

She was still looking at him with a troubled expression. She wanted to tell him that even if she didn't actually need to go back home today shopping for clothes was the last thing she could afford. Her salary was wiped out paying for her living expenses and Pauline and Chloe's extravagances! But even as she thought it she felt rebellion stir. If *they* could fund their lavish lifestyle by selling off paintings from Haughton, well, so could she!

In the deep pocket of her robe she could feel the weight of the jewellery she'd worn last night, which she would hand back to Max as she must, however reluctantly...

A stab of anger bit at her, hardening her resolve. Her expression changed as she made her decision. Max saw it and was glad.

* * *

He was even more glad, later that afternoon, when she emerged from the changing room of one of the most upmarket fashion houses, finally looking the way her natural looks deserved.

It hadn't been completely plain sailing—she'd balked as they'd walked in, a look of near panic on her face, and he'd had to steer her firmly towards the serried racks of clothes.

'I don't think there'll be anything to fit me!' she'd said nervously, her eyes casting about at the stick-thin customers who all seemed to be Chloe clones.

Doubt had suddenly assailed her. She'd been wearing, perforce, the dowdy old-fashioned suit she'd worn yesterday, and there, surrounded by elegance and fashion, she'd felt her fragile new-found confidence waver. Panic had bitten at her throat.

They're all looking at me—wondering what on earth a lumpy frump like me is doing here! Wanting me to get out, to stop inflicting myself on their eyesight!

The old, painful, mortifying self-consciousness had come back, drowning her, trying to send a tide of humiliated colour back into her face. The urge to run out of the shop, to take herself off to the station, to rush back down to Haughton, seeking its refuge, hiding there in solitude, safe from condemning eyes, had almost overpowered her.

Then Max had spoken, ignoring her protestation. 'This will suit you,' he'd said decisively, reaching for a knee-length dress in warm caramel, soft jersey with a draped neckline. 'And these.'

He'd taken a teal-blue dress and a tailored jacket off the rack. He'd handed them to her and then started sorting through the trousers, pulling out a black pair and a chestnut-brown pair, before picking up a couple of cashmere sweaters. He'd guided her to the changing rooms.

'In you go,' he'd said, and he'd given her the rest of the clothes and a gentle push. He'd had no intention of letting those chains start winding themselves around her mind again.

As she had headed, still reluctantly but obediently, into the changing rooms he'd beckoned to a sales assistant, giving her a particularly engaging smile. 'We're going to need a lot more clothes,' he'd said, nodding at Ellen's back.

The sales assistant had cast an expert eye over her, taking in the tight, ill-fitting suit. 'Definitely.' She had nodded and glided off, returning with a large selection of separates, plus shoes, belts and some costume jewellery.

With a smile at Max, who'd settled himself comfortably into one of the leather chairs conveniently placed nearby for attendant males, complete with magazines about cars and fitness to while away their time while they waited for their womenfolk, she had whisked them into the changing room.

It had taken quite some time for Ellen to emerge...

CHAPTER EIGHT

'TELL ME,' MAX SAID, 'how are you with helicopters?'

Ellen stared. 'Helicopters?'

'Yes. I've got one on standby,' he informed her. 'There's a property out in the Chilterns I want to take a quick look at, and a helicopter is the fastest way.'

'I've never been in one,' Ellen said.

Max grinned. 'Great—a new experience. You'll love it.'

He bore her off towards the kerb, where his car was hovering. He wasn't giving her a chance to object, just as he hadn't given her a chance to run out of that fashion house. When she'd finally emerged from the changing room he'd wanted to punch the air, like he had the night before. And now she had looked—fantastic!

Straw-coloured trousers neatly hugged her trim hips, and a casual cashmere sweater in oatmeal superbly moulded her generous breasts. A long jacket and a swish leather handbag completed the outfit.

Behind her came the sales assistant, with more clothes, and they all totted up to a good half-dozen or more capacious carrier bags.

His driver climbed out of the car to put the bags in the boot as Max helped Ellen into the back of the car.

She was in a daze—no doubt about it. She'd handed over her credit card, wincing at the huge total, but then tightening her mouth in defiance. Another watercolour would have to be sold—but this time *she* would get the benefit of it.

And it was money well spent—she'd seen that the moment she'd taken in her reflection, seeing not frumpy, lumpy Elephant Ellen but a tall, good-looking, athletic, fashionably dressed woman who could stride through the world with assurance and poise. It was a good feeling—a brilliant feeling!

A bubble of happiness rose in her, as if she'd just drunk a glass of champagne. She was going to enjoy this—enjoy *everything*! Including the novelty of a ride in a helicopter.

Her eyes widened in excitement as the noisy machine rose into the air, skating high above the River Thames. London became increasingly miniature, and then was left behind as the countryside approached. She gazed spellbound as they flew, then circled over the property Max wanted to assess.

It was another large country house, Victorian gothic in style, and far larger than Haughton. Only then did a shadow cross her eyes, for it reminded her of the danger to her home. Oh, he could buy anywhere he liked—so why insist on buying the one place in the world she so desperately loved?

Conflicting emotions swirled in her. Max had been so *good* to her, and even though she knew why he

JULIA JAMES 563

was doing it, it did not detract from the gift he had
given her.

I will always, always be grateful to him.

It was a gratitude she voiced yet again that evening,
as they dined in the Michelin-starred restaurant at the
hotel.

'All I've done, Ellen,' he said, and smiled, 'is show
you what was always there—that's all. You've always
been like this—but you hid it. And now you don't any
more. It's as simple as that.'

His eyes washed over her, liking what they saw.
She was wearing the teal-blue dress he'd instinctively
known would suit her, and it did—much to his satisfaction—and her hair was loosely gathered into a chi-
gnon at the back of her head. Her make-up—another
purchase that day—was not as striking as it had been
for the ball, but it gave her smoky eyes and long lashes
and a soft, tender mouth...

He dragged his gaze away, returning to his study
of the wine list. The arrival of the sommelier diverted
him some more, and when he was done with his discussion and selection he turned back—to find Ellen
looking around the dining room and getting the attention from male diners that she well deserved. He was
glad to see it—it would do her good.

All the same, he reached out to touch her arm, with
an atavistic instinct to show the other males she was
spoken for.

Her gaze came back to him. 'So, will you buy that
place you looked at this afternoon?' she asked.

As she'd glanced around the room she'd become conscious that she was being looked at by other men, and whilst it had given her a little thrill of confidence in her new appearance it had also, with her not being used to it, been somewhat disconcerting. She was grateful to have Max with her. He seemed…reassuring.

How odd that Max Vasilikos should seem reassuring to me—yet it's true.

A thought flickered through her mind. Could this man who had wrought this seismic revolution within her, with whom she'd spent the most amazing twenty-four hours in her life and still counting, really be the same man who was threatening Haughton, threatening to wrest from her all that she held most dear? It was hard to think of it.

'Maybe.' He was answering her now. 'Of course I'll need to look over it in person. But it ticks a lot of boxes. It's on at a good price, I like the look of it and it's close to London.'

'Much closer than Haughton!' she heard herself say quickly.

Max's eyes veiled. 'Haughton is quite different,' he said. 'I have…*other* plans for it.'

'*If* you manage to buy it!' Ellen riposted, her chin going up.

But even as she spoke she wished she hadn't. She didn't want to talk about Haughton, about how he wanted to buy it. For now—just for now—she only wanted to enjoy the present, this wonderful time with him. Nothing more than that. All the difficult, painful stuff could be left to one side. For now at least.

He gave a guarded smile. 'As you say,' he murmured, offering nothing more than that.

The sommelier returned with his choice of wine and he busied himself sampling it, nodding his approval.

He glanced across at Ellen. 'So,' he said, 'did you enjoy the helicopter ride?'

'It was amazing!' she exclaimed. 'A completely new experience.'

His long lashes dipped over his dark eyes. 'Well, new experiences are what you *should* be having, Ellen. Lots and lots of amazing new experiences!'

Was there a subtext to what he was saying? He was conscious of it. He was determined for her to have experiences with him... But he also wanted to indicate to her how her life could, and would, open up once she was free—not just of the chains that had made her think herself plain and unattractive, but of those that bound her to a house that had become a weapon against her stepmother and stepsister.

'Tell me,' he said, taking the subject further, 'when were you last abroad?'

She thought. 'Um... I took a school team to the Netherlands in the autumn term,' she recollected. 'And I did a field trip to Iceland with some sixth-formers— that was extraordinary. The geology and geography is breathtaking!'

Skilfully Max drew her out, and then equally skilfully drew her into contemplating where in the world she might yet like to go, exchanging his own views and experiences with her as their food arrived and they started on their meal.

An idea was forming in his head, but it would be premature to voice it now. He *could* sound her out, however, in general...

'And what about sun, sea and sand—tropical beaches and all that?' he ventured. 'Or did you do all that as a child in holidays with your parents?'

She shook her head. 'No, my mother preferred cultural destinations—so I've been to places like Florence and Paris and so on. Done all the museums and art galleries. I'm not sure I'd like to go back to those places again,' she said. 'They'd have sad memories for me now.' A shadowed look permeated her expression.

He nodded in sympathy. 'I've never gone back to where I was raised except once. And that,' he said, 'was to buy out the *taverna* my mother once slaved away in. I bought it, and now run it as a place to train unemployed young men—of which Greece now sadly has all too many—in useful skills.'

She looked at him. 'Would you never live in Greece again? Never settle there?'

He shook his head. 'I've let it go, Ellen. Cut my ties to a painful past and made a new life for myself. A better life by far! One I'd never known I'd dreamed of until I started to make the dream come true.' His eyes rested on her, his expression intent, challenging. 'Maybe, Ellen, it's time for you to do the same. Make a new life for yourself. Think about the future instead of clinging to a past that is gone.'

He'd spoken deliberately. It had to be said, after all. For her own sake as well as his.

She needs to be free—free of her chains. Free to move on. She needs to see the truth of that.

But a mutinous look had closed down her face and her eyes dropped, refusing to meet his gaze. 'This isn't a subject for discussion,' she said tersely. 'I don't want to sell you Haughton and that's that.'

Inside her head thoughts were teeming. She was immediately wary, reminding herself just who this man was and why he was interested in her, in spending time with her.

He's a stranger who wants to buy your home—and he'll use any means to get it. Including all this that he's doing for you now. Oh, he may have given you a priceless gift, freeing you from what that witch Chloe did for so long, but don't think it's for your sake he's done it—it's for his. That's why he's done it.

From the corner of her eye she saw the waiter approaching with their dessert and was glad of the diversion.

For a moment Max went on gazing at her, fulminating. Her constant obdurate stonewalling was frustrating. Then, with an intake of breath, he let it go. He'd made his point—he would let it be. He hoped she would take it on board internally, even if she did not accept it yet. Besides, he thought as he rested his gaze on her closed face as she doggedly focussed on her food, he wanted to dismiss the subject himself. He didn't want to think about the house she was refusing to sell, or her convoluted reasons for that. No, what he wanted to think about right now was something far more immediate.

The effect that she was having on his libido.

He'd been resolutely repressing it all day, but now, sitting opposite her, with her newly revealed beauty playing havoc with his senses, he knew without a doubt what he wanted to happen between them.

Even if she didn't own a single brick of the house I want to buy from her I'd still be doing this—still be spending the day with her, the evening with her.

And the night too…?

His eyes drifted over her face, visually caressing the curve of her cheek, the length of her lashes, the sweep of her hair, the lush, inviting richness of her mouth whose sweetness he had tasted so tormentingly as he'd bade her goodnight. He tore his gaze away, only for it to slip downwards, to see how the soft material of her dress shaped and pulled across the generous swell of her breasts, and into his head leapt the memory of how they had danced last night, her body so intimately close to his. He wanted to feel her in his arms again, closer and closer still…

He reached for his glass of wine, started to speak again to take his mind back into safer territory for the moment. Besides, he wanted to remove that fixed, closed look on her face. Wanted to see it soften again, become animated with interest and engagement with him. Wanted to see her smile at him again.

'So, tell me,' he opened decisively, 'this eco-resort of mine in the Caribbean—do you think it's the kind of place that would appeal to someone keen on an active holiday?'

It was a deliberate trail—something to catch her attention, make her look at him, take her away from that dark mental interior where she brooded on her father's resented second marriage. It seemed to work, for she lifted her head, blinking for a moment.

'What sort of activities will there be?' she asked.

Max waved a hand expansively. 'Well, water sports, definitely. Nothing motorised—that would be out of keeping—but sailing, windsurfing, kayaking…that sort of thing. Snorkelling and scuba diving, of course—the reef is notable, and I'm hiring a marine ecologist to advise me on the best way to preserve and nurture it. All the sports will have to be outdoors, but to be honest there probably isn't room for a tennis court. Plus it would require a hard surface—again, out of keeping. We'd run beach volleyball maybe,' he finished.

He found himself on the receiving end of an old-fashioned look. 'Well, that would be popular as a *spectator* sport—for the male guests, certainly,' she commented drily.

Max's riposte was immediate. 'It would be popular with me if *you* were taking part, even more certainly.'

The sweep of his long lashes over his revealing glance gave him the satisfaction of seeing her dip her gaze as his compliment registered. He followed through seamlessly.

'So, does it tempt you to come out and check over the place yourself? Try everything out before the first guests arrive later in the season?'

Ellen stared at him. 'Go to the Caribbean?' she said, as if he'd suggested a jaunt to Mars.

Max lifted a hand nonchalantly. 'Why not? You've

got time before term starts again, haven't you? Plenty of time to cross the Atlantic.'

She opened her mouth, then closed it again. Gave a slight shake of her head as if that was all she could manage. He let it go. He'd planted the idea—he would harvest it later. When the time was right.

He started to talk about coral reef conservation. It was as good a subject to pass the time as any. He was enjoying the meal, enjoying spending this convivial time with her—no doubt about that. And there was even less doubt that he was looking forward to what he wanted to happen afterwards...

The elevator, when they walked into it some time later, seemed too small, too empty. And as it whooshed them up to the top floor of the hotel Ellen could feel her stomach dropping away. But it was not just from the effect of the lift. No, it was caused by the man she was sharing it with.

He stood a few feet away from her and gave her a quick smile as the doors opened, waiting for her to emerge. The soft, deep carpet of the penthouse-level corridor muffled all sound. It was completely deserted. A strange sensation of electricity started to run in her veins, along her nerve fibres, just as it had throughout dinner, in little jolts and quivers, every time she'd let her eyes rest on him.

Inside the suite, only a table lamp was lit, creating an atmosphere that was...intimate.

'Nightcap?' Max asked, strolling towards the drinks cabinet.

For a second—just a second—Ellen heard in her head the answer that she could give—*should* give. *Thank you, but no. It's been a long day. I really must turn in.* But instead she heard her voice saying, 'Lovely.'

She walked to the sofa. She could feel her heart thumping in heavy slugs, feel that electric current setting off again, humming through her veins. Carefully she lowered herself down, deliberately kicking off her shoes, tucking her legs under her and resting her elbow on the sofa's arm. A moment later Max was placing a small measure of liqueur on the coffee table in front of the sofa and then lowering himself on to the far end, his free hand cupping a cognac glass. It was a large sofa, but it suddenly felt very, very small.

She took a tiny sip of the sweet, orange-scented fiery liquid—no more than a sip, for it was strong, she knew, and she'd already drunk wine at dinner. A supreme sense of self-consciousness filled her—but not like anything she'd ever known before. This was nothing like the embarrassingly awkward consciousness of her ungainly body, her unlovely appearance that she was so bitterly used to feeling.

No—this was utterly different.

A lioness—that's what he called me last night!

And that was what she felt like—with her lithe body toned and honed, not an ounce of excess fat on it, yet rounded and womanly. She was supremely conscious of the way her hip was indenting the cushions of the sofa, the way the soft jersey of her dress was stretched over her breasts. Breasts that seemed fuller, somehow... heavier.

She felt the alcohol creaming in her bloodstream, heating it. Making her feel different…oh, so different. Free…bold…daring.

Daring enough to sit there with the devastating homage to manhood that was Max Vasilikos, whose lidded eyes were resting on her, whose sensual smile was playing around his mouth. His long lashes were veiling but not concealing the expression in his deep, dark eyes. That thrill came again in her…electricity crackled along her nerve fibres. She was no longer the person she had been—she was someone else now. Someone new.

Someone a man like Max could desire?

Because why else was he sitting there so close, so intimately, his eyes holding hers as if by a silken thread that was drawing her towards him, closer and closer yet? Why else—unless he desired her?

Wonder and hope welled up in her. Was this truly happening? All those long, lost years when she'd been trapped in despising her body, her face…were they really over? Was it possible that she could now reach out and take what was surely every woman's right—could taste and enjoy the sensual pleasures of the flesh?

A memory pressed at her of her time at university, studying sports science, when all about her everyone had been pairing off, partying…and she had not dared. She'd felt excluded, forbidden from trying to join in. Had drawn back and hidden away, feeling herself unworthy—for who could want a woman like *her*? Men could only possibly want women like Chloe…who was the total opposite of herself.

I banished myself—did not dare to try and claim the place that every other woman was claiming.

But now—oh, now she *did* dare! She *did* dare to lean back into her end of the sofa, to relax and take a deep, easing breath.

And the absolute proof of her right to dare was the expression in Max Vasilikos's eyes now, as he twined his gaze with hers. The dim light cast shadows, created an atmosphere that was as heady as the liqueur she was sipping. She felt relaxed, languorous. And yet that low electric current was humming all the time, fuelling the charge that was building up in her, circuit by circuit.

Desire quickened in her veins. Desire made her eyelids heavy. Her breathing was shallow, her awareness of the sheer, raw physicality of Max becoming heightened...super-aware, ultra-aware.

I want this! I want what is to happen. I want it with all my being. To taste what I have denied myself so long...what I have never dared to take...

Yearning filled her, fusing throughout her being.

He moved first.

Wordlessly he placed his cognac glass on the table. Wordlessly he reached to remove her glass from her hand and do likewise. Wordlessly he curved his hand around the nape of her neck. Silently, his heavy-lidded eyes lambent upon her he drew her lithe, pliant body towards him.

And as his mouth closed over hers in the sweet heat of his kiss there was only one conscious thought left in her head.

If Max Vasilikos desires me, then I am desirable indeed!

And then all conscious thought fell from her.

Now there was only sensation—sensation so strong, so overpowering, so arousing, so incredible, so blissful, so pleasurable, so *fantastic* that there was room for nothing else at all in her entire existence. His kiss was as skilled as it was consuming, unhurried—leisurely, even—as touch by touch, graze by graze, his mouth explored hers, slowly at first, skimming her lips, then deepening moment by expert moment, deepening until she was lost, yielding to what he was arousing in her, igniting in her, as each touch of his lips set new fires within her. Fires that he stoked, and stroked as his fingertips explored the nape of her neck, grazed the tender lobes of her ears, as his mouth moved to nuzzle at them softly, sweetly, arousingly.

She felt her breasts engorge and strain, and then a hand was cupping one, and a whole explosion of sensation ignited within her. A soft gasp sounded in her throat as he coaxed her cresting nipple to exquisite arousal. Her hand pressed against the hard-muscled wall of his chest, fingers splaying out, finding as if by instinct the shirt buttons, reaching between, within, slipping one and then another undone as if this were a skill that had been innate inside her all her life.

She heard him groan as her palm slid across the bare skin of his chest, slid down to where his belt snaked around his hips, eased along the rim of it. And he groaned again, his hand tightening on her breast, his mouth devouring hers now.

Excitement ripped through her, raw and intense. She pulled her mouth away, gazed at him, lips parted, eyes flaring, spearing her free hand into the hair that feathered at the base of his skull, shaping it with her fingers. There was an urgency in her now. A sense of power. She felt ripped, pumped, with adrenaline flowing in her, strong and purposeful. She knew what she wanted. *Who* she wanted.

A lioness seeking her mate…

His mouth curved into a smile. A smile of triumph. She knew it, gloried in it.

Their eyes twined together as they half lay upon the sofa that was suddenly much too small.

With a single fluid movement he got to his feet, scooping her up with him. She gave a cry that was half a gasp, for she knew just how much she weighed, even though it was muscled mass, not fat, but it didn't faze him in the slightest. As if she were a feather he carried her through to his bedroom, lowered her down on the bed. But he didn't come down beside her, remaining on his feet.

He wasn't idle, though. He was shrugging off his unbuttoned shirt, ripping the tie from him, ripping everything from him. Her eyes widened—how could they not?—and then, belatedly, she started to work off her own dress.

A hand stayed her.

'Oh, no,' growled Max. 'That's for *me* to do.'

He drew her back to her feet, utterly shameless in his own nakedness, his own rampant arousal. And she, because of that, was shameless too, standing there in front of him, fully clothed, her hands reaching up to her head, pulling off the hairclip so that her tousled locks fell with a single sensuous shake of her head, rippling down her back.

She heard him growl in satisfaction, saw his eyes flaring in the near darkness, for the only light came from the dim lamp in the lounge beyond. It was all the light they needed, and now he was stepping towards her, his hands catching at the hem of her dress, drawing up the soft jersey material in a slow, unstoppable movement until he'd eased it clear off her shoulders and freed her from it, casting it unwanted to a nearby chair. Now it was just her, with her hair rippling down her back, and the underwear she stood in.

But not for long.

Her own hands reached behind her back and she unhooked her bra deliberately, displaying herself, her eyes holding his all the time, her chin lifted, lips parted, knowing *exactly* what she was doing. Her breasts were freed, the bra discarded to the floor, and she stood there, showing her body to him as he was showing his to her.

His expression changed. 'My beautiful lioness...' he said, and his voice was low, deep, husky. His hand reached forward and the tips of his fingers simply grazed across her peaked nipples, so that they flowered even more, and a whisper of delight, of pleasure so exquisite, rippled through her so that she gasped and her head fell back, her long tousled hair brushing across the lower reaches of her arching spine.

He cupped her full, engorged breasts, heavy in his

hands, and then his mouth found hers again, slowly, sensuously, with an intensity of arousal that she knew, with a kind of glory inside her, was the beginning of ultimate consummation.

She let him press her down upon the bed, let his body come over her, felt the crushing, arousing weight of him. He was kissing her still, one hand still enclosing a breast, the other now despatching the last remaining obstacle to his imminent possession. She lifted her hips as he discarded her panties and then she let his hand slide between her thighs, parting them for him. Whirls of pleasure rose within her, each one more intense than the last. A mist descended over her consciousness. She was no longer a thinking being—only a feeling one. Giving herself to the ultimate sensation.

He nestled himself within the apex of her body, and she felt with a mix of shock and exultation just how ready he was for this. How ready *she* was…

He took her hands, lifted them above her head so that the peaks of her breasts lifted too, and she gazed up at him. He smiled. Slow, intimate—possessive.

With an instinct older than time she felt her hips lift a little, straining towards him, yearning for his possession. His name was on her lips. An invitation—a plea. His smile deepened. And then, in a sudden fluid movement, he pulled away from her—only a fraction, but it was enough to cause alarm to flare in her eyes. Until she realised what he was doing—reaching into the drawer beside his bed…finding protection. *Her* protection.

She shut her eyes—there were things that even as a

lioness she could not cope with! She heard him laugh, as if he realised that. A kiss nuzzled at the tip of her nose.

'Safe to peek now,' he said.

Amusement was in his voice, but it was only on the surface. Below was something deeper, and far more primal. She opened her eyes, looked deep into his, and even in the semi-darkness the naked desire there, the raw arousal, shocked her like electricity jolting through her body— her inflamed, aroused body.

For one long moment he gazed down at her. 'My lioness,' he murmured. 'My strong, beautiful lioness!'

And then, with a slow, deliberate tensing, he lowered himself to her as her thighs parted for him, as her hips lifted to his, as her body opened to his. Taking possession of her.

As she did of him.

There was tightness, but no resistance. She drew him into her, her body welcoming his, glorying in it, her delicate silken tissues gliding him in, sending a million nerve endings firing, shooting volley after volley of pleasure through her.

How could it be so good—so good to feel like this? How could this fullness be so incredible? This fusion, this melding of their flesh?

She dimly realised that for a moment he did not move, with supreme self-control, letting her body accommodate itself around him, letting her revel in the fullness of their fusion, letting her body reach the same level as his, poised at the brink.

Her hands were on his shoulders, braced against

him, and his hands were bearing his weight, for he did not want to crush her. He wanted to see her face—a face that was raised to him in wonder, in beauty—in the moment before the ecstasy took her...took him...

And then, with the slightest shift in muscle, he moved, letting himself release.

He saw it happen in her face, saw her eyes distend, and then he was beyond everything but his own conflagration which swept up through him like a firestorm, burning him to ashes. Burning her with him.

She cried out in wonder, in amazement, in pleasure, and the sound of her cry shook him to his core. Her spine arched, her hips straining at him, nails clutching at his shoulders, head thrown back so that he could see the ecstasy that was in her face, the wonder and the joy. He felt her body thrash around him, pulsing with consummation, felt her thighs straining taut against his, and then his arms were around her, holding her, cradling her, keeping her safe within his embrace as her body burned.

And then slowly, oh-so-slowly, she slackened in his arms—slowly, oh-so-slowly, she stilled, her eyelids fluttering, her breath ragged, her skin dampened with a silken sheen. He held her tight against him, still half possessing her, then slackened away from her. He smoothed her hair, so fine and soft, and spoke to her in his native tongue. He knew not what he said. And she was like one who had gone beyond—gone far beyond, to a place she had never been before.

He held her while her taut muscles relaxed, released their tension, became soft and lax. She was letting him rock her gently, oh-so-gently, and he held her, still murmuring to her, as he brought her back slowly, carefully...oh-so-carefully.

He kissed her forehead, with scarcely any energy left in him to do so, and then a great lassitude swept through him. An exhaustion of the senses, of the passions. He turned her in his arms, her body still damp, her eyes still glazed, and kissed her bare shoulder, nestling her into him, holding her close and safe and warm against him.

'Sleep,' he said, his voice a murmur. 'Sleep now...'

He saw the ghost of a smile cross her mouth. It was all that she could manage and he asked for no more—not now. She had given all and taken all, and now they would rest, exhausted and complete, embraced by each other.

Sleep took them both.

CHAPTER NINE

ELLEN STIRRED. SHE was cradled against hard, warm muscle, and an arm lay heavily around her. She could feel Max's breathing, low and steady, feel his breath on the nape of her neck. As she came to wakefulness her own limbs felt heavy, tired, and there was an ache between her legs. Yet it was not pain. Oh, no, not pain...

A sense of wonder suffused her. Was it real to be lying here in the dim morning light, with Max's arms around her, holding her so closely? Could it possibly be real? But it was—oh, it *was*. That was the wonder of it—the miracle. That after all those long, miserable years of thinking herself repulsive, repellent, all the misery, the dreary self-torment, was over.

Gratitude flooded her. She knew why Max had done this, knew what his reasons were—to wean her away from clinging to the home she loved so much, that he could only see as her hiding place—but she didn't care. How could she care when his strong arms were warm around her? When her body had discovered the bliss he could arouse in her? No, whatever his motives, she could only be grateful for this wondrous, incredible gift that he had given her—the gift of knowing herself to be desirable.

It was gratitude that she gave voice to when Max awoke and made love to her again, bringing her once more to a peak of ecstasy that left her breathless with wonder. Then another appetite struck, and they wrapped themselves in voluminous bathrobes, padded through to the suite's dining area to partake of a large and filling breakfast.

She caught his hand, staying him. Her eyes huge. *'Thank you...'* she breathed.

He turned her hand in his, winding his fingers through hers, turning them towards him. Amusement danced in his eyes, but there was another expression there too.

'Oh, the pleasure was all mine—be very, *very* sure of that!'

He kissed her nose, lightly and humorously, squeezing her hand, his free hand brushing the loosened locks of her hair caressingly. She was gazing up at him wide-eyed, with that wonder in her expression that did strange things to him. There was wonder in him, too. He'd awakened her senses—but she had awakened in him senses he had not known he possessed.

Satisfaction—deep, consuming and very...well, very *satisfying*—creamed through him. Whatever his original motives for setting Ellen free from the chains she was bound with, he knew with absolute certainty that what had happened between them—what was still happening—was for quite different reasons. For reasons that had only to do with him being a man and Ellen being a woman, desiring him and being desired.

That is all we need. All I want.

He sat himself down opposite her, reaching for her glass and filling it with fresh orange juice from the jug on the table. His eyes rested on her, appreciating what he was seeing—her loose, tousled hair, the deep vee of her robe exposing the swell of her breasts, the softness in her face, in her eyes, the deep, sensuous glow of a woman who'd spent a night of passion in his arms.

He poured his own orange juice and drank it in one draught, setting down the glass. She was sipping hers in a more genteel fashion, and her gaze was flickering to his, as if she wanted to feast on him but felt a touch of shyness yet. Hunger rattled in him—and not just for the croissants nestling in their napery. He helped himself to one, tearing it open with strong fingers. Then his eyes went back to hers, holding them.

'We need,' he announced, 'to get hold of your passport.'

Ellen started. She'd been in a daze, wanting only to let her eyes gaze across the table at him, to drink him in—the way his jaw was roughened right now, and how enticingly piratical the dark shadow of regrowth made him look, and how there was that glint in his eyes again that could melt her bones like water, and how the towelling robe he wore with such casual ease was so incredibly white against the gold tan of his smooth, half bared chest, and how his strong, lean forearms were reaching for that croissant with fingers that had stroked her body to shuddering ecstasy.

'What?' Her eyes widened in confusion.

'Your passport,' Max repeated. His expression changed, become amused. 'So we can visit my eco-resort in the Caribbean. I told you over dinner last night that I needed to go out there.' Long lashes dipped over his dark eyes. 'Surely,' he said softly, 'you did not think that a single night with you would be enough—did you?'

He watched his words sink in. Words that he had already formed in his own head as soon as he'd awoken. A single night with this woman? No, not enough! Not anywhere *near* enough!

Across from him he saw her reaction—saw for the fraction of a second indecision hover in her eyes and then vanish.

Her face lit, and inside her head words were singing suddenly.

Go with him! Go with him while he wants you—because he does want you. Because this time is the most wonderful of your life so far. So seize it—seize it all. Take what you've never had before and wring from it every last drop. After all, why not?

Max Vasilikos had given her a gift she had never, never thought to possess—the gift of her own beauty. The gift of himself desiring her.

Wonder, joy and gladness filled her to the brim.

'There are no walls!' Ellen exclaimed as they walked into the room. It was situated in one of the cabanas that had already been constructed, at one end of the resort, and was cantilevered over a low, rocky bluff that jutted right out over a sheltered bay on the tiny islet.

'Just mosquito nets,' agreed Max. He strolled up to the missing outer wall, where an area of decking gave some outside space to meld interior and exterior seamlessly. 'Like it?' he asked as Ellen walked up to join him, resting her hands on the balustrade above the tumbling rocks.

A little wooden staircase to their left led down to the white sand beach a few metres below. An azure sea lapped lazily, beckoning to her with seductive allure.

She twisted her head to look at him. Made a face. 'Oh, no, it's awful—honestly, how could you bring me to such a place? I mean, there isn't a nightclub for miles, and there's no gourmet restaurant with a signature chef, and, I mean, there isn't even a *wall*, for heaven's sake!'

In the hours it had taken them to arrive here the very last remnants of her shyness and uncertainty in his company had vanished. Gone completely. Now she was at ease with him, daring to laugh with him, be confident with him, to tease him as she was doing now.

He kissed her to silence her and they both laughed into the kiss, and then Max tightened his hold and deepened his kiss. 'There is, however,' he told her, 'a bed—a very large, king-sized bed—and the mattress is very, *very* high spec... I promise you.'

It was, too, and suddenly all jet lag was gone, and energy and the fires of arousal leapt within her, dismissing all other thoughts.

'I wanted to swim in the sea,' was her last muffled cry as he swept her off to the bed.

'Later...' Max growled.

Afterwards, as they lay exhausted in each other's sated embrace, it came to him that for a woman who had only a handful of days ago regarded herself as completely repellent to the male race, she was, in fact, taking to this like a natural. As if she'd been born to be in his arms...

Ellen waded out of the water, feeling the heat of the sun on her body immediately, even through her sopping wet T-shirt. Her snorkel and mask dangled loose in her hand.

'Lunch?' asked Max, glancing at her and admiring the way the wet T-shirt material clung to her generous breasts. Desire stirred in him. Maybe they could wait for lunch for a while?

'Definitely,' agreed Ellen, dashing his hopes, or at least deferring them until a post-lunch siesta.

Ellen glanced fondly at him. The days had slipped by, one after another, each one glorious. They'd swum and snorkelled, sailed and kayaked, and Ellen had done a beginner's dive while Max, with years of experience, had gone for a serious deep water session.

She'd accompanied Max as he'd inspected the resort site, talking to his project manager, the architect and the work crew who came across from the main island, where they lived. It had been revealing to see him with his staff, because even the most junior of the work crew got a word of appreciation from him, and she'd been able to see they regarded him as a good boss.

That said a lot about a person…things she could admire, respect. No mere venal money-grubbing property developer was he—his values were those she could share and approve of.

'There are places in the world where new construction is fine—and places where it isn't,' Max was saying now as they relaxed, replete after dinner cooked over an open firepit, down on their little beach, leaning back against a rock with the water lapping gently a few metres away and overhead the tropical stars wheeling their slow arc across the midnight sky. 'Places where we should tread lightly on the land, as I'm trying to do here, or not tread at all—places where we should save and repair what is already there, conserve what earlier generations have built.'

She glanced at him, liking what she'd heard him say. 'Maybe being Greek helps—growing up amongst so much antiquity?'

But her words drew from him a glance that seemed, she felt, to admonish her.

'We cannot live in the past—it is not healthy to do so. Sometimes,' he said, 'we have to let go. Let go of the past and make a new future for ourselves! A new life.'

Ellen's eyes slipped away. Discomfort snagged in her, and she wished he had not said that. This was the first time he'd referred to the underlying reason he was in her life at all. Up till now there had been no mention of it—as if that troubled situation thousands of miles across the ocean did not exist. And certainly it had not intruded into what they had here.

Here, she knew—with a gratitude that in itself was revealing of how much she did not want to think of anything beyond this bliss—she could merely revel in what was happening. Day after day, just her and Max—wonderful, *wonderful* Max!—who'd transformed her, transformed her life, and to whom she would be grateful always! Walking barefoot on the sand, hand in hand beneath the sun, beneath the moon and stars. All cares and concerns far, far away.

But now he was reminding her of them. Making her think about them…making her face them once again. She didn't want to hear him say such things. He'd made no mention before—none at all—of what was for this brief space of time an ocean away. Nor did she want him to.

I don't want this time with him spoilt in any way at all. I don't want to think about Haughton, how desperate I am to keep it. Nor to be told that I should let it go…

But Max was speaking again, gazing up at the starry night sky.

'I remade *my* life,' he was saying. 'My mother's death forced me to do so. I wish so much she'd lived to see what I've achieved, but it was not to be.'

His gaze flicked back to her, trying to read her expression in the dim light. But he could not see it. And nor could he bring himself to tell her how struck he'd been by the house he wanted her to yield to him—how it had called to him immediately, arousing in him for the first time in his life an urge to cease his wandering, rootless lifestyle.

Instead he focussed on what he so wanted her to realise for herself. 'Do you not think,' he ventured carefully, weighing the impact of each word upon her, 'that your father's death is also a turning point for *you*? Allowing you to be free at last to do what you want with your life?' He chose the word 'allowing' specifically. 'Allowing you,' he finished, his eyes on her, 'to move on. To claim your own life for yourself?'

With a sweep of his hand he indicated the whole expanse of the beach, the starry tropical sky, the lap of the gentle waves.

'It's a good life, isn't it?' he said softly. 'Here—and everywhere! The whole world lies before you, Ellen, and now you know how beautiful you are, how desirable, what is stopping you from walking out into that world? Living your life. *Your* life, Ellen—unfettered and untrammelled. Not trapped in an unhappy past.'

She let him speak. She knew why he was saying it—knew it was because he wanted her to stop fighting him, stop clinging to Haughton. Knew that he truly believed it would be for her own good. But she could make no reply. Inside her, like a festering wound, was all the bitterness she felt about what Pauline's marriage to her father had done, and it could not be so easily lanced.

I don't want to think about them—what they did to my father, to me—not while I'm here, having this precious time with Max. I don't want to tell him what they're like, how vicious and ruthless they are—greedy

for everything they can get their hands on. I don't want
this idyll with Max spoilt.

So she looked away, giving a slow shake of her head,
closing her eyes momentarily. Shutting out what he
was telling her. Then she felt his hand on her arm, not
pressing firmly, almost as a message to her.

'Think about what I've said...' His voice was low,
compelling. 'That's all I ask for now.'

He paused, instinctively knowing that he must say
no more now, that she must ponder his words, let them
soak into her. Make sense to her.

He shifted his position, hooking his arms loosely
around his splayed bent knees. 'So,' he said, his tone
quite different now, 'what shall we do tomorrow? How
about if we take the catamaran out?'

Gratefully, Ellen followed his lead. This was the
Max she wanted. Carefree and easy-going. Revelling
in the days and nights they spent here.

And she was grateful, too, the next day—to experience the thrill and the speed of skimming over the
azure swell as she clung to the tarpaulin between the
twin hulls of the wind-hungry vessel, with Max com-
mandingly at the helm.

'Enjoying it?' he shouted to her over the rush of
wind.

'Fantastic!' she yelled back, and then gave a cry,
snatching more tightly at the tarpaulin, as with a careless answering laugh Max spun the helm, heading right
into the wind, and the catamaran tacked with a lift of
one hull before coming about again.

Exhilaration filled her as he headed downwind back

to shore. With easy strength she helped him haul the vessel up on to the beach, then flopped down on the hot sand.

Max lowered himself beside her. Her eyes were shining, her face alight. There was sand in her hair, and it was windblown and tangled. A memory of how Tyla had hated getting her hair in a mess sifted through him—how she'd fussed endlessly about her appearance, wanting him and every other man to admire her constantly. Desire her.

His eyes softened. Ellen—his own beautiful lioness—was fit and fabulous. She'd believed no man could desire her, and even now that he had convinced her how very, very wrong that misconception had been, so that she now finally accepted the truth of her own appeal, there was still no trace of the fussing and self-absorption that Tyla had indulged in endlessly.

How easy that makes her to be with—she accepts my desire for her as naturally as breathing now, returns it with an ardour that takes my breath away!

And it was much more than simply the time she spent in his arms, breathtaking though that was. It was her enthusiasm, her sheer enjoyment of everything— from food, to sunbathing, to swimming, to gazing up at the stars—everything they did together.

I like being with her. I like her company—I like her thoughts and views and opinions. I like it that she likes this simple place and that she does not yearn for bright lights and sophisticated glamour. I like her laughter and her smiles.

She was smiling now—smiling right up at him as he loomed over her.

'Good fun?' He grinned, and she laughed again exuberantly. 'You can sail her tomorrow,' he promised, and then busied himself with kissing her.

From kissing her it was an easy progression to sweeping her up into his arms and carrying her up to their open-air room, making use, yet again, of the very large bed.

His last conscious thought, barely forming in his head, was just how good it was to make love with Ellen—how very, *very* good. And then there was no more thought, no more conscious awareness of anything at all, only rich, sating fulfilment.

Max's hand was resting lazily over Ellen's warm, sand-speckled thigh as they lay in partial shade on their little beach, having breakfasted on their terrace after an early-morning workout at the open-air gym in what would shortly be the reception and central services area of the resort. They were sunning themselves, waiting for enough wind to rise so they could take out the catamaran.

It was their penultimate day there, and Ellen was only too conscious of a sense of deep, aching reluctance for this blissful, wondrous time to end. She could feel a little tug on her insides—a sense of yearning for this time not to be over, not to be done with. She glanced over the sparkling azure water to the curve of the tiny bay edged with vivid glossy foliage. The fronded roofing of their wooden cabana was barely visible, blending into the verdant greenery.

She gave a low, regretful sigh. These past days—one slipping effortlessly into the next, so that she'd all but lost count of them—had been so wonderful. So idyllic. They had been cocooned on this lush tropical island, living as close to nature as they could. Away from all the rest of the world, away from all its problems and difficulties.

A little Eden—just for the two of us. And I was Eve—woman new-made. Discovering for the first time just how joyous being a woman can be.

New-made, indeed—and from Adam's rib. A smile tugged whimsically at her mouth.

Max made me—he made me a woman, sensual and passionate.

Oh, he'd done it for his own purposes, his own ends—she had no illusions about that. He had been perfectly open about wanting her to discover what life could be like beyond what she knew he saw as the prison of her childhood home. The place that had trapped her in misery, in the past, in her bitter feud with Pauline and Chloe. But she didn't care. How could she? His motives could never detract from the effect his liberation had had on her. The wondrous, glorious gift he had given her!

The gift of his own desire for her.

And hers for him.

Her eyes went to him now with familiar pleasure as he lay beside her on the sand, dark glasses shading his eyes so that she did not know if he was dozing or awake.

It was the latter. 'Why the sigh?' he asked, turning his head towards her.

'Oh, I guess it's just that I... Well... This time tomorrow we'll be heading back to London.'

She felt his gaze on her through the opaque lenses. 'You've enjoyed it here?'

There was a little choke in her voice. 'Of *course* I have! It's been idyllic.' It was all she could manage to say.

'Yes,' he agreed, 'it's certainly been that.'

His hand moved a fraction on her thigh, and he turned his head away to look up into the sky. She could hear a pause in his silence. Then he spoke.

'Tell me...'

His voice was different—almost, she thought, speculative.

'What do you think about Arizona?'

She frowned in surprise. 'Arizona?'

'Yes. Or actually it might be Utah. I'll have to check.' He turned his head towards her again, pushing his dark glasses up on to his head. 'Ever heard of Roarke National Park?'

She shook her head, still frowning slightly.

'Well,' Max continued, 'it's not as well-known as the more famous National Parks in the American West, such as Zion and Bryce—let alone the Grand Canyon. But, anyway, the lodge there is hosting a seminar on sustainable tourist development which I've a fancy to go to.'

He paused again, his eyes suddenly unreadable.

'So what do you say? Shall we head there next? We can fly from Miami. Once the seminar's done we could add a few days' hiking, maybe. Pick up boots and kit when we're there. Does it appeal?'

She was silent. Then suddenly she propelled herself up on her elbow, looking down at Max. '*Yes!* Oh, yes.'

In an instant her heart was singing, her mood soaring into the stratosphere. More time with Max—oh, yes, more time!

A grin split his face. 'Great,' he said.

He reached up a hand to her nape, drawing her mouth down to his, letting her hair fall like a veil around them. Satisfaction filled him. And a sense of triumph. Another new place, another new experience for Ellen to savour—to tempt her to stay out in the wonderful world that could be hers if she left her past behind her.

And, best of all, another stretch of time to enjoy all that she bestowed upon him.

His kiss deepened, and soon all thoughts of taking the catamaran out that morning faded completely.

CHAPTER TEN

ROARKE NATIONAL PARK proved to be an experience ideally suited to Ellen. She loved it—loved the wild beauty of the American West, loved even more experiencing it with Max.

They flew in to Salt Lake City, then drove down through the increasing grandeur of the landscape as it rose in a vast stone flight of inclined steps from the south. The park itself was still relatively quiet at this early time in the season, with parts of it still closed by snow, but in the sheltered canyon it was warmer, and the sunlit orange sandstone rock was a vivid contrast with the deep blue of the sky and the dark green of the pines.

The timber-built lodge fitted into its remote setting perfectly, blending into the landscape, a tribute in itself to the kind of design that worked best in places where nature was pre-eminent. And Ellen found the seminar fascinating—as fascinating as learning about the geology and geography of the park and the wider landscape beyond. Already she was planning a field trip here, making appropriate notes with which to broach the project with her headmistress on her return.

She made no mention of that to Max, however. She did not want to trigger another attempt by him to persuade her to abandon what he was so convinced were the confines of her life at Haughton. She did not want that upset. Wanted only to enjoy this time with him to the hilt.

And enjoy it she did.

As he'd promised, after the seminar they kitted themselves up with hiking gear and took to the trails that were open at that time of year.

'Boy…' she breathed as they reached the summit of one trail that had ascended up out of the canyon and on to a rocky plateau where the chill wind seemed only cooling after the heat generated by their hard-pushed muscles. 'You don't need a gym at this place, do you?'

Max gave a laugh, leaning back on a rock to take a long draught of water from the flask that hung around his neck—an absolute necessity for hiking, as they'd been firmly instructed by the rangers—and she did likewise.

'No, indeed,' he agreed. 'We're going to feel it in our legs tomorrow, though, I suspect. But it's worth it ten times over.'

'Oh, yes.' She nodded, her eyes sweeping out over the grandeur of the wilderness that stretched as far as the eye could see and much further still. Her gaze came back to Max. 'Thank you,' she said.

He smiled, warm and affectionate. 'I knew this was

a good idea,' he said. He lowered his backpack to the ground. 'Right, that hike's made me starving—time for lunch.'

They settled themselves on a sun-warmed rock in the lee of a boulder that sheltered them from the keening wind and companionably started on the packed lunch prepared for them. Ellen lifted her face to the sun. Happiness filled her. Complete and absolute happiness.

Her eyes went to Max.

You...you make me happy. Being with you makes me happy. Whether we're making love or sitting like this, side by side in the silence and the grandeur of nature's gift to us. It's being with you that makes me happy.

Yet even as the thoughts filled her head their corollary came. If being with Max made her happy, what would being *without* him make her?

For being without him was what awaited her. It had to—there could be no escape from that. In days they would be heading back to England.

And even if it were not mere days...even if it were weeks...even months...at some point I would have to be without him.

Shadows clouded her mind and through the shadows words pierced her. Pierced her with painful knowledge.

The longer I am with him, the harder being without him will be.

There was a little cry inside her head as the piercing knowledge came. Instinctively she sought to shield herself. To hold up a guard against the thought that must come next but which she would not permit. Dared not permit.

Fiercely she fought back.

Enjoy only this! Enjoy this for what it is and don't ask for more.

Yet even as she adjured herself to be cautious she knew with sudden certainty that it was already too late for caution. Awareness opened out within her like a physical sensation, and the words that went with it took form in her consciousness—loud and unstoppable.

Am I falling in love with him?

She pulled her mind away, tried to silence the words. Sought urgently to counter them. To deny them. No— *no*—she *wasn't* falling in love with Max. She was only *thinking* she was!

And it was obvious—wasn't it? Max was the first man in her life…the only man to have made love to her, embraced her, kissed her, spent time with her. It was obvious that she should fancy herself falling in love with him! What female *wouldn't* fancy herself falling in love with him when he was so incredibly attractive, so devastating, from his deep, dark eyes and his curving smile to his strong, lean body?

That was all it was—just a natural and obvious reaction. It was only that, nothing more—it was nothing real…just her imagination.

Beside her, Max was packing away his now empty lunch box and fishing out his phone.

'Selfie time,' he announced, hooking one arm around her while holding out his phone ahead of them.

'Big smile!' he instructed, and set off a flurry of shots of them both. 'There,' he said, showing her the images.

Ellen smiled, but she could feel a pang inside all the same. A sudden sense of impending loss.

This is all that's going to be left of my time with him—photos and memories.

She took a steadying breath. Well, she would deal with that when she had to. Right now, as Max slipped his phone away and got to his feet, hefting his backpack on to his broad shoulders again, she would make the most of this time with him. So she got up too, and set off after him on the descent.

More hiking, cycling along the paved valley trails and even horse riding—with Ellen discovering the novelty of a Western saddle—comprised their days, and dining at the lodge in rustic comfort passed their evenings. Roaring log fires in the lounge and no TV or other electronic distractions all added to the ambience and mood. Yet all the same the days passed, one by one and ineluctably, taking them nearer to their return to the UK.

Ellen's mood, as they finally headed north to pick up their flight from Salt Lake City, became increasingly sombre as mile after long mile ate up this last time of being with the man who had so utterly transformed her.

Inside as well as outwardly.

An ache caught at her. Soon they would be parting. One plane journey away and she would be heading back to Haughton, and he—well, he would be heading to whatever was next on his busy schedule. This time tomorrow he would be gone from her life.

JULIA JAMES601

A silent cry went up inside her. And a savage admonition.

You went into this with your eyes open. You knew why he was doing it, what his reasons were—so don't bewail it. Think of it as...as therapy!

She shut her eyes, blocking the sight of him from herself. There would be other men in her life now. He had made that possible. Made her see herself as desirable, as beautiful. That was the gift he'd given her, even if he'd given it to her for reasons of his own. From now on she knew that men would desire her—

But even as she told herself that she could hear that voice cry out again in silent anguish.

But what man could I desire after Max? What man could ever compare to him? Impossible—just impossible! No one could ever melt me with a single glance, could make love to me as he does, could set the fires racing through my veins as he can! No one! No one else ever will.

A shiver went through her, as if she had stirred ghosts from a future that had not yet happened but was waiting to happen. A future without Max Vasilikos in it. An empty future.

No, she mustn't think like that. A future without Max in it would not be empty. Could not be—not while she had to fight for her beloved home, keep it as long as she possibly could, safe from those who wanted to take it from her. Including Max.

Her face shadowed. Here, on the far side of the Atlantic, she had been able to forget that it was he who wanted to oust her—for her own good, as he believed—but that bitter truth was not something she must ever forget.

And it was a truth that loomed larger with every hour on the plane as they flew back to the UK.

Her mood had darkened as they flew into the night, and she had slept only patchily and uncomfortably. She knew she had a sombre air about her as they arrived at Heathrow in the bleak early hours of the morning. She was facing the end of her time with Max and the resumption of her battle for her home.

After the tropical heat of the Caribbean, and the crisp, clean air of the American west, the wet spring weather of the UK was uninviting and drear as a chauffeured car drove them into London through the rush hour traffic.

Ellen sat huddled into a corner, groggy from the red-eye flight, and Max let her be, busying himself with catching up on his emails on his laptop. Thoughts were racing across his mind.

As they stepped out on to the pavement outside the hotel he shivered extravagantly. 'It's freezing!' he exclaimed. He ushered her inside the hotel, and as they reached the warmth of the lobby said, 'Thank goodness the Gulf is our next destination!'

He didn't notice Ellen's sudden start at his words, only guided her into the elevator. Back in his suite, he elaborated, watching as room service departed after setting breakfast out for them.

'I've just had confirmation via email that my appointment with the business adviser to the Sheikh there is the day after tomorrow. It will be a bit of a rush, but we can fly out tomorrow. You can cope with that, can't you?' He smiled. 'We'll stay on—go camping in the Arabian desert. Stargazing, camel rides, dune-bashing—you'll love it.' Then his expression changed. 'What is it?' he asked.

Concern was in his voice. Ellen was just looking at him in consternation.

'Max... Max, I can't,' she said.

He frowned. 'You've still got a while before your next term starts,' he said.

She shook her head. Her expression had not changed. 'It's not that,' she said.

'Then what is it?' he demanded.

There was an edge in his voice he could not suppress. Emotion was starting up inside him. An emotion he did not want to feel, but that was happening all the same. Why was she hesitating like this? Making objections? Didn't she *want* to come out to the Gulf with him?

Because I certainly want her to come with me. I don't want to let her go—not yet. Definitely not yet.

Emotion swirled within him. He was certain—two hundred per cent certain—that he had no desire whatsoever to part company with Ellen now. That conviction had been growing with every passing day they'd spent together, and had come to a head on their overnight flight, when he'd realised he did not want their time together to end yet.

She'd been a revelation to him—a total revelation. Not just in her new-found physical beauty, which had knocked him for six from the moment she'd walked out looking so incredibly fantastic in that Edwardian ballgown, but ever since... And, no, not just in that respect. But more—oh, *much* more!

I like being with her. She's good company. Fun, intelligent, with a great sense of humour. She's easy-going, undemanding. She enjoys everything, is good-tempered, isn't self-obsessed or demanding of my attention—though I'm more than happy to lavish it on her because I so enjoy being with her.

The litany ran on in his head, concluding with the most obvious reason of all. In bed, he and she set off fireworks!

Ardent, passionate, sensual, sensitive, affectionate...

The litany set off again. And was cut brutally short as she shook her head again. He saw emotion flash across her face, then vanish. There was something different about her suddenly. Something that reminded him, with a sudden flicker of concern, an inward frown, of the way she'd looked when he'd first gone to look over Haughton and succumbed to its charms. As if she were locked inside herself. Shutting out the world. Shutting *him* out.

And he didn't want that. He didn't want it at all.

OK, he allowed, trying to rationalise her reaction, so she was jet-lagged. Flying the red-eye was never a fun experience. But her wavering was more than just sleep deprivation and grogginess. His thoughts raced on swiftly. Was it because although *he* was two hundred per cent sure he had no desire to call it quits between them, *she* might not realise that? Was she feeling uncertain about him? About what they had between them?

He took her hand in his, squeezed it tight. Time to reassure her.

'Ellen—we are *good* together. Never doubt that. So let's go on making the most of it until your term starts. Don't cut this short unnecessarily—come with me to the Gulf! I want to show you as much of the world as I can. I want—'

But she tugged her hand free, stepping a pace away from him, her face working. Emotions were swilling within her—a turbulent mix. All the way back on the flight it had been worsening with the knowledge that her time with Max was ending. And it *must* end. That was the blunt truth of it. She would be back at school, and Max would either be pressing ahead with his proposed purchase of her home—although Pauline would have to start legal proceedings against her to force a sale—or else he would be backing off and leaving Haughton alone.

Whichever he did, her time with him would have ended. And while part of her—the part that had her heart leaping at the thought of what his words meant— was saying, *Go with him now—take these last few days with him!* she could not let herself listen to it. A few more days and then she would be back here again, just as she was now, and their time together would be over.

Better for it to be over now. Because the longer you are with him, each and every day, the worse it will be for you when it's finally over. The more you will fear that you're falling in love with him—which you must not do. You must not!

Because whether she was falling in love with him, or whether it was just an obvious reaction to her first romance, it was going to hurt, doing without Max— it was hurting already…had been hurting all the way across the Atlantic…this prospect of her time with Max running out, reaching its close.

I'm going to have to do without him. I'm going to have to go home, back to my life, and keep fighting for Haughton to the bitter end.

So she had to crush down the rush of joy that came from the knowledge that Max wanted to spend more time with her.

She sought for the right words to say to him. 'Max, I can never thank you enough for what you've done for me. *Never!*' Emotion filled her voice, though it was low and strained. 'You've given me a gift I never thought to have—and this time with you has been…*miraculous.* I'll always be grateful to you—'

He cut across her. 'I don't want your gratitude! I want you to come to the Gulf with me, make the most of our time now, before your term starts again. It's not too much to ask of you, is it?'

His tone was persuasive, compelling, but there was an edge to it as well. Didn't she *want* to be with him for longer? That bite of emotion came again, and with it another spiralling upwards of frustration.

She was staring across at him, her hands lifted as if—damn it—as if she were holding him at bay. Ellen was holding him off—

Emotion bit in him again, more painful this time.

'Max—it isn't that. It's…it's just that it'll only be postponing the time when I have to get back to Haughton. And it seems to me that it might as well happen now, rather than in a few days' time, when I'll just be right back here, facing the same situation. I *have* to go back to Haughton. And it isn't just because term is starting, it's because it's where I *want* to be—'

She broke off. Echoing bleakly in her head were the unspoken words—*while I still have it.*

But that was too painful even to think—too painful to say to the man who was trying to take it from her. Even though she knew that if it was not him who wanted to buy it at some point someone else would, and Pauline and Chloe would force the sale through, and she would lose the place she held so dear to her. The place where all her happiness was centred.

Yet even as the clutch of emotion that always came when she thought of Haughton gripped her, so did another.

All my happiness? And what of the happiness I've had with Max? What of that?

But her mind sheered away. Whatever happiness she'd had with Max, it was never, ever going to be anything other than temporary. How could it be otherwise? He'd transformed her into a woman who could finally indulge in her own sensuality—a gift she would always be grateful for, just as she'd told him. But for him…? Well, she was just a…a novelty, maybe, made all the more intriguing by the revelation of her desirability for him. Whatever her appeal for him, she had to accept that she was no more than a good companion, in bed and out, while they were together.

'*We're good together,*' he'd said, and it was true.

But it did not make it anything more.

Time for me to go home.

She shook her head, her expression anguished now. 'I just want to go home, Max,' she said. 'It's all I want to do.'

Even as she spoke she could feel that anguish spearing her. Yes, she wanted to go home—to be there while she still could, before it was torn from her—but it was not all she wanted. She wanted Max—oh, how she wanted him, to be with him—but even if she stayed now it would only be putting off what must be the inevitable end, only be making it worse for herself. So best for her to go now—go now and have precious time at the home that she could only lose in the end.

He saw her expression and hated seeing it. Hated hearing her say what she had said. Telling him she didn't want to be with him—wanted instead to return to the place he was trying to free her from. Frustration boiled up in him—more than frustration. It was an emotion he did not want to name, *could* not name. It boiled over. He stepped towards her, closed his hands around her arms, fastening her to him.

'Ellen, don't do this. Your obsession with Haughton isn't healthy. It's poisoning you. Chaining you to a life you should not be living!'

His voice was urgent, his expression burning. Here they were, not an hour back in the UK, and she was already reverting to what she'd been like when he'd first known her. He had to stop that—right now! He had to make her see what she was doing to herself. Had to convince her, finally, that she *must* set herself free from her self-imposed chains. Chains that were as constraining and as deadly as those of her belief that she lacked beauty or desirability had been.

He took a shuddering breath, surged on with what he *must* say to her now to set her free.

Free to seize life with both hands. Free to take all it offers. Free to be with me—

Words were pouring from him. He could not stop them. He'd tried to be gentle on her during their time together, tried to ease her into seeing how she had to let the past go, not cling to it, had to move forward with her life, not stay trapped in the mesh of resentment she so obviously felt about her father's remarriage, unable to free herself of it. He had to make her see that now— in all its stark, unvarnished truth—or she'd just go right back into it all again. And be lost…

Lost to *him*…

An even greater urgency fuelled his words. 'You call it home—but it's a tomb, Ellen. *Your* tomb. Don't you see? You've buried yourself in it, clung to it, and you go on clinging to it because you can use it as a weapon against Pauline, who dared to marry your doting father and give him a second chance of happiness—'

A cry broke from her but he did not stop. Could not stop.

Frustration surged in him, boiling up out of the long, sleep-depriving red-eye flight that had taken them from their passion-filled carefree travels together to land them back here.

Ellen—*his* Ellen—whom he'd freed from her self-imposed mental prison of thinking herself unlovely and undesirable, was now determined to go straight back to the destructive life he'd released her from. He couldn't bear to let it happen. He had to make her see what she was doing to herself, consumed by bitterness as she was. It was a bitterness that was destroying her. Changing her from the wonderful, carefree, passionate woman she'd been when she was with him. Changing her back into the embittered, resentful, anger-obsessed person he'd first encountered.

He couldn't let that happen. He couldn't!

He plunged on. 'Ellen—look at yourself. You've let your anger and resentment eat into you. For years and years. You never gave Pauline and Chloe a chance—you never wanted them to be part of your family. You were fixated on your father—understandably, because of the loss of your mother—but now you've become obsessed with punishing them by hanging on to Haughton.'

She thrust him away, lurching backwards. Her eyes were wide and distended. Emotion battered at her. Stress, weariness and anger rushed up in her.

'It's my *home*, Max! Why *should* I sell it so that someone like you can turn it into a hotel? Or sell it on to some oligarch or sheikh who'll only set foot it in once a year, if that!'

He shook his head vigorously. 'That *isn't* what I want to do with Haughton. What I want is—'

She didn't let him finish. Dear God, why was he choosing now, of all times, to lay into her again? Why couldn't he just leave her alone? Stop going on and on about it?

'I don't *care* what you want! I don't care because I will fight you to the last—fight Pauline and Chloe to the last. Haughton is my home, and all I want—*all* I want—is to live there in peace!'

Max's hand slashed through the air. Exasperation and anger and emotions that were far more powerful than both of them fuelled his outburst. 'Then do it! Just damn well *do* it! Stop your venomous, vengeful feud with your stepmother, which is twisting you and poisoning you, and buy them out.'

He saw her freeze, his words stopping her in her tracks.

'Buy them out...' It was not a question, not a statement. Merely an echo. Her face was blank—quite blank.

He took a heavy breath. 'Yes, buy them out. If that is how you feel, Ellen, then simply buy their share from them so they can make a new life for themselves somewhere miles away from you, since I'm sure they feel the same way themselves. And then there'll finally be an end to this sorry saga. God knows I've tried to show you how good your life can be, but while you cling to your vendetta, keep punishing Pauline and Chloe, the poison is destroying you.'

He shook his head. He was beating it against a brick wall, he could see. He turned away, pouring himself a cup of coffee and knocking it back, as if to restore energy levels that were suddenly drained dry. Could *nothing* make her see what she was doing to herself?

There was the lightest touch on his arm. Ellen was there, drawing his attention. He put down the drained cup and turned.

There was something strange in her expression—something he'd never seen before. And it chilled him to the core.

Her voice, when she spoke was thin...thin like a needle. 'You said I should buy out Pauline and Chloe's share of Haughton...' Something flared in her eyes like a black flame. *'What with?'* The words were spat at him.

Exasperation lashed from him. 'Ellen, don't be melodramatic,' he said crushingly. 'You could easily buy them out if you wanted. Pauline told me that you'd inherited everything else your father left—his stocks, his shares, all his other assets. She told me herself he was a very wealthy man.'

He saw her face whiten like a bone. Bleach-white. The hand on his sleeve seemed to spasm. But when she spoke her voice was very calm. Too calm.

'Let me tell you something, Max.'

Her hand dropped like a dead weight from his arm. There was something odd about the way she was looking at him. Something that made him think of a mortally wounded animal.

'Do you remember the night of that Edwardian ball? The jeweller who arrived with all that jewellery for hire? Do you remember I chose the rubies immediately?'

There was something wrong with her voice too, and it made Max frown.

'It was not just because they went with my gown. It was because—'

And now there was definitely something wrong with her voice—with her eyes—with her white face and stiffened body.

'Because they once belonged to my mother. I recognised them instantly—especially the ring. It was her engagement ring. And it was my great-grandmother's before that—as was the rest of the parure. My mother liked the old-fashioned setting. But Pauline did not.'

And now Ellen's eyes had a different expression in them—one that Max found was causing the blood in his veins to freeze.

'So she sold it. She sold a great deal of my mother's jewellery, only keeping what she liked. Or what Chloe liked. They both like pearls, as it happens, in particular. The double pearl necklace Pauline was wearing when you came to lunch was my father's tenth anniversary present to my mother, and the pearl bracelet Chloe wore was given to me by my parents for my thirteenth birthday. Chloe helped herself to it—said it was wasted on me. Wasted on me because I was nothing but a clumsy great elephant, an ugly lump, totally *gross*. And she never, ever missed an opportunity to remind me of that! Wherever and whenever. She made me a laughing stock at school for it, and has gone on laughing ever since—she's mocked me mercilessly ever since her mother got her claws into my poor, hapless father!'

Max saw her take a breath—just a light, short breath—before she plunged on. There was still the same chilling light in her eyes, in her voice.

'When Pauline married my father he was, indeed, a very wealthy man. It was his main attraction for her, his money—she just loved spending it. And so she spent and she spent and she *spent*! She spent it all. *All* of it! She spent it on endless holidays to expensive places—spent a fortune on interior designers both at Haughton and for the flat in Mayfair she insisted on. And she spent it on couture clothes for herself and Chloe, and on flash cars that were renewed every year, and more and more jewellery for themselves, and endless parties and living the high life at my father's expense.

'She burned through the lot. He sold everything in the end—all his stocks and shares, and some of the most valuable paintings. He cashed in all his funds and his life insurance, just to keep her in the luxury she demanded for herself. He died with almost nothing except Haughton—and he left two-thirds of that to Pauline and Chloe. Pauline made sure of that when he had to make a new will once he'd remarried. Made very, *very* sure!

'So you see, Max—' there was a twisting in her voice now, like the wire of a garrotte '—there is absolutely *nothing* left of my father's wealth except what Haughton represents, so it would be hard for me to buy out Pauline and Chloe on my teacher's salary. That goes on paying for groceries and council tax and utility bills—and for my stepmother and stepsister's essential expenses. Like having their hair done. Their little jaunts abroad, of course, are paid for by systematically selling off the antiques and paintings left in the house.'

Her voice changed again, becoming mocking in its viciousness.

'To be fair to them, that's how I've decided I'm going to pay for the clothes I bought here in London. After all, why *shouldn't* I get just a fraction—a tiny, minute, minuscule fraction—of what my father's wife has taken? And by the same token, Max...'

The pitch of her voice chilled his blood once more, and the venom in her eyes was toxic.

'Why shouldn't I be just a tiny, teeny bit...*reluctant*...to let that pair of blood-sucking vampires sell my parents' home out from under my feet? *Why damn well shouldn't I?* Because it's all I've got left. They've taken everything else—everything! They bled my father dry and made his life hell—*and* mine! And I will loathe their guts for it till my dying day.'

A shuddering breath escaped her, as if she were at the end of all her strength.

'So now, if you don't mind, Max, I'm going to go back to the place where I was born and raised, where I was once entirely happy until those...*vultures*...invaded it. The home I so fondly thought would one day be mine to raise my own family in, where I'd live out my days, but which is now going to be torn from me by my grasping, greedy, *vile* stepmother and stepsister, because it's the only thing left they can take. And I'm going to make the most of it—the *very* most of it—until

the law courts, or the bailiffs, or your security guards
or whatever it damn well takes drive me out of it.'

Her face contorted. She whirled around, seizing up
her suitcase. He watched her stalk across the room,
yank open the door, slam it shut behind her. Watched
her while he stood motionless.

Quite, quite motionless.

CHAPTER ELEVEN

HAUGHTON WAS BATHED in watery sunlight, turning the house and gardens to pale silver, but as she stepped inside misery filled Ellen to the brim—for her father's ruin, her stepmother's avarice, for her angry parting with Max, for parting with him at all.

And for the loss of her home, which must come—now, or later, come it must.

As she went into the kitchen she could feel a dull, dread awareness forcing itself into her consciousness. A new, bitter truth pushing itself in front of her.

I can't go on like this. I just can't—not any longer.

Stark and brutal, the words incised themselves into her consciousness. She felt a pit of cold, icy water in her insides, a knot of dread and resolve. She had to face it—accept it. She could not stay locked in her vicious, destructive battle with Pauline and Chloe. It was a battle she could not win in the end. A battle that was indeed twisting her, deforming her.

I can't stop them taking it from me. I can't stop them and I can't go on the way I have been. So all I can do is give in. Give up. Give up my home.

More words echoed in her head, stinging even more painfully. Max calling this house a tomb. *Her* tomb. She felt her hands clench as if in desperate denial. But his accusation stabbed again. Forcing her to face what he had launched at her. Forcing her to face another truth as well.

I've changed. Max has changed me—changed not just my outer appearance but what is inside as well. I'm not the same person any more. Being with him, seeing the world with him, has changed me. He's opened my eyes to the world beyond here, given me the means to make the most of it, to stride through it with confidence and assurance.

I won't have him and I won't have Haughton—but I will have myself. And that must be enough. It must be enough because it is all that I can have now.

She knew it, accepted it—had no choice but to accept it.

But it was with a heavy heart and a sick feeling of dread and painful anguish that she went to make the phone call she knew she must make.

Max sat with an expression of polite interest on his face, as his meeting with the Sheikh's development minister proceeded. The meeting was going well, mutual benefits from his proposal were being agreed, relations were all extremely cordial and everyone all around was very pleased.

But Max's thoughts were far, far away, burningly consumed by a project that was small fry compared to the one being set up here, but ultimately far more important to him. One that was crucial to his future. His UK head of legal affairs had phoned him just as he'd arrived for his meeting and Max had mentally punched the air with relief.

The meeting finally over, with an entirely satisfactory conclusion, Max walked out to his waiting car. The heat of the Persian Gulf engulfed him. So did spearing emotion.

Ellen should be here. She should be at the hotel, by the pool. I'd join her and then enjoy a sundowner as the day cooled, looking forward to dinner together followed by an early night.

Then tomorrow we'd explore the souks of the old city, with the scent of a thousand spices and the fragrance of frankincense everywhere we went, with gold glinting from a hundred stalls! We'd cruise along the coast at sunset in a dhow, *watching the sun set over the city like a ball of crimson flame.*

The next day we'd drive into the desert, camp out in the Empty Quarter, sleep under the stars burning holes in heaven's floor...

He tore his mind away. He must not indulge in such wishful thinking. He must only look to the future now—must get back to his hotel, phone London, get matters expedited, concluded with all possible haste. No delays could be tolerated. The rest of his life depended on it.

Ellen glanced at her stopwatch, lifted her whistle to her lips and blew sharply to call full time on the match that was taking place on the pitch in front of her. She shivered. A cold wind was blowing, seemingly straight off the tundra hundreds of miles to the north—the Canadian spring was later to arrive than the English one.

But she was grateful that her headmistress had looked to her to accompany the school's lacrosse team's visit to a school in Ontario at short notice when a fellow games teacher had had to pull out. Even more grateful for the invitation she had just received from the principal here—to spend the summer semester as an exchange teacher.

New horizons, a new life—Max would approve.

She sheered her mind away. *No—don't think of Max. Don't think of anything to do with him.* He was gone, out of her life now—gone from everything that had ever been anything to do with her. Except… She felt emotion twist inside her like a spasm, except from the one place on earth she had sought so desperately to keep—the place that a single phone call to her solicitor had severed from her for ever.

Maybe here, as she forged a new life for herself, she might start to forget the home she had lost. Maybe here, in the years to come, she might forget the man who had given her more than she had ever thought to have—who now possessed what she had feared so much to lose. Maybe. But she could not believe it. Because there was only one place on earth she wanted to call home. Only one man on earth she wanted to share it with.

Max! Oh, Max, why am I missing you so much? Why do I want only to rush back to you? To go with you wherever in the world you go, for however long you want me? Why do my dreams torment me? Why does

longing fill me—useless, hopeless longing for some
fairy-tale world where it would all have been different?

A world in which Haughton was hers. In which Max
was hers.

But what was the point of such longings? What
would be the point, now, in standing here in the cold
wind, in this alien land, and dreading a future on her
own, without Haughton, without Max? What would be
the point of admitting that what she had tried to pass
off as merely a predictable reaction to the first man in
her life was so much more?

What would be the point in admitting she'd fallen
in love with him?

Max turned the powerful car on to the long curve of
the gravelled drive, flanked at either side by a crimson
blaze of rhododendrons, misted with bluebells along
its verges, until the vista opened up to reveal the lawns
and gardens beyond, and then the house itself, with the
pale mauve of wisteria coming into bloom tumbling
over the porch.

Haughton was, indeed, looking its best in the late
spring sunshine. Satisfaction overflowed in him.

He had achieved exactly what he wanted, and as he
parked his car in the kitchen courtyard his mind went
back to the first time he had done so.

I fell in love with this place the moment I saw it and
nothing has changed.

Except that Haughton was now his.

Satisfaction curved his mouth into a smile, putting a gleam into his dark eyes as he strode up to the

back door. Haughton was *his*. His to do exactly as he wanted! With no more blocks or obstacles or impediments.

His keys were at the ready—after the completion of his purchase they were in his possession—and he unlocked the back door, glancing briefly into the kitchen where Ellen had hurled at his head her refusal to sell her share of the property unless it was forced from her by a court of law. Yet again satisfaction filled him. Well, that had not proved necessary.

He walked down the stone-flagged corridor to push open the green baize door and walk out into the front hall. It was chilly there, with no heating on yet, but that would be easily remedied. He paused, and gazed around, feeling the silence of the old house lap at him.

It's waiting. Waiting for its new owner to take possession. To live here and make a home here. To love it as it wants to be loved, to cherish it and value it.

Into his head came the memory of how he'd stood on this very spot, recognising his self-discovery, his sudden determination that he should make a home here for himself—recalling the moment he'd first felt that overpowering urge so strongly.

For a fleeting moment regret showed in his eyes for what he had done. Then it was gone. He had done what he had done, and it was what he had wanted to do. He would allow himself to feel nothing but satisfaction at having accomplished it. Nothing but that. He would have no regrets at how he had achieved it—at the price that had been paid for it. None.

He strode to the front door, throwing back the bolts

and locks and opening it wide. Only one more signature was required to fulfil his purpose, to achieve what he wanted to do. And that would be supplied soon— very soon. He stood and watched over the gardens. Waiting...

Ellen sat in the back of the taxi taking her from the station to Haughton. A grief so profound she could not name its depth filled her. This was to be her very last time walking into the house that had been her home—that was hers no longer. Now, after landing that morning from Toronto, her charges having been safely bestowed upon their waiting parents, she was coming here only to remove her own personal possessions and the few keepsakes she still had from her parents before returning to Canada.

Everything else was included in the sale. A sale that had been conducted at breakneck speed the moment she'd made that fatal phone call to her solicitor to yield victory to Pauline and Chloe.

Now all that remained was for her to put her signature to the contract. She'd be calling in at the family solicitor on her way back to the station. Where Pauline and Chloe were she did not know and did not care. They'd signed the contract and taken themselves off— presumably to await the transfer of their share of the sale price into their accounts and then spend it as lavishly on themselves as they had spent all the rest of her father's money.

She closed her eyes. She must not let bitterness and anger fill her again. *She must not!* Max had been right—those harsh emotions had eaten away at her for too long. Now she had to make a new life for herself. A life without Haughton. A life without Max.

She felt her throat constrict, felt pain lance at her.

I've lost my home and I've lost my heart as well. I can bear neither of them, and yet I must.

'Stop! Please!'

The words broke from her as the taxi driver turned between the stone pillars on to the drive. Startled, he braked, and Ellen fumbled for money, pressing it into his hand and scrambling from the vehicle.

Dragging her pull-along suitcase behind her, she started along the drive. Emotion poured through her, agonising and unbearable, a storm of feelings clutched at her heart. Soon…oh, *so* soon…all that would be left to her of her beloved home would be memories.

I was happy here once. And no one can take those memories from me. Wherever I go in the world I will take them with me.

She took a searing breath. Just as she would take the memories of her time with Max—that brief, precious time with him.

I had Haughton for a quarter of a century and I had Max for only weeks. But the memories of both must last my lifetime.

An ache started in her so profound it suffused her whole being with a longing and a desire for all that she had lost—the home she had lost, the man she had lost.

As the massed rhododendrons in their crimson glory gave way to lawn she plunged across the grass, cutting up towards the house, her eyes going immediately to its frontage.

This is the last time I shall see it! The last time...the very last time! The last time—

She stopped dead. There, standing on the porch, was a figure—tall and dominating and already in full possession.

It was Max.

Max watched her approach. He'd timed his own arrival perfectly, having obtained from her school details of the flight she'd be on, and calculating how long it would take her to reach here. He had the paperwork all ready.

As she reached the porch he could see her face was white, the skin stretched tight over her features. He felt emotion pierce him, but suppressed it. No time for that now. He must complete this business as swiftly as possible.

'What are you doing here?' The question broke from Ellen even though the moment it was out she knew how stupid it was. What was he doing here? He was taking possession—as he had every right to do.

His long lashes dipped down over his eyes. 'Waiting for you,' he said.

He stood aside, gesturing for her to step into the house.

His house. That's what it is now. Not mine—not once I've completed the final step that I must take and put my signature on the contract for my share. That's all he is waiting for now.

She swallowed. Anguish seared her. Dear God, why did he have to be here? Why must she endure this final ordeal?

How can I bear it?

How could she bear to see him again? How could she bear to feel that terrifying leap in her pulse, which had soared the moment her eyes had lit on him? How could she bear to have her gaze latch on to him, to drink him in like a quenching fountain after a parched desert?

He was crossing to the door to the library. 'Come,' he said to her, 'I have the paperwork here.'

Numbly she followed him, her suitcase abandoned on the porch. She was incapable of thought. Incapable of anything except letting her eyes cling to his form. She felt weak with it—weak with the shock of seeing him again. Weak with the emotion surging in her as she looked at him.

He went to her father's desk and she could see the documents set out on it. He indicated the chair and, zombie-like, she went to sit on it, her legs like straw suddenly.

She looked at him across the desk. 'I was going to do this at the solicitor's later today,' she said. Her voice sounded dazed.

He gave a quick shake of his head. 'No need,' he said, and picked up the pen next to the paperwork, holding it out to her.

Ellen took a breath, ready to sign. What else could she do?

Do it—just do it now. It has to be done, has to be

faced, has to be endured. Just as seeing him again has
to be endured.

She lowered the pen to the paper. Then, abruptly,
before she could start to write, she stopped. The enor-
mity of what she was about to do had frozen her.

She lifted her head to stare helplessly up at Max.

'Ellen—sign the contract. Go on—sign it.'

There was something implacable in his face now.
Something that made her eyes search his features.
Something, she realised, that was making her flinch
inwardly. Making her forcibly aware that this was a
man who dealt in multi-million-pound deals as casually as he ordered a bottle of vintage wine. That to him
this purchase was nothing but small fry—a drop in
the ocean—when it was the whole ocean itself to her.

Did he see the flash of anguish in her eyes, hear the
low catch of her breath—suspect the emotion stabbing
at her now? She didn't know…knew only that he had
placed both his hands, palms down, on the edge of the
desk opposite her, that his tall frame was looming over
her. Dominating, purposeful.

She tried to remember how different he could be—
how he had stood at the helm of that catamaran, facing
into the wind, his dark hair tousled, his smile lighting up the world for her. How laughter had shaken his
shoulders as they'd laughed at something absurd that
had caught his humour. How his dark eyes had blazed
with fierce desire as he'd swept her into his arms and
lowered his possessing mouth to hers…

'Just sign,' he said again, wiping all the anguished

memories from her. His eyes bored into hers. 'It's for your own good,' he said.

His voice was soft, but there was a weight of intent in it that pressed upon her.

She lowered her head, breaking the crushing gaze that was bending her to his will. His words echoed hollowly. Forcing her to accept their truth. The truth as he saw it—the truth as he had made *her* see it. She could not go on as she had sought to do, locked in a toxic, unwinnable power struggle in the bitter aftermath of her father's death.

Slowly, carefully, she set her signature to the document before her, on the final page of it. The only clause visible was full of incomprehensible legal jargon she did not bother to read. Then, swallowing, she sheathed the pen and put it down. It was done—finally done. She had no claim on what had once been her home. Now it was just one more property in Max Vasilikos's investment portfolio.

Emotion twisted inside her. Impulsively she spoke. 'Max! Please… I know that the future of Haughton is nothing to do with me…' She swallowed and her voice changed, becoming imploring. 'But this was once a happy family home. Please—think how it could be so again!'

She saw a veil come down over his eyes. He straightened, took a step away, glanced around the room they were in. The original dark panelling was still there, and the serried ranks of books, the smoke-stained fireplace with its hearthrug and her father's worn leather chair. Then his eyes came back to her.

'When I first came to Haughton,' he said slowly, 'my plan, if I decided to buy it, was to realise the value in it and likely sell it on, or rent it out for revenue. But...' His eyes flickered to the tall windows, out over the gardens beyond, then moved back to her again. 'But as I walked around, saw it for myself, I realised that I did not want that.'

He looked at her. His expression was still veiled, but there was something behind that veil that caught at her, though she did not know why.

'I realised,' he said slowly, and now a different note had entered his voice, 'that I wanted to keep this house for myself. That I wanted to make this house my home.'

He looked at her. The veil was impenetrable now, and yet she gazed at him fixedly still.

'I still want that—for it to be a home,' he said.

For just a fraction of a moment his eyes met hers. Then she pulled her eyes away, closing them tightly. Emotion was sweeping up in her.

'I'm glad.' Her voice was tight with emotion. 'Oh, Max, I'm glad!' Her eyes flew open again. 'It deserves to be loved and cherished, to be a happy home again.'

There was a catch in her voice, a catch in her heart. To hear that this was what Max wanted—that Haughton would be protected from the fate she'd dreaded for it—was wonderful! And yet her heart ached to know that he would make a home here for himself...only for himself.

Until one day he brings his wife here!

Images forced themselves upon her. Max carrying his bride over the threshold, sweeping her up the stairs…his threshold, his stairs, his bride. Max running effortlessly on untired limbs around the pathway beside the lake, taking in his domain, making it his own. Max surrounded one day by children—a Christmas tree here in this hall, where she had once opened her childhood presents—their laughter echoing as hers had once done.

Max's children. Max's bride and Max's wife. Max's home.

And she would be in Canada, or any place in the world. For where she was would not matter—could not matter. Because she would be without Haughton.

Without Max.

Pain lanced at her and she got to her feet, scraping her father's chair on the floorboards. She faced Max. He was still standing there, his expression still veiled, still resting his gaze on her.

'Yes,' he said. 'It does. It does deserve that.'

He spoke the words heavily, incisively, as if they were being carved into him. He looked at her, held her eyes unreadably for one last moment longer, then spoke again.

'And I hope beyond all things that it will be *my* home—'

She stared at him. Why had he said that? It *was* his home now—her signature had made it so.

But he was speaking still. 'That, however, depends entirely on you.'

Bewilderment filled her. There was something in his eyes now—something that, had the sombreness and the despair of the moment not overwhelmed her, she would have said was a glint.

'You should always read what you're signing before you sign it, Ellen,' he said softly, and his eyes were still holding hers.

'It's a contract of sale,' she said.

Her voice was neutral, but she was trying desperately in her head not to hear the seductive, sensuous echo of his naming of her, that had sent a thousand dangerous whispers across her skin.

'Yes, it is,' he agreed.

'Selling you my share of Haughton.'

'No,' said Max, in measured, deliberate tones. 'It is not that.' He paused. 'Read it—you've signed it... now read it.'

Numbly, she turned back the pages to reach the opening page. But it was full of legalese and jargon, and the words swam in front of her eyes.

Then Max was speaking again. 'It *is* a contract of sale,' he said, 'but *you* are not the vendor.' He paused. 'I am.'

CHAPTER TWELVE

MAX'S EYES WERE holding hers and not letting them go—not letting them go for an instant...a single second.

'You see...' he said, and he spoke in the same measured tones, but now there was something else in his voice—something that was an emotion rising up to break through, an emotion that was possessing every cell in his body. 'You see, I am selling you the two-thirds share of Haughton I have already purchased from your stepmother and stepsister. Which, Ellen—' and now the emotion broke through finally, unstoppably, blazing through him, lighting up his eyes with the fire he had banked down with every ounce of his strength since he'd watched her walk up to him across the lawns '—which I now restore to *you.*'

For one last moment he held on to his self-control.

'I've given you a very good price,' he told her. 'I believe even on your teacher's salary you can afford to pay me a hundred pounds. How does that sound? I hope it's acceptable—because you've just put your signature to it.'

She wasn't saying anything. She was just staring at him as incomprehension, shock, disbelief, all flashed across her face.

'I don't understand…' It was a whisper, faint and scarcely audible.

For one long, timeless, endless moment the tableau held. Max standing there, his face expressionless, and she seated across the desk from him, as white as a sheet with shock etched across her features. Then, like a dam breaking, all the emotions Max had been holding in check burst from him.

'Did you truly think I would take your home from you—after you'd ripped the scales from my eyes?'

He took a shuddering breath, making himself calm. His gaze was on her, holding her like a magnet.

'The moment you hurled what you did at me, before you stormed out, I knew there was only one thing to do. Only one! And now…' A sigh of profound relief went through him. 'Now it's done. I put my legal team on to it straight away, the minute you'd gone, and they got hold of your stepmother out in Spain and told her I'd buy their share even without yours.'

A hard, cynical look entered his eyes.

'She jumped at the chance like I was dangling a diamond necklace in front of her. My lawyer phoned me their agreement when I was in the Gulf, and then I knew, finally, that I was free to do what I have just done.' He paused, and an expression moved across his face that showed all that had possessed him until this moment, the driving urgency to accomplish what he had. 'Make Haughton safe for you,' he finished.

She heard him, yet still she dared not believe what he was saying. Dared not believe that she had just bought her beloved home back for herself—for a song—for a gift...

For of course it *was* a gift! How could it be otherwise at so paltry a price? A gift that Max had given her—a gift so wonderful, so precious that it took her breath away, squeezed her lungs so tight she could hardly breathe, could hardly feel the beating of her heart, though it was hammering in her chest.

'Why?' It was the only word she could say, as faint and low as her breath could make it. 'Max—*why*?'

She took a searing breath through the constriction in her throat and made herself speak again, forced the words from her though they were still low and faint.

'Why should you care what Pauline and Chloe did to my father and me? Why should you give me so fabulous a gift?'

He was looking at her still, and the expression in his face made the hammering in her heart pound in her ears.

'Why?'

His voice echoed hers. But he gave her no answer. Only strode around her father's desk, catching at her hand and drawing her to her feet. Her legs were like jelly and she had to cling to his arm lest she collapse, so overpowering was the shock shaking her.

In her head she kept hearing her own voice, saying over and over again—*Haughton is mine! It's mine! It's mine! Dear God, it's mine for ever now!*

It was a paean, an anthem, ringing in her head like

bells. She gazed helplessly up at Max. At the man who had done this, made this happen. Into her head, flashing like a strobe light, came the memory of the moment Max had given her that first wonderful, miraculous gift—the moment when he'd shown her her reflection the night of the ball, transformed beyond recognition. Made beautiful by him.

He freed me from Chloe's hex—and now, oh, he's freed me from Pauline's too!

Emotion overwhelmed her. Gratitude and wonder and so much more.

'Why?' His voice came again, husky now. He caught her other hand, held it, cherished it. He towered over her, his strong body supporting her stricken one. 'Oh, Ellen—my beautiful, lovely, passionate, wonderful Ellen... Have you really not the faintest idea why?'

He held her a little way from him, the expression on his face rueful.

'Did you not hear me when I told you that the moment I saw this house I wanted to live here? That something about it called to me? That after all my years of wandering, never having had a home of my own, having existed only on sufferance at my stepfather's *taverna* and having lived in hotels and apartments anywhere in the world, I had finally come across a place that urged me to stop...to stop and stay. Make my life here.'

Now the rueful expression deepened.

'That was what drove me so hard to buy it—to make it mine. What drove me to do all I could to achieve that aim. Including...' his eyes met hers wryly '...whisking you off to London to show you how good your life could be if only you would let go of the place I wanted for myself.'

He gave a regretful sigh.

'I went on and on at you. I know I did. But you see...' and now a different note entered his voice '...I'd sought an explanation for your stubbornness, your refusal to agree to sell your share, from your stepmother and stepsister.' His eyes shadowed as he remembered that scene in the drawing room when he'd made his initial offer for Haughton. 'And they told me that you'd become obsessed with the house, that you'd never accepted Pauline's marriage to your father, that you had rejected them from the very first, seen them as interlopers, invaders.'

He gave a shake of his head.

'I remembered my own childhood—how my stepfather never wanted me, never accepted me into his home, always resented my presence even though he made use of it. I was always the outsider, the unwanted brat of my mother. Maybe,' he said slowly, 'that was why I was so ready to believe what Pauline and Chloe told me. So, while I could make allowances for your reaction to your father's remarriage, all I could see was how that resentment was poisoning you....chaining you to this place. Making you think it was the only way you could punish Pauline for marrying your father, seeking to take your mother's place.'

He felt Ellen draw away slightly. Her eyes were full of grief. Her voice when she spoke was low and strained, her glance going to her father's empty chair by the hearth.

'I was *glad* when my father told me he was marrying again. So glad! He'd been grieving for my mother and I desperately wanted him to be happy again. If Pauline made him happy, then I knew I would be happy. I tried to welcome them, tried to befriend Chloe...' A choke broke in her voice. 'Well, I told you how they reacted. But even then if they'd only made my father happy I could have borne it! But within months of marrying Pauline my father realised that her only interest in him was his money.'

Her mouth set.

'He was powerless to do anything about it. If he'd divorced Pauline she'd have taken half of everything he had—forced him to sell Haughton and split the proceeds. So he kept on paying out and paying out and paying out. I had to hide from him all the spite and venom that came from them—hide from him how Chloe had tried to make my life hell at school, and how she constantly sneered at me because I'm tall and sporty, told me how repellent I was because of it until I believed her completely...'

Her voice broke in another choke before she could continue.

'I had to hide it all from my father because he'd only have been hurt all the more, worried about me more, and felt yet more trapped by Pauline. So when he died I was almost relieved, because finally I didn't have to pretend any longer. I could find my backbone and re-solve that even though I knew it was impossible to stop

Pauline and Chloe from getting their claws into Haughton eventually I would do everything in my power, for as long as I could, to make it as hard and as expensive as possible for them to force a sale.'

She took another choking breath.

'I was—just as you said—using Haughton as a weapon against them—my only weapon.' Her gaze shifted again, became shadowed. 'But when I came back here after leaving you I knew...' She paused, then made herself go on. 'I knew that I'd changed—that you'd been right to say that I was poisoning myself in my battle against them. That it was time...finally time...to let go. They had won and I had lost and all I could do was leave and make a new life for myself somewhere else. *Anywhere* else.' She took another searing, painful breath. 'This—today—was to be my very last visit, my last sight of my home.'

He drew her towards him again and his voice was gentle...very gentle. 'And now it is yours for ever.' His eyes poured into hers. 'No one can ever threaten it again.' His mouth curved into a smile. 'Look around you, Ellen—it's yours, all yours.'

A strangled sound was torn from her throat, and then a sob, and then another, and then tears were spilling from her eyes and Max was wrapping his arms around her, and she was clinging to him, shaking with emotion, with the relief and disbelief that all this was really true, that all the stress and fear and anguish at losing her home was over—over for ever. Because Max—wonderful, kind, generous Max—had made her dream come true. Haughton was hers, and it was safe for ever now.

He held her while her body shook with the tears choking from her, convulsing her, while her hands clutched at him and she was finally purged of all that her stepmother and stepsister had done to her for so long. And when she was finally done he stroked her hair with his hand, murmured things to her in Greek.

She didn't know what they were, but knew that he was the most wonderful man on earth. And that she had now taken from him something he had wanted from the moment he'd first set eyes on it.

Her thoughts whirled in her head, troubling her. She lifted her face from his shoulder, looked up at him with an anxious look.

'Max, I still don't understand. You've given me this miraculous gift and I still don't understand *why*. Why would you do it when you've told me yourself that you fell in love with Haughton and wanted to make your home here? How can you bear to give it away to me like this?'

He looked down at her, his deep, dark eyes holding an expression she could not recognise.

'Well, you see, Ellen, I'm forced to admit that I am a shamefully devious character.' He cradled her to him, his hands resting loosely around her spine. '*Shamefully* devious. Yes, it's absolutely true that I was…devastated…' his voice was edgy suddenly '…when I realised how wrong I'd been about you—about your behaviour towards Pauline and Chloe over this house—how deceived I'd been by their appearance of solicitude towards you, how disgusted I felt at their exploitation of your father and their cruelty to you. It made me absolutely determined to redress this final wrong, to restore your home to you, out of their clutches. But...'

His voice changed again, softening now, taking on a hint of wry humour.

'But even while I was set on being the one to save Haughton for you, because you love it so much and have been through so much because of it, I also knew perfectly well that I had... Well, let's say an ulterior motive all along.'

There was a glint in his eyes now, blatantly visible. It did things to Ellen's insides that even the flood of emotion over regaining her home could not quench—things that took her back instantly to the time she'd spent with Max abroad, setting loose a quiver inside her, a quickening of her pulse that made her all too aware of how Max's body was cradling hers, of the lean strength of him, the taut wall of his chest, the pressure of his hips, the heat of his body...

'I told you when you signed my contract restoring Haughton to you how much I was still hoping to make it my home,' he was saying now, 'but that it would depend entirely on you. So...' He raised a quizzical eyebrow. 'What do you think? Could you bear to share Haughton with me?'

She looked at him, not understanding. 'Do you mean some kind of co-ownership?' she ventured.

He shook his head. 'No, I don't want you ever to have to worry about not owning Haughton one hundred per cent,' he said. 'I was *thinking*,' he went on, and now the glint was even more pronounced, and she felt a sudden tightening of the arms around her spine, 'of a *different* way to make this my home.'

'I don't understand…' she said again. But her voice was weaker this time. Her whole body was weaker.

'Then maybe,' said Max, 'this will make things clearer.'

He let her go suddenly, and she felt herself leaning back on the desk as his hold on her was relinquished. She clutched the edge of the desk with her hands. Saw him reach into his jacket, draw out a tiny square box. Felt her heart rate slow…slow almost to a standstill. The breath in her lungs was congealing.

Before her very eyes she saw him lower himself upon one knee and look back up at her.

'Will you…?' he said, and his eyes pinioned hers as she gazed down at him, her own eyes widening until they could widen no further. 'Will you, my most beautiful, most wonderful, most lovely and fit and fabulous and incomparable Ellen, do me the honour, the very *great* honour, of making me the happiest of men? Will you…?' he asked. 'Will you marry me?'

He flicked open the box and her eyes went to the flash of red within. She gave a gasp.

Max quirked an eyebrow again. 'I'm sort of hoping,' he said, 'again quite shamelessly, that this might help persuade you.'

He took the ring out, got to his feet, lifted Ellen's nerveless left hand and held it. His other hand held the ring. The ring she'd worn at the Edwardian ball that had changed her life for ever. The ring that had been her mother's engagement ring, given to her by her father. The ring that had once belonged to her grandmother and her great-grandmother.

'How did you get it...?' Her voice was faint again.

'I bought the ruby parure you wore to the ball. And by the same token I also bought back all your mother's jewellery that Pauline and Chloe helped themselves to—it was in the fine print of the terms and conditions of their sale contract. As for everything else—all the other jewellery and antiques and paintings they sold—I've got a team searching them out and I will buy them all back as and when we find them.' And now that glint was blatant again. 'You see, Ellen, I want to do absolutely everything in my power to persuade you to do what I want you to do more than anything else in the world—and, my sweet Ellen, you haven't actually answered me yet.'

Was there tension in his voice, lacing through the humour, turning the glint in his eyes to something very different?

She gazed at him. Her heart was suddenly in her throat—or something was. Something huge and choking that was making it quite impossible for her to do anything at all except gaze at him. And force out one breathless whisper.

'Did...did you just propose to me?' she asked faintly.

A tidal wave of disbelief was sweeping up through her—the same as when he'd told her he'd gifted his newly acquired share of Haughton to her.

A rasp broke from Max. 'Do you want a replay?' he said, and he started to go down on his knee again.

She snatched at him to stop him. 'No! No—*no!*'

He halted, looked at her quizzically. 'Is that no, you won't marry me?' he asked her.

She shook her head violently. She could not speak. Emotion was pounding her, crashing in on her consciousness, overwhelming her.

'So, that's a yes, then, is it?' Max pursued. He paused. 'I'd just like to clarify this, if you don't mind. Because it is, you see, somewhat important to me.' His expression changed suddenly. 'It's going to determine my entire future happiness.'

She swallowed. That huge, choking lump was still in her throat, and the tidal wash of emotion was still pounding in her.

'Why...?' The single word was faint, uncomprehending.

'Why, what?' he said blankly.

His self-control was under the greatest pressure he'd ever experienced in his life. Even worse than that very first night of the revelation of her beauty to him, when she had offered her mouth to him and he had swooped upon it with all the hunger of a starving man—and then, with the feast before him, had had to draw back, let her go and get the hell out of her bedroom before he'd succumbed to the most intense temptation he'd ever known.

Even worse than that...

'Why...?' She swallowed. 'Why are you asking me to marry you?'

And Max lost it. Finally lost it. It had all been just too damn much. Too damn much from the moment

Ellen had laid into him in his hotel suite, telling him the truth about the vultures who were feeding off her. In that single instant he'd known exactly what he was going to do—and he'd spent the last fortnight pulling out every stop, racing to get the paperwork done, the contracts drawn up and completed, and to drive down here to do what he had just done. Hand her back her home and gain her for himself.

'Will *this* help you understand?' he demanded.

He swept her up to him, his strength easily crushing her against him, his mouth swooping down on hers. And instantly she went up in flames, her mouth opening to his, melding with his. Her arms wound around him, her fingers spearing into his hair. She was hungry for him. Desperate for him. When finally he released her she was shaking, breathless.

Max's hands splayed around her face. 'I've fallen in love with you,' he said.

His voice was quiet but there was an intensity in it, a strength that came from the very core of his being.

'Somewhere along the way I've fallen in love with you. Oh, I admit that my motives in taking you to London were entirely self-interested—you knew that... knew I was seeking to open your eyes to what your life could be like beyond the narrow confines you'd imprisoned yourself in with your vendetta against your stepmother and stepsister once you'd discovered your own beauty. But once I'd discovered it too—and helped myself to it!' His voice was wry. 'Once I'd whisked you off to enjoy it to the full... Well...' Warmth infused his voice now. 'It dawned on me that I was enjoying your company in a way I'd never experienced with any other woman.'

'Even Tyla Brentley?' Ellen breathed.

A dismissive sound came from his throat. 'Tyla was lovely to look at, glamorous to be with—and totally self-absorbed. You… Ah, *you* were utterly different. Even before you had your makeover I knew that. You're intelligent, clear-sighted, and I approve of your efforts with all those deprived city children.'

He dropped a kiss on her nose.

'We had a good time together, Ellen, on our travels. We were good together—incredibly, fantastically good. And when you stormed off I wasn't just appalled to discover how vicious your step-relations were, I also knew I desperately didn't want you to leave me! I knew I *had* to try and get you back—get you back so we could go on being good together. Good together for the rest of our lives, Ellen—that's what I so hope for.'

Something changed in his voice again now, and an urgency speared it.

'And if somewhere along the way you happen…just happen to come to feel for me what I feel for you… Well…'

She didn't let him finish. She reached up her hand, snaked it around the back of his head, hauled his mouth down to hers again. She pressed her lips hard against him to silence him. Then, as she drew back again, emotion burst in her.

And so did a storm of weeping.

For the second time in a handful of minutes she clutched at him as wave after wave of emotion swept through her yet again—and again and again. Max loved her—he *loved* her! He'd given her the inestimable gift of her home to her, and he'd given her a more incomparable gift as well.

Himself. His heart. His love.

'Max! Oh, Max!' It was all she could say. But it seemed to satisfy him.

As she finally came down on the other side of the tsunami inside her he patted her back and reached for the ring box, sitting abandoned on her father's desk.

'That's *got* to be a definite yes,' he told her, with satisfaction in his voice and the love in his eyes pouring out over her, embracing her and caressing her.

'Of *course* it is!' She gulped. 'I kept telling myself that because you were the first man in my life of course I'd get the idea in my head that I'd fallen in love with you—but it wasn't just that. It was real. Completely real what I was feeling for you. When I stormed out on you it was tearing me to pieces, and being out in Canada, facing the rest of my life without Haughton and without *you*—I... I just couldn't bear it!'

Tears threatened again, spilling into her watery eyes.

'And now I've got both—I've got my beloved home and I've got something even more desperately precious to me.' Her face worked. 'I've got *you*. And you, my dearest, most adored and most *wonderful* Max, are my heart, my life—the love of my life.'

'Excellent!' he said, and his satisfaction was total now. 'So,' he said to her, taking the ruby ring from its case, 'do we finally get to the ring bit now?'

He took her hand again and, not waiting for an answer, slid the ring carefully over her finger. But he did not relinquish her hand. Instead he gazed down at her.

'When I first walked into this house I knew it was the place I wanted to call my home,' he told her. His face was serious now—completely serious. 'I had a sudden vision…a vision of myself here, with the woman I love, making our home here together, raising our family here together.' His eyes had a rueful glint in them again. 'I thought that I would have to bring her here, having found her somewhere out in the world beyond. And yet all along—' His voice changed, and there was a crack in it, he knew. 'All along she was here. Waiting for me to find her. Waiting,' he said, 'to find *me*.'

He paused minutely.

'And now,' he said, 'we're done with waiting. Done with finding. We can just enjoy, Ellen. Enjoy the rest of our lives together.'

His mouth lowered to hers and he kissed her softly, gently, before withdrawing. He felt her fingers tightening over his as his lips brushed hers, felt the sudden constricting of her throat, saw the misting of her eyes as he drew his head away.

'So…' he said, because he wanted to make sure—to make absolutely, totally sure of his future happiness…a happiness that was already flooding through him, soaking through every cell in his body, radiating from him like a beacon. 'Have we finally got everything sorted? I love you, you love me, and we're going to marry and live here together in this house we both love, make it a home again, for you and for me and for all the children we are most definitely going to have! A happy family home for a happy family—just as we both wanted. Did I leave anything out?' he asked.

Ellen leaned into his shoulder. Her sigh was pure happiness. 'No,' she said. 'I think you've just described heaven on earth.'

Max smiled. A warm, approving smile that melted her all the way through.

'That's what I thought,' he said. He dropped another kiss on her nose. 'I do like to be right,' he told her.

He straightened up.

'OK, it's a lovely day—actually the best day in my entire life so far—let's get outdoors. Let's get into the sunshine—the sunshine of our lives, my adored, beautiful goddess and lioness.'

She looked at him. 'Can I be *both*?' she queried, with a teasing smile in her eyes.

Max's mouth quirked, his expression doting. 'You can be everything you want, my beloved, providing you go on loving me.'

He started to lead the way out of the library and across the hall, his hand wound in hers and hers in his. Side by side and shoulder to shoulder.

'And you me,' said Ellen.

He paused at the door. 'Deal,' said Max, and kissed her once again.

Then, with a squeeze of her hand, he opened the front door and they stepped through it, into the sunshine, into the happiness of their life together, into their love for each other.

EPILOGUE

MAX WRAPPED HIS arm around Ellen and drew her closer against his shoulder as they leant back against the sun-warmed stone. They were sitting on the step of the little folly, looking out over the lake to where the setting sun was turning its reedy waters bronze. Ellen gave a sigh of deep contentment as she nestled into Max's sheltering embrace, her knees drawn up and slanting against his thighs.

'You're really sure you're OK with us spending our honeymoon here at Haughton?' she asked him, glancing up at his profile.

He nodded, his gaze going to her. 'My beautiful, adored Ellen—don't you know that I am happy wherever *you* are? And if you are happiest here, then here we shall stay for all our days,' Max finished with a fond smile, and let his lips brush across her hair.

'Maybe,' she mused, 'I feel that if I ever leave Haughton I'll return to find that this heaven was only a dream, and I'm back here again with Pauline and Chloe still trying to sell it from under my feet and force me out,' she said.

Max shook his head. 'Oh, no,' he said decisively. 'This heaven is real, believe me. And as for your stepmother and stepsister—well, they'll never set foot on your property again, I promise you. If they even come back to the UK I'll know about it!'

She looked at him quizzically. 'Are you really keeping them under surveillance?' she asked.

'I'm keeping tabs on them, yes,' Max admitted. 'So that wherever in the world they go, if they try and home in on anyone wealthy but vulnerable, like your father was, then their target will be warned. Of course,' he went on, 'it could be that they won't need to target money any more—they have pots of their own. And I don't mean just their ill-gotten gains from selling me their share of Haughton!'

Ellen's quizzical look intensified and Max elucidated.

'I just happened to mention to them, at some point while I was acquiring their share of Haughton, several new property hotspots that were emerging, where substantial profits could be made. They seized on it, and my latest information is that they're now investing substantially. However, if they're prudent they'll take on board that where there is the chance of high return there's also the chance of being wiped out financially.' He smiled, and it was not a wholly benign smile. 'Let's just say that if they *do* get wiped out financially...well, I for one will not be weeping.'

Ellen looked away, out over the lake. She had come so close to losing her beloved home that it was hard to feel any concern at the prospect of Pauline and Chloe losing the money they'd made on selling up to the man who'd saved Haughton for her.

'Karma,' she murmured now.

'Yes, indeed,' agreed Max. 'And it was fate, too, that brought me here...let me find you here.'

He turned his head to look across the lake, beyond the lawns, to the mellow stone house that was now home to both of them, safe and secure for ever, for themselves and for their children to come. Contentment filled him. With his free hand he reached sideways to lift the bottle of champagne from its ice bucket.

'Time for a refill,' he said, and Ellen picked up her empty glass and held it tilted while he topped it up, then held his glass while he did likewise.

He set down the champagne bottle and raised his brimming glass, clinking it against hers.

'This is to us,' he said, and now his eyes wound into hers, his love for her glowing like an eternal flame. 'To our marriage, to our lives together, to our love—and to our beautiful, most precious home.'

'To us,' she echoed. 'To you, my darling, wonderful Max, who has made all my dreams come true!'

He dropped a kiss on her upturned face, then took a deep draught of champagne as she did likewise.

'It's going to be quite a busy honeymoon,' he observed. '*Un*decorating the house from all that interior design, getting it back to the way it used to be... It's great,' he added, 'that so much of the original furniture got stashed in the attics.'

'We *will* need new curtains, though, and soft furnishings,' Ellen commented.

'We'll choose them together. Did I tell you?' He cast a wicked look at his bride. 'I've always had a thing about spots. I think curtains made from a polka dot fabric would be ideal…' He trailed off.

She laughed. 'Let's save that for the nursery, maybe,' she said.

He cast her an interested look. 'Are you trying to tell me something?'

His voice was casual, but Ellen was not deceived.

'Well, no,' she admitted. 'But maybe this time next year? That should give my headmistress time to sort out maternity cover.'

'You really want to go on teaching?' Max asked.

'Oh, yes,' she answered. 'I can't just be the idle wife of a rich man! And besides…' it was her turn to throw him a wicked look '…if I don't teach Games I might go off the boil about exercise in general. I might run to fat,' she said dulcetly. 'And *then*,' she finished dramatically, 'you wouldn't love me any more!'

A growl came from Max and he set down his champagne glass, removing hers at the same time. His arm around her shoulder tightened, and with his free hand he cupped her face.

'My goddess—my lioness—you could turn into a morbidly obese rhinoceros and I wouldn't love you an iota less. Don't you realise it's *you* I love, and to hell with anything else?'

'Oh, Max!' She gave a little choke, feeling her eyes misting suddenly.

How blessed she was—how unutterably blessed—that Max should love her!

He kissed her, warm and tender, deep and passionate.

Increasingly passionate.

Gently he drew her down upon the stone floor of the folly, and their bodies were limned with the light of the setting sun as desire flared between them—rich and ardent, sweet and eternal. Desire that was the manifestation of a love that would not end—that *could* not end. That could only bind them, each to the other, all their days…

* * * * *

Keep reading for an excerpt of a new title
from the Modern series,
HIS BILLION-DOLLAR TAKEOVER TEMPTATION
by Emmy Grayson

CHAPTER ONE

THE TOWERS AND high-rises of New York City glittered against the backdrop of a darkening summer sky. Adrian Cabrera raised his glass of Merlot to his lips and took a long drink, soaking in the sight of the metropolis from the second-floor balcony in the crowded Grand Ballroom of the Kingsworth Hotel.

The view was a preferred distraction from the vapid comments coming from the woman plastered against his side. Jackie—if he recalled correctly from her hurried introduction when she had appeared behind him—had wasted no time attempting to seduce him.

"Cabrera," she purred. "Such a sexy last name."

"A proud last name," he countered, making no attempt to keep the irritation out of his voice. "Traced back four generations to an ancestor who planted the first grapevines at the base of the Sierra Nevada in Spain."

"Like the Sierra Mountains in California?"

Adrian gritted his teeth. "The Sierra Nevada is a mountain range in southern Spain."

"A winery at the foot of a mountain." Jackie giggled. "How thrilling!"

Yes, being at the helm of Spain's most successful winery and a member of the ultra-wealthy Cabrera clan *was* thrilling. But he doubted his over-eager lady-friend would understand the excitement of a business acquisition, the anticipation of tasting a new wine that was the result of years of hard work…

No, all she cared about was a night spent with the mysterious Adrian Cabrera and perhaps a few weeks being jetted around the world on one of the family's private planes.

He risked a glance down. A skintight orange gown enhanced Jackie's slender figure, including the generous amount of cleavage that threatened to burst free at any second. Dark curls fell in an artfully arranged waterfall over her shoulder, accentuating sharp cheekbones and a large, blindingly white smile any model would envy.

But, other than the vaguest stirring of a physical response to her amply displayed breasts, he felt nothing. After years of entertaining himself with models, politicians, business leaders and actresses, he was very selective in his choice of bedmate. Married women and overly attentive ladies who wore their greed on their sleeves topped his off-limits list.

"I'd love to know more about your winery." She smiled again and pressed her breasts flush against him.

The move jostled his arm. Ruby-red wine sloshed out of his glass onto the white cuff of his dress shirt. His mild irritation flared into icy displeasure.

"Oh, no! I'm so sorry..." Her voice trailed off as their eyes met. "Um... I'll just let you get cleaned up."

She scuttled down the length of the balcony and hurried down the stairs. He watched as she reached the ballroom floor and disappeared into a sea of evening gowns and tuxedos.

A glance down at his shirt made him sigh. He had plenty of dress shirts in his closet upstairs in the Roosevelt Penthouse Suite. It would only take ten minutes to change and rejoin the party. But the deviation to his routine annoyed him. He always spent the first half-hour of a wine release alone, surveying whatever grand room his event planner had booked and savoring the success that had brought him to this moment.

From evaluating the mineral levels in the soils of the vineyards to collaborating with his head of marketing on the international campaigns that had taken Cabrera Wine to the top of the industry, each wine release marked the end of a long, demanding journey.

As a Cabrera, he could have asked for much

more by way of reward. All he wanted was thirty minutes to himself.

She's gone. Focus on the party. Don't let her ruin your night.

Tiffany chandeliers cast a sparkle over the golden ceiling as partygoers milled about the ballroom. Waiters expertly danced in and out of the guests with silver trays full of culinary treats like brie-stuffed mini burgers and pork chop bites with a tangy orange barbeque sauce.

Adrian's blood had curdled when Cabrera Wine's event planner, Calandra Smythe, had read the menu to him. Did Americans have to put barbeque sauce on everything?

Yesterday's final tasting had altered his view somewhat, when he'd been forced to admit that the unique recipes brought out the velvety flavors of the Merlot. And the surprisingly tasty offerings had been a hit with both his American and international clients.

Down below, he watched Calandra flit through the crowd, her eagle eyes seeking out every tiny imperfection with laser precision. From relighting candles to adjusting the angle of the tall vases overflowing with Spanish bluebells and white carnations, she had everything under control. As always.

He'd started to turn back to the arched window, to pull the curtain aside and take just a moment longer to enjoy the sight of the skyline, when he caught sight of a woman gliding in and out of the hordes of people. Her confident, graceful movements, coupled with the tumble of blonde hair cascading over her shoulders, piqued his interest. Elegant, yes, but something about her seemed out of place compared to the stiff-necked men and women milling about.

The crowd broke for a moment. He could see her below him, illuminated by the golden light of the chandeliers and the glow of the hundreds of candles that lit the ballroom. Her head snapped up and their gazes collided, caught and held.

The distance between them didn't diminish the sudden heat in his blood. Who was she? And why, after months of no one catching his interest, was he suddenly so drawn to this random stranger?

The woman looked away and the crowd surged once more. His eyes narrowed. He wasn't used to women turning away from him. Between the handsome looks he'd inherited from his father, his family's fortune and his fondness for ensuring his romantic partners left his bed feeling completely sated, he never had to seek out female companionship. It always came to him.

A grin tugged at the corner of his mouth. It would be a novelty to pursue a woman who had dismissed him with a glance. Perhaps novelty was just what he needed.

"Are you hiding, brother dear?"

Adrian rolled his eyes and turned his attention from the ballroom to Alejandro. His younger brother walked down the length of the carpeted balcony, his broad shoulders barely contained within the tailored sleeves of his tuxedo. While both of them sported the dark hair and chiseled features of the Cabrera family line, Alejandro's stockier build had led many a tailor to curse when designing his suits.

But his rugged appearance served him well as head of Cabrera Shipping. Alejandro never shied away from hopping on one of the freighters that crossed the Atlantic and working alongside the deckhands as they braved rough seas to deliver cargo around the globe.

"I'm not hiding. Just taking a break from the crowds," Adrian retorted as he turned his back on the party and moved toward the window. He drew the curtain aside to gaze out into the night.

Alejandro joined him. "I saw Jackie Harold rush downstairs. You're supposed to seduce the women, not frighten them off."

Adrian ignored his brother's jibe and swirled the remaining wine in his glass. "The Cabrera Merlot is a success."

The teasing smile disappeared from Alejandro's face as he clapped Adrian on the back. "It is. Congratulations, brother."

For a moment they stood side by side, surveying the impressive layout of New York. While Adrian's heart would always rest in Spain, his jaunts to America provided a brief respite from his chaotic life in his home country.

Cabrera Wine had grown from a small operation just outside of Granada into a respected international brand under Adrian's guidance. The resulting success came with a price—specifically the demand of time. Between meetings with the heads of marketing, business and accounting and trips to the various vineyards and wineries scattered across Europe, his schedule left little time for pleasure.

He shrugged off his musings. The success of Cabrera Wine would always take precedence. He'd made that choice eleven years ago and hadn't looked back since.

"How's Antonio?"

Alejandro chuckled. "Baby brother is celebrating the success of his most recent launch with a model in the Caribbean."

Despite Antonio's wild youth, the youngest Cabrera brother had surprised everyone by assuming control of a small real estate firm attached to the family's name. Antonio's opening of a luxury hotel in the French Riviera marked his third consecutive success since he had taken over three years ago.

Pride swelled in Adrian's chest. Nothing could diminish the success he and his brothers had achieved.

"Madre is worried, of course, but she still acts like he's five, not almost thirty years old."

The mention of their mother momentarily over-rode Adrian's pleasure and crushed it under the old, familiar sense of anger. He squelched it and focused his attention back on the crowd beneath them, where energy and laughter pulsed through the ballroom.

He'd achieved this on his own. Other than the occasional visit, his *madre* had no place in his life.

"Antonio can take care of himself," he said.

Alejandro picked up on the thread of warning in Adrian's voice and swiftly changed the sub-ject. "Are you coming back down?"

"I am. Although first I'm going to enjoy the rest of my drink. Alone."

Alejandro held up his hands. "I'm going. While you savor your solitude, I'll see if I can track down a suitable companion for you to celebrate with," he threw over his shoulder.

Adrian ignored the jape. Yes, his brother was right. He hadn't been tempted by anyone since the day he and his last lover had amicably parted ways. The release of the Merlot had consumed his every waking hour, even his dreams. He'd had no time for sex. And, with the aging of the Tem-pranillo almost complete, the next year would demand even more of his time.

But, while he preferred relationships with

agreed upon terms, perhaps one night of passion was just what he needed.

Not with a woman like Jackie, he added mentally. *A woman who was intelligent, savvy and sophisticated.*

"Mr. Cabrera?"

The husky feminine voice slid over his senses and sent a flash of heat over his skin. He took another deliberate sip of his wine before turning his attention to the second woman who had invaded his space this evening.

Her.

The blonde woman he'd locked eyes with before Alejandro's arrival now stood before him. The neckline of her dark blue gown plunged down in a V to the silver ribbon wrapped around her slender waist. From there the dress flowed into a long, billowing skirt that reminded Adrian of the waters of the Mediterranean before a storm.

His eyes drifted back up to her face in a slow, deliberate perusal. Lush silver-blonde curls enhanced her delicate features. Violet eyes stared back at him, and her caramel-colored lips were set in a firm line.

"Yes," he finally responded, his voice cool, showing that, despite the unusually intense effect she was having on him, he was still in control.

She stepped forward and held out her hand, bare except for a simple silver band on her wrist.

Adrian grasped her fingers, pleasantly surprised by her firm grip.

"My name is Everleigh Bradford. Congratulations on your Merlot. It's exquisite."

"Thank you." He arched a brow. "While your compliments are appreciated, was it necessary for you to ignore the 'Balcony Closed' sign and invade my privacy?"

Everleigh's chin came up and her eyes flashed with stubborn fire. "Yes."

Intriguing... There were plenty of men who would have cringed at the slightest hint of his disapproval. But not this woman. She stood her ground, shoulders thrown back, lips now set in a determined line.

"You're a busy man, Mr. Cabrera. I need to speak with you on an urgent matter. I'm sorry for breaking the rules, but it was necessary for me to have a moment alone with you."

Her honesty was refreshing. A night with someone as bold and beautiful as Everleigh would more than make up for his past few months of celibacy.

He infused his smile with sensuality as he raked his gaze up and down her slim form once more, this time letting his appreciation for her body show. "I would greatly enjoy a moment alone with you."

Everleigh's cheeks flushed pink. The blush caught Adrian unawares. Was she an innocent or just playing a role? Much as it would disappoint him, she wouldn't be the first to go to such lengths to catch his attention.

"This has nothing to do with sex, Mr. Cabrera."

"Adrian."

Her lips parted. "I… Excuse me?"

"Please call me Adrian."

Those beautifully shaded violet eyes narrowed. "This is a business discussion, Mr. Cabrera. First names are for friends and family."

"We could become friends, Everleigh."

What was wrong with him? He never teased a woman like this. He complimented, touched, seduced… But with this woman he just couldn't help himself.

Perhaps it was the blush. Yes, that had to be it. The delicate coloring that even now crept down her throat toward the rising slopes of her breasts…

"We will never be friends, *Mr.* Cabrera," Everleigh snapped. "I'm here to discuss your proposed purchase of Fox Vineyards."

Desire fled, replaced by the cold calculation Adrian wielded in every business meeting. "Then let's talk."

He watched as his quick change of personality threw her off balance. She glanced out over the ballroom, her chest rising and falling with a deep breath. He waited, never taking his eyes off her. It was a tactic that had served him well and caused many a nervous business partner to blurt out something they wished they hadn't.

At last she turned back to him and speared him with an angry gaze. "You're trying to bully my terminally ill father into selling the vineyards and the winery that have been in our family for generations to your international conglomerate. I want you to stop all communications with my father and allow me to step into his role."

He finished off the last of his Merlot while he processed her words. He'd met with Richard Bradford on several occasions as they'd negotiated the sale of Fox Vineyards to Cabrera Wine. The older man had been thinner the last time they'd met, but Adrian had chalked it up to the hectic lifestyle of owning a winery.

While Fox Vineyards only maintained one location in upstate New York, their wines had grown in popularity these last two years. Adrian had made it known that he wanted to expand Cabrera Wine into the States, so when Richard's attorney had contacted him about selling Fox it had been a welcome proposal. Not once had Richard mentioned any illness or a spoiled daughter wanting to take over the business.

It didn't matter. Adrian wasn't about to turn down the opportunity just to appease this brassy young woman. The fact that he hadn't made the connection between her last name and Richard signaled that he was too distracted. Better to put

Everleigh's jaw dropped. "Are you denying that you're—?"

"Threatening a man well-respected in the wine community? Yes, I deny it because it isn't true."

He leaned in, expecting her to back up, but she didn't. No, she just jutted that stubborn chin up another notch until her lips were just a breath away. A mad desire gripped him to haul her against him and kiss her senseless until she apologized.

No. He would never kiss a woman who disrespected him like this.

"Never accuse me again of something I haven't done, Everleigh Bradford. Tonight, I'll walk away and leave you with the embarrassment of knowing you were wrong. Next time, I will not be so generous."

as much distance between Everleigh and himself as possible.

"Just so I'm clear, Miss Bradford, you believe I've intimidated your father into selling Fox Vineyards?"

"Yes." For a moment her eyes glittered.

Dear God, please don't let her cry.

Adrian had zero interest in comforting a bawling woman in full view of hundreds of guests.

"I see. Have you spoken with your father about how he and I came to be doing business together?"

Everleigh's hands curled into fists. "He refuses to talk about it. All he'll say is, 'I had no choice.' You may be a successful businessman, and well-respected in some circles, but I also know you're ruthless. I will not have you run my family out of our own vineyard."

Adrian set his glass on a small end table, his movements slow and deliberate. The simple action kept him from displaying the wrath that was rapidly boiling to the surface. He was a determined businessman who went after what he wanted, but he wasn't heartless. The accusations this upstart American was leveling at him—and on the night of his own party—angered him as nothing had in a long time.

"Miss Bradford, I could have you arrested for slander."

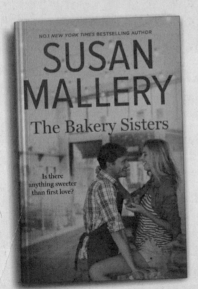

MILLS & BOON

Book Club

Have your favourite series
delivered to your door every month
with a Mills & Boon subscription.

**Use code ROMANCE2021 to
get 50% off the first month of
your chosen subscription PLUS
free delivery.**

Sign up online at
millsandboon.com.au/subscription-2

or call Customer Service on

AUS **1300 659 500** or NZ **0800 265 546**

**No Lock-in
Contracts**

**Free
Postage**

**Exclusive
Offers**

For full terms and conditions go to millsandboon.com.au
Offer expires June 30, 2021